THE
LAZARUS
SUCCESSION

KEN FRY

THE LAZARUS SUCCESSION
Copyright © 2016 by KEN FRY
Second Edition

First Edition March 2015
Originally published by Matador
A division of Troubador Publishing Ltd.
Kibworth Beauchamp, Leicester

Second Edition December 2016
Published by Ken Fry
Surrey, UK
ISBN-13: 978-1542913621
ISBN-10: 1542913624

Copy Edited by Eeva Lancaster
Cover Design and Book Interior by The Book Khaleesi
www.thebookkhaleesi.com

www.booksbykenfry.com

A LEGEND to SLAUGHTER FOR...
A TRUTH to DIE FOR

The Lazarus Succession is a modern-day thriller with a medieval mystery attached to it. The discovery of which could change mankind forever.

Praise for The Lazarus Succession and Ken Fry:

"A brilliant read. Could be screenplay for the next Indiana Jones...."
Amazon UK

"...we are treated to a fast-paced page-turner of cat and mouse intrigue. A very exciting story indeed, which kept me on my toes right up until the end with twists and turns all of the way."
Goodreads Review

"Ken Fry writes with such fluidity that characters and situations spring to life."
Goodreads Review

OTHER TITLES by KEN FRY

The Brodsky Affair

Suicide Seeds

Check Mate

Is That You, Jim?

Dying Days

Join Ken Fry's Circle of Readers and get free eBooks

www.booksbykenfry.com

PROLOGUE

Bethany, nr. Jerusalem
The Tomb of Lazarus

T he crowd pressed in tight behind me, so much so that I could not turn around. The pressure of the people pushing and jostling, trying to see, caused consternation and anger amongst those caught hard in the middle of the pack. I was fortunate to be in the front rank.

They had come to see the man called Jesus. It was said he was a magician, a holy man, a prophet. I've heard stories, but whatever he was, it was known that he had performed astounding acts; like curing lepers and causing the blind to see.

His followers had linked arms and formed a ring, preventing the crowd from overwhelming him.

Rumour had it that a friend of his, named Lazarus, had died four days ago, and was now entombed behind the large stone in front of the cave. His friends and relatives were sobbing and talking to Jesus; some looked sad, others sounded angry. The man, this Jesus, asked for the stone to be rolled away. It was, and he walked to the entrance.

He muttered words we couldn't hear, but then after only a few seconds, his voice broke the stillness and thundered, "Lazarus, come on out!"

And we all understood what this Jesus did.

It was hard to believe, but from out of the darkness of the cave, Lazarus, still draped in winding bandages, walked out into the light and knelt before Jesus.

Like the crowd around me, I was astonished. No ordinary man could do this. Surely it was an act of God. As an artist, I knew I had to capture this event. It was the most unbelievable thing I had ever seen.

Lazarus had stepped out of the bandages, and for a reason I cannot explain, I knew I had to collect them up. I moved forward to gather what I could. One of his men tried to stop me. But this man, Jesus, prevented them.

"Let him," he said in a clear voice. Then, he stared at me in a way that I have never been looked at before.

His eyes shone with such brilliance, I was transfixed. I knew then he knew everything about me; who I was, what I did, all my aspirations, hopes and failures.

He spoke. "Annas Zevi, you are blessed. You shall paint what you have witnessed today and it will radiate a power for all those who truly choose to see it."

Well, I don't know why, but I fell to my knees and closed my eyes as he placed his hand on me.

To this day, and that was twenty-one years ago, I remember his words.

"Others, through its power, will all be superseded until the end of days."

I couldn't understand what he meant, but when I arose, he had gone, and with him all the people. I was left alone with the burial trappings of the man, Lazarus.

That day, I rushed home determined to start painting what I

witnessed. One week later, it was finished. It didn't feel like I was painting it. I was guided. Don't ask how, I can't tell you. But I *knew* it possessed power of some sort. I was determined to preserve it. Wrapping it in the bandages from Lazarus's body, I hid it away in a secret place.

I wept, as I swore never to paint another picture again.

CHAPTER 1

**Bodega de Vinos Universal
Cafayate, Argentina
Three years ago…**

T he 4x4 jeep, unlocked and bearing false number plates, the key still in the ignition, was parked off track amongst thick bushes and undergrowth. It stood ready for a fast exit.

He checked his watch. Two-thirty.

Above, a spectral moon spread a pale light around the area, revealing their objective as a murky silhouette.

"You okay there?" asked Brodie.

"Fine," replied Ulla. "You got everything?"

"Affirmative."

"Hoods and gloves."

"Okay, let's go."

He watched her pull on the black balaclava, masking her chiselled features. He leant forward and pulled down the corner that had snagged on the rope she had around her shoulders. She nodded. He made one last check on his equipment, ensuring there were no mistakes or omissions. There were none. Everything in their backpacks was secure and in its place; wire-cutters, flashlight, small crowbar, knives, handcuffs, more rope and finally the item he hoped not to use, a suppressed Glock 19 pistol that Ulla had insisted on bringing in case the going got tough.

He pointed in the direction of the large, concrete, block-like structure that stood on the summit of a small hill. It overlooked endless rows of symmetrically planted vines that stretched out and down to the area they were now beginning to move through.

Broderick Ladro didn't doubt his research. He was seldom wrong. Research was what he did for a living. The concrete structure was the home of Bernhardt Higuera. He was the only known living relative; the son of the deceased Aldric Vogel, a former Nazi SS Commandant who had fled the Allies in 1945 following the defeat of the Third Reich. Vogel, had changed his name to Pedro Higuera, but had been tracked down to Argentina where he had established a successful wine producing business, employing considerable numbers of locals. It was for this reason that attempts by the Allies at extradition had been blocked by the Argentinean authorities. They wanted him for his involvement with the *Einsatzstab Reichsleiter Rosenberg* or ERR as it was known. The ERR looted, and logged with careful precision, every valuable piece of art they could find across Europe. Vogel had made a mistake. He gunned down a prominent French art historian and his aide for standing in his way, when they attempted to stop him from removing various masterpieces. The murders were witnessed by several people, and recorded. Aldric Vogel guessed what his fate would be if captured. In 1945, he fled, taking with him every valuable artefact and artwork he possessed. A brain tumour forty years ago denied the hangman his prize.

It wasn't Vogel's son that Brodie was after; it was what he had in his home. Ulla had gleaned from her research into the *Einsatzstab's* meticulous archives that there would be more in there than the two icons their commission requested. One was Greek, a

5

rare eleventh century work depicted as *Christ's Sermon on the Mount*. The other was Russian, twelfth century, described as *Mary, Our Lady of Bliss visited by the Archangel Gabriel*. They had their instructions. They were to take only what was ordered.

Ulla set a brisk pace. In stooped postures, they began to thread their way through the vines as they drew closer across the eight-hundred metre approach. The estate was bristling with security devices, dogs and guards. Traversing through the vines presented the least chance of activating any form of security.

It was at times like this that Brodie wondered why he did this for a living. What did he get out of it? Frequently, he came close to calling it a day, but it was Ulla, little Ulla Stuart who always persuaded him otherwise. She didn't have to say anything. Being with her and feeling the adrenalin coursing through his body as they embarked on another dubious enterprise, was enough.

He never forgot his first serious mission with her. She had organised it after he'd met a high ranking British Cabinet Minister four years ago at an Arts Foundation soirée. The minister had lamented the loss of a very early and rare illuminated edition of Chaucer's *Canterbury Tales*. It had been stolen by his mistress, and for obvious reasons, he couldn't do anything about it. He was willing to pay handsomely to see it again. On their behalf, Ulla took him up on his offer.

The sheer thrill of breaking into the mistress's apartment, finding the volume, and then making love in her silk-sheeted bed before walking away and leaving it in a mess, was the biggest turn-on he'd ever experienced. Ulla had agreed. She loved risks. The more challenging it was, the more determined she'd become. She never ceased to amaze him. They both agreed their line of work held more rewards than money.

As he had guessed, the security lights were switched on, pointing directly at the building's corners. Peering harder, he watched as two guards paced in different directions around the structure, passing each other every two minutes and forty-seconds.

Somewhere, two dogs gave intermittent barks.

"Do we get danger money? Those dogs are running loose," Ulla whispered.

"If we don't get what we came for, we won't get anything."

"The dogs worry me."

"They'll be taken care of. I've got four fat slabs of meat here, each laced with curare." He patted his rucksack. "It's almost instant and should keep them quiet for a couple of hours. Okay?"

"I bloody hope so. Now, let's look around and work out how we'll deal with the guards."

"What a god damned awful place." Brodie pointed to the building. "It looks like a German war bunker."

Ulla counted fifteen deeply recessed square windows in straight lines, complemented by what looked like defensive observational slits at odd intervals. At one point, an overhanging balcony projected from the wall and was surrounded with massive black iron railings.

"It looks as if it was built to withstand an attack. Nobody's going to climb in that way."

"Hopefully, they're not expecting small assaults like ours. Let's move around the back."

Keeping low amongst the vines, out of sight from the guards, they reached the back of the house. They found a solid smooth concrete wall with a thick iron door set into it, and a pathway leading down to two cemented helicopter landing areas, each inscribed with a large white letter 'H'. They were vacant.

"Looks like nobody's home," whispered Ulla holding Brodie's arm.

"And it looks like the dogs have got our scent. Ulla, don't move!" Brodie knelt and thrust his hand into his rucksack. He'd placed the carefully wrapped meat on top of the contents. "Don't use this unless you have to!" He handed her the Glock.

One large barking German Shepherd, together with a Doberman, covered the distance from the building with pounding speed, before breaking into a circling movement and coming at them from two sides. Brodie had the meat unwrapped, keeping his eyes fixed at Ulla. She held the Glock and pointed it at the Doberman now only thirty metres away. Brodie lobbed the meat as hard as he could. Two chunks landed on the ground ten metres from them both, followed by two more in quick succession.

"C'mon, you ugly bastards, eat it," Brodie shouted in a whisper as he grabbed a large hunting knife. The German Shepherd's nose went upwards. He turned in mid-air and slewed to a skidding halt. The dog saw the meat and lunged, his huge jaws shaking and tearing at the treat in a frenzy of greed. The food disappeared in a gulp. It turned and saw the second piece a few metres in front of him. He lunged forward to grab at it with his mouth wide open. He didn't make it. A vacant expression passed through his eyes. Without a sound, the dog toppled over sideways into a clutch of vines. It attempted to stand, but its rear legs kicked out. It fell back down and then was still, unable to move, glassy eyed, its tongue hanging loosely from the side of its jaws.

The curare worked on the German Shepherd, but the Doberman wasn't hungry. Its target was Ulla. She straightened the arm holding the Glock and didn't hesitate. The shot penetrated the dog's throat. With a piteous moan, it attempted another attack before dropping sideways with one last gasping breath.

"It was you or me, chum. Nothing personal," Ulla said to the dead dog.

"No time for that." Brodie's urgent tone cut through the air. "The guards are coming."

They were making their way at speed across the lawn, heading towards the area where the dogs attached them.

Brodie pushed Ulla down amongst the vine foliage, her head resting on the dead Doberman's back. "Give me the gun."

Ulla placed it in his outstretched hand. "I thought this was going to be an easy exercise."

The guards came to a halt, looking for the dogs.

Brodie stood up. "You guys looking for me?"

They looked startled, but the one on the left took aim and fired his rifle. The shot missed Brodie and whined into the vines. Brodie's shot was more accurate. The guard dropped to the ground without a sound, clutching at his arm. The second guard threw his rifle to the ground and put his hands in the air.

"Please. No kill. Please!"

"Flat on the ground, face down, if you want to carry on living." Brodie waved the gun at him.

Ulla stood and knew what she had to do. The frightened guard needed no second asking. Within minutes, the two guards were bound and gagged with duct tape. She checked the gunshot wound and saw it wasn't serious. He wouldn't bleed to death.

"Well done, Ulla. They're not going to move for a very long time. Let's check the house and get what we came for."

Vogel and his wife were staying overnight at a reception being held at the Vintner's Heath Golf Club, just outside the town's centre. There was no need for stealth now, but they kept their hoods on. In the glare of the security lamps, Ulla produced a set of plans for the interior of the building. She had stolen them from the municipal offices two months previously, when she learned what their objective would be.

"Now we've seen the place," she said after looking carefully at the plans, "the easiest way in, would you believe, is through the front entrance. Everything else is barred and alarmed."

"The door won't be a problem. I've got these." Brodie produced a small wedge of pen-sized explosive, and tapped the small crowbar in a sheath strapped to his leg.

Ulla looked up and around the door. "How long do we need?"

"Assuming nobody knows we're here, we have as long as we like."

"We agreed to a time limit. I want to get this over with fast and get out of this place."

"You're right. Patrol guards are normally required to make

contact at regular intervals, either with Vogel or their HQ. If they don't, another batch would turn up from somewhere to see what the problem could be. How are we doing for time?"

"We're four minutes to the good."

"That's great. Let's go for it."

Brodie slipped the crowbar between the lock and the door jamb. After one hard twist of his wrist and a hefty shove, the door lock splintered and the heavy oak door swung open. He slid the tool back into its sheath as Ulla pushed him into the dark interior. No need for the explosives,

"We need some light," she said. "There's nobody in so we can risk it. These flashlights are not going to help much. I'll find the control box. There has to be one somewhere in the front area." Within thirty seconds, she had located it, mounted on the wall behind the door. She pulled down the Perspex view panel, activated the large red control switch, and the house blazed with light.

The entrance hall floor was covered in solid white and black marble. Works of art hung from the walls, sculptures and bronzes stood on plinths or in recesses that pointed the way to other areas. Bookcases and writing tables gave an air of culture, enhanced by the wide spiralling staircase leading to the upper floors. That culture, Brodie knew, was a stolen one. A phoney. For that reason, he had no qualms about the nature of his work.

"Wow! Look at all this," Ulla whispered as if she thought someone might hear her.

"No need to whisper, Ulla," Brodie whispered back as he walked past a Picasso. He stopped and pointed. "I don't believe it!"

"What is it?"

Brodie pointed at a painting. "It can't be, but it is!" Staring down at them was a very obvious Vincent van Gogh. "It's the *Painter on the Road to Tarasco.* That was supposed to have been destroyed in the last war, either by bombing or burnt as an example of degenerative art by the Nazis. This is amazing."

"Well, here's one Nazi plunderer who didn't think it was so degenerate. We're going to leave it where it is. Don't touch it, Brodie... *please*. I know you're an artist, but leave it... *please*. We know where it is now and I'm certain some museum or institution would love to acquire it. We can contact them and make a proposition."

Brodie sighed. "What else is here?" He moved towards a large wall-mounted bookcase groaning with leather-bound first editions. "These are worth a mint, Ulla. Perfect for my collection at home, don't you think?"

"No, you don't... leave them be. Remember, we're ethical robbers not common thieves." She pushed him away and pointed upstairs. "Our information indicates the icons are mounted in the main bedroom. So, let's get up there, grab them, and get out of here."

They reached the top of the staircase and headed for the main bedroom at the far end of the corridor. It had two large grey Gothic style doors.

"There it is." She pointed.

"How are we doing on time?"

Ulla checked her watch. "We're on par. We have seven minutes to get back to the car."

As expected, the bedroom was huge; circular with en suite facilities, walk-in cupboards and closets. It was perfect and neat, with nothing out of place. But there wasn't time to admire the fixtures and fittings. Brodie swung his gaze around the walls and saw what they had come for. Positioned on each side of the bed were two icons, resplendent in golden and red hues. With their reproachful Byzantine facial expressions, they stared down at him.

"Not my cup of tea." Brodie gestured at the pair.

"Nor mine. God knows what our client sees in them."

"Something to do with his family. He has a connection with these icons. That's his business. So, let's get them wrapped and bagged and leave this place."

Eight minutes later, the 4x4 fired up and headed back the way it had come. The Martin Miguel airport at Salta, the provincial capital, was a good two-and-a-half hour's drive. A private jet was waiting for them.

CHAPTER 2

Toledo, Spain
1553 A.D.

B ecause he was twelve years old, and busy with producing drawings and paintings that were the love of his young life, Francisco's periods of prayer were not as frequent as he would have wished. Yet, in the last few days, he felt an overpowering desire to put that right.

For his age, he was not atypical. His build was slight, with dark hair and curious deep brown eyes, s staring out from behind his smooth olive skin. As if giving evidence of his prodigious artistic ability, his hands and fingers were slender, elongated, and tapering off almost to a point. He promised himself he would set aside his paints one morning and attend mass at the Cathedral.

Later that evening, his father, who rarely spoke about prayer or church, but often of his vineyard and wine, had discussed the awfulness and sinful nature of one of his worker's reckless remarks concerning God. He'd overheard the man cursing Him, shaking his fist at the sky and calling Him a bastard. For that, his papa announced, he was going to get rid of him. At the same time, he fixed Francisco with a withering stare.

"Don't ever let me hear you say such things, son. There are mysteries in this world that only God knows of, or those with whom he chooses to share them with."

Francisco bent his head and cast his eyes downward. "Yes, papa. I could never say such things."

"Promise?"

"I promise, papa. I promise."

That night, after he had gone to bed and said his prayers, Francisco thought about what his father had said and what sort of mysteries he meant. Unable to come up with an answer, he drifted to sleep, but not before he resolved to go to the Cathedral in the morning. That would please his father. It would also satisfy the strange longing he was experiencing. He'd enjoyed going to church, and it was time to feel that pleasure again.

The cries of the crows woke him early. Francisco had never got used to their noise. They were always fighting. Spring had arrived and daylight broke much sooner. As he prepared, what his father said the night before remained with him. The thought of saying such an awful thing about God made him uncomfortable.

The Cathedral was an hour's brisk walk away, and that morning his father was unable to go with him. He was expecting wine merchants, and his mother would have to stay and see to the cooking.

"You're old enough, and the way is straight. So yes, Francisco, I would be pleased to see you go. And while you're there, say a prayer for us both. Don't dawdle back or get in with those gypsy boys. They can only get you into trouble."

After breakfast, he waved goodbye to his parents and left. On the way, he saw many people he knew and exchanged greetings with. Some were his father's customers, and some were people he knew from the market. He avoided the gypsy boys. But this morning, he felt no desire to be with others and preferred his own company. He strode with purpose along the track.

In the distance, he could see the small city of Toledo dominated by the imposing silhouette of the Primate Cathedral of Saint Mary. Francisco lifted his head towards the sky to feel both wind and sun shower down their offerings upon him. It gave him a happy glow. Soon, he was passing into the narrow, shady streets, squares, and beneath numerous archways surrounding the great building.

— — —

Francisco sat in blissful devotion within the coolness of the Chapterhouse, the *Sala Capitular*. Such was the ardour of his immersion, he lost awareness of time. To open his eyes would be an affront to the sanctity that now possessed him.

He listened hard but heard no external sounds.

He was cocooned in an awareness of the overwhelming wonder of God's breath entering his young mouth, accompanied with the unique aroma of the Cathedral's frankincense. It was heady, luscious, and more exotic than his paints and their inimitable smells. He held the moment, letting it stretch into a timeless realm.

Of their own accord, his eyelids fluttered open and he suspended his quivering breath.

Things were as they had been one hour ago, except they now possessed a beauty he'd never seen before ... a beauty of bewildering colours, of dazzling gold and silver, never ending perspectives of harmony, and perfection of structure and dimension.

He looked down at the wooden stool he was sitting on and saw the large crack running the full length of the leg. He could only smile, for he now knew that the crack, insignificant, and for some a blemish, contained a symmetry equal to any of the great works of art to be found in Spain. Lifting his head, he enjoyed a feeling of serenity, asleep and cocooned in his mother's womb was the closest image that came into his mind. Where this wonder and timelessness came from, he couldn't explain. It was then his eyes were drawn to the many frescos around the walls painted by Juan de Borgoña. These were hailed as the most magnificent religious paintings of their genre in Christendom. They were depicted in a glorious variety of reds, blues, purples, and vibrant yellows, scenes depicting the healing miracles performed by Christ. They completed the sacredness of the Chapterhouse.

Francisco marvelled at Borgoña's work, its vibrancy, its realism, unique for its time. Although he had not been taught, he found he understood Borgoña's technique intuitively ... the positioning of his characters blending into a perspective, highlighting the subject matter. He sensed the structure and the passion behind his interpretations. Each work showed a healing — the blind made to see, the lame to walk, the lepers cured and the raising of the dead. It was the huge fresco on the far wall depicting Lazarus being brought back to life that captured his attention. Francisco was transfixed. The whole of his being responded in a mysterious rapture as he gazed on the yellow shroud that covered Lazarus and the white-robed figure of Christ, who with one hand raised, was addressing Lazarus's dormant body.

As he studied the work, it seemed to move! Francisco gasped out loud and struggled for breath. The shroud had shifted and the form of Lazarus had become visible as he appeared to support himself on one elbow to look into the face of Christ, whose body was surrounded by a golden aura. Christ then lowered his hand, turned his head, and directed His gaze towards Francisco.

Francisco collapsed.

How long he had lain there on the stone floor, Francisco had no idea. He sat up. His head buzzed and he could see he was alone. Everything was as it had always been in the *Sala Capitular*. Had he just fainted? he wondered. He sensed that an extraordinary event had occurred.

His entire body tingled. The colours around him remained the same, and the dimensions no different to his previous visits. The frescos were as magnificent as ever. The Lazarus fresco was as it was, unchanged. Yet, he was looking at it in a different way. There were no clues or signs to tell him what had happened.

He stood with caution. A blaze of colours played through his mind, vanishing as fast as they appeared. His whole being, physical and mental, had a lightness that left him feeling as if he could fly. He turned, paused to think, and decided to return home. Perhaps his parents could give him an explanation.

He walked through the city and observed along its walls the ancient and uneven brickwork formed with rough mortar, and wondered how he could capture its texture and colour with his paints. He passed old alleyways with crumbling arches, bricks warm and weathered, and questioned why he'd never noticed them before. Entering the market place, he was astonished to realise it was a living thing. It was alive with colourful foods, meats, fish and vegetables from all regions; plus, clothes and textiles being hawked by their merchants.

Francisco became conscious that a door he'd not known of had opened in his mind. Was this one of the mysteries of which his father had spoken?

Stepping outside of the city's main portal, the gentle wind possessed warmth, although the sun's glare caused him to shield his eyes. He strode out of the city and once outside the walls of Toledo, Francisco set off in a daze along the dusty brown track that zigzagged its way back to his father's house.

CHAPTER 3

**The Hofburg Palace
Vienna, Austria
The present day…**

T he *Juristenball* was in full swing. An atmosphere of struggling elegance pervaded the ballroom as dresses swirled, perfumes wafted, and men of all ages in starched shirts and evening dress attempted to look casual.

Sir Maxwell Throgmorton, former UK High Court judge, stood alone on the balcony, smoking as he gazed around at the building's curvature and down at the cultural magnificence of the Heldenplatz and the statue of Prince Eugene of Savoy on horseback. The ball was an annual event and primary for those involved in the legal profession: judges, lawyers, students and others involved in the judiciary. He'd been formally invited.

His hosts knew nothing of his reasons for retiring early in his career.

He'd left London and hadn't been practising for three years. His departure had been an escape from the ignominy of facing possible arrest and police charges. He could imagine the headlines in the papers, *Famous Judge Arrested. Possible Criminal Charges.* A discreet voice in his ear had said all would be forgotten if he disappeared. If he didn't, they could not guarantee what might happen to him.

Drawing deeply on his cigarette, he mulled over the events that led to his exodus. Too many important establishment figures had their fingers in the pie. They'd been afraid he'd expose them and he would have. So, to avoid more trouble, he announced his retirement. He was fifty-three. It didn't appear unreasonable although judges went on for many years past that age. He had moved to Vienna, a city he had always adored. Now, three years later, he looked fitter than ever. At a trim six feet and in good health, he was in better condition than ten years ago. His face was pale as he avoided sunlight as much as possible. It remained unlined and he had a full head of tangled hair. Too many people didn't want him back in the UK. He feared for his freedom and safety, yet the thought of returning was never far away. So, he'd learned to be content living his life as a disaffected expat, scouring around the rich and famous notaries of Europe.

The night was warm, sticky, and a quarter moon hung without enthusiasm in the sky, offering its faint glow across the plaza. The filtered gaiety from behind him contrasted with the silence that stretched out for what seemed like forever. He couldn't deny that the sight of Austria's top legal fraternity dancing and drinking was a sharp contrast to his introspection as he stood gazing into the heavens. He let the ash drop from his cigarette, reached into the inside pocket of his tuxedo, and pulled out a gold case that he'd filled with twenty cigarettes before he'd left for the ball. There were twelve left. Smoking was a habit he wished he could abandon but had never mastered. He lit another and found himself reviewing his whole life and the past activities that had brought him to this moment.

He'd never escaped the notion that his privileged background,

his education, Charterhouse and Cambridge, gave him superiority-
--a natural assumption that he wasn't of the herd. He'd always
known he had the ability to do whatever he wished. It was in his
blood. He found the process of study boring for its unbelievable
easiness. With a first-class degree, he went into law. The mandatory
processes applied and his rapid rise ensured that at forty-six, he
became the youngest High Court judge ever. Successful as he'd
become, it lacked real challenge. It was too simple. He would have
preferred a more risqué life. However, he discovered that
convention and the route into respectability had advantages. Both
his marriages gave him access to the wealthiest strata of society.
Lady Isabella McKenna was his first choice. She'd possessed
enormous wealth and it hadn't been for her good looks that he'd
married her. She was by any degree plain... plain in the extreme.
She perished in a yachting accident off the coast of Cannes. His
grieving picture made the national newspapers, as did his next
wedding eighteen-months later to Ruth Overberg. She was pretty,
intelligent, and the only daughter of the international financier and
banker, Donald Overberg.

Maxwell exhaled another lungful of cigarette smoke and
watched its greyness rise lazily into the cool night air before it
vanished forever.

His thoughts turned to love. It was an emotion he had little
experience of. Ruth got as near to that for him as was possible. He
still thought of her and was surprised to feel pangs of sadness at
her absence. The never-ending social whirl of their life together
ended once she'd discovered the true reason for his retirement. She
left him. Now living in Zurich, she had, apart from the divorce,
granted him one thing. She promised him she wouldn't reveal
anything of his circumstances. He still didn't believe that. Ruth had
never been able to keep her mouth shut.

Crooks, villains, bent bankers, financiers, politicians, judges,
lawyers, solicitors, all had added spice to his life, making it
interesting, more rewarding. For the right fee, anything was

possible; reduced sentence, acquittal, procurements, insider trading, and anything else that required a legal stamp of some sort. He had the right contacts. There was always someone who could help.

A perk of the job, he reasoned.

For many years, he had managed to keep his double life hidden. That secret had teetered on the edge of exposure. A journalist, Desmond O'Keefe from *The Times*, had been tipped off about possible irregularities between government and the judiciary. Through a process of elimination, O'Keefe's investigations had pointed directly at him and a handful of his associates.

He paused and lit another cigarette. The memories were raw, stressful, and caused him to tighten his lips.

It had been an almost fool-proof idea.

Two government ministers had negotiated with a contractor to build three major privately run prisons: one juvenile in Penrith, and the other two in Anglesey and the Isle of Dogs. Without their input, the prisons would not have been built. The ministers were on a kick-back, and the price had been over inflated. Prisons require prisoners. The more prisoners and the longer they stayed locked up, the more money went to the operator and contractor who, unknown to anybody apart from those involved in the scam, were close cousins. Throgmorton considered what he had done. Using two other judges who were important to the success of the scheme, they handed down severe maximum sentences for every offence, no matter how minor or ludicrous. The prisons were kept full. Between them, the three judges netted a cool £3.5 million.

What the ministers required was action to prevent O'Keefe from exposing the entire scam. They leaned on Throgmorton to use his knowledge of the underworld. He did. O'Keefe's body was later found drifting down the Thames. The report that he'd entitled *'Lags for Cash'* plus all traces of his records and research … vanished. The ministers were pleased but decided that he, Throgmorton, was now a liability. If he retired quietly, nobody would be any the wiser. If he didn't ... well, he too might be found in the watery coldness of the Thames. He considered the proposal. Why not? He'd made a small fortune together with added excitement. *It's time for some new venture.*

He gave a start and turned around with a scowl as somebody tapped on his shoulder. He recognised Dr. Marcus Urbanek, Public Prosecutor from the Federal Ministry of Justice. He didn't know the woman with him. He disliked disturbances unless they were of his own making.

"Sir Maxwell, I'm so sorry to startle you but I've been looking for you all evening, and then I thought it was you standing here." Peering over his steel rimless glasses, he offered his hand.

Throgmorton shook it. "Hello, Marcus. Good to see you." He wasn't sure about that statement and the man's hand remained as damp and podgy as it had been the previous month when they had met at the opera.

"Allow me to introduce you to a close friend of mine, from Spain, the Condesa Maria Francisca de Toledo." He stepped back and with a flourish of his arm, ushered her forward.

She was a tall, spidery looking middle aged woman, dressed in black with a severe countenance that oozed a confidence born of her upbringing and the certainty of years. Her dark hair was pulled back into a tight bun, with no attempt to disguise the obvious grey streaks that reminded him of aircraft vapour across a dark night's sky. Deep brown eyes hinted at a long and distinguished history. The jewellery had an expensive aura. He couldn't fail to notice the discreet diamond and pearl Riviere necklace and the hefty ring on her finger, a large oval sapphire surrounded by diamonds worth God knows how many hundreds of thousands. This had to be a lady worth knowing.

She made no move towards him and he had to make the journey to her as she emitted a thin smile and shook his hand. She barely made contact, as if she were doing him a favour, and withdrew her fingers as fast as she was able.

"Sir Maxwell, I would like to speak to you about a certain matter, but not here." Her request sounded like a summons, and her voice, with its Spanish accent, had the texture of ice about to crack.

Before Throgmorton had a chance to speak, Urbanek interjected, "The Condesa has heard that where others fail you can often succeed. She is on a spiritual quest and ..."

The Condesa waved her hand at him and stopped him from explaining further. "Let Sir Maxwell speak."

Urbanek's eyes betrayed his minor embarrassment.

What Urbanek had said was not the sort of statement he wished to hear bandied around. Throgmorton's response was cautious. "The Condesa must not believe everything she hears. Often, anything said about anybody is exaggerated, don't you find?"

"I don't have time to check all the details of what I hear about people. I am far too busy."

"And what keeps you busy, My Illustrious Lady?" He saw the momentary lift of her eyebrows at his correct address in Spanish.

"I'm conducting research on the impact of religious art on the human psyche. How it can alter our perceptions and viewpoints. It also covers the realm of miracles. Do you believe in miracles?" Her inquiring tone had the warmth of a glacier.

"I know nothing about those sorts of things."

Urbanek, attempting to restore some worth, explained. "But you do, Sir Maxwell." He turned to the Condesa. "He told me he has a portfolio of important Byzantine and Renaissance religious artefacts." He turned back to Throgmorton. "Isn't that right, Sir Maxwell?"

Throgmorton's insides cringed and before he could speak, she asked, "Are you a collector, scholar, or both?"

"More of a collector, you might say. I'm just an interested layman. I enjoy art and fine things. I find them rewarding, enjoyable. Don't you?"

"So, it's just for pleasure that you acquire things. That was not what I was hoping to hear, but it will do. I will contact you very soon. You will excuse me?"

"A remarkable woman," Urbanek observed as he watched her walk back into the ballroom.

Feeling as if he'd just been dismissed like an errant waiter, Throgmorton ignored the Public Prosecutor's observation. He agreed she had quality, as had many other people he knew. Not many people could treat him the way she had with so little demonstrable effort. Their next meeting would be interesting.

CHAPTER 4

Florence, Italy
The present day...

O verlooking the River Arno, Ulla Stuart sat alone drinking coffee beneath a large red umbrella at a pavement café. The area was thick with tourists but she had a distant view of the iconic dome of *Il Duomo* which helped soothe her irritation. She'd been waiting forty minutes for Brodie.

Four days previously, a small but very fine marble and ivory statuette of *The Death of Remus* by Bernini had been 'liberated' from the premises of Count Luigi Falcone di Milani. It had been stolen a century previously by the Count's ancestor. Brodie and she had secretly returned it to its rightful home at the estate of Mario Finelli. Finelli could trace his lineage back to Giuliani Finelli. Giuliani had been a student of Bernini and had worked with him on producing the piece. As Bernini's patron for the work had died before it was finished, Bernini had presented it to Finelli, in whose family it had remained for centuries until it was stolen.

The humidity and its accompanying flies didn't help her

patience. To help calm down, she watched the sun casting a thousand reflections across the surface of the waters. It never failed to fascinate her. Every so often, she looked around the café, across the other tables and back down the aisle of the interior, but the place looked deserted. Brodie hadn't appeared yet, and true to form, he was running late.

She activated her mobile to check for messages; there were none. Her nimble thumbs and fingers began tapping out a text, *"Where are you?"* She paused before sending it, as when she turned her head, she saw him talking to a waiter in the foyer. The first thing she saw was the pony tail, and then the craggy, life-worn lines of his lived-in face as the waiter pointed in her direction. Brodie smiled and began walking towards her. She ignored the small wave. He was dressed in his usual fashion: T-shirt, a safari style jacket, jeans, and desert boots.

"Where've you been?" She tried to keep the snap out of her voice. "I've gone through two large cappuccinos waiting here, looking like a tart trying to hook a client. Don't tell me you couldn't find it because you've been here before."

He gave the suggestion of a smirk but looked apologetic. "Ulla, sorry for being so late. I had too much to do. I asked the waiter if there was a single woman here, possibly looking irritable, and staring into a mobile phone. He pointed to you."

Brodie never failed to disarm her and she gave a weak smile. He was of Scottish-Italian descent, aged forty-three and wasn't tall, just five feet ten inches. At thirty-three years of age, she hadn't let their ten-year age difference become an issue. He had many surprising talents. The one she admired most ... his paintings and drawings. With several exhibitions and reviews to his credit, it fitted in well with their line of work. He had often said that he'd missed his true calling in life.

She too had a Scottish connection and believed that was part of the attraction between them. Her father, an oil worker from Aberdeen, had married her Ukrainian mother. Brodie had told her that she had that indefinable Russian beauty about her. Her striking blond hair, green eyes, and a figure no woman would be ashamed of, were attributes she gave little thought to. She met Brodie ten years ago by pure chance, or so he thought. In truth, Ulla had planned it.

Brodie was on her list. She'd spotted him on several occasions in the Renaissance Room at the Stephen Chan Library in New York. She soon got talking. He'd told her he was doing research for a client, and ran a small fine art and antiques agency. When he asked her what she was doing, she'd replied, "Looking for where I can find something to steal." She still remembered his shocked expression.

"You must be joking."

"Not really." She'd offered her hand. "My name's Ulla." He had qualities that attracted her.

Later that night, in bed together, she recalled his reaction when she'd asked him what he thought about making a living from something more than just research.

"Clandestine search and rescue, Brodie. Putting things back where they rightfully belong or removing them from those who shouldn't have them or don't deserve them. Honest robbery."

"What? I wouldn't know where to start, and besides, we'd end up in jail."

"With our knowledge, we can access areas others wouldn't even know about." She saw the look on his face. "I can see you think I'm joking, but wait until we get back to the UK and I'll show you how easy it is, believe me."

Two weeks later they met and she stayed with him in Harrogate. Brodie had allowed her to persuade him to embark on what she had described as an enriching evening stroll. He looked at her delicate face; it had a fearlessness that shone with what he could only put down to her Ukrainian blood. Her beauty was enigmatic. He knew now she was a risk taker, but never impulsive. It hadn't taken long to understand that every decision she made was an exercise in studied patience leading to the desired result.

Twenty-minutes later, they had strolled casually by the outskirts of the black expanse of The Stray, close to the large houses that bordered it. He knew what was about to happen and he wished he wasn't there, but to walk away would have made him look stupid. She stopped outside a large darkened house and moved into the blackness enveloping it.

"This way," she whispered, "follow me."

He followed her, aware of his rising excitement. There was nobody home and access was simple. Using a flashlight, she manoeuvred around the house until in the bedroom she found a bedside table. It contained jewellery and the beam from the torch caused the gems to sparkle.

"I'm not a thief, but it won't do harm to let them know we've called."

He remembered she'd taken one single pearl earring and left the drawer wide open. She'd come alive, overflowing with energy. Just being able to do it, the risks involved, gave her joy like nothing else she knew.

He'd been following her through windows and doors ever since. He'd never met a woman like her. She came to life when presented with a risky challenge. His concern was how to control her unbridled passion for the extraordinary.

He leant over and kissed her on the cheek as she took yet another sip of lukewarm coffee.

"I thought Florence might be a break from the last six months of hectic Milan and Rome," he said, "but looking around here, I don't think that's quite correct." He indicated the endless procession of cars and scooters passing by. "What're you reading there?" He pointed to a small clip of papers she'd pulled from a large plastic UPS envelope. It was addressed to them both; to their hotel, and in parenthesis, 'care of' their small but successful company they had named, not without a certain irony, 'Gordian Knots.'

The company's purpose was primary art research, which allowed them to produce low budget TV documentaries, investigating and seeking out the lost, the stolen, and the unbelievable. Moving up from small freelance assignments, they'd pooled their expertise and established a first-class reputation in finding long-lost paintings, gold, porcelain, jewellery and other items. The potential was endless. It also gave them privileged access to their true and secret passion, clandestine theft on behalf of genuine clients ... mainly.

"Our next project perhaps?"

"What is it then?"

"It arrived by courier when you were out this morning. How we were found, God knows."

"Well, who's it from?"

As much as he tried to see, she wouldn't let him

CHAPTER 5

Toledo, Spain
1555 A.D.

F rancisco lay awake but his eyes were closed. He thought back to the event in the Cathedral two years ago. He'd told nobody apart from his father, Diego. To do otherwise seemed unworthy.

His father was a short, dark, strong man who always said what was on his mind. At forty-two years of age, he was not known for expressing emotion. Yet, when Francisco told him, at first faltering, and then a second time at his father's demand, he remembered his startled expression. He had said little, but looked grave. From the narrowing of his eyes, Francisco thought his father looked like he knew something ... something he couldn't reveal. His father swore him to secrecy, told him to keep the event to himself because others wouldn't understand. Francisco kept that secret. He'd revisited the Cathedral many times attempting to recapture the vision ... but it eluded him. It would not return. His memory of it had begun to fade as his father said it would.

He'd continued to paint, attempting to capture and portray the essence of his vision through art. He never could. His other works were admired by those who saw them, who said they were dazzling and that he had a natural gift. For one so young, he was considered a marvel. His portraits and market scenes were only surpassed by his depictions of the healing miracles of Christ. Despite what he heard from admirers, he knew he needed to learn more about technique and the subtleties of paint, tone and texture. He had little satisfaction in his accomplishments.

That afternoon, Diego was preparing his schedule for the next day's work. His vineyards produced fine wines and they had helped him prosper. His wines were sought after and visitors were frequent. Macaria, his wife, was kept busy preparing small meals and drinks to keep potential buyers happy. She was six years younger than Diego, and the daughter of a prosperous wool merchant from Toledo.

Francisco sat outside and thought about his life. It was comfortable and his father continued to send him to Toledo to be schooled in Latin, mathematics and languages. He wanted Francisco to go to University, become a lawyer, and make a success of his life. Francisco's passion, though, was his art. He found the scholarly processes of formal study restrictive, stiff, and joyless. Pencils, charcoal, paints and brushes gave him freedom ... an almost guilty pleasure. The last thing he wanted was the stifling life of a lawyer.

He began sketching several versions of a gnarled pair of hands reaching out towards a bunch of grapes, complete with vine leaves. His father stood close by. Talking to him with serious gestures stood a tall, charismatic looking man in a black wrap-around cloak. He wore a large, black gathered velvet hat, braided with gold thread across a small peak beneath which shone dark kind eyes. Every so often, the conversation would stop and they would look across at Francisco. Sometime later they walked over to him.

"Francisco, this is Señor Salvador Méndez." His father

gestured for him to stand.

Francisco stood and extended his hand. "I'm pleased to meet you, Señor." He grimaced at the strength of the man's handshake.

"The feeling is mutual, Francisco. I've heard much of you." He looked at his drawing. Méndez's smile revealed crooked teeth with a prominent chip in the front.

Francisco noticed a large gold ring set on his finger, with a bright, black emerald cut into an eight-pointed cross. "Your work is exceptional." Without another word, he turned, placed a friendly arm around his father's shoulders and walked off with him.

Two hours later, the sunlight had clouded over. Francisco had had enough and as ever, was dissatisfied with his efforts. He packed up his materials and went inside. Macaria and Diego, both wearing serious expressions, were sitting side by side behind the large oak dining table. Señor Méndez had gone. His father pointed to the vacant chair opposite them.

"Francisco, we need to speak to you."

As he sat, his mother reached for his hand and squeezed it gently.

"What is it?" he couldn't prevent the concern in his voice and rubbed a knuckle across the side of his mouth.

His father placed his hand on top of his; an unusual gesture. Francisco experienced a flush of embarrassment.

He began to explain. "God has whispered to you, Francisco. He gave you a vision and a rare and wonderful gift, which would be wasted as a lawyer. Your mother and I are agreed. In life, we get few opportunities and you now have one that we hope you will appreciate. Señor Salvador Méndez, whom you met earlier, is a highly-regarded art master, and has received numerous commissions from the Pope himself and from our King. I showed him more of your work. He was impressed and has agreed to take you in, to study and develop your talent as an apprentice at his studio in Valencia."

— — —

A week later, his mother handed him one last bag to place in the cart as his father secured various small chests and a larger trunk for the journey. Francisco could feel tears in his eyes as he gave her a final embrace, before she turned with a cry and ran back into the house.

His father held up his hand. "Don't cry. It won't be long before we see you again. Trust and take note of what Señor Méndez tells you. There's more to him than being an artist. He has God's blessing, as have you." He handed Francisco a small package. "Take this, it is now yours, and God speed."

The wagoner flicked his whip and the cart moved off in a swirl of reddish dust. Once out of sight of the figure of his waving father, Francisco allowed himself to sob. When he had exhausted his sadness, he looked up at the wispy stretches of clouds. In the distance, reaching out to touch them, the towering facade of Toledo's Cathedral. He picked up his father's package and unwrapped it. What he saw caused him to gasp. There was a note in his father's handwriting, which simply said, *Méndez knows of Lazarus.* With it was a small gold ring inset with a white stone on which lay a black emerald cut into the shape of an eight-pointed cross.

CHAPTER 6

Heiligenblut, Austria
The present day...

Putting down his magazine, the guard pushed his beer out of sight under the shelving. The sound of an approaching car on the twisting road leading up to the Condesa's Austrian home, alerted him to check his visitor file. There was only one name on it.

Sir Maxwell Throgmorton.

From his cabin, he watched the sleek blue Bentley roll to a halt and stop outside the massive ornate iron gates. He stepped outside to check as a tinted window lowered. A face with a head of thick silvery hair appeared.

"Sir Maxwell Throgmorton to see the Condesa Maria Francisca de Toledo."

The guard nodded. "I will need ID please, sir."

Throgmorton raised his eyes upwards. "Did she not let you know?"

"She did, but whoever it is sir, I am required to check before I log you in and open the gates."

"It's not a problem. Driving licence okay?"

The guard took the licence and scanned it on his system. He handed it back. "That's fine. You'll find the visitors' car park in front of the chalet. I'll alert her that you've arrived. She'll be on the steps to meet you. If not, please wait in your car until she arrives."

Throgmorton wound up the window, not enjoying the smell of alcohol on the guard's breath. Driving slowly in, he checked for hidden security cameras. He could see none. The four and a half hours drive from Vienna had been more relaxing than he dared hope. There should be some reward for his perseverance.

Her phone call had been more of a summons than a social invitation. He couldn't refuse. There was something about her that intrigued him. He hadn't forgotten the way she'd dismissed him at the ball.

The car park had the only visible camera, which was mounted on a steel support above the circular layout. It was positioned in front of the decorative three storey chalet, a luxurious eighteenth century wooden structure with an ornate scalloped fascia ablaze with Austrian and Spanish flags. He eyed it over. *Hardly modest and I expect it's not her only cottage.*

— — —

10 mg of morphine sulphate slid down the syringe, through the needle, and into her outstretched arm, as she watched his arrival on the CCTV screen. She leaned her head back and released a low sigh, then took a deep breath and stood. The pain was constant and the only thing that masked it was morphine. It didn't take long to begin its work.

Sir Maxwell Throgmorton could be her only hope.

— — —

He saw her on the top step, dressed in black from head to toe; statuesque, severely elegant, and her dark hair in the same tight bun he remembered her wearing before. He could only wonder what she wanted to see him for. She ignored his outstretched hand but with a small sweep of her arm, ushered him into the main part of the spacious chalet, whose expansive windows offered a spectacular view of the Grossglockner Mountains. Around the walls were packed countless volumes of books on the afterlife, near death experiences, miracles, psychology, ancient and modern medicines, the power of the mind, holy relics and religions.

"Sir Maxwell, you are welcome and thank you for coming at such short notice. I trust you had a pleasant journey. This part of the world can be quite spectacular." Her voice hadn't lost the iciness of their previous encounter.

He stared into her impassive brown eyes and detected a moment's uncertainty. "Yes, it was better than I imagined. Thank you for inviting me. Please call me Max. What shall I call you?"

"You may call me Maria."

"Maria." He pronounced it as if he were chewing a sweet. He lifted his head slightly. "Do I detect the aroma of tea brewing?"

"You do indeed. It has been an old family custom to greet guests with tea rather than alcohol. I trust you approve?" She indicated a chair near a small log fire where a silver *art nouveau* tea service was placed on a matching tray. "Please sit. How would you prefer your tea?"

"Black would be fine."

"Likewise."

She sat down and he noticed the slight wince as she leant forward to pour from the teapot.

"Maria, I'm not one for small talk. It seems improbable that after meeting me for a few minutes over a week ago, you just want the pleasure of my company."

"Max," she hesitated as if the familiarity of using the first name of a virtual stranger was an anathema to her. "I did say at the time that I wanted to discuss something with you. You've obviously forgotten." Her mouth had tightened as if she had tasted something unpleasant.

He sipped his tea and paused. "Not entirely. I just wanted to make it easier for you. I didn't drive over four-hundred kilometres just to sip your excellent tea. I think you'd better tell me."

"Of course."

Throgmorton sensed she'd be economical about the real reason, but he'd have to go along with it, especially as there had to be money involved. She looked up at him with an odd expression, and again, he saw her suppressed flinch.

"I've been researching into the effect of religion and its art on the mind and body, especially where miracles or healing appears to have occurred. I have studied this subject for many years and I'm now finishing my fifth book on the subject, *The Healing Power of Sacred Art*. As part of my study, I've travelled around the world and seen many inexplicable occurrences. I've seen stigmata appear by gazing on the supposed true cross, people unable to walk begin walking after manifesting hysteria in front of images of Christ. On that level, there isn't much I haven't seen over the years, including weeping and bleeding Madonnas whose excretions could supposedly heal any known illness or condition. Much of it has been fraudulent, but on the odd occasions, no explanation can be offered."

Throgmorton remained impassive and wished she'd get to the point. It was like a junior barrister doing a long winded summing up. He poured himself another cup of tea. "Max, I can trace my ancestry farther back than the thirteenth century. My family came from an aristocratic and wealthy lineage. This is my third home." She waved her arm expansively. "I have one in Toledo, this one, and another in Zurich."

She fixed him with a blank stare. It was then he saw the yellowness of her skin that even expertly applied makeup failed to hide.

"I am a close friend of your ex-wife, Lady Ruth. As you know, she lives in Zurich. You needn't know how and when we met, but with what she told me, plus Herr Urbanek's input, who incidentally has represented me on occasions, I arrived at the conclusion that you might be of assistance. I hope I'm not going to be disappointed."

"You *know* Ruth. That's very strange, but now I know our meeting was more deliberate than I realised. As far as your anticipated disappointment is concerned, there's no way of knowing unless you tell me what it is you have in mind." He shifted uncomfortably. *What does she know?* There was no way he was going to allow himself to ask questions about Ruth, or show any sign of surprise. *Just what has Ruth been saying?* He attempted to look unperturbed as he drummed his fingers on the table top. At the same time, he noticed her sharp intake of breath, her eyes closing for a moment before a look of calm relaxation crossed her face. *She's in pain.*

"Your reputation, Max, no matter how much you've attempted to disguise it, is well known in certain quarters. You're regarded as a person who has fallen from grace, but has the ability to influence, find things that shouldn't be found, and lose things if necessary. Am I making myself clear?"

"Crystal." He couldn't suppress his tight smile. Flattery, even if convoluted, was music to his ears. The way the Condesa was handling this, suggested that her discretion would be paramount.

"I need something found… a painting. It should rightfully be mine and belongs also to Toledo. All I can tell you is the artist's name. Francisco Cortez. The work was painted in the latter part of the sixteenth century. I need it for my research, you understand?"

Her momentary eye contact told him that she may be good at being a Condesa, but like many felons who'd stood before him in the dock, she wasn't good at lying.

"All relevant information is contained in this file." She reached down beside her chair and produced a dark blue leather-bound binder. "To explain it all would take too long and I'm feeling very tired right now. Please take this with you to study."

He took the portfolio from her. It looked and felt expensive, secured with a decorative solid silver clasp. "What next?"

"An intriguing question, Sir Maxwell. I'm hoping you can get the wheels turning on this. Your skills in sifting through evidence and discovering truths are, I've been told, of legal legend. I'm giving you the opportunity to resurrect those skills. You know people who could help, perhaps people you shouldn't know. To be frank, I don't care about who you mix with. I want that painting and I don't want to have to wait too long. Before you ask, because I find it distasteful to discuss, you will find in the dossier details of money, fees, expenses and commissions. You'll find there's more than enough allocated to support a third party, should you require it. In your own time, read what is there and then contact me directly. Now, forgive me, I must ask you to leave. I am far too tired. If you wish to stay, there are good hotels in town or perhaps you want to drive back." She stood and indicated the main door where he had first entered.

Throgmorton again experienced the sensation of dismissal, like dirt being wiped off her shoes. His angry look, the vein twitching on the side of his head, if she noticed at all, was ignored. Within minutes, he found himself alone on the outside steps and walking back to the car park. He decided to leave the area and find himself a place to eat or stay on the way back to Vienna. In his own good time, he would study her file. Her arrogance had irked. Right now, his overriding wish was that somehow, he could engineer her come-uppance.

— — —

She watched him drive away, deciding that former High Court judge or not, he was still a slithery reptile. She balanced that observation by telling herself that reptiles were excellent at getting under closed doors. Her pain had diminished, leaving her with a yawning tiredness characteristic of her morphine use. Diagnosed with Stage 11A pancreatic cancer, barring a miracle, doctors gave her a twenty per cent chance of survival over the next five years. Having thought that she was impervious to infections and illness, the prognosis had given her a profound shock.

Since that date, her research assumed a more serious aspect. What had been a harmless, light hearted investigation into charlatans, fraudsters and missing relics, had now turned into a quest to find a genuine symbol, artefact, or whatever could possibly hold the power to cure her of the all-consuming cancer. She'd tried many prayers, reliquaries, relics like the Virgin's Veil, sacred sites including Lourdes … all without success.

Recently, while trawling through the 15, 000 records of the *Institución Columbina* in the Cathedral of Seville, she had come across a reference to the artist Francisco Cortez. It was simple. It stated that he came from Toledo, and that he was an apprentice of Salvador Méndez, and his works were highly regarded. Only three were known to exist. Two could be found at the El Prado museum in Madrid, and the other at the Cathedral-Basilica of the Assumption of Our Lady of Valencia, otherwise known as the Cathedral of the Holy Chalice. It was stated that the true Chalice of Christ displayed there was the one used at the Last Supper.

There were rumours of other paintings, but one had been regarded as his most influential. It was said to have been painted after he had a profound religious experience in the Toledo Cathedral. It was believed to have miraculous healing properties. Those who touched it or gazed upon it in sincere repentance, would be cured. It had never been found, nor was the title ever known. The records indicated that Cortez and his painting had vanished in mysterious circumstances and were never seen again.

Her first reaction had been one of annoyed astonishment. She had lived in Toledo most of her life and had never heard of him. With her condition, she couldn't prevent the thought that this was too much of a coincidence. The two works held at the El Prado were not on display. They had been stored. Using her title of Condesa, it hadn't been difficult to persuade the museum to allow her access. She remembered the Curator walking her down a cold and spiralling staircase into an immense space, like a warehouse where rack upon rack of paintings, no longer fashionable or showing their years, were stored for inspection and restoration. The Curator explained that humidity was always a problem and temperatures had to remain constant. Some paintings reacted badly to light and could only be shown for limited periods of time. Cortez's paintings had their own resting place. The Curator had written its location on a large white card taken from the database. He had found them without difficulty. With care, he slid them from their bay, placing them next to each other as if he were holding a new born baby. Both works were of identical proportions and framed in heavy gilt surrounds. She gasped at her first glance. They were like nothing she had seen before. They looked like superior amalgamations of El Greco, Correggio and Murillo.

Both depicted healing miracles of Christ. One showed a leper and the other of a herd of swine being driven over a cliff top. For their time, they had an almost abstract quality; swirling dark and light colours, blacks and blazing reds, with suggestions of triumphant yet penitent figures emerging from the swirling eddy of colours.

"Wonderful. Oh, they're just wonderful." She experienced the strangest emotion, a feeling of disembodiment, a spark of rare happiness. It went as quickly as it had come.

"Yes, they're truly superb," agreed the Curator, holding them at arm's length, "and they are due for showing in another two years. I think then we shall see a reappraisal of Cortez. The shame is that after he vanished, it was said that his works were destroyed in a large monastery fire. But nobody can verify that. According to stories, he apparently thought his life was unworthy, and later rode off into the desert and disappeared forever. Sadly, nothing has ever been found."

The Condesa nodded. The Curator had confirmed her findings. She took several photographs of the works. The images she had seen and the story surrounding Cortez haunted her for the rest of the day. They caused her to tremble. She tried looking at other works but Cortez kept flooding into her mind.

Her intuition sent her an invitation.

Later, she booked a flight from Madrid to Valencia, before her scheduled return to Zurich.

— — —

The busy streets of Valencia had lost little of their ancient history and the city remained wrapped in the atmosphere of its past. It wasn't long before she found herself in Our Lady Square, leading into the Cathedral's entrance at the Apostle's Gate overlooked by the medieval Transept Tower.

Placing a black lace mantilla on her head, she stepped inside. The cool quietness propelled her into a mood of reverence. She wished to speak to nobody, not even for information. She was on a mission, and something told her she would find what she was looking for.

She was alone. Her footsteps rang across the flagstones, and as if pulled by an unseen power, she proceeded up the nave passing panels by Jacomart depicting *Saint Benedict,* and *Ildephonsus* without giving them a second glance. Then, she remembered. Stopping at the small arched portal of a side chapel, she turned to look. It contained a confessional, chairs, and a central altar surmounted by a crucified Christ wrought in silver and wood above which hung a painting.

This is Cortez. I know it is.

Walking in, she knelt, crossed herself, recited the Hail Mary three times and the Apostles Creed at speed as if the Cathedral was ablaze, anxious only to inspect the painting. Leaning forward, she needed no telling that it had been painted by Cortez. The unusual style, the swirling blend of colours suggesting the anguished expressions of Christ and of Holy Mary, were unlike anything that came before. It gave confirmation of her search, and she knew she'd been led there. Her gaze wandered across the picture for minutes on end. She still had the photographs she had taken on her tablet. One thing had heightened her curiosity. Alongside a small signature was the even smaller but unmistakeable shape of a black eight-pointed cross…

followed by the letters *KORL*

She sat in the chapel for over an hour, alone with her thoughts, emotions and feelings. There had been no miraculous cure of her condition. That remained the same. It didn't surprise her. Yet, her hope had been ignited. Never before could she recall feeling like this. She believed she'd been guided to this place. Any doubts she'd had about miracles, and she had investigated hundreds, could now be disregarded. That she had been led by Cortez to the same sacred place where Christ's Chalice was also stored … was no accident. That alone was a minor miracle. Her conviction had increased that Cortez, in some way, held the answer. The enigma of his last missing work called her.

Where is it?

It would be found. She believed that, and that a cure for her would be there. The play of synchronicity reverberated too strongly for recent events to be mere chance.

Subsequent research had ended in a cul-de-sac. She no longer had the strength to travel far or make aggressive investigations, or harass people. Apart from her doctors, the only person who knew of her condition was Lady Ruth Throgmorton. It was one afternoon in a Zurich restaurant along the Langstrasse that Maria had confided in Ruth. She had told her of her recent disappointment. She had hit a brick wall and was slowly losing whatever hope she had of a cure for her cancer. She needed to find the painting.

That was how, in strictest confidence, she had learned of Sir Maxwell; his past and what he was capable of.

CHAPTER 7

**Hotel Machiavelli,
Florence
The present time...**

HIM." Brodie gave a snort of derision. "The dodgy judge ... friends in low places guaranteed."

"What are you on about?" Ulla's brow creased into a frown.

"Some years back, there were strong whispers about him, his past, his criminal mates, and a major storm he was involved in with government ministers. There were allegations of corrupt deals concerning the building of prisons and filling them with over-sentenced offenders. He wriggled out of it and retired early. What does he want?"

"Here, read this." Ulla took a sip of her cappuccino and thrust the letter into his hands.

There is a painting I have been asked to locate by a titled and very wealthy lady whom I now represent. Sadly, I lack the expertise to do so but she has made provisions for me to hire a third party. I am hoping that with your vast and undoubted expertise you may care to fulfil that role.

A location fee of £200,000 sterling is envisaged. On top of this all expenses will be paid. In anticipation of your acceptance I have enclosed two open-ended first class air tickets to fly to Vienna.

On meeting, full details will be given. Please inform me of your intended arrival.

Truly,
Sir Maxwell Throgmorton

Ulla pulled the tickets out of the package and waved them in his face. "Look, we've nothing on at the moment, and at the very worst, it's a free weekend in Vienna."

"No, not that crooked bastard. Forget it." He screwed up the letter and jammed it back into the envelope.

"You getting cold feet?"

"I can see what's going to happen. We find whatever it is and he steals it off us in some way and then offers it back to his sponsor at a hugely inflated price. Ulla, we both know how this game works, we've seen it a thousand times."

"If he's prepared to pay us *that* sum of money, how much must it be worth?" Ulla's face hardened.

"With that sort of money involved, he's bound to have hired guns. I don't doubt it. People could end up getting killed for something this valuable. I wouldn't put it past him. Remember the Rosicrucian issue? We found their stupid casket and they ended up killing each other over it. No more of that. People got killed and I felt responsible, and so should you."

"I don't care about them, Brodie. If they couldn't handle it then that has nothing to do with us."

"Throgmorton's painting, whatever and wherever it's supposed to be, you can guarantee for certain it won't be a legit operation." He grimaced and gave a shake of his head. "There's so much shit flying around about Throgmorton it would fill a sewer. If people heard we were involved with him, it'd be the end of the road for Gordian Knots and for us. No, the answer is no way. To be honest, Ulla, we're doing well enough without taking any more risks."

"What are you trying to say?"

"I'm just saying we don't need to take risks. We don't need that anymore. We have enough without them."

"Enough?"

"I want to finish with our extra activities."

The pause was lengthy. She couldn't prevent her voice from rising. "I could see this coming for months back. I can read you like a book."

Brodie stared at her. The effect of what he'd said was obvious. He was about to hear where that left their relationship.

"What you've done, the stealing, the break-ins, they all point to one thing, Brodie. A leopard can't change his spots. You're a great thief, not the normal type, you don't do it for personal greed, and true, we've helped ourselves here and there, but you have helped put a great deal of good back into society. Why can't you accept that?"

"What I'm accepting is that I love you. That's the only thing that's not going to change. I don't want you dead or banged up in jail."

"I know that. It's a bit like love me, love my dog. By that I mean, if you love me, love what I do."

"That's ridiculous and you know it. Aren't you ever going to call it a day?"

"No. I'm still enjoying it."

"Sooner or later one of us *will* get killed. Shots have been fired at us aplenty, and only bullet-proof vests have prevented that from happening."

"A self-fulfilling prophecy?"

"I want a normal life, Ulla."

"Then find yourself a normal woman."

"Look, this is getting out of hand."

"Brodie, I'm not joking. I'm serious. If normal is what you want in life, we can say goodbye and we can say it here and now."

"Don't be stupid. I know you like taking risks. Isn't our legitimate work sufficient? Sure, we can add in risks if that is what you want; rock-climbing, base jumping, freefall parachuting, anything. Whatever you need, but please no more guns or shootings. You've been hit twice. How far do you want to take this before you quit?"

"And let's say I don't want to stop. What then? You leave me?"

There was challenge in her eyes. He thought he could handle it, but now that he was being put to the test, his certainty wobbled. He wasn't going to make it easy for her.

"I'll have to think about it."

"It all seems plain and simple, so what do you have to think about? It looks like you've done that already."

Her confident stare didn't waver. He'd never seen her like this before. He reached for her hand but she wouldn't let him hold it.

"It's make your mind up time, Brodie."

He remained expressionless as the events of the last few years spun through his mind. They'd made a million between them and that was without Gordian Knots. At his age, he'd guessed it would one day come to this. There was a price to pay and there was no such thing as a free lunch. As a robber and burglar, he'd never doubted that statement. They'd had weapons training and now routinely carried arms on their excursions, which had increased his uneasiness. A man had been shot and he still didn't like to think of it. Ulla had missed that possibility on her well-planned agenda. It had added another unwelcome factor to the risks they were taking. *Is there a limit to what I would do for her?* He didn't know the answer. Life without her would be bleak. For the time being, that had to be the deciding factor.

After what seemed like time being stretched to breaking point, he spoke. "It looks as if Sir Maxwell Throgmorton will be having visitors this weekend. What's his number?"

— — —

Clutching a briefcase, Throgmorton walked at a brisk pace along the Mariahilfer Straße and headed for Hotel Das Tyrol where Ladro and Stuart were booked for two nights. It was better than them turning up on his doorstep. Phone numbers or email prevented people from getting too close. He turned into the hotel entrance between two pillars and into the elegant reception and lobby area, where he hoped they would be waiting for him. The two sitting in the corner were the only people there. He didn't need an introduction to realise who they were. They both stood as he approached.

He'd never felt comfortable in casual clothes. Even the smartest he regarded as one step removed from the vulgar. Brodie Ladro and Ulla Stuart fell into that category, with their jeans and safari style jackets.

"Miss Stuart, Mr. Ladro?" He extended his hand, aware of their lack of enthusiasm. "I can only tell you how pleased I am that you are willing to have a look at the problem I have. But first, let me order some drinks."

Brodie ordered a lager and Ulla, scotch on the rocks. He had a gin and Dubonnet.

"My grapevine told me that if anyone could find what's in here," he tapped the leather-bound file, "it would be you two. At first, I didn't realise who you were, but then I remembered your exploits on TV when you found the lower left panel of the Ghent Altarpiece on that programme about the Van Eyck brothers."

"Yes, we were pleased about that one." Ulla smiled but Brodie remained silent. "To cut a long story short, the thief tried to get money from the Belgium government, who weren't going to play ball. On his deathbed, the thief revealed that he was the only one who knew where the masterpiece was hidden, and that he would take the secret to his grave. Although several people claimed to know its whereabouts, the painting had not been seen since. All sorts of people claimed they'd found it, but if you remember, Sir Maxwell, we found it a short distance away from the Cathedral, on the wall of a back room in a hardware store. It had been there for years."

"Yes, it was that and other things that I'd heard that drew me to you." His smile was cryptic. "I hope you're not going to ask how I found you, that's my secret."

"Well, you would know that wouldn't you, Sir Maxwell." Brodie received a sharp kick under the table from Ulla. "So, can we get to the point now? What exactly do you expect us to do?"

"In this file is the strangest information I have ever seen. It beats by a mile any case I have ever come across. Do have a look and ask me whatever you want." He pushed it across the table. "There is a work by this artist Cortez," he jabbed a finger at a series of photographs, "that my client desperately needs to find for her research work. Please look at these. They are the only known examples of his work. Take as long as you wish. While you are doing that, I'll adjourn to the bar for twenty minutes."

"Thank God he's pushed off," Brodie muttered.

Ulla opened the envelopes and spread the contents around the table top.

"Two hundred grand says to me I hope he's not going to be too long. What do we know of Cortez?"

Sheets of paper full of notes and headed: _Francisco Cortez (1541-?)_ stared up at them.

"Never heard of him. Have you?"

"No, but look at these." She pushed several photographs of three paintings by Cortez closer to him. All had been taken at different angles. The Leper's Redemption, The Swine of the Gadarene, and Christ Crucified and the Mother Mary.

Brodie went quiet and gazed for some while at the

photographs. "I would say they're powerful, masterly, and disturbingly mystical. What d'you think?"

"They're all that. It's odd there's so little known about him, and neither of us have come across him before."

"What do the other notes say?"

Ulla noted Brodie's gathering interest. "He came from Toledo, rumoured to have had a vision and later studied under Salvador Méndez, the Court and Papal artist. It also says something happened and he and all his works vanished off the face of the earth."

"That's a shame. They're superb. What year?"

"It doesn't say. All it mentions are the three we have photographs of, two in the El Prado and one in Valencia Cathedral."

"That's not much to go on. Any clues on Maxwell's client?"

"None that I can see, but he did let us know she was titled and wealthy."

"It mentions that the *Institución Columbina* in Seville may be able to supply background information"

"I think we'd need to start at the beginning, Toledo, and work forward from there."

"Look, he's on his way back. Let's see how much more he's prepared to tell us."

Throgmorton strode over, still holding on to his drink, with a large manila envelope under his arm. He didn't wait for a reply. "I have here" he said, placing the envelope on the table, "a contract for you to look at and hopefully agree to. Well, what do you think of the assignment?"

Ulla guessed what Brodie could be thinking and he spoke before she could say anything.

"There's not much to go on, and what makes you think we want to sign up for something that could tie us up for God knows how many months, for expenses only money, looking for a missing work that may not even exist?"

Ulla nodded. "I agree, we're not working for nothing. We don't have to."

There was a pause. Throgmorton tilted back his head, ran his hand through his hair and proceeded to pucker his lips. "I guessed you might take that approach and I can't fault it. There are other factors in my submission that you should consider."

"They'd better be good or Ulla and I will be out of here tomorrow morning."

She nodded her agreement.

"I have access to a considerable amount of what I call 'social information.' I know that my client writes books ... lots of books. They are mainly about the impact religion has had on art and the subsequent healing powers of certain works and artefacts. Personally, I don't believe a word of it, but money can be persuasive. I'm certain you'll agree. I also discovered, though she would never tell me, that her life expectancy isn't going to exceed five years. She has cancer, and I have witnessed evidence of that. God knows why she wants to find Cortez's painting, but from what she has said and given her interests and writings, I suspect that she believes this missing painting could hold the cure for her cancer. She has nothing to lose and will spend whatever it takes to find and possess it."

He paused. He raised his eyebrows and began smoothing down non-existent creases from his clothes. "Can't you see," his voice ascended a pitch. "if there is any substance in her story, how much that could bring? People from all around the world would be willing to pay God knows what to see or touch it or whatever they need to regain their health. I intend to at least give it a chance. Whether this *is* true or not, my wealth would be unbelievable, and you could be part of it. Just imagine the kudos and spin offs you'd get for such a discovery." His eyes hardened like a hawk.

"It's pie in the sky. I don't believe a word of it," Brodie sounded annoyed. "Even to start, we'd need an immediate advance plus substantial monthly retainers up front, or a large sum to cover a three-month period. And that doesn't include expenses. If you're prepared to do that, we might consider it. It's that or nothing."

Ulla knew Brodie well. He'd taken a personal dislike to Throgmorton, and his bargaining had become abrasive. Not a half-hour ago, he was about to walk away from the proposal, but curiosity had always been his weak point. She squeezed his arm hard.

"That's as it is, Max." She cocked her head to one side and gave him her sweetest smile.

Throgmorton crossed his arms, attempted to smile, but could only register a pinched expression. "It's like that, is it?"

"Yes, it's like Brodie says, deal or no deal."

"What amount do you have in mind?"

Brodie scratched at an invisible mark on the back of his hand. He didn't look up, but replied in a flat tone. "Twenty thousand right now and ten on the first of each month, in sterling. That's without the expenses, of course. One late payment and it's off."

Throgmorton's expression soured but he gave a small nod, "Agreed, but for a three-month trial period only, and then we'll assess where we are." He pulled out the made-up contract, filled in the appropriate details, and Brodie and Ulla signed every entry as he did, retaining a copy for himself.

"I hope for your sakes you two are as good as they say you are. Take this file, I have the original and we will be in touch within a week. Twenty thousand will reach you tomorrow." With a grim expression, Throgmorton handed them the file, stood and walked towards the door.

"Was he making some sort of threat?"

"Ulla, yes that *was* some sort of threat. Don't doubt it. Should we ever locate this mysterious painting the first thing he'll do is short-change us, and as I said, steal it, and then offer it back to his client for a vastly increased sum of money. Should it have powers, which we all doubt, including him, he'll keep up the pretence, and cash in on its fame. Exciting enough for you?"

"Exciting and different."

"I suggest we start early next week, make a trip to Toledo, and begin by tracking down his client. That shouldn't be too difficult. What d'you think? Throgmorton's not expecting that line of enquiry."

Ulla suppressed a giggle. "And you wanted to give this all up. What was that all about?" She leant over and kissed his cheek.

"I don't like mysteries and I admit, I'm curious. But I'm more curious to see Throgmorton's face when he realises that if we find something, he's never going to get his hands on it."

CHAPTER 8

Within two and a half hours of the Boeing landing at Madrid's Barajas airport, Brodie and Ulla were on the A-42 freeway, driving the seventy plus kilometres down to Toledo.

"Whether Toledo is the place to start, I'm not sure, but I think we need to absorb the atmosphere of the place."

Ulla's reply came across as distracted, "Yeah, okay."

"You don't sound too certain. What's wrong?"

"Nothing really. Look in your mirror."

"Okay, what am I supposed to be looking at?"

"The dark blue car. See it?"

Brodie took another long look in the driving mirror. "What about it?"

"It's been behind us ever since we left the airport. Every move we make, it follows. When we stopped to check the route, it stopped too. I think it's following us."

"I doubt it, but I'll pull over to see what happens." Brodie swung the wheel hard to the right, pulling onto the hard shoulder. The dark blue car appeared to hesitate before it powered past them. The two men inside didn't give them a second glance.

"Sorry," said Ulla, "paranoia must be setting in."

"Don't be too sorry. For a moment, that man didn't know what to do."

"Throgmorton?"

"If they were tailing us it, would be on his orders, for certain."

"Let's not think about it. Besides, we can't prove we were being followed."

— — —

Their hotel, Hotel Pedro Sanchez, was small and located in quiet, narrow medieval streets close to the Cathedral, near the city centre. They sat in a walled garden beneath a leafy pergola surrounded by a meandering path bordered with ranks of climbing roses. The owner had told them these were descendants of original thirteenth century stock.

They spread the contents of Throgmorton's file across their table. It included three glossy A5 sized photographs of Cortez's paintings. Ulla was studying Throgmorton's directives.

"I think he's slipped up. He didn't want us to know who his client is and all he was prepared to tell us was that she's a titled and wealthy woman. In her notes, she mentions her annoyance for not knowing of Cortez and his works although ..." Ulla paused for effect. "Guess what? She says he came from her home city of Toledo." She handed him the notes.

Brodie looked up with a grin. "Well done. That's going to help. All we have to do now is track down a local aristocrat; a Duchess, Condesa, Marquesa or a Baronesa, who happens to write a lot of arty-religious books. Shouldn't be that difficult to find."

She didn't hear him. With a large glass magnifying lens, she was bent over the photographs of Cortez's works.

"What d'you make of that? It's on all three." She pointed to the signature and what was beside it, hard to see but clearly identifiable beneath the lens: a black cross followed by initials.

✠ KORI

"It's some sort of religious cross, but I can't make out the initials too well."

"Doesn't Malta have a society known as the Sovereign Order founded back in the times of the Crusades? They were originally dedicated to helping lepers, and sick and poor pilgrims to and from Jerusalem."

"If I recall, they do, but back in medieval days, they were full-blown Knights who went into battle if needed. They spread across the known world."

Brodie gasped as he peered even closer. "What in God's name is that?"

CHAPTER 9

Monasterio de San José de Nazaret
Nr. Segovia, Spain,
1604 A.D.

Brother Alfonso arose early. The sky remained dark and a million pin pricks of light were beginning to surrender to the approaching day.

He shaved using cold water and the one small broken mirror he was allowed for doing so. He never liked what he saw in the reflection. The marred face staring back at him was thin, bony, and dominated by a squashed nose that had spread like a flounder – the result of an agitated disbeliever when he was a young monk. His skin had grown blotchy and his face and arms had a spread of red and bulbous lesions like mud bubbles in a pond. The disease remained, but his impetuous days had gone. His world now was of the spirit, of contemplative beatitudes.

He walked across the grey flagstones of the Square of the Blessed Virgin. The fine mist of early morning rain from nearby hills dampened his brown scapular as it flapped across his white tunic. He pulled up his hood and tightened the rope-tie around his waist. On this special day, he needed an extra hour of solitary contemplation before first prayers.

Seated on a long, low oak bench, he recited the Psalms asking for purity and cleansing. He needed to be viewed as worthy for what was about to happen this day. He reviewed his life before he succumbed to the call of God—his lusts, his rampant sexuality, his greed, his imperfections from the day of his birth forty-two years ago, then to his undying shame, he had been branded a bastard. A sense of sanctity filled him. For over twenty-five years he had rebuilt his life, attempting to erase the follies of his past. They paraded through his mind like water cascading over some giant fall. He had followed the vows of poverty, chastity, and obedience. Had he not devoted himself to the Rules of the Monastic Knights that had shaped his life and made him willing to defend Christ's sacred Order to the death?

Lord, inflame our hearts and our inmost beings with the fire of Your Holy Spirit, that we may serve You with chaste bodies and pure minds. Through Christ our Lord. Amen.

Tonight, there would be a reward for him for his toil. The Abbey's secret, guarded with jealous zeal, was to be made known to him.

Wiping away tears, he bent his head low and pulled the hood of his habit further over his head. It would be a long day and night, but he was ready.

Later that evening, the two large wooden gates that sealed off the monastery from its outside perimeters, swung open in a cacophony of creaks and groans to reveal the surrounding hills, bathed in hazy moonlight and standing like tired sentinels. In the middle of the exiting procession and surrounded by twelve monks, each wearing a white cloak emblazoned with a black eight pointed cross, walked Brother Alfonso. Weighed down with a sense of unworthiness, he lost himself in spiritual contemplation. The slow-moving column was led by the upright and dignified figure of Grand Master, Abbot Aelred.

They descended a rocky gulley before passing through a narrow cleft that led into a hidden cave. The light of their flaming torches cast exaggerated shadows off damp pockmarked walls, punctuated with crucifixes and images of the Blessed Virgin. Alfonso drew a sharp breath of astonishment. For all his years at the monastery, he'd not known of this place. He had an increasing sense that this was no ordinary secret.

The procession, led by the Abbot, took up the Templar's chant, *Salve Regina*. Misty breaths arose as a deep resonance filled the descending cavern. Alfonso quivered, his body shaking with an intoxicating emotion he'd never experienced before.

This was being done for him.

They moved through numerous passages and tight tunnels before the flickering torches lit up a central area that echoed with a thousand chants from ages past. One monk went to the left and the other to the right, until they formed a semicircle with Grand Master Aelred centrally placed. In front of him, concealed by a large gold mantle emblazoned with a black cross, stood something ... he had no idea what. It stood on a low altar surrounded by candles.

The chant came to an end.

Silence engulfed the cavern like a grave.

"Brother Alfonso, step forward and kneel before what you do not understand." The Abbot's voice reverberated around the clammy walls glistening with the flicker of torchlight. He gestured to where Alfonso should kneel.

Alfonso moved forward, hesitating before he reached the spot.

"There is nothing to be afraid of, Brother. There is only joy to be welcomed. You have been considered worthy by the council that now stand around you. You are to be one of us. Your vows have been wholeheartedly fulfilled, and what we cherish, protect, and would willingly lay down our lives for now stands before you. What you will witness is our sacred secret, never to be revealed. Do you, Brother Alfonso, with your immortal soul to forfeit if you break this trust, swear to uphold your vows to God and of us Holy Knights, to help spread the goodness and healing you are about to be privy to?"

"I swear it." Alfonso's voice had descended to a low but loud disembodied whisper.

"Then look now." The Abbot lifted his arm and in one swift movement removed the gold covering cloth, letting it drop to the floor.

Before he lapsed into unconsciousness, Alfonso saw a large intense painting shimmering in shades of purple and yellow, depicting Lazarus stepping from his tomb and reaching out to the resplendent figure of Christ. From Christ's eyes shone a dazzling white light that Alfonso knew could not be paint. It physically glowed.

It was real!

The eyes shone and looked straight into his own.

CHAPTER 10

L ooking through the lens at the dark yellow signature scrawled across the bottom of *The Leper's Redemption*, Brodie looked puzzled. "Ulla, am I seeing things? What do you make of this?" He jabbed his finger at the photograph and handed her the lens.

She peered long and hard at the signature. Around the feet and ankle of the leper were clay pots, urns, and small glass bottles, and from one appeared to be emerging an evil looking snake, its forked tongue forming an inverted heart resembling a bottle label. The label completed Cortez's signature.

"I see what you mean. It's as if Cortez was making a statement. The snake's tongue clearly spells out, *Bodegas de* and that is above his signature of Cortez."

"A clue of some sort? The evils of drink, message in a bottle, or was there a wine-making concern called Cortez? Could even be a Conquistador —let's check it."

A Google search revealed the name Cortez as the sixty-fourth most used Hispanic name. Clearly not prolific. In the immediate area, though, there were just a handful. Then came the clue they had been looking for.

Thirty minutes later, Ladro and Stuart were driving north-west of Toledo. Their objective lay an approximate twenty kilometres distant. The *Bodegas de Cortez.*

Brodie whistled. "If this place has anything to do with Cortez, the medieval artist, then that will be one amazing coincidence."

"We're soon going to find out." Ulla looked up into the driving mirror. "Oh no!"

"What?" Brodie grimaced

"Look behind."

Brodie turned around. "Is it the same blue car as last time?

"It is. What do we do?"

"Nothing. My bet is they're reporting back to Throgmorton. If and when we find something, then they'll make a move. I guarantee it."

"I'll give them a friendly wave." Ulla lifted a finger and waved it with some vigour at the following car. It dropped back "Now they know we're on to them."

The car didn't pursue them when they turned to follow a signpost with a large black index digit, directing them to *Bodegas de Cortez.* It led up a narrow track leading into a private estate and a vineyard. They watched the car behind them pull up into a nearby lay-by.

"What's the betting that when we come out, they'll still be there waiting?" Ulla swung the wheel to avoid a large pothole.

They drove past row upon row of symmetrically planted low bush vines that led up a gentle gradient towards the small main building and its equivalent car park. A barrier stood in front, bearing the company logo.

"Look familiar?" He indicated a large yellow coloured inverted heart garlanded with vine leaves. The complex was far from a simple rustic set up. In one direction stood numerous outbuildings and rows of tall stainless steel vats looking like columns of armoured knights. Built with ancient bricks and featuring arches, the main building had a small restaurant where the reception area and visitor's centre were located. It was surmounted by a towering spire on which a weather vane dominated, featuring the same vine leaves around which curled a large snake.

Ulla gave a small gasp. "This is getting spooky." She brought the car to a stop, and they slipped on their Gordian Knots ID tags. No sooner had they stepped out when a petite, pretty woman with a sunny smile walked towards them from the front entrance.

"Buenos Días. Bienvenido a Bodegas de Cortez!"

"Thank you. My name is Ulla and this is Brodie." They shook her outstretched hand. "Evita." Ulla had read her name tag. "I'll get to the point. We're not here for the wine. We are researching a lost Spanish artist by the name of Cortez and we're wondering if we may speak to the owner?"

Evita stiffened, lost her smile, gave them a probing gaze, but managed to say, "I will see. Señor Cortez is usually very busy. Please wait." She turned and walked back in.

They both looked at each other with raised eyebrows.

Some minutes later, the door swung open and a slight wiry man stepped out. He looked like a septuagenarian, but held himself upright. "I am Raúl Cortez," he said, moving towards them with a suspicious glint in his eye. "What is it you want?" His voice was snappy and he didn't offer his hand.

Ulla thanked him for his time and showed him her company ID tag. Cortez read it but remained impassive. She went on to explain their mission.

"Not much is known of him. Only three paintings are acknowledged to exist, but it was suspected there were others." Still, Cortez retained an aloof, poker faced expression.

Brodie interrupted. "Señor Cortez, tell me what you make of this." He pulled the photograph out of his briefcase, together with the lens. He thrust it at the old man, pointing to the leper's ankle and the signature. "Now look at it through the magnifier. Tell me that's not the same as your company logo."

64

Cortez pushed it away without a glance. "There is no need for me to look, Señor."

"But..."

"Follow me, please." He turned, signalled with a small wave of his arm, and walked to the swing door, holding it open for them.

"If I didn't know better, I'd say he was smiling," Brodie whispered.

Raúl walked at a brisk pace. His shoes clip-clopped across a highly polished wooden floor until he came to a halt before a small central wooden doorway at the far end of the room. He reached for a key hanging an arm's length above.

"We are nearly there," he said without explanation and still with a trace of a smile.

The door creaked open to reveal an oak panelled room with a vaulted and beamed ceiling. An array of glass display cases and what looked like a library collection, spread out along the walls. He ushered them in.

"Our museum." He gestured around the space. "I'm sure you are wondering why you are here."

"Why are we here then?" Brodie didn't know whether to smile or scowl.

"Please sit while I explain." He led them to a small sofa. "I'll get to the paintings in a moment. The Cortez family have been producing wine as far back as the thirteenth-century, if not before. Around you here are examples of what we have produced through the ages: the equipment, bottles, and glasses that helped us to the finished product. As you will see, we have kept bottles of unopened wine for centuries. But, this is not why you are here. The painting in the photograph you attempted to show me, I am well aware of." He paused as Evita walked in with a tray on which stood a bottle of Tempranillo and three large tulip shaped glasses. Without asking, she poured and handed out the wine.

"Our finest," she half whispered.

"You are correct, Señor Ladro. It is true that the painting in your photograph depicts our emblem and it has not changed since it was first introduced back in the middle ages." Raúl Cortez paused, ran his hand through his grey hair, tilted his chin, and looked at them both with an enquiring expression.

He's teasing us. Ulla leant forward. "I don't doubt that what you say is true, Señor. The signature of Francisco Cortez suggests he must have been part of your distant family and therefore you, Señor, are a direct link to him."

"What more can you tell us?" Brodie asked with an expectant look

Again, the pause, as Raúl took a long sip of his wine. "Yes, all that you say is true."

Another lengthy silence.

"What I'm about to tell you, only a few know. I think the time for that is now over. The paintings at El Prado, shown in your photographs, were not Francisco's true intentions."

"What are you implying?"

"He repainted them rather than make alterations or adjustments. El Prado, in my opinion, holds inferior versions. There can be no doubt that he had intended to paint something else. I like to think that in the versions you are about to see, his true intentions are hinted at."

Ladro looked across at Ulla whose jaw had dropped.

"What! There are others?"

"Say nothing." Raúl had a grave expression as he raised a hand, his palm stretched out towards them. "Francisco, as I told you and the records show, painted two of each, of the Leper and of the Gadarene Swine. He was unhappy with his first attempts. He refused to alter them, but elected to redo them for reasons we can now only guess at. The Cortez family, from generation to generation, became keepers or guardians of his true paintings to this day."

"You have the paintings and records, Señor Cortez?" said Brodie, aware of a familiar and accelerating excitement.

66

"Please be patient ... Evita, would you?" He signalled to her and pointed to the panelled wall.

Evita nodded, said nothing, and moved across to dim the lights. She reached down behind a small cupboard and there followed the sound of a switch. Two large panels on the opposite wall slid silently open, one to the left and the other to the right. Overhead, halogen picture lamps shone down and illuminated side by side *The Leper's Redemption* and *The Swine of the Gadarene*

Ladro gave a low whistle. "Phew! They look so much bigger."

"That is because they are. They are half the size of the two held by El Prado."

"Your emblem is clearer on the signatures and so are the black crosses and those initials. Let me check for other differences." Brodie held the photographs against the paintings. "Yes, look here Ulla." Brodie skimmed his finger over the pointing arm in the photograph. "Look, the fingers are pointing downwards. Now, look at them on this painting—the hand is positioned upwards and the index finger points towards a small hill on the distant horizon." He bent his head closer. "And look, there's a suggestion of a building there. Can you make it out?"

Ulla squinted hard. "Without the lens, I would say it's an abbey, monastery or church."

"Well, it's certainly not a synagogue because that's an unmistakable cross there." "What's it doing there? Historically, it's out of context. The continuity is wrong."

Raúl stepped back. "Look at the swine now. What do you see?"

Brodie quickly counted. "On your painting, there are thirteen of them, and the El Prado version shows twelve. Look, what's that man doing?"

"He's pointing at what looks like the same building as in the other painting. It seems also to have been placed in exactly the same spot. What is it?"

Ulla, using her tablet, took several close-up photographs of the area around and including the building.

Raúl turned to Evita. "Please."

Evita closed the panels and restored normal lighting. "Somebody has come into the reception. I must see to them. Please excuse me." She gave the hint of a smile and walked out.

"You say you are looking for Francisco's missing paintings. You've now seen two." Raúl's brow wrinkled and he pointed a finger at them both. "You say that's your intention, but I suspect there is something else you are looking for. Am I correct?"

Ulla raised her eyebrows and looked across to Brodie.

He looked down at the floor, then lifted his head and nodded. "You've been very frank with us, Señor, and yes, you're right, there is something else. There is rumoured to be a missing last work. It is alleged by some to have miraculous powers. Personally, we doubt the truth of that, but our client is insistent we locate it—should it exist at all. What you have shown us is amazing and gives us some hope. If we've been less than truthful, please accept our apologies."

Cortez leaned back in his chair, placing his chin on his hands. "None of us here have time for extensive research. I know of your company Gordian Knots from television. Maybe we could help each other. I have here the Cortez archives since the late thirteenth-century. They do contain reference to the Cortez line, and it includes Francisco and his parents. There are also personal diaries and his early sketches and thoughts. These, I imagine, would be invaluable in attempting to find what you are looking for. You would not get far without them."

"We are contracted to another party, Señor, but what would you expect from us?"

"All we ask is that … anything you discover should belong to the Cortez family." He pointed to a vast, glass fronted bookcase that stood in permanent semi-darkness. It contained rows of hefty volumes, scrolls, diaries, almanacs, and ledgers—the Cortez family records. "If you agree, you can have unlimited access." He extended his hands with open palms. "Is that acceptable? If so,

Evita will be at hand to assist you in every way, and I will draw up a contract."

"We weren't expecting this, but if Ulla agrees, we'll do it."

Ulla looked at him with a quizzical expression. "Okay, if that's what you want."

An unexpected and loud noise like a thunder flash filled the room from outside. *What on earth!*

Evita crashed through the door, her head soaked in blood.

CHAPTER 11

Valencia, Spain
1559 A.D.

S pluttering candlelight caused his shadow to dance across the coldness of the thick stone walls. He clutched at his throbbing head. Red wine and birthday celebrations the night before were collecting their fee. Shaking his head from side to side, Francisco blew out a slow agonised breath. No matter how fragile he felt, the day's work had to be prepared.

His daily task was to organise the paints, grind up the pigments, and set out the brushes for his master and the other students. All this preparation had to be set out in long rows down the length of a very large table. He performed the daily routine in a rush. The part he enjoyed most was grinding up the pigments.

Today, it didn't feel so good.

There was a difference between students and apprentices. The abilities of the apprentices exceeded those of the students, and would one day be expected to surpass those of the master's. Salvador Mendez had only two apprentices, Francisco and the newly appointed Greek boy, Kadmos. After last night's revelries, he didn't doubt that Kadmos would be feeling as unwell as he did. In two hours' time, an interval that would pass in a flash, the day's real work would begin.

The entire operation, thought Francisco, reminded him of a monastery. The early morning starts with the washing, the daily duties, prayers, and then breakfast, all watched over by the unsmiling gaze of Salvador Méndez. It led him to wonder if his life would ever be his own. The painting Francisco had been appointed to involved the Danish astronomer, Tycho Brahe, holding a copy of the *Alfonsine Astronomical Tables,* which had recently been revised in Toledo. Francisco would get lost in the structure of the work, the juxtapositioning of objects, the subtle metaphors and symbolic meanings he could construe.

But it bored him.

Famous people from society, the arts, science, and political figures, were familiar visitors at Méndez's paint-stained studio. He would perform the major features of the work and ask apprentices to execute certain other aspects to bring in their own ideas, colour, and brush work. He would supervise and contribute where required so the painting would have his stamp upon it.

This was not what Francisco wanted to paint. *Painting portraits is for career artists. There are greater things to paint.* The emotional impact of the religious vision of his youth had faded, but was not forgotten. The memory, although distant, continued to leave him awe-struck. It wasn't often that a day passed when he didn't think of it and suspect his future was connected to it.

Something else was on his mind. Love. Her name was Paloma. If he had to do a last ever portrait, it would be of her. Tall, slender, olive skinned, with luminous intelligent hazel eyes that brimmed with vitality, she was the daughter of the studio's materials supplier. Francisco was a frequent visitor, often sent to buy paints, pigments and canvases for Salvador.

That evening, when the day's work was over and his hangover

gone, he sat in the darkening studio and imagined her face; recalling the touch of her hand on his that morning—a touch that he thought was no accident. Was it his imagination that whenever he walked into the shop she would appear in a rush of laughter? When he left, did he also imagine her sadness as she whispered for him not to take too long before his next visit?

There had to be a way they could meet without her father or his tutor knowing.

Francisco's dreamy thoughts broke when the door swung open and Salvador Méndez walked in. He had a serious expression. Francisco stood as studio etiquette required.

"Sit back down." Salvador, sounding solemn, seated himself opposite Francisco. "It is time for me to speak to you most seriously."

"Have I displeased you, Señor?"

"Just the opposite, Francisco." He stared hard. "I can say, without any doubt, you have been my best apprentice—ever. From you I have learnt things I would not have believed possible. The way you can construct a scene, capture the essence of somebody and their family ... the olive merchant, Sanchez and his wife, for example. You seemed to have caught his entire life with your colour and brushwork. It was quite extraordinary."

"But Señor..." Salvador's look and the wave of his hand stopped his interruption.

"You remember when I first met you at your father's house. You were drawing a pair of hands, always difficult to get right. I was impressed. I didn't arrive that day by accident, it was your father who invited me. I promised him not to have the conversation we are about to have until after your eighteenth birthday. That time has now arrived."

Salvador's voice dropped to a loud whisper, and he turned his head left and right as if he expected someone to be there. "What I am about to say to you this night is secret, and must never be revealed. You must promise never to make known what I'm about to tell you."

Francisco swallowed hard. "A secret? You want me to keep a secret?"

"That's what I'm asking."

Francisco ignored the butterflies that jumped inside his stomach, aware of an overwhelming need to know what his master had to reveal. "I promise." His voice was loud and clear.

Salvador looked relieved. He leant forward. "Your father and I have been colleagues for many years, and it was he who told me of the experience you had as a young boy in Toledo's Cathedral."

"He told you that!" Francisco didn't know whether to be angry or flattered.

"He was obliged to."

"*Obliged!* What on earth do you mean?"

"The fresco of *The Raising of Lazarus* you were so moved by in the Cathedral, was painted by Juan de Borgoña. He was a mystic, deeply religious, and a member of our Order—as is your father, and his father, and his father before."

He paused, raising both hands again to cut off Francisco's intended question. "I will explain as I go along."

"Borgoña had the self-same vision with a similar painting, as you had, before he painted that fresco. He had a disease and it was cured. Part of that experience revealed to him that whoever had a similar vision, would be compelled to paint a picture so miraculous that whoever gazed upon it with complete faith … would be healed. That has yet to happen. Your father and I believe that you are the person Borgoña has chosen. We know of no others who have had that experience after him. That task has fallen to you, Francisco. His fresco will someday vanish or be destroyed as have all other paintings linked to the original painting of the Lazarus miracle. Yours will replace it."

The colour drained from Francisco's face. He felt giddy, as if he were losing his mind. He had difficulty breathing. He bent forward and clutched at his stomach. His voice quaked when he finally spoke.

"My father, an Order … what does this mean?" He slumped back into his chair and felt the comfort of Salvador's arm around his shoulders.

"Your father Diego, as I am, is a lay member, a follower of the monastic Order of the Knights of the Risen Lazarus. Our emblem is the Black Cross of Christ. Our knights have fought in every Crusade since they began. But the Order's main work is to heal, not to kill or injure. We nurse the sick and the lepers of this sad world both in body and mind."

Francisco leant into Salvador's shoulder. At the same time, he could feel tears in his eyes and rushing blood as his heart began to pound. He struggled to speak. "What has this got to do with me?"

"That, you alone must decide. We suspect you were chosen that day. Borgoña said there would be few to be so blessed, that the next one would be creative and pure in heart. We have not known of any. You are the first. Your father recognised what had happened and informed me, especially when he saw the scenes of Christ's miracles that you painted with such fervour. When you left, your father gave you his ring. It was not given lightly. That action reveals what he wants from you—to accept and join our Order. But you must make your choice, not now, and only when you feel ready. You are free to say no. The vows required are obedience, chastity, piety, and poverty. You, I suspect, have a God-given power, for the benefit of all. Latent it may be, but it is waiting to blossom."

Francisco lifted his head and stared with a blank expression up at the ceiling. Mendez's words had mesmerised him.

His destiny had become clear …. Any doubts fell away like a crumbling wall.

He stood, bowed his head to Mendez, turned and walked from the room.

— — —

Toledo, Spain
The present day...

Her expression contorted as pain slid through the thousand nerve endings of a body that grew more emaciated, unnoticeable on a daily basis, but striking to those who saw her infrequently.

In her private chapel designed as a smaller version of the Medici family's at the Church of Santa Croce in Florence, a chapel she had greatly admired, the Condesa Maria Francisca de Toledo struggled with her mental Litany to Saint Peregrine.

O good Saint Peregrine, patron of those suffering from cancer and incurable diseases, I beseech you, relief from my suffering...

She repeated this over and over until her devotions obstructed every other thought.

The one thing that wasn't blocked out — pain.

Morphine had become the saint who interceded on her behalf. Its usage, she knew, was the ultimate death-dealing helter-skelter. She thought Satan lurked behind its deceitful respite.

Doctors had been unable to cure her and neither had the other therapies and weird techniques she had championed. In desperation, she had placed all remaining hope, but with reservations, on Sir Maxwell Throgmorton. High Court judge he may have been, but there was something worthless about him. How on earth Ruth Overberg married him, she didn't understand.

She no longer had the luxury of choice. Her standards and beliefs were coming apart like wet tissues.

From another room, she heard the phone ring. She didn't need to be told who it was. Her maid tapped the door and opened it. She was holding the telephone.

"Thank you, Donna." She stretched out her hand and took the phone from her. "I know who it is."

"Sir Maxwell."

75

"My Lady Maria."

She detected a tone of mockery in his voice. "You have news for me?"

"Early days yet, Maria."

She winced at his descent into the familiar.

"My researchers are following several possibilities and are in Spain as we speak. I hope to hear from them soon with positive news."

She tried to read behind his words for something to grab hold of. "Is there nothing else?"

"I'm afraid not, but believe me, if there is anything to be found, which I think there is, my researchers would be the only people capable of finding it."

"You truly believe that?" Her guard dropped and the icy tone melted a fraction.

"Maria, if I didn't believe so, I wouldn't have undertaken this project."

"Who can tell?" She resurrected her cynicism. A sharp blaze of pain in her lower stomach cut off thoughts of what else she intended to say.

"Relax, Condesa. I'll call within seven days and should have news for you."

She switched off the phone and sunk onto a fat cushion placed on a pew, hugging her arms around her abdomen. Intuition whispered that she had less time than the doctors had predicted.

God, come to my assistance.

O Lord, make haste to help me!

She looked up at the prismatic array of colours; blues, reds, yellows and a dozen flickering hues streamed through the window's stained glass. It caused her to take a deep breath and realize that her life hung on to the one small vestige of hope available, and the crook who had just put the phone down.

CHAPTER 12

E vita let out a low moan and crashed to the floor.
Ulla rushed to reach her, followed by Raúl. Brodie sprinted out of the door and down the few steps towards the main reception entrance.

He saw the backs of two men running towards the car park. As Brodie rushed forward, one man stopped, turned, and pointed a gun at him. Brodie had no weapon and dived to the ground, shielding his head with his arms.

There was no shot.

By the time he leapt back to his feet, the car was speeding out of the car park, throwing up a dust storm. He didn't even get a look at who it was. He thundered back into the building.

Evita was sitting on the floor supported by Ulla and Raúl. Blood was being wiped from a gash on her forehead. The colour had drained from her face and her bottom lip quivered.

"What happened?" Brodie asked out loud. "You okay, Evita?"

Evita nodded but winced in shock. "I'll survive. Two men. One asked for my father..."

"Raúl's your father?"

"Si, Señor, ever since I was born." She managed a weak smile.

Raúl spoke, "Quick, I'll call the police. What did they want? Do you know? Was it money?"

"No, they only wanted to see you. I told them to leave and make an appointment as you were busy. He said that was unacceptable, pulled out a gun from under his jacket, and just hit me with it … twice. He fired a shot through the roof and that was when I collapsed through the door."

Brodie looked anxious. "Evita, you could have been killed. Did they say what they wanted?"

"Only what I've told you."

"Throgmorton?" Ulla looked thoughtful.

"Why would he jeopardise our work before it's got under way?" He turned to Raúl who had the phone in his hands. "Not yet, Señor, please."

"Are you thinking what I'm thinking? A crude warning?" Ulla asked.

"Too right."

Raúl looked perturbed. His arm was still around Evita who clutched her head. He rose to his feet. "Armed robbers. We've had them before."

Ulla looked at Brodie and shook her head just enough for him to notice. He nodded back. "Evita, do you want an ambulance?"

"No, nor any policemen. They're bad for business. I don't think they'll be back."

"You're going to just let this go?"

Pressing a large tissue to her head, she glanced up enquiringly at Raúl.

"I'll get security guards starting tomorrow. Besides, police ask too many questions and put off customers."

"Do we still have a deal, Señor?"

Cortez extended his hand. "We still have a deal. When do you wish to start?"

"We already have. We shall be back later in the week to start going through your records. Is that okay?"

"Si, Señor."

Ulla helped Evita to her feet, making sure she wasn't going to have anything worse than a head bump and a minor gash. "You and your father have lived here all your lives. Do either of you know of a wealthy titled woman from these parts who writes religious self-help style books? She could be an important factor in what's been happening here."

Raúl replied. "Spain has numerous nobles and they can live anywhere in the world these days, although Toledo has its fair share of them. The wealthiest belong to the House of Alba, headed by Cayetana Fitz-James Stuart. That line had something to do with your King James the Second. An illegitimate son, I believe, from whom she descends. She's fantastically wealthy, owns much priceless art and properties, worth millions. I hear she's selling furniture and art to help with the upkeep of it all. I don't know whether she's written books." He turned to Evita. "You read a lot, Evita. Do you know if any of these titled aristocrats write books of any sort?"

"Not that I know of. Ulla, I can send you a list of known dignitaries and titled people, and a small background of those who live within a twenty-mile radius of Toledo. Would that help?"

"We need all the help we can get." Ulla gave her a hug.

— — —

The drive back to the hotel was uneventful. Ulla scoured the roads, on the alert for any sign of the attackers. Brodie drove fast. She guessed his speed ran parallel to the anger he was suppressing.

"If this has anything to do with Throgmorton, not only will he not get what we find, but he's going to end up with some serious injury, I promise you." His knuckles whitened on the steering wheel.

"I agree. Let's stop guessing and start making plans. We might even enjoy the process." Beneath the surface, Ulla sensed an intense buzz of excitement.

"I'll check out Evita's list when it arrives, and we'll both visit Toledo's Cathedral. I'll then go to the Prado and you go on to Valencia. That way we cut down on time. After that, we start going through Cortez's records. What d'you think?" Ulla was hoping her ideas would distract Brodie's combustible rage.

He said nothing. She knew then that he agreed.

Thirty minutes later, they'd navigated the narrow, congested streets of Toledo, making their way back to the hotel.

The owner, Miguel, greeted them. "Ah, there you are. You missed your friends by about thirty-minutes."

"Friends?" Brodie's face looked quizzical and Ulla frowned. "Did they say who they were?"

"No, Señor, but they said they may call again later."

"Thank you, Miguel." He paused. "Ulla, I've nasty feeling about this."

"So, have I. Let's get to our room."

Brodie unlocked the door to their room and pushed it open to see all their things strewn around the room. "Shit, we've been ransacked."

"Holy God!" Ulla thumped her fist on the wall.

A quick check through wardrobes, cupboards and drawers, revealed that nothing had been taken. Brodie shook down a discarded novel as if expecting some clue to fall out. "What on earth did they want? We have nothing."

"This has everything to do with our mission. Someone is trying to find out what we've achieved or where we are going next. It's obvious, and they don't care that we know it either." Ulla began throwing items and clothing into piles, but not knowing why. "Throgmorton. It has to be him. He's the only one who knows anything."

Brodie brandished his phone. "We owe him a progress call." He paused. "Do we tell him or not?"

"Let's not. If he had something to do with this, not hearing anything might make him nervous, and the nervous make mistakes."

Brodie nodded. "I think you're right. Let's clear up first."

— — —

Thirty-thousand feet above the Pyrenees, Lufthansa flight VIE441 gave a small dip in a swirl of turbulence. The Captain had warned them of it and seat-belts had been fastened.

Sir Maxwell Throgmorton, travelling first class, didn't give it a second thought. His mind was full of a miraculous painting by Francisco Cortez. Regardless of how accurate that story was, his only thought was of how much money he could make out of it. Faith and money equated to power ... power he could have in so many spheres.

His cell phone vibrated, alerting him to a call. As usual, he disregarded airline regulations about their use.

He answered with muffled caution. "Yes?"

"They will begin in Toledo."

"Then we are close?"

"If it exists, and once they search the records, it could be found."

"Good. Very good. What do you need from me?"

"Just how far do we go with Ladro?"

"As far as Ladro and the woman are concerned, let them get on with it. Their next fee is never going to reach them, and should they find what I'm after, they are just as likely to disappear with it as tell me. It will do no harm for them to know they are being trailed. Is that okay?"

"Okay." The phone switched off.

Throgmorton's heart speeded up. He was about to get richer.

He gazed out at the mountains down below and the rolling expanses of massive clouds, lost in thought. The possibilities of the plot he had put into motion overwhelmed him.

Who'd want to be a judge?

CHAPTER 13

O verhead, a gathering thunderstorm wrapped the city of Toledo in a sweltering blanket of humidity. Ulla and Brodie stared at the magnificence of the medieval High Gothic built Primate Cathedral of Saint Mary of Toledo.

The rain began to hammer down.

"Where do we start?" Ulla asked, balancing a magazine on her head.

The facade stood close to the lofty one-hundred-and-forty-foot tower that had surveyed the city since the early Conquistadors. Brodie began climbing the steps towards the main doors. "Let's go in the front entrance. The main façade has three named entrances: Forgiveness, The Last Judgement and Hell on the left. Take your pick."

"I'm not quite ready for Hell, Brodie boy." Ulla chose Forgiveness.

"And remember, sweetheart," Brodie replied, "we're not gawping tourists. We're here to locate paintings that suggest healing miracles or even better, something by our mysterious Francisco Cortez. I've got the camera." He thought not being allowed to take photographs was outrageous, especially when they were charging eight Euros admission fee. He tapped a concealed miniature camera fixed into the lapel of his jacket. "Much better than cell phone shots."

Once inside, he could only gape at the astonishing demonstration of light emblazoned from windows, vaults, candles, and the staggering multi-foiled arches towering far overhead. It was a dazzling rich architectural display of lost craftsmanship that repeated itself throughout various chapels and cloisters.

"Oh wow! Just look at this." Ulla spoke in hushed tones as she scanned the overhead riches, festooned in countless golden carvings.

Brodie refused to be overwhelmed. Unseen, he began taking the pictures he wanted. He took photographs of works by El Greco, Caravaggio, Luis de Morales, but not one by Cortez could be found.

Ulla began moving more quickly and Brodie followed her as she turned left from the ambulatory into the Chapterhouse, the *Sala Capitular.*

"Who are these by?" Ulla indicated a powerful array of frescoes that filled the walls around the structure.

"It says here," said Brodie flicking through his guide book, "Juan de Borgoña.

"And at last, some miracle healing subjects. But no Cortez by the looks of it."

"Look at this one." Brodie pointed to a huge fresco, *The Birth of the Virgin.* "Astonishing colours and composition … how did he do that? Makes my efforts look a bit pitiful."

Ulla hesitated. "I see what you mean, but they're not my cup of tea. I prefer what you do, would you believe? C'mon, take your pictures. We've been here long enough. It's time we left."

Brodie turned to go. He needed to get back to the hotel to study the photographs. It was then he caught sight of two men staring straight at him from beyond a nearby pillar.

They ducked away. A little too obvious, he thought.

He pulled Ulla across the marbled floor and out towards the

ambulatory. "We're being watched." There was nobody there. It had become devoid of tourists. They passed slumbering effigies of long dead cardinals and saints that flickered in an amber glow from the overhead lighting.

Ladro sensed danger.

"Ulla, we need to leave quicker than I thought. They're following us." Dragging her around a fat carved edifice, he prepared to exit into the downpour outside.

"Wait, Mr. Ladro."

The voice spoke in toneless English.

Brodie and Ulla spun around.

From behind two other pillars, two male figures moved out but remained in the gloomy shadows of the columns and the paltry light of wall-mounted candles. Their features, shielded in shade, were unrecognisable. They stood in a dark line, their arms by their sides. Both stood motionless. His first impression was that he was in a Quentin Tarantino movie.

He whispered to Ulla. "Did you bring a gun?"

"Of course," she replied from the side of her mouth.

"Who are you and what do you want?"

The darkness concealed whether they had weapons.

"Who we are doesn't matter, but there's no need to be afraid," the voice said. "Look upon us as your insurance policy, your protectors."

"What do I need you for?"

Ulla, Brodie could see, had her hand behind her back, reaching for the pistol tucked into the back of her belt.

"Just to let you know that you and your delightful companion are not alone."

The other man spoke, but this time with a Spanish accent. "You are here to discover the secret of Cortez. You may or may not find it. But if you do, we will ensure that what you find will not disappear or fall into the wrong hands. Do we make ourselves clear?"

"What do you mean ... wrong hands?"

The first man spoke again. "That is not your concern, Mr. Ladro. We make those decisions. Let's just say we wouldn't want you walking off with your prize somewhere. Am I making myself clear?"

"So, you think we are potential thieves?" Ulla blurted out.

There came a chuckle. "That's a rich statement coming from you and you know it."

Brodie stood in the dull glow of filtered light amongst the dead saints and marble columns, and allowed his anger to rise.

He could hear the rain splattering outside and smell the incense wafting across from various altars.

Whoever these men were, it was dangerous that they knew more about Ulla and him than was safe. She had stopped reaching for her gun and now held on to his arm. He chanced a wild card.

"Who sent you? Throgmorton?"

Another chuckle. "Ladro, do you always give out names so easily? Let's just say you have been warned."

He signalled to his companion, and the two melted back into the shadows. Before Brodie and Ulla could move, they had vanished.

Brodie breathed hard. He was accustomed to risks, but this assignment had shifted to a different level. Being followed, then threatened, placed a new dimension on both him and Ulla. That was dangerous. It had never happened before, and whoever was behind it seemed to know a lot about them.

Breaking through his apprehension, he could hear the choir and the priests going about their devotions.

Ulla interrupted. "You're rattled and I know what you're thinking. We're *not* giving up. We're pressing on. If that little demonstration is enough to deter you, then you are not the man I thought. Am I making myself clear?"

He didn't know what was worse, the men or Ulla. He ignored her challenge. "Who d'you think they were?"

"Something to do with Throgmorton, I'm certain."

"If it is, he doesn't trust us."

"Would you?"

Brodie pushed open a side door and stepped out into the rain, his gaze attempting to penetrate the downpour. "I can't see anybody. Whoever they were, they've gone"

"C'mon back to the hotel."

Francisco Cortez was becoming an unsafe mystery.

— — —

They slumped back into bulky armchairs.

Ulla's excitement didn't abate. She'd always had a sense of rebellion — a desire for excitement. A love-hate feeling was how she would describe her reaction to it. Since she could remember, it had been part of her character — it had delivered her endless trouble, and she could hate herself for it. Apart from Brodie, she'd made a mess of her life.

But, she had no time for regrets. She never really had— she was addicted to the buzz. That was her driver. She loved Brodie, but would never marry him. He was too problematic. He'd asked her several times and her answer had always been no.

The way the relationship stood suited her just fine. Anything else could get too damn cosy. She wasn't used to that, and it made her uncomfortable. Most of her younger years had been spent in an orphanage, and absconding had become a way of life. She'd never been shown love, and in place of that, she substituted high risk adventures and action to give herself a sense of worth. Brodie and Gordian Knots satisfied her aesthetic self, but the circle wasn't complete. Burglary and all that went with it completed the loop.

She looked across at him and he was deep in thought. It was tough for him, she guessed. He was on the wobble, and more so of late. She didn't want to get into a tug-of-war of will right now. She switched on the laptop to check for messages. There were two. She read them out aloud.

One from Evita gave a short list of known female aristocrats living in the Province of Toledo. She'd given five names.

The other email came from Throgmorton. *Awaiting news. Please let me know.* She looked up. Brodie didn't react.

He stood and walked to the window. "Look down there."

Ulla followed him and glanced out. Cars were crawling by in both directions along the narrow street. The rain had stopped and the sun had begun to shine. Passers-by moving along the tight pavements revealed two men standing and looking at the hotel entrance.

"They followed us all the way back here."

"Our friends from earlier?

"Who else?"

Something was not right.

Whoever these men were, how did they know so much? If it was Throgmorton, what was he doing sending emails asking for a progress report? What did threatening them achieve?

Ulla braced herself for what she expected he would say next. It was bag packing time.

But it wasn't.

"Ulla, what happens to you is my concern. And no, I don't want to quit. We've had narrow escapes but this has gone up a few levels. Are you up to this and are sure you want to carry on?"

"And I thought you were about to split." She held on to his arm. "You know me. I can't wait to see where this is leading. What do we do now?"

"We stick to our plan and when we get back tomorrow, we go for the aristos and then on to Cortez's archives."

"What do I tell Throgmorton?"

"I'm certain he knows, I'd put money on it. Don't tell him anything yet. Let him stew."

CHAPTER 14

Monasterio de San Vicente de Valencia
1561 A.D.

O bedience, piety, poverty and chastity.
The same vows applied to the Lay Brotherhood as to full
members of The Knights of the Risen Lazarus.

Francisco Cortez loved God as much as any man alive. With Salvador Méndez's permission, he had become a lay brother of the Order. He longed to be a full member, a monk. For three evenings each week, he would devote the time to helping administer supplies for the monastery and the knights, plus small duties managing finance. He was also about to commence painting a picture of Abbot Covas. Before picking up a brush, he would lose himself in prayers and contemplation. He would thank God for his life, his parents, his sponsors, and his artistic gift.

He often thought of the fresco of Lazarus by Borgoña, and had been to see it in Toledo several times. Its magnetic force always caused him to gasp.

But he could never bring himself to dare paint something of

the same episode. The thought overwhelmed him and rendered him powerless.

I am unworthy.

There were moments while meditating when he became suffused by an inner light and thoughts of monastic life would surface.

There was a difficulty … Francisco's other love, Paloma.

I love her more than ever.

— — —

Before setting out for the studio, ready for the day's work, Francisco, amidst the aromas of paints, pigments, chalks and charcoal, knelt in silent prayer. He prayed that his hand would be steady and his eye true, and what he produced would be for the greater glory of God.

Today, like many others of late, his prayers would be distracted by visions of Paloma. He could see her beauty, feel the softness of her skin, the lustre of her eyes, and smell the sweetness of her *eau de cologne.* What meetings they had were in secret. They would meet on the hillside woods, in a hidden bower away from her father's beady eye, and the seminarians of the monastery.

There they learnt the ways of love. Shy kisses, lingering caresses, evolved into fleshy breathlessness. Fingers touched buttons, hooks, and farthingales undone. They became one and their union complete.

— — —

The Abbot arrived earlier that morning for his sitting. He was a small man with pale but kindly features. His age caused his limbs to creak with aches and pains. Forty years of monastic life and never venturing beyond the walls of the monastery had given his skin the texture of ancient parchment.

He would not be easy to flatter in paint.

Francisco studied him with an impersonal gaze. Did he look better in sunlight or half-light, and what angle best hinted at or revealed the Abbot's humanity?

Francisco then made a bold decision. He would break with convention and paint the Abbot kneeling in prayer. This would add reverence to his subject and give Francisco the opportunity to work on the Abbot's hands—Francisco's forte. Abbot Covas, his face close-up and in detail, would be gazing upwards. His eyes would be imploring and his features exuding veneration and humility. His hands would be in prayer and directed at the figure of Mary, the Blessed Virgin, and in her arms, the new-born infant Jesus.

Mary would be painted swathed in white and blue robes, bedecked with lilies symbolic of the Virgin. Jesus would be wrapped from the waist downwards in white, gazing up at his mother.

With rays of light radiating from her and enveloped in an ethereal luminosity, Mary would have the likeness of Paloma.

Abbot Covas was an excellent subject. He could keep still and silent for hours. For him, this was not difficult, stillness and silence had long been part of his life. After two hours, Francisco gave him a break. He had enough material to know how to capture the sanctity of the Abbot.

The Abbot spoke to him, the creases around lips shifting. His voice was clear, soft as warmed oil.

"Brother Francisco, I'm certain that what you are painting will be, as usual, excellent. I don't want to see it until it's finished. You've given us many examples of your work for our beloved building. For that we are grateful. What I'm about to say may come as a surprise to you."

Francisco looked wary. *He's found out about Paloma.*

"You've been coming here for two years now. You are diligent and there can be no doubt that you love God. He has also given you a rare talent. Have you considered becoming a full monk? I have spoken with your father and with Señor Méndez. There is no disagreement. You would, of course, have special dispensations for your art. Don't rush your decision. Take a week or two and let me know what you think when you are ready."

Francisco had known this day would come. It had arrived sooner than he wished. He grasped the Abbot's outstretched hand and knelt before him. "Father, I am honoured, but I am unworthy."

"There isn't a monk here, and we have forty, who hasn't said that."

"Forgive me, Father. There is much to consider. Part of me would like nothing more and part of me has to consider how I wish to live the remainder of my life."

How could I possibly tell Paloma and leave her?

"It is wise that you consider all aspects, Francisco. We will not talk of this again unless you ask me. Agreed?"

"Agreed, Father."

Abbot Covas turned to leave, but before he did, he made the Sign of the Cross and bestowed his blessing on the still kneeling Francisco.

Outside could be heard the mealtime refectory bell summoning the monks to eat. Francisco wasn't hungry. A thousand thoughts ran through his mind.

— — —

The winter passed.

Torn between his two loves, Francisco had yet to give his reply to Abbot Covas, whose frailty had become more defined, for all to see.

He told Paloma of his predicament and sensed her anxieties that he would choose God and not her. They continued making love and he found that hard to resist. It was passionate and overwhelming for them as they struggled with uncertainties.

Neither her father nor Abbot Covas knew of their relationship. Her rival was ever present — the memory of a twelve-year-old boy and a mystical event, as paint and colour transmuted, but just for a moment, into living flesh.

That brief moment haunted him. He knew Paloma's ambition was for them to marry. In the past, he had alluded to it, but of late, had said nothing — not a hint. The last thing he had said was that the Abbot would be mortified if he knew what was on his mind. For good measure, he had added that her father would murder him if he found out.

— — —

The rain had stopped that afternoon as she turned off the muddy track towards the tumbledown barn they had taken to using as a rendezvous. Francisco was due to meet her there as they had arranged a week ago. She, as usual, had brought a basket of fruits, cheeses and meats. They would eat the food and what was left over Francisco would take back with him, either to Salvador's studio or to the monastery. Paloma ducked under the overhanging branches, moving them to one side as she pushed open the rickety door of the barn.

Rays of light filtered through gaps in the walls and roof. The barn was empty. It was, she thought, unusual.

The rain must have kept him.

She stood by the door hoping to catch sight of him coming along the track. He'd always been the first to arrive.

There was no sight of him.

An hour had passed before she realised he wouldn't be arriving. Her mouth had gone dry and she found herself sitting and then standing repeatedly, not knowing what to do. Butterflies fluttered in her agitated stomach. This hadn't happened before.

There's something wrong.

She made the decision to leave. On the way back, she would

stop off at Salvador's studio on the pretext of seeing if there were any supplies he needed. Perhaps he would be there.

Thirty minutes later, she entered the muddy street where the studio was located. She'd been there many times but this time her heart pounded with anxiety. Standing outside the door, she looked through the small window next to it. Candles were burning, so somebody was in. She took a deep breath and rapped hard on the door. When it opened, Salvador Méndez stood there, bespattered in paint and holding a large paintbrush in his hand.

He looked annoyed. "Paloma?"

"Sorry to interrupt you, Señor, but as I was passing, I wondered if there was anything you needed from our shop?" She couldn't help herself from straining her neck a little to see if Francisco was there.

His face relaxed and a thoughtful look took over. "Well, maybe our usual canvases wouldn't go amiss. Can you do that?"

"Of course, Señor. Will Francisco be collecting them?"

"Oh, I don't think so. Haven't you heard?"

Paloma's insides went cold. "Heard what?"

"Good news. Tomorrow is his initiation ceremony. He's to become a full monk of the Order so we won't be seeing too much of him, apart from when I go up there."

Her heart sank like a wounded songbird. It was as if she was falling into a pit of black emptiness. "Dear God. Dear God. I don't believe it. That can't be true!"

"Oh, it's true alright, Paloma. I've spoken to the Abbot and so has his father. It's all going ahead."

The colour drained from her face as she began to tremble. Without another word, she turned and walked away.

Mendez stood there, looking puzzled. "I'll be around tomorrow," he shouted, but his words went unheard.

— — —

That night Paloma's fears and agonies multiplied. Her lover had betrayed her. He had not even told her and he must have known what he was about to do. *I love him. He loved me! It's not true! It can't be. How could he? He never told me. He said he loved me and would never leave me. I gave myself to him freely and he took what I offered. I'm finished. My life is over.*

Paloma lost herself in a surge of sobbing as she buried herself deep into a pile of blankets and straw. She now knew the unique agony of bereavement.

A week came and went and she had not seen or heard from Francisco. She had important news for him.

I am pregnant.

CHAPTER 15

Valencia
The present day...

C atching a bus was easier than trying to park a car, so Ladro elected to use the service that skirted around the Turia River. The waters had been diverted in the sixties after severe flooding, and transformed into gardens at the *Plaça de la Mare de Déu.* Commemorating that event was a central fountain with seven maidens around it, representing the tributaries of the former river. Close by, he could see the dome of the Cathedral. He didn't know what he expected to find, but there was one painting he needed a good look at, *Christ Crucified and the Mother Mary* by Cortez.

He got off the bus at the Cathedral and headed for the Almonina Gate entrance where there were throngs of people. He wasn't surprised as it was the weekend. *If the Holy Chalice, declared as authentic by the Church, can't attract visitors, what would?*

The building had a nine-hundred-year history. Once inside, he could see it was crammed with religious artefacts, but all were overshadowed by the presence of the alleged 'true' Holy Chalice. Inside, the atmosphere oozed with religious sanctity, heightened by an overwhelming display of statues, gold, and the smell of incense.

A service was being held in front, at a small side altar. About thirty people knelt in prayer and sacred music from a hidden organ floated around the pillars.

He was determined not to be distracted.

Ladro found the art of greater interest. He noted there were paintings by El Greco, Goya, Valázquez and Jacomart. But where was Cortez? There were numerous chapels set off from the main aisle and it had to be displayed in one of them. Each chapel had to be inspected.

Most had been set up with the ducal funds of some long dead aristocrat. The majority of chapels were short on visitors, which gave him time to reflect. Only a week ago, he was prepared to pull out of this sort of thing, lose Ulla, and vanish into obscurity with nothing else to do but drink himself to death. She had been right. He couldn't deny the buzz that fed his never-ending curiosity.

There were times when it didn't feel right, but being at a certain crossroad in his life, if he wanted to feel alive, he had no other choice. Ulla was made of harder stuff. She was never going to marry him, but together, as a pair, they worked and loved well. Doing what they were doing was the best it would ever get between them … and that took some beating. Nothing else came close.

Every painting had to be inspected. It was tiresome, foot aching work and after two hours, he began to flag. He found himself underneath the plain undecorated curvature of the dome that was supported by a display of Corinthian pillars. There were eight chapels, four on each side plus others, at least four more at the far end. He suppressed a groan.

It has to be here somewhere.

It was then he saw it in the first chapel on his left, named the Chapel of Saint Lazarus of Bethany.

The painting was on the far wall behind the altar. The chapel was deserted, and not being religious, Brodie ignored protocol. He bent his head to look respectful, walked in, and decided not to waste time. There were rows of seats and a confessional that looked like it had never been used. Moving up behind the simple altar, he faced the painting head on.

No doubt at all, it was the same as Throgmorton's photograph which did the painting little credit.

The work was full of vigour, life, and sadness. that was devoid in the two-dimensional photograph. Muted colours flowed in and around the body of Christ, splattered with dark blood raised and congealed by a technique little used in those times ... a palette knife. *Amazing.*

The red, white, and torn purple robes surrounded a mortified Mary, as she attempted to hold his body and wash away the blood.

The figures looked alive, as if they could walk out of the paint and canvas that bound them. Ladro gave another start. Above the pattee and the mysterious letters *KOBL* next to his signature, stood a disconsolate figure of a woman. It was not visible on the shot he had. She pointed upwards, not at Christ, but in the direction of a distant hill on the horizon. On it was a small, almost indistinguishable building with what looked like a cross mounted on it.

It's the same building as on the other two paintings Raúl Cortez has, but this time it's a woman pointing, not a man. It's so out of context. This whole affair is an enigma.

He thought it profound with artistic ability, the equal of, if not better than many established Masters. It had a mesmerising quality full of clues and hints. He zoomed his lens in to take separate photographs of the hill, the signature, the woman, Christ and Mary. He took twenty shots.

— — —

THE LAZARUS SUCCESSION

El Prado Museum
Madrid
The same day...

Ulla elected to travel to Madrid using the AVE high speed train from Toledo's main train station. She boarded the nine-twenty departure and arrived in thirty-five minutes at the Atocha Renfe, the High Speed Terminal in Madrid.

From the station, she boarded the Metro, and within twenty minutes of arriving, was walking up the steps between the Corinthian columns and into the structure and magnificence of Spain's finest eighteenth century building and a top world museum, El Prado.

She had made the necessary arrangements beforehand. Passing under the curvature of the domed glass roof, she made her way to the reading rooms with her head kept down. She wasn't a tourist to look at the art.

One brief halt was all she allowed herself.

She couldn't pass by her favourite painting though. She had included it in her University dissertation — *The Dog* by Goya. She gazed at it and as it always did, it moved her. In less than a minute, she walked away.

In the Reading Room, she had arranged for digital access to the archives and its 3500 boxes of documentation, the library catalogue, and further related papers and notes. Copies of what she wanted could be made available from the technical advisors on hand.

She tapped out what she was looking for ... *All information and documentation — Francisco Cortez, 16th Century. The Leper's Redemption, The Swine of the Gadarene, et al.*

The two paintings flashed on the screen, allowing her to home in on every corner and detail. Raúl Cortez was correct. The two held by the museum were not identical to the two he held at the Bodega. The paintings were smaller and the mysterious initials were absent.

Ulla thought Raúl's versions were superior. What interested her more was the information and documentation that followed.

Francisco Cortez born in the district of Toledo *circa* 1541. Died...? Reputed to be the son of a vineyard owner.

The museum holds two of his works, *The Leper's Redemption* and *The Swine of the Gadarene*. (Neither on display). Another of his works, *Christ Crucified and The Mother Mary* is held at the Valencia Cathedral.

It is known that he painted many more, but their whereabouts has remained a mystery to this day. It is suspected they belong to a closed monastic order. The few known examples are considered by some historians and art experts to be of outstanding quality, and forerunners of the later Impressionist movement. Many regard them as superior to such greats as El Greco and Velázquez. An *aficionado had bequeathed them to* The Museum.

Attached is documentation relating to the two held by this Museum. Cortez left them behind in the studio of his tutor Salvador Méndez, the renowned Court and social painter, after he disappeared. [See attachment]

It would suggest he was experiencing a crisis. What became of him is not known.

Ulla clicked on the attachment. A faded and tattered document, presumably of parchment, flashed on the screen. It was hard to read although Ulla spoke perfect Spanish, and the language hadn't changed much across the centuries.

THE LAZARUS SUCCESSION

Señor,

I have been a monk but eight months and I know not what I can do, for I have sinned greatly. My shame I cannot reveal.

You need know that I am unworthy of my calling. I am also unworthy of the trust and time you placed in me. I have brought discredit to the Order and to the good name of your studio.

I have made my confession to the Abbot. I am to do penance for forty days and nights in solitude, and I am to do one last painting. It is to be my last and is to reflect my remorse. After completion, I am forbidden ever to paint again.

If I am found to do so, I shall be expelled and excommunicated. A just punishment for my sin and errors.

I am uncertain if I can do this and the thought of it all besets me with the notion of not wanting to live.

I give you two examples of my latest works...

At this point, the translation ceased and was in harmony with the tattered original, where what was written had been shredded and obliterated beyond recognition.

Oh wow, we make progress. Ulla called the technician over and asked for copies of all she had viewed. She realised that Cortez's records and library back at the Bodega had to hold vital clues.

She had time to look around further before her train departed for Toledo. Feeling at ease, she walked along the various galleries, entering deeper into the building, taking time to examine the exhibits. For a moment, she turned to look around, and twelve metres away, she saw a familiar face...

It can't be.

Sir Maxwell Throgmorton.

He was supposed to be in Vienna.

There was another man with him.

Seeing him unnerved her, and if he'd seen her, he was making no attempt to approach. She had two choices; to go over and speak or to avoid him. She chose the latter.

This isn't a coincidence.

She thought about stopping and confronting him. What was the worst thing that could happen? The fact that he had allowed himself to be seen deterred her from doing that. Wherever she turned, they turned, keeping the same distance behind her. She quickened her pace and passed through a series of small galleries before taking a sharp left towards the exit.

A tall man stood there, barring her way with folded arms.

"What is this all about?" she shouted at him. He had no time to react. She walked straight up to him and before he could move, she rammed her knee hard into his crotch.

He gave a sharp, surprised yelp followed by a groan and sank down on one knee, clutching his groin.

People around looked aghast and began backing off as Ulla moved towards them, heading for the exit. She held up her Gordian Knots ID tag knowing that onlookers would assume it was a police or security tag. There were CCTV cameras everywhere and she knew what had happened would be recorded and security would be swarming like an army of ants in her direction.

She had no intention of letting that happen. What Throgmorton was playing at left him with a bagful of heavy questions to answer.

Beads of sweat gathered on her brow like tiny blisters. She could see the glass doors up front and the sunlight shining through, beckoning her. Nobody stopped her and moments later, she was out, pushing through throngs of people, past the souvenir stalls, and heading for the Metro.

CHAPTER 16

A re you sure it was him?" Brodie asked as he paced around the hotel room.

"I could have been mistaken but I'm not short-sighted." Ulla looked puzzled.

"I believe you. I've called his Vienna number several times and there's no reply. It's odd he never left a mobile number." "No, it's not odd. Looking back on what's been happening, I'm sure that was deliberate." She paused and he saw her querying look. "What d'you want to do? Whatever you decide I'll go along with it. D'you want to quit, take the money and call it day? We're in the spotlight here, and that's something we both agreed we'd avoid at all times, for obvious reasons."

That, coming from Ulla, was atypical. She always saw projects through to the bitter end. And that included their extra-curricular activities.

His reply was blunt. "No, I want to carry on. There're two reasons; one, I want to mess up that devious slime ball and get him nailed one way or another. The second is, there's something behind this story that's nagging away at me. There's a mystery here that's crying out to be discovered. All my instincts are on full alert, and that's rare."

The phone rang, cutting him short.

Ulla reached it first. "Hola. Ulla Stuart."

"Miss Stuart, Sir Maxwell speaking."

— — —

Her gaunt fingers clacked along the string of rosary beads. She could no longer kneel without enormous effort. Condesa Maria Francisca de Toledo believed she was out of favour with God.

Hail holy Queen, Mother of mercy...

Her concentration wavered. The smallest task required effort. She put this down to her past sins. The thought of them had become overwhelming. God was punishing her.

For too long she had flirted with suspect practices, had been tempted by other religions, and not of God and his Catholic church. She had lapsed and denied her baptismal and confirmational promises. She hadn't attended confession for a decade. Now, she asked for mercy and prepared for surrender.

Surely such action would bring release and a new life away from the humiliations of the cancer eating her body.

She believed with a fervour that miracles did happen, were possible, and God would reward her. Hadn't he directed her to the paintings of Francisco Cortez? Had she not located the chapel instantly in the very Cathedral where, of all places, Christ's Holy Chalice was to be found? And why had she been led to learn of Francisco Cortez and the possibility of a miracle contained in his missing work?

The answer was obvious. These were signs from God. He wanted her well, but repentance—lots of it—would be required. She knew that her contrition would not just be a few Hail Marys, Our Fathers and a matching number of Glory Be to the Father and the Creed. No, it would be heartfelt, sincere and nothing less than full devotion to Him. She will live her remaining life in an almost monastic condition.

The missing work would be found and she would be made well once more.

Throgmorton had his uses. As for his honesty and integrity … that was another issue. She knew her strength had diminished and conducting her own research had become almost impossible. But from what Ruth Overberg and Marcus Urbanek had confided in her, she believed he was resourceful enough to conduct a clandestine operation. What would be discovered was to be hers and kept a secret.

After that, and if need be, Throgmorton would be fed to the dogs.

For safety, she had held back various pieces of information from him. In front of her lay a long wooden coffer. Its contents had remained there for centuries, handed down from one generation of her family to the next.

The lid, felt heavy as it swung open with a groan.

Before her lay the personal and private legacy of nine-hundred years of her family. It came from the twelfth-century Mozarab nobility, and then followed by the various Dukes of Alba through the Middle Ages up to the present day. Apart from her brother, Fernando, an ageing hippy living in Ibiza, she remained the only living descendant of her branch of the family.

Layers of tissue paper separated one generation from another, each a personal token to be passed on to the next generation. She removed jewellery, porcelain objects, early photographs and various certificates rolled and bound in coloured ribbons. Others were laid out flat. Fine old dresses, boots, diaries, documents and early umbrellas, jewellery and artefacts, she removed with care.

At the very bottom, she found what she was looking for.

The once pure white tabard made of wool and cotton linen was old, very old, and threadbare, discoloured from centuries past. It looked charred and battered in places, and the note attached to it revealed it was the bequest of her distant ancestor the third Duke

KEN FRY

of Alba, Don Fernando Álvarez de Toledo y Pimentel. That dated the note as being in the mid sixteenth century.

Her body, rotting in terminal decline, had not yet interfered with her memory. Seeing the small black cross on the painting in Valencia Cathedral, she made a connection with the long-forgotten tabard in the chest. It too had emblazoned on its front, a large black cross. The time period of the third Duke had to be about the same period as that of Cortez's painting.

Why, she thought, had the Duke left the distinctive tabard in the family chest? Could there be a connection with the painting?

She liked to think and hope that there was.

This is more than coincidence. She ran her hand across the tattered cloth and lingered on the cross. A feeling of warmth passed through her ... a willingness to believe that everything would be all right.

— — —

"Miss Stuart, how nice to hear from you. Now tell me, was that you I saw in the *Prado* earlier?

Ulla was taken aback. Her eyes widened. "What?" Her instincts took over. She couldn't admit to seeing him or he'd want to know why she was rushing away from him. "Yes, I was there but..."

"I thought it was you. I tried to reach you but you seemed in such a hurry."

"I've been doing research ... but what were you doing there?" She glanced at Brodie. Tight lipped, he grimaced and shook his fist at the phone.

"I've friends here and I've business to see to."

Ulla couldn't help thinking she could have made a big mistake. It could be genuine. But what about the heavy who tried to block her way? He hasn't mentioned that. He must have seen it.

He continued. "What progress are you making? I was

expecting a report."

Ulla handed the phone over to Brodie. "He wants a progress report."

He grabbed the phone. "Throgmorton, it's Brodie Ladro you're speaking to. There's nothing much to report and when there is, you'll know. Let me ask you a question. Are you following us? If you are, the deal is off. Is that clear?"

"Mr. Ladro, that's an extraordinary observation. Why would I want to do that? Far from it. Seeing Miss Stuart was a total coincidence. You have my word on that."

"What about the man who tried to stop her from leaving?"

"Man trying to stop her—what are you on about?"

Brodie had the phone on loudspeaker and Ulla could hear every word. She shook her head.

"Well, what about the men who surrounded us at the Toledo Cathedral? One sounded like you."

"I haven't the faintest idea what you're talking about." He paused. "Mr. Ladro, you came to me highly recommended. Don't let me revise that opinion. I'll say this. On one thing, you are correct, the deal will be off—sooner than you think, unless something concrete materialises in the very near future. I'm sure I don't need to spell that out."

"I think we understand each other well enough. Let's leave it at that. You'll hear from us soon." Brodie slapped down the phone. He stared at Ulla. "God, I hate that bastard."

"I agree. But let's not give way to emotion. We've a job to do and when it's finished, we can sort him out in a way he won't expect. Agreed?"

"Okay, agreed. Can you contact those names Evita gave you? I'll make notes on what we've achieved so far, and then I'll start looking at Raúl Cortez's archives. Who knows what we'll find there." He hesitated. "I've a feeling we could be in for more shocks."

CHAPTER 17

T he red franking mark of the *Banco Popular Español* accelerated his desire to vomit.

He knew what the envelope contained. With shaky hands, he tore it open.

Raúl Cortez was running out of time.

He read through it with a rapid scan, too fearful to digest the full force of the words used. *Urgent ... action will be taken ... unless ... fourteen days ... legal ... let us know your proposals.* With moist palms, he screwed up the letter and threw it across his desk.

Five minutes later, he reached out for the crumpled ball of paper, straightened it out and read through it, but this time he absorbed its full impact.

Nobody knew, not even Evita.

What did the bank care that three years of unseasonal weather had all but destroyed his annual yields? That weather had produced successive seasons of Berry Rot and Crown Gall disease, almost impossible to control under the conditions. He was in no position to pay back the accumulated overdraft given on the expectancy of bumper harvests.

He faced ruin.

Yet something had happened ... almost as if it was meant to. A lifeline had been thrown to him.

He was being offered money, enough to fend off the bank and give him breathing space. It was tempting enough to dispel any moral qualms he had. All that was required was for him to supply his caller with anything that Ladro and Stuart came up with. It also included their itinerary, information about or sight of any paintings that might be discovered. Further rewards were hinted at.

His caller had also promised protection for his home, family, business and staff from any unwarranted attacks.

That promise removed any doubt about the source of the call. It had everything to do with the recent attack on Evita. He still had the two paintings unknown to the outside world. They had to be worth a lot of money. Validating them and liquidising assets took time ... and time was something neither he nor the bank had. Besides, he fiercely wanted to keep the Cortez paintings. They were part of his flesh and blood, and it was important to know where you came from.

If he went under, he'd have nothing to leave his daughter and they could end up in poverty. Ladro and Stuart hadn't offered money, only the hint that if they found anything, he could transform his fortunes.

I can't live on dreams.

Passing on information wasn't harming anybody. If he worked it well, no one would know and his business could be rescued.

He rubbed his hand across his wrinkled brow. *I'm seventy-three. What time I've left on this earth, God only knows.* He pushed aside any uncertainty about his decision.

He reached for the phone.

— — —

Ulla threw her hands up in despair. "Shit!" she shouted as the answerphone message cut in.

This was her fourth call to the names on Evita's list. Two had told her not to trouble them again, one didn't reply, and now this. She left her message.

"... and my name's Ulla Stuart from the TV production company, Gordian Knots. We are researching a Spanish artist from the sixteenth-century, Francisco Cortez, and are eager to find out what information we can about him and his life. We believe he came from Toledo and painted portraits and scenes from this area. If you can give any information about him, however insignificant, your call to this number would be appreciated."

Ulla had two thoughts. Using the company name legitimised the operation. Flushing out Throgmorton's mysterious client could short-circuit his plans.

Neither she nor Brodie had the slightest doubt he'd screw them to the deck as soon as he could.

— — —

Condesa Maria's fading brown eyes seemed to shine as she stared out of the window, hearing the far-away bells of Toledo's Cathedral, her wiry fingers steepled under her chin.

She wanted time to think.

Ulla Stuart's message had sent a jolt through her body. She found herself muttering. "This is a sign. Please let it be, please, dear God." It was too much of a coincidence. It couldn't have anything to do with Throgmorton as she had forbidden him to reveal anything about her or the project. He had promised not to.

Hell, I dislike the man, but he knows if he broke his promise ... he's finished. Not only with me but with all his smart friends in Vienna. With Marcus Urbanek's help, I'll make certain of that.

The sudden flood of energy startled her. It was a rare and almost forgotten experience. It felt good, a memory of times past. It didn't last long.

An unexpected talon of pain hooked into her, breaking the

euphoria. It was time for her needle. As she reached for it, she made the decision to call Ulla Stuart.

CHAPTER 18

L adro stood back as Cortez emerged from the dark basement with the last box of his family records. There were six in total. A thick sheen of ancient dust billowed about in a powdery protest at being disturbed.

Cortez brushed himself down. "There they all are, Señor. That should keep you occupied for some while. I've no idea where you would want to start but the last boxes are the oldest. If I remember, I was told some even span the thirteenth century upwards. Shall I leave you to it?"

"Yes, thanks." He breathed in deeply and pulled on a pair of thin white cotton gloves. He took photographs of the chest from every possible angle.

"Here goes."

He dragged over the last box, dusted off the debris and undid the metal clasp. *This hasn't been opened for decades.* Without a sign of rust, it was in good condition. With care, he eased open the lid supported by two adjacent brass chains. He pushed it up to its furthest extent.

More photographs.

The light of day shone on the earliest records of the Cortez lineage.

In all his years of research, Brodie had never failed to experience a respectful awe at what he saw or discovered, whether it was some old statue or tomb. The Cortez records were no different. History came alive at moments like this.

For a brief moment, he knew this was where he differed from Ulla.

Beloved Ulla.

Vital to their research processes, he knew her of old. She would be making links as to where existed possibilities of *liberation*. That side of their work had lost its attraction for him. He made a mental note that this was to be his last venture, *ex officio.*

He knew that decision could split them. He loved her more than he was prepared to tell her, and that was from the first time they met in New York. He was going to hold on to her as long as possible.

At that moment, he caught sight of two small, faded, red leather bound volumes. He reached in and lifted them out, placing both books on his table.

The sixteenth century pages crackled as he began to turn them. The first volume was a treatise on agriculture and the art of wine making titled, *Obra de Agricultura* by Gabriel Alonso de Herrera, dated 1513. The pages revealed diagrams of wine presses, grapes, and instructions on fermenting musts. Linked to this were comments on the weather and probably the earliest records of grape varieties and subsequent diseases.

Ladro's investigative self took hold. "Amazing! They're of museum quality."

The second volume related to the property, Bodega Cortez. Signed by Sebastian Cortez, it was dated 1474. Inside were details of assets. Listed were horses, mules, tools, the number of vats and barrels, pitch, gesso and wine presses, together with the names of workers and their wages. The faded pages also revealed the extent of the winery, and mapped out were diagrams of the location of all the land. It was divided into even sized plots, descending from the top of the large hill down to the river. Not much had changed in terms of geography.

Brodie received his first surprise.

A religious connection had existed. The winery had received the patronage of Cardinal Ximenes de Cisnores. Side notes revealed that both Sebastian Cortez and his father Manuel had been personal friends of the Cardinal.

The next was intriguing.

The present day winery was made up of fifty hectares of arable land. Back in the time the book was produced, the extent of the arable land was listed as one hundred *fanegdas.*

That was big. Four or five times the size of most. Whether it was all utilised, it didn't say, but the area converted to fourteen hectares *more* than the present day. The business hadn't grown. It had shrunk and was smaller than it was in the sixteenth century. With today's costs, it didn't take much to work out that Raúl's enterprise could be in difficulties.

Brodie's immediate thought was that something bad had happened, but he wasn't there to sort that out.

Following his notes, he took more photographs of both volumes and of selected pages. The next item that grabbed his attention was a small painting. It was no bigger than an A6 sheet of paper. It was a head and shoulders portrait of an unnamed middle aged man, by his clothes, a Spanish merchant or trader.

Sebastian Cortez?

He thought it odd that he was holding a sword almost as if he were in prayer. There was no signature or date, but Ladro gasped when he turned it over. Staring up at him was a solitary symbol. It was the same as what he'd seen on Francisco's paintings.

The painting can't be by Francisco Cortez, it's not his style and it's too early. It must have been done before he was born. What does that insignia refer to? Is it a religious order of some sort? What does it mean?

He spent time making notes, copying and photographing everything. Buried in these chests, he hoped his intuition would be correct.

Two hours later, covered in ancient dust, surrounded by maps, papers and various artefacts, Ladro came to a halt. He leant back in his chair and shook his head. *There's nothing here of any use.* He put the small portrait to one side. That would require closer examination.

He took a deep breath and plunged his hands to the bottom of the chest and rummaged through the remaining items. His fingers wrapped around a bulky package. He tugged it out. There were two thick but brittle journals separated by a document. They were tightly bound together by a leather thong that had not deteriorated over time.

His stomach tingled. He set the item down on his desk and stared at it. To open it was almost sacrilege.

He reached for it, and at that moment, the door opened.

CHAPTER 19

Valencia
1562 A.D.

P aloma's nakedness absorbed the heat of the noonday sun knifing down onto her body. Stretched out on her back, both arms and legs spread-eagled, she could see the full bloat of her belly

Francisco's legacy.

The drought blighted field had been the only witness to their sins. Once more, she opened her fruits to its pitiless gaze. She wanted death for herself and the unborn child. No matter how much she willed it, her prayers remained unanswered. God was intent on her punishment. Tight cords, herbal remedies and stays had not worked, nor had lifting heavy weights or drinking vast amounts of wine and sherry. The birth would happen.

At first, she had taken to wearing large billowing clothes, but her pregnancy was huge. She had not been able to hide it or prevent the gossip. Her sin was there for all to see.

Her father had been the last to know. Not a man given to

violence or anger, he had wept. With help from friends, he had secured an arrangement with the new foundling hospital in Madrid, to care for her and the child.

She recalled his chilling words that morning.

"I shall never say your name again. I will call you by your true name ... Whore. You have degraded the memory of your beloved mother. You have disgraced me, ruined my business, and brought everlasting shame on yourself. Your life is over. It is finished ... Whore. You are no longer my daughter. God will for certain punish you. It would be better for us all if you died. Tomorrow, you are to go to Madrid, to the General and Foundling Hospital where you are expected. I never wish to see you ever again nor the stained bastard festering in your womb."

Why has Francisco deserted me? Why hasn't he contacted me? His eternal promises were like a soldier's drum ... lots of noise but empty inside. Bewilderment coalesced into a spleen of poisonous hatred against herself, Francisco, and his bastard child. He loved God and God had stolen him from her. Her disgrace had devastated her father and she had become an outcast. She blamed God.

She stood. Stretching up her arms and clenching her fists, she cursed God and Francisco to the end of time.

"God, I spit on you and your lying son, Jesus, and his wanton mother. May every hurt and harm befall your disciple, the coward Francisco Cortez."

Naked, smeared with dirt, cloaked in madness, cursing and screaming at God, she turned and walked back to the town.

The kicking inside her womb became stronger.

— — —

117

Madrid
The Foundling Hospital
Two months later...

The nursing mother had finished preparing the meats for the evening meal. It was then she heard the shouts.

With vigour, she wiped her bloody hands down the sides of her shawl and hurried towards the room where three beds were kept for fallen women and diseased prostitutes.

It was small, dirty, and the floors were covered with matted straw. The walls were smeared with the blood and stains of previous patients.

Through waves of gripping pain, Paloma called out for her.

The rapid clip-clop of the woman's wooden shoes announced her arrival.

Paloma, her complexion ablaze, hauled herself onto the birthing chair. "It's coming."

The woman said nothing, knelt in front of her, surrounding herself with wooden trays, buckets of water and majolica bowls. She hauled up Paloma's skirts and pushed her legs as wide open as they would go. Watching for signs of movement, she scrutinised her vagina before oiling it with unguents to help prevent the perineum from tearing.

Paloma knew the time had arrived. Water had flown from her and she began to push.

"Harder!" shouted the woman.

Blood seeped onto the straw.

Paloma screamed and continued screaming as she pushed and strained, screwing every tendon, sinew and muscle into tight bulges. Her belly began to shift and change shape. Through agonised gasps and heaving breaths, she shouted through cramping, sweaty knots of pain.

"I want this thing out of me. Get it out! Get it out!"

The only thing coming out was blood.

The woman leant forward. "It's stuck. Its head is stuck."

"Get it out! For the love of Christ, get it out!"

The nurse had seen this many times. The head was showing and it needed help to bring it out. It was dangerous. She inserted her hands into Paloma, gently grasped each side of the baby's head, and began the process of gentle tugging to inch the infant out of her. But it was stuck fast, causing Paloma to throw back her head, grind her teeth, and with every sinew throbbing in her neck, scream with excruciating pain.

"I'm dying! O God, let me die!"

The nurse pushed in deeper and found the child's shoulders. She began to ease the bloody head and body into the world.

"God, you've punished me enough. Let me be. I beg you. I…" A massive painful contraction cut her short. Together with the nurse's efforts, the baby was born; half pulled, half pushed.

"*El hijo de puta,*" the nurse muttered as she held up the bloody bundle. The bastard.

Paloma's last sight was of her baby boy. Pain and fatigue caused her to close her eyes.

"Forgive me. Dear God, forgive me." Her voice was but a whisper. There was something wrong, she could sense it. Her life force was draining away.

God was finally granting her prayer.

The placenta had not come free, and Paloma had a blood-pumping haemorrhage. In spite of the attempts by midwives to stop the bleeding, within the hour, she died … contorted in agony.

It was agreed the baby boy was to be provided for until he was older, and then placed in an institution for orphans.

— — —

A month had passed. Salvador Méndez needed supplies for the studio and rode out to the art shop. He was dismayed to see it was closed and boarded up. He banged on the door, rattled at the lock, but there was no reply. Peering through the gaps in the wood, he could see the place was empty.

"What's happened here? Where are they?" he asked an old woman passing by.

She spat. "They've left. Didn't you hear? His daughter, that Paloma, a whore with child. She died weeks back and her father closed up and left. She brought shame on him and left a bastard son. Good riddance to scum." She spat again and hobbled off.

Mendez looked stunned. *Paloma dead! Pregnant!* Apart from wondering where he was to get his supplies, he found it hard to believe that she had a baby. *That can't be true.* He'd always found her kind and helpful. She'd been a friend of Francisco. *He'll be shocked. I must tell the Abbot. He'll pray for her soul.* Remounting his horse, he turned and headed out to the monastery.

CHAPTER 20

L adro looked up. Evita walked in followed by Ulla, closing the door behind her.

"This looks like a delegation."

Ulla spoke. "Brodie, I've made some headway with Evita's information. I was telephoned earlier by a Condesa Maria Francisca de Toledo. All very grand. She said she was most interested in our research as she had tried to find out about Francisco Cortez but found nothing. She wants to meet us. And guess what? She writes books."

"Bingo! Well done. This could well be Throgmorton's mystery client."

"She said we can meet her anytime."

"When and where?"

"Anytime. She has a country home just south of Guadamur, not a long drive from Toledo. Shall I fix it?"

"A S A P."

Ulla stretched her neck to see what he was doing. "Have you found anything?"

"Not yet, but it's getting interesting."

"Señor Ladro, Ulla, I would like to speak to you both." Evita looked serious.

"What is it, Evita?" Ladro sensed she was uncomfortable.

She reached into her pocket and pulled out a crumpled letter that had been folded in half. She spread it out in front of them and smoothed out the creases. "I found it in my father's waste bin when I was cleaning up. Please read it."

Ladro could see from the logo and the dull red banner that it came from the *Banco Popular.* He didn't have to read it. He knew what it would say. He fixed his gaze on her and passed the letter across to Ulla. "I guessed as much, even from the old documents I've been looking at. How much?"

"I don't know. There is something else you should know." She began twirling the end of her hair around her small finger.

"What's that?" Ulla asked, putting down the letter. "We're not here to get involved in your business affairs."

"Indirectly, you are involved. The Bodega is in financial trouble. My father doesn't know how much I know. We have two paintings he refuses to part with, and they would go a good way towards clearing our debt, and possibly there would even be money left over. You are here to investigate the rumours of Francisco Cortez's last painting. If you find it, it would create a stir. Why? I do not know. You mentioned a name earlier, Throgmorton, was it?"

Brodie's eyes widened and he heard Ulla's sharp intake of breath. "What do you know about him?"

"Not much, but enough to suspect that this man was behind the attack you saw last week. You see Señor, I overheard my father talking to this man…"

"What?" Ladro's face creased with anger. "Are you telling me your father spoke to Throgmorton? How can that be?"

"I don't believe it! That's all we need to hear." Ulla cast her eyes upwards.

"I'm sorry to tell you, but it's true. Everything you discover, what you say, where you go and anything else, my father will tell him. For any information, he will be paid, and the money he gets will go to the bank. It is not easy for me to tell you this, and my father must not know that I told you. It seems our future rests on you and what you find." Her voice, imploring, choked, and she spread her hands wide.

Ulla put her arm around her. "Evita, I don't know what to say." She gave Brodie a questioning look.

Ladro looked at Evita. Her head hung down and she looked vulnerable, her shoulders shook. Her obvious shame stirred him. His memory went back to the time when his father was prosecuted for embezzling money from his employer. He had said it was to pay for his son's school fees. When he needed help, there had been no one.

He knew what Evita was asking. It would be easier for them to walk away.

"Evita, there's more to this Cortez painting than meets the eye. I've an odd feeling about it and I want to see it through to the end. But to do that, we would need your cooperation. Throgmorton is an unprosecuted criminal. He will steal from your father and your estate anything that is found. Don't doubt that. He's paying us to do research, but that was before we found out the full extent of what he's prepared to do. It's an arrangement that is about to come to an end ... Ulla?"

"I agree. You know me well enough to know what I think about him." She turned to Evita who had regained composure. "Evita?"

Evita gave a sad smile and wiped a tear from her cheek and squeezed Ulla's hand. "Thank you both. I will help you. I promise."

— — —

Ulla swung the rental car out onto route CM-40, heading out of Toledo on the drive south of Guadamur.

Ladro leant back in the passenger seat and thought about

Evita's disclosure. The visit to the Condesa might throw even more light on Throgmorton. Her profile already ticked a number of boxes. She was rich, wrote books and was titled. It was almost perfect. If she happened to be ill, and hoping for a miraculous cure from a missing painting or a number of them, then she should be able to throw some light on their mission.

It was vital that they revealed nothing, especially of their connection with Throgmorton.

Guadamur had about 2000 inhabitants, all who must have been at siesta as they passed through its narrow streets. The name was Arabic in origin, dating back to the Moors, and meant *River-Valley*. Dominating the area stood the imposing Castle of Guadamur, like an iron fist built over the ruins of an Arab fort.

The sat-nav indicated they needed to make a left turn. Brodie checked behind. They weren't being followed.

The Condesa's home was situated about four kilometres up the twisting track that cut upwards through the rocky hillside. Brown and dry, the land was bespattered with shrubs, discarded olive trees, goats, innumerable rocks and boulders. The records across the centuries catalogued many battles in the area. It was easy to imagine Templars and Moors riding across the landscape, ready to fight each other. As they rounded a small rise, Ulla stopped the car and switched off the engine.

"That must be it." Ulla pointed to a large white painted building about two-hundred metres in front.

"Someone wants to be alone." Brodie pointed his camera at the building. "Listen."

Deathly quiet.

The click of the camera.

Stillness and not a ripple of a breeze.

Ulla restarted the car, letting it idle for a few moments. "I've an odd feeling about this." She looked pensive.

"This whole mission is odd. It has been from the day we agreed to do it. Don't forget, whatever is said, we know nothing about

Throgmorton."

"Agreed. What do we call her?"

"I'm sure she'll tell us."

The house got bigger the closer they got. It had a monastic look. Verandas and pergolas adorned with multi-coloured bougainvilleas flanked white walls, arches and clay pots brimmed with pelargonium and hibiscus. Close by stood a row of palm trees giving needed shade to a cool blue swimming pool. This was all topped by a large, overhanging brown tiled roof. A small 4x4 was parked in the shade of a thatched car port.

"This is her country home. How many has she got?" Ladro said.

"She did say she'd recently returned from Austria. Who knows?"

"That must be her."

A tall, statuesque woman watched them from beneath a leafy pergola. On a table beside her stood a pile of books, and a maid was bringing out two large ice boxes. A tray stood nearby with several glasses and a large crystal jug.

"Perfect timing. Let's meet her." Ulla jumped from the car followed by Brodie, whose first impression was of an imperious looking, tall, scary, regal middle-aged lady who wouldn't tolerate fools of any sort ... the type of person who was used to getting her own way. Her dark hair, streaked with grey, was pulled back into a tight bun and fastened with a large silver clasp. She wore a white, full length kaftan.

She moved forward to greet them. Her face gave a small but welcoming smile, one that Ladro thought was not given easily. His next impression was that the woman was not well. Not well at all. There was a yellowy sheen to her skin and her brown eyes possessed a faded glow.

The boxes were almost ticked.

"Miss Stuart and Mr. Ladro, you are most welcome." Her voice wavered as she extended a long thin hand. She gestured for them to sit.

Brodie was the last to sit, a little awed at the woman. Something about her fascinated him. She could have been beautiful once, but that didn't matter. Her obvious intelligence was magnetic.

"I'll dispense with formality, you may call me Maria, and you?"

"Broderick's my name but people call me Brodie, and this is my partner, Ulla."

"Ulla and Brodie, how gratifying it is to meet people on similar quests. Before we talk, do have some refreshment. Donna, please."

Donna stepped forward and opened the ice boxes to reveal an array of fruit juices, wines and beers packed in ice. Ulla went for the fruit juice and Brodie chose a chilled white wine.

The gripping silence was broken by self-conscious sips while the landscape breathed with a secret life of its own.

Ladro gave a gasp and looked startled. "Aah!" He clutched at his head with tight fingers.

Crusaders, flags flying with their black pattée on shields and tabards. Knights brandishing swords on horseback, and solemn monks wearing white and brown robes standing in a semi-circle, chanting.

"This can't be!" It passed almost as soon as it had appeared.

She stared at him. "You have seen them?"

Ladro shook his head and widened his eyes. "How do you know what's going through my mind? What happened just then?"

"Don't be afraid. You're privileged indeed. What you saw is part of our life and history. Those monks and knights live in the soul of this place, Guadamur ... the earth, the trees and the hills. They also live in the collective unconscious of certain people here, and they are part of me also. That you have glimpsed them is a good sign. Few ever do. It means, Broderick Ladro, we have much in common."

Ladro swung his head to look at Ulla, who looked baffled.

"What's going on?" she asked.

"I've no idea. I just picked up on a whole load of knights and monks..."

"Ulla," interrupted the older woman, "it's nothing we need talk about now. I want to talk about Francisco Cortez. I believe, from the examples I've seen of his paintings, they exceed anything of El Greco. What you know and hope to know, I want to understand." Her tired eyes flickered. "God himself knows how much I need information. For that reason, I shall be frank and honest with you. That a minor Spanish artist is, generating such interest is, I suspect, less than a coincidence. God, I believe, sent you to me."

Ladro prevented himself from saying, *no, it was due to a man named Throgmorton.*

"I've employed the services of somebody to help locate Cortez's works, who told me he is getting close to solving the riddle."

Ulla leant forward. "Then why do you need to talk to us?"

"I need all the help I can get, and frankly, I believe this man to be suspect. He was all that I could find at the time." Her faced softened, her eyes moistened.

"I have pancreatic cancer. I believe I've not long to live, unless a miracle occurs. There are around this Moorish area of Spain many legends and rumours of relics, bones, and true crosses. I've never believed any of them. Look at the books I've written on the subject." She indicated the pile standing on the table. "They debunk most claims, but there are a few that remain unexplained. Cortez, I have of late discovered, had painted a work that supposedly possessed healing powers. I've no evidence of that, but I'm now hoping that miracles do exist. I may be stupid but I have no other lifelines. You do understand, I hope."

Brodie glanced at Ulla who smiled with a gentle nod.

All the boxes were ticked.

She continued. "My family lineage can be traced back to the tenth century. We were Mozarabs, Iberian Christians living under

Islamic rule, in the province and in what is now the city of Toledo. There were the usual political and religious upheavals but we never deviated from the Catholic faith. Many converted to Islam. My book, *Conversion: The Islamic Effect in Medieval Spain,* covers that in detail. We were cousins of Alfonso, the first King of Aragón who joined the crusades. Muslims eventually killed him in one of his battles. He died childless. My line goes down through the House of Alba, our foremost aristocratic family, which can be traced back to the earliest Mozarab nobility from where we originate." She paused, placed her hand on her chest and struggled for breath.

Ladro stood and poured a tumbler of water.

"No, it's fine. I'm used to it, but thank you." She waved her hand in the direction of the door. "I'm telling you this because I wish to show you something. Follow me."

Walking through the coolness of her house, with its fresh marble floors and white washed walls, Ladro realised it was far bigger than it first appeared. They descended to a lower level not visible from outside. The Condesa said nothing as they glided down a wide passageway. The marble gave way to flagstones and the corridor got narrower. On either side, the walls were mounted with icons and religious statuary.

Ulla whispered from behind her hand. "We're underground. It looks like an old abbey or the remains of a disused monastery."

"It was a small thirteenth century monastery." Maria had heard her. "It fell into disuse and in the late fourteenth century, the monks moved to Valencia. The lands belonged to my Mozarab ancestors before the first Duke of Alba was born in 1429. It seemed a fitting place to build a home. Look, we are here."

A few steps led downward to a stout black door embossed with ornamental ironwork. It was unlocked. Maria pushed it open and ushered them into a small low ceilinged room. Two old stone archways divided the area into three sections.

It smelt of incense.

"This is my private museum, study, and library. Around the

walls stood scores of ancient, precious leather-bound volumes, with pennants and old weapons filling in the gaps between the shelves. "I am told I have an *incunabulum,* my Gutenberg Bible. It is very rare and almost priceless. The collection has grown over the centuries."

Ladro raised his eyebrows amazed that she sounded so indifferent to the importance of what she had. "What are you going to show us?"

"This." She indicated a large red silk cloth. Pulling it back, she stood to one side to reveal the time-worn tabard with its black cross.

Ladro was transfixed.

The room went silent, like a great brooding mountain.

Ladro's head sunk to his chest. "Oh, my God!"

It was the almighty clash of battle. Centuries passed in a few heartbeats.

Like a radio, it switched off as fast as it had begun and Ladro collapsed onto one knee as Ulla looked at him with astonishment.

CHAPTER 21

U lla looked down at his craggy face as his head rested in her lap. Ladro's eyelids fluttered before they opened. He looked stunned.

"What happened?"

"You tell me?" She stroked his forehead. "Are you okay?"

"I think so." He sat up and shook his head. "Where's the Condesa?"

Her soft voice answered. "I'm here." She was standing in a corner, but she moved and knelt beside him. She looked ecstatic.

"I saw and heard the same as *you* did." Her hand pressed her lips. "It's a miracle."

"Well, I saw and heard nothing." Ulla spoke.

"The only miracle is that I didn't crash my head as I fell." Ladro pulled himself up. "I think I just had a rush of blood to the head."

I'm lying, it was definitely more than that.

He looked at the Condesa. An enigmatic smile betrayed her expectancy.

"Señor Ladro, what you saw and heard was real. I know that … and whatever you say, you know it too."

Ladro looked annoyed. "I saw and heard nothing. Look, I'm

feeling okay now. Can we get on with why we are here?"

Ulla gave the Condesa a long cool look. "There's something odd here. I can sense it. What *is* that?" She pointed to the tabard.

"The tabard is very old. It found its way to my ancestor, the Third Duke of Alba, some time in the sixteenth-century. These garments were worn by Knights, Crusaders, and Templars. Unlike Hollywood would have you believe, the crosses on these tunics were not always red. As you can see, this is black. What date the Duke received it is not known. Why he kept such a shoddy garment is not known. I can only guess why. What is known is that invariably, the knights, whether monastics, nobles or lay brothers, would often form an order like the Knights of Jerusalem, take vows, and live and die by them."

"I can see where this is going," Ulla said. "You said earlier that Cortez painted something rumoured to possess miraculous properties. The black crosses on his works are identical to that on this tabard. Are they connected in some way?"

"I believe they are. I have shown this to nobody but you two. The experience Brodie had when we first met told me that you were meant for this search."

Ladro still didn't believe a word of it. "I nearly passed out due to the change in humidity … that's all. Are you suggesting that Cortez was some sort of monastic knight?"

"I don't doubt it. Why else would he add the cross on his paintings? And I don't doubt he wants to come to rest, to be found. I feel something remains unfinished. What I've experienced today tells me that you are the person who must solve this."

Ladro had one thought ... Throgmorton. But Ulla beat him to it.

"Condesa, we're here to locate missing paintings and that means we don't plan on getting mixed up in some *Indiana Jones* adventure. What you thought you saw or heard is your experience and not mine, nor possibly Brodie's."

"What about the man you also have searching. What does he

131

know of all this?" Ladro asked and winced at his deception.

"He has not seen the tabard, nor will he. You two are the only living people to have seen it. There's no need for him to see it ... yet. He's in Spain also and sends me regular reports. He told me he's going to La Alberca with his researchers. That's a small town about two-hundred plus kilometres from Madrid—a place of some mystical significance, I've heard."

Baloney! The lying bastard. He's around Toledo or Madrid waiting to see what we come up with.

"What's his name?" Ladro continued the deception.

"I can't tell you that."

"Maria, I can't see what we can do for you. You've given us no real information. We've seen a tabard that doesn't really tell us much and you have somebody researching for you. We have our own line of enquiry and that doesn't embrace miracles."

She paled. "Wait." She held up her hand and walked over to the bookshelves. Running her fingers along the volumes, she came to a halt at a very large thick book. The cover, bound in reddish brown leather and board, were worn and tatty. Four fragile thin leather tapes were tied onto the front board, securing the pages inside.

"Would you please?"

Ulla moved across, and with care, slid the hefty volume from its shelf, before placing it with a slight thud on the table. "What's this?"

The Condesa blew the dust off from the pages and sat down.

Ladro saw she was struggling. Her eyes had fixed on him. He wouldn't admit it, but she was right, there was a connection between them. Unlikely, but from within, he couldn't deny it. He found himself reaching out and placing his hand on hers. He smiled.

"What's in this book?"

"There were battles around here between Moors and Christians as the Crusaders and Templars attempted to remove the

Muslim influence. Skirmishes and conflict continued for many years in this area. One bloody incident known as the Battle of Guadamur was an immense battle in which thousands died. As a tribute to the dead, the monastery was built. You will find it all in here." She tapped the book. "It is a record of the Monasterio de Santa Maria de Guadamur from 1280 until 1361 that once stood on this site. As it was so small, it was abandoned and the few monks that were here moved to a larger abbey in Segovia and Valencia. The last entries in this volume were by Abbot Covas from Valencia who died in 1570 or thereabouts. I have never read it thoroughly. It was found with the fifth Duke's possessions and passed on to me. Please use it for your research."

"Thank you," Ulla said, pressing her lips into a fine line, "but how is that going to help us? Cortez lived around Toledo not Valencia, well after the date this codex began."

"Before I became ill, I scanned through this volume. These areas and the tabard are in some way connected. There is a monastic link." Her voice rose. "I found a small sketch for a much larger painting in the fifth Duke's archives, passed down from the third Duke. It was lodged amongst the last pages of the monastic records. This is it." She opened a drawer from the table and pulled out a small package, wrapped with care in a black velvet cloth and secured by a delicate red ribbon.

Ladro glanced at Ulla. Her expression registered what he was thinking. The Condesa might be ill but she hasn't missed a trick. Much of this has been planned.

Her skeletal fingers began unravelling the ribbon.

"Stop," snapped Ladro, his hand pressed hard on hers.

She looked startled. "What's wrong?"

"There's a burning question here that neither of us can get our heads around. You tell us all this, show us important material, and are now about to show us some sort of painting. You've been playing and leading us along. You've not told any of this to your researchers. Why? There's something not adding up here. What is it?"

For a moment, there was silence.

Ladro had an uncomfortable feeling as he watched her begin to laugh.

"What is it? What is it?" She mocked his last words in between more croaky laughter. "Señor Ladro, Señorita Stuart—playing games, leading you along—if anybody has been doing that, it's you two. I might be frail, but my brain is as sharp as it's ever been. I'm not stupid. I had you both checked, and know of your standing through your company, Gordian Knots."

His face reddened and his thoughts raced for an answer. He knew what was coming. Ulla remained stone-faced.

The Condesa continued. "Indirectly, I believe I've been funding you. Correct?" There was a flash of anger in her eyes.

Brodie knew he was cornered and said nothing.

"You haven't been alone on your travels from the Hotel Pedro Sanchez, Toledo Cathedral, and the Bodega."

"They were your men, in the Cathedral?" Ulla blurted out.

"Of course, but they were following other men who I then discovered were following you."

"Throgmorton?"

"I wondered how long it would take you to get to that."

"But, you employed him. It's not making sense."

"It makes a lot of sense. I used him to help locate a painting I desperately want. I gave him a wide brief. I know his estranged wife, Ruth Overberg, who told me he had many contacts and knew people who didn't mind cutting corners. She also told me, High Court Judge or not, his dishonesty is unprecedented and inherent— part of his genetic make-up. He is capable, she said, of stealing sweets off a child, just to enjoy the thrill of getting away with it.

"If you knew all this, why did you commission him?" Ladro shook his head.

"I am so sorry now that I chose him, but I was desperate. I should have known he would be as incapable of the task as I was.

He would have to find someone to locate it for him. He found you. Whatever you did that attracted him, I've no wish to know. I've had him followed as I don't trust him. Like you, I have an instinctive dislike for the man. I am aware that he might have other reasons for helping me."

She paused, placing her hand on her chest. Her breath moved fast and shallow. She opened the small bag she carried around her body, tipped two green pills out into her hand and swallowing them in one dry gulp.

Ulla moved over to her. "Are you okay?"

"I am. Let me finish while I can. I'm afraid we both deceived each other. However, it was necessary for us both."

She turned to stare at Ladro. "As soon as I saw you, Brodie, I knew. Don't deny it. You've had two experiences in the space of an hour. I saw you, and believe me … I know. If that's not a heavenly sign, I don't know what can be. It convinced me that you are the right person."

He gazed at her and her smile was disarming, as was the sweet softness of her voice. She squeezed his arm.

Am I going soft? This fearsome woman has got to me. I want her to get well. I don't want her to die. She's a one off. I can't lie to her or myself. I did see and hear things.

"If there's any truth in this legend, that, Broderick Ladro, will be reward enough."

A surge of hope passed through him. For a moment, he became light headed. He felt released.

"Ulla, I'm carrying on with this. How about you?"

"I want to, money or not. What are we going to do about Throgmorton?"

"He's both our concern. I shall terminate my contract with him today. If you agree, I will provide you with anything you wish, and that includes money." Maria extended both her hands towards them. "I trust you both."

They embraced her.

Money wasn't an issue. Ladro knew that and so did Ulla. "Throgmorton," he said "can now go forth and multiply."

CHAPTER 22

Staring through his binoculars, Throgmorton thought her home looked like part palace, part church. He hadn't known where her other home was. Now, he did. The surveillance device concealed on Ladro's vehicle had done its job.

He cursed.

Underestimating a person had never been his weak point. This time, he'd lost. He should have realised trained researchers were single-minded predators. There wasn't much that was beyond them. Now, they were with the Condesa and that spelt trouble. Apart from her money, whatever happened to her was fast becoming irrelevant. It was the information Ladro and Stuart could glean that held the key to his operation. He had to let them continue. Raúl Cortez's input could be vital to the success of his scheme.

It didn't take him much to realise that the Condesa could dispense with him altogether. But, she was vulnerable. Being vulnerable, she could still be manipulated. Her illness wasn't going to go away.

He chewed on his finger. He knew where he would find help.

A short smile.

Stefan de Witt should still be in prison, the one he had sent him to four years back.

— — —

The drive back to the hotel passed in silence. Ulla balanced her options. She wasn't happy about any of it. It had all become messy. "What are we going to do about Raúl?"

"We can't say a word. That would bring the mission to a close. We need to examine his records in conjunction with the codex. If there is any information to be had, it must be in those volumes. We also need to look more closely at the two Cortez paintings. If those pointing figures aren't geographical clues of some sort, I'd be surprised."

She caught the burning expression in his eyes. For once, she didn't share it. In the back of her mind, she still remembered his desire to quit. If he does, their relationship could slip. A gap had begun opening between them.

There was still time to recover it.

— — —

Back in the hotel, Ladro called the Bodega. Evita answered.

"Evita, we'll be coming in tomorrow. Could you get out all the records, papers and anything else relating to Cortez, and also the two paintings you have? Let your father know." He told her what had happened at the Condesa's, but not the strange occurrences.

"Señor Ladro, it is good you are coming. I've found something you and Ulla will be pleased to see. I will show you when you arrive."

"I look forward to that." He said goodbye and put the phone down.

"Why," said Ulla, "do you want her father to know. Wouldn't

it be better if he didn't know?"

"The more he knows, the more Throgmorton will trust him. This way, we can also feed in some dodgy data."

"Okay, but what about the Condesa?"

"She's telling him he's off the case. But we both know he won't let that stop him. You heard his ideas. If there's the remotest shred of truth in this, he's up to coining a fortune. If we let him, he'll milk it for all its worth. Sick people, like the Condesa, will pay a fortune if they believe there's a scrap of truth in it. I loathe him."

"Where does that leave us?"

"We're ending our business with him but that doesn't mean we're finished with the search. It goes on. If there's anything to be found, Maria will get it."

Ulla noticed the first name term. "She really got to you, didn't she?"

"She did. It's about time I did something decent ...."

The sharp tones of the hotel phone cut through the conversation. Ulla picked up. It was the Condesa. Her voice had an urgent edge.

"I had a long conversation with Throgmorton. He knows he's off the project and he also knows of your situation. He told me he is within a whisker of locating what I'm looking for. I asked where he was, but he refused to say."

"Him finding it is total rubbish."

"I told him that. I also said any attempt to continue would be publicly rebuked, and would ensure that all my social contacts would learn of his sinister past. It was then he said I'd be sorry, and that when he found the painting, I wouldn't get to see it. Any attempts to blacken his name and he would kill me."

"Oh God. Have you reported this to the police?"

"No. We have our own way of dealing with these sorts of things around here. I have a recording of the phone call." She paused for breath. "Forgive me, Ulla, I'm feeling unwell right now."

"Condesa, please rest. We'll be in constant touch and don't worry about Throgmorton. There's little he would dare do."

— — —

A light morning breeze rippled through vine leaves as Brodie drove the rented car towards the reception area of the Bodega.

"I wonder if Cortez will still be paid by Throgmorton?" asked Ulla.

He brought the car to a stop. "Maybe, but I doubt it. No Condesa, no money. Look, there's Evita."

Dressed in a red two-piece suit, she walked over and welcomed them before ushering them inside past the main office area. "Señor Ladro, Ulla, our previous discussion remains private, yes?"

"Of course."

"Thank you. My father must not know, that is imperative. I have prepared everything you asked. I also made my own small search. As I told you, what I found could be of interest to you. Buried amongst the early stock and harvest records of the early vineyard, was this portfolio." She produced a large, faded yellow packet tied loosely in black cotton material and handed it to Ulla. "I have not told him about this."

"What is it?" Ladro took the packet from Ulla.

"There are drawings, sketches of this area and people. I don't know who made them, there are no signatures. They look very old, though. Francisco perhaps?"

"Wonderful, Evita." Ladro wanted to hug her but drew back. "We'll open them up when we've gone through an order of preference. The first is this codex we received from the Condesa. You can tell your father that we'll let you know if we have more news." He gave Ulla a knowing look.

For a few moments, they stared at the ragged leather cover. Ulla, wearing white cotton gloves, opened the medieval volume and with care, began turning the ancient pages. The early pages were in a Latin script complete with illuminated lettering. Looking like a musical score, they formed a series of thick colours. The second part of the book was older, written in early Spanish, containing land and building diagrams related to the House of Alba.

"Majestic. This book alone is worth a fortune." She turned back to the cover page. There was a date and a title, written and painted in black, gold and red, as if it had been done yesterday.

MCCXVII
MONASTERIO de SANTA MARIA de GUADAMUR

"It's early thirteenth century, 1217 A.D." Ulla peered at it intently. Screwing up her eyes, she ran her finger along the ancient text, scanning the calligraphy and mouthing the Latin script to herself as she translated. "Brodie, this is written by an unknown scribe. Listen to this. You're not going to believe it. It's about the time of the Fifth Crusade."

The people of this area have become poorer both in land and in spirit. They are the Mozarabs. Both our Archbishop, Rodrigo Jimenez de Rada, and our king, Alfonso, are not well disposed to their presence. Their lands are being taken from them. They say Mozarabs have come too much under Muslim influence. We at Santa Maria do not find this as true. They are devout and gifted.

Our monastery has been under attack in the past from the Muslims, but now we are able to live together. Our Pope Innocent III has requested our King to visit him in Rome to discuss the situation, but the King is reluctant. He wishes to muster an army of Templars and Crusaders to rid Jerusalem and the Holy land of Muslims.
His Holiness is anxious on two counts: The Mozarab Missal of Silos, which is now over 100 years old, is not to be harmed or desecrated in

any way. It is a gift from God himself. There is also the matter of our sacred relic. Inspired by a vision of our Blessed Virgin and her Holy Son, sweet Jesus Christ, the Son and Lamb of God, is the painting by our founder, Abbot Xavier of Galicia, in the year of Our Lord 1145. Our present Abbot Montez, allows the work to be shown on holy days only. To this day, even in these evil times, those who are dying from sicknesses and are true believers and are penitent need only to look into the eyes of Christ, who, in his divine mercy, may heal them with the light from his eyes. I myself have seen this happen.

It is said the painting will vanish 100 years from now, but its secret will be passed on to a worthy one who will recreate its power. We knew our Abbot was a sick and dying brother whom God took pity on, giving him this miraculous and most sacred of gifts. He founded our holy building.

We, the Benedictine monks of Saint Mary of Lesser Toledo and Guadamur, are the guardians of this most holy relic we call The Eyes of Christ. It is known that the Archbishop wants the painting to be enshrined in Toledo's Cathedral. Our Abbot has declared that we will resist this. It belongs to the monastery.

Ulla looked up at him, her eyes wide. "That's what I call a giant step for two researchers."

"Twenty-four hours ago, I didn't believe in miracles. Does this mean our Condesa could be right?" Ladro asked.

Ulla nodded. "Could well be. But if the painting was destroyed after a hundred years, it is said there would be a successor. Where would that be?"

"There could be a series of successors. I never found one in Toledo Cathedral. But that doesn't mean there isn't one."

"We don't even know what we are looking for."

"The codex was written in several different hands. From what I can make out, Latin was superseded by early Spanish before the volume passed into the secular ownership of the Dukes of Alba. It could mean the monastery was destroyed or abandoned."

A puzzled Ulla moved her chair closer to the codex, bending forward as if she was about to command it to give up its secret. "If the Condesa has written all those books about this sort of thing, why hasn't she found this piece of evidence? It's been under her nose for years."

"History shows the best kept secrets are often kept in full view and nobody realises they are there. People spend too much time creating impossible solutions. But, I think I have the real answer."

"What's that?"

"She knows nothing of Latin."

"*That* simple?"

"No, not necessarily. A woman of her intelligence could have had these words translated years ago, but she didn't. She knew the story behind the painting but was afraid to investigate it further. She's scared that if it's not true, she would have to give up her last hope … and will die. She doesn't want to find that out personally. She's also part of a noble family who protect their secrets with a wall of iron. An assault on these would bring an unwelcome spotlight on their current lineage, and could bring her into disrepute. You've seen the way she behaves; imagine what the rest of them could be like. Illness apart, she's up against an equally strong force, the family. So, she activates a clandestine mission, allowing herself to be removed from the activities. But she makes a colossal mistake; Throgmorton. A blessing in disguise, though, since it led us to meet her."

Ulla frowned. "If the original painting, *The Eyes of Christ*, did exist, it would have been destroyed centuries ago according to the prophecy. What is it we're looking for?"

"I don't know."

"As you said earlier, the answer could be staring us in the face. We have every written piece of documentation relevant to this mystery. There must be clues here. If you work on the codex, I'll start on the family records."

"Okay, I agree."

She added, "I don't understand what happened to you at the Condesa's home. Something between you two was obvious. In the last twenty-four hours, there's been a subtle shift in your attitude. I think you believe all this stuff, don't you?"

"Yes, I think I do."

———

A grim smile spread across Throgmorton's pasty face. "Raúl, you have been most helpful. You say they are there now and going through old records?"

"Si, Señor, lots of them. My daughter will help them where she can, and she will tell me what's happening."

"You look after her now. She could be most useful. I'll arrange a money transfer for you when I'm next in the city." *That will be his first and last but should keep him going for a while longer.* "Should there be anything dramatic, you will let me know at once."

"Si, Señor, at once."

The judge gave him his mobile number.

He beckoned to his two guards to follow him back to his rented villa. This was going better than he had expected. Ladro and Stuart were now off his payroll, and would be no match for his men. A surge of excitement reminded him of the thrills criminals must experience when hatching and executing their plans. He was beginning to understand what law and crime were about. They were dependent on each other.

144

CHAPTER 23

Deciphering the manuscript revealed to Ulla that at least six scribes were responsible for the work. The first part spanned a period of over one hundred years. *The Eyes of Christ* was mentioned whenever a holy day appeared. True believers and penitent sinners would be allowed to gaze on it, but no record of miraculous events had been recorded.

Attempts by the various Bishops of Toledo to obtain the painting had been recorded in detail. On more than one occasion, it was recorded that armed soldiers representing the Bishop had made forays to the monastery. It was this entry that caused Ulla to gasp and call out to Brodie

"Listen to this. . ."

They were about fifty strong, armed with swords, shields and bows. We monks, one score, Knights of the Risen Lazarus, formed a tight circle around our beloved treasure. Wearing our blessed tabards showing the black cross of Christ, we held up our swords to show we were warriors of the Son of God. Our Abbot blessed us and gave to us Extreme Unction. After he had done this, he turned to face the robbers. In a loud voice, he shouted to them, "Dare you kill or maim those whom God has blessed? We are not afraid to die. You are. You will all burn for eternity in the hottest hells. Look upon this." He stepped back so they could see our treasure. I believe it dazzled them. One by one they bowed their knees, then turned and walked away from battle.

"𝒦𝒪ℛℒ... Knights of the Risen Lazarus," Brodie ran his fingers through his hair and smiled. "We now know two things we didn't before: who these people were and what those initials stand for."

Ulla smirked. "Those initials unravel one mystery but there're no historical references to them."

"For the moment, that doesn't matter too much. Have a look at these." He pointed to a row of faded sketches; small preliminary workings of the unsigned artist. "These are what Evita gave me. I've arranged them by subject matter, faces, people, buildings and locations. Anything you notice?"

She bent her head forward, peering hard at each work. She said nothing. When she had finished, she lifted her head. "There's a story here."

"Exactly. Let's assume these are by Cortez. The style and texture would suggest that they are. The first few show a landscape that doesn't look a lot different from the approach off the road coming into the Bodega. Look at the line of hills in the background." He pointed at a dark background of undulating shadow. "That is identical to the line of hills you can see from this window."

"Without a doubt." Ulla traced her finger along the line of hills. "So, this drawing could show the Bodega back in the sixteenth century?"

"It would seem so. Now, look at this sketch. It shows two people." He pointed first at a stocky, middle-aged man. He had a small beard and was dressed in a short doublet. He was bent over what looked like a large map, and alongside him, holding his arm and pointing out of a small open window, stood a woman. Her expression looked enquiring. From her clothing, she looked prosperous. The sketch had been done from an open door and gave a view of a small well-furnished room.

"The draughtsmanship is superb. Pass me the lens, will you?" Ulla bent closer and scoured the drawing. "Well, we know who it is. It's his mother and father. It says so here, written beneath the table. Look." She handed it back to Brodie.

He peered at where she pointed. Written in small letters, the words *mamá y papá* had been inscribed, almost as if the artist had been shy about it.

"You're right—this is turning out to be quite a morning. Now let me show you something else before we tell Evita. These are preliminary drawings that lead up to a finished work. You can see they are by the same artist who did 'Mum and Dad.' It seems they were done at a later date, judging from the maturity that shows in the way the composition is handled, and the confident expressions. Look closely, and tell me if you see what I think I see."

Ulla didn't know what she was supposed to look for.

One drawing was of a pious, older looking man, a monk, pictured from the side on his knees. He wore a scapular covered by the suggestion of a tabard. He was praying to a *Pietà,* an image of the Virgin Mary, her head uplifted, and her arms cradling the crucified Christ. Inset were two more sketches of thin, tapering and gnarled hands.

If these hands are by Cortez, he had unbelievable skills. She looked across to Brodie who had an air of triumph. She shrugged.

"Okay," he said, "now look at this." He placed it in front of her.

It was a head and shoulders study of a pretty young woman. She was looking at the artist from over her left shoulder. Her eyes were wide and bright, mounted above high cheekbones. An earring could be seen through locks of hair. A suggestion of sadness shone from her that the passing centuries had failed to eradicate.

"Superb, but what am I supposed to be looking for?"

"Look at Mary in the other drawing."

147

Ulla shifted her gaze from one to the other. "Oh wow, they're identical. They're one and the same woman."

"The head and shoulders version hints at a relationship closer than just being a study for the work. What d'you think, Ulla?"

"Agreed. It's a visual sonnet ... very intimate. Do we know who she is?"

"Not yet. I'd make a hefty wager that the answer is somewhere in this material. I'll call Evita. She needs to know and that information will find its way to Throgmorton. Then, we can only guess what he'll do next."

— — —

Sir Maxwell Throgmorton contemplated his options. It was useful to have contingency plans and he had several. What Cortez had told him to date was interesting, but it didn't add up to anything useful enough to act upon.

To be dismissed and threatened like an errant employee by a sick, ageing and crazy countess was something he wouldn't tolerate. Somehow, she had converted Ladro and Stuart to her cause.

Both acts were unforgivable.

His determination strengthened when he thought of the fun he would have making millions at her expense. Once the work was discovered, and even if it was not, she'd be none the wiser.

Ladro and Stuart would be easy to handle and put out of action ... permanently.

Stefan de Witt wouldn't say no to the right proposition. His career as a master forger was about to be resurrected. There was nothing he wasn't capable of, artistically. A visit was needed.

The saying is right. Revenge is a dish best served cold.

CHAPTER 24

**Monasterio de San Vicente de Valencia
Valencia, 1562 A.D.**

S norting vigorously, Salvador Méndez's horse clattered beneath the stone arches into the central compound of the monastery before Méndez reined it to a halt. Dismounting, he made the sign of the cross before tethering it to a rickety post.

As a valued Lay Knight of the Order, he had access to the Abbot and to any Brother he chose. His business was with the Abbot.

— — —

Abbot Covas was seated at a large oak desk. His morning devotions had ended quicker than he had intended as his arthritis was bothering him again. His jaw thrust forward like a craggy rock. Thinning hair straggled downward across his pinched face. He was looking forward to commencing his important work on the illumination of his script for the Little Office of the Virgin Mary. It will hold a special place in the liturgy of the monastery. It would be central in the oath of compassion sworn by the Order and its Knights.

He might never have undertaken the task had he not dreamt that their past glories would return. The Knights were blessed by God. That had been proven by the power of their sacred painting, *The Eyes of Christ.* Many true and afflicted believers after gazing upon the figure of Christ with penitent hearts, had been healed miraculously. As prophesied, the painting had been destroyed by fire in the Toledan conflict a century and a half ago. It was said to have mysteriously self-combusted.

Never before had he seen a miracle or had a dream such as he had the former night. Its power was so real he was convinced it was *bona fide.* It had told him that their former glory would soon be restored.

It did not say where or when.

Before plunging his dip-pen into a horn of mosaic gold ink, he gave a deep sigh and gave thanks to God, and asked that he be alive to witness His wonder.

A sense of irritation passed through him on hearing a knock against the door.

He cleared his throat. "Enter," he croaked.

The door swung open and Méndez strode in.

— — —

His cell was sparse, consisting of washed brown walls, a straw bed, one bench, a chair, and a rough table. The bareness of the wall was broken only by an agonised crucifix. Sitting alone in front of the cross, Francisco Cortez, now Brother Francis, contemplated the nine months that had passed since his ordination. It had not been easy. It had been harder than he imagined it would be. He loved God and he also loved his fellow brothers, but his love was stained by remorse.

If my love for God was true, I wouldn't be regretting my decision to become a monk.

He missed the banter and camaraderie of the studio, his Greek friend Kadmos, the daily routines, the paint mixing, the smells and the unexpected tasks and projects that Méndez would surprise them with.

Above all, he longed for Paloma.

He had not seen or heard of her since the day he had left for the monastery. He had abandoned her.

In her absence, his love for her had grown. There was hardly a moment when he didn't picture her in his mind. He imagined her at the studio, at her shop. He remembered the tantalising swish of her dress, and how he delighted in her furtive smiles and the warmth of her fingertips brushing secretly against his when others were around. The secrecy of their love had heightened their passions. He remembered its heady intoxication, so much so that his devotions had become meaningless, replaced by constant thoughts of her. He could almost feel the wetness of her lingering kisses when taking the wine of communion, and hear the softness of her voice whispering, *I love you, Francisco, as* he recited the Nicene Creed.

"I love you too, Paloma." He would say aloud when alone. "Forgive me, please, I am not worthy of your love."

He had denied her and now felt only the deepest of shame. Yet, he knew his love of God had not diminished even if he loved another. But, God would punish him for what he had done. Unless asked, he knew he could never leave the Order.

Worse still…

He had never confessed his carnal sins. He had tried closing his mind to her pleasures and what they had done together, but it would find ways of entering his consciousness. He couldn't stop it. So intense, he became afraid of climbing into bed at night or waking in the morning.

His failed attempts to banish her from his mind made him

think she was the work of Satan.

Would God ever forgive him? Why had God led him here and what was he asking of him? Why had he been tempted so?

In his turmoil, Francisco attempted to gain order from his situation. God had led him here, of that he didn't doubt. Paloma had been sent to test him and prevent him from becoming a monk. He had almost succumbed.

Haven't I remained faithful to the order? The Abbot has declared me as Artista del Monasterio, and I have dutifully carried out the tasks asked of me.

He remembered his painting of the Abbot, completed before he became a monk. Since then, he had brought with him several of his other works. All of them portrayed various miracles performed by Christ. He had also completed a fresco for the church entrance, a triptych to surround the altar, and was now working on plans to complete the new ideas for the Fourteen Stations of the Cross. Yet, within, Francisco had become aware of something missing from his life. It lacked fulfilment. Something was deficient, that in a mysterious way was connected to his art … his vision as a twelve-year-old boy in Toledo's Cathedral.

Lazarus.

He'd encouraged a repeat of the experience many times. Each time, it eluded him. He thought it beyond him and came to realise the futility of grasping for that which was not his to have. Only Christ could permit this. And Christ had withdrawn from him.

Punishment.

So, why was I shown this … for what reason? It was a question he had asked himself many times before.

His thoughts were broken by a sharp knock on the door.

In front of him stood Abbot Covas and Lay Brother Salvador Méndez, his art master. Their expressions were unhappy.

— — —

For several seconds, Francisco stared at them without speaking. He heard the wind blowing, the sounds of birdsong through the open window. But something was not right.

All three made the sign of the cross.

"I am honoured, Brothers. Please take a seat." Francisco gestured to the rough wooden bench in the corner. He sat on his bed. He noticed that the Abbot and Mendez looked quickly at each other.

Mendez spoke. "Brother Francis, I must congratulate you on your work of our Abbot at his devotions. It exceeds my highest expectations of you. It is masterly."

"Thank you," Francisco replied, with as much humility as he could muster.

Abbot Covas held up his hand to speak. "Brother Méndez has given me some worrying information. He will wait outside whilst we discuss this." Méndez nodded, stood, and walked from the room.

Once the Abbot was certain Méndez was out of earshot, he spoke with a slow and serious voice. "Brother Méndez tells me the Blessed Virgin in my painting has the face of your art supplier's daughter. Is that true?"

Francisco lowered his head and whispered, "That is true, Father."

"Why did you use a shopkeeper's daughter?"

"I knew no other and she had the same innocent quality as our Beloved Virgin. It seemed right to capture that."

Francisco saw the Abbot lean forward, and for a man of his years, a surprising hawk-like glint emanated from his eyes. His next question took Francisco by surprise.

"Have you ever dreamed or fantasised about her in an inappropriate way?"

Francisco stared back into the Abbot's questioning eyes. He hesitated, lowered his head and spoke in a whisper, "Yes I did."

"What was her name?"

"Paloma."

"Did you lust after her?"

"Yes, I did."

"Did you lie with her in a carnal way?"

A hot flush made Francisco's face burn. His voice descended lower. "Yes."

"You have not confessed this before. Brother Francis, it is a serious mortal sin you have committed."

"Forgive me father…"

Abbot Covas cut him short. "If Brother Méndez had not informed me of this girl, I would not have known, although God does. You are to be punished for this deliberate and serious omission, in more ways than one. The girl no longer suffers. God have mercy on her soul." Standing as tall as he was able, he made the sign of the cross twice. The second was over Brother Francis. "Because of that, you are saved from ex-communication. Seven days from this moment, you will be taken out to the desert. There you will spend forty days and nights as did our Blessed Lord. You shall not eat, but only drink. You will also be supplied with appropriate means to chastise yourself three times daily. *Deo Gratias.*"

The rest of the Abbot's words were lost, as Francisco, in cold horror, understood what his Abbot had said.

A descending sensation swept through him as the colour drained from his face. His stomach knotted, causing him to cry out. "Paloma! Please, Father, what's happened to Paloma?" he implored the Abbot.

He looked into a face that had the expression of a tombstone.

"For her sins, she was taken by God some weeks back. She was pregnant and died giving birth. She left a bastard boy, which I suspect was yours. That is all you need to know. You will remain in your cell until you are ready to be taken from here. Time enough to start your penance." Covas turned, and without a sound, left the cell.

Francisco knew the child must have been his. That thought caused him to shake uncontrollably. With it came the crushing burden of horrifying guilt, shame, and remorse. He passed from shock into unconsciousness.

CHAPTER 25

E xtraordinary," Ladro whispered under his breath. In front of him on the massive library desk lay a collection of sixteenth-century diaries and manuscripts written from around 1550 and covering a twenty-year period to sometime in the 1570's. They seemed to recount how the vineyard developed during that time, but of major interest were the year-on-year recollections and written entries by their subject, Francisco Cortez.

The script was in Early Spanish. The letters had long tapering strokes and words with elongated letters with added flourishes and swirls.

"Ulla, listen to this."

August 9, 1550

Today is my ninth birthday and it makes me happy. I have given thanks to God. My papa says I will go to University when I am older and become a lawyer. I want to be a painter...

"He's even done a small sketch of himself. It's called, '*Me.*' Ulla looked at it. It showed a boyish face, yet with a mature and serious expression, almost as if he knew something you didn't.

"Even from that you can see his talent shining through."

"True, but what would be better is, if we could find clues to the so called miraculous painting supposedly in Toledo's Cathedral." Ladro picked up another volume. "It might take a while."

An hour later, and Ladro was still turning pages with care, reading closely but anxious not to damage or tear the delicate paper which crackled on occasions like a box of cereals. Many of the entries were mundane and what he regarded as domestic trivia.

And then, a passage caught his attention. It was what he looking was for.

The language was simple, that of a young Francisco Cortez. Every entry opened up a vista into medieval Spain. The pages were decorated with illuminated drawings and sketches of buildings; the countryside, animals, plants and flowers, and people's faces with their names written besides them. Ladro could sense himself being drawn in as he began reading.

He called Ulla over. "We've got something here."

March 19, 1553
The Feast of Saint Joseph

My parents are too busy today to journey with me to Toledo. So, I have to walk alone. I want to speak to God, to ask him to let me become an artist. I washed myself more than usual and put on fresh clothes and sandals. I had to look clean and pray with dignity, or he might refuse my request.

It is hot today and (Cortez's writing here is indistinct and words are crossed out.)

There are men and women with carts and mules. Many have fruit and vegetables. Others have chickens or pigs. They are going to the market. Most of them I know as they buy wine from papá.

I can see the tower from here. It looks grand.

I hope God is not too busy today.

Ulla pointed at the script. "It looks as if the writing has been interrupted, and the remaining entry written later that day. The ink colours are different."

"Not only has the ink colours changed, but the whole tone. Why?"

Crowds were around, but I was alone. People were speaking, but it was silent. The bells chimed, but no sound came from them. I knew where I had to be. I walked through the cloisters and turned into the Chapterhouse, the Sala Capitular… Incense. Around me are the religious frescos by Juan de Borgoña, I've been told. I knew I should be here for God has told me so. I was compelled. I have been led here. For the first time in my life, I prostrated myself three times and then knelt in prayer and contemplation. I beseeched God to allow my talents to benefit mankind. How long, I have no idea. Time did not exist. I had a feeling I never had before. I felt the breath of God.

I opened my eyes and saw the fresco of Christ raising Lazarus. The shroud moved and Lazarus sat up. Jesus turned and looked straight at me with rays of golden light coming from his eyes. I heard his voice in my head. He called me by name … FRANCISCO CORTEZ! I think I fainted.

When I awoke, I knew.

I knew I was to paint the next resurrection of Lazarus to benefit all men and penitents. I could tell no one. For in each period, man would destroy that which he could not understand, as they had destroyed him.

Why me? What am I to do? Who can I tell? Who will understand? Perhaps papá? I shall praise God forever. This is a miracle, a true miracle! LAUDÁTE DÓMINUM!

"Praise be to God, indeed." Ladro's voice was louder than he intended. "Result!"

Ulla clapped him on the back. "Hey, Brodie boy, now it looks as if we have something to work on."

He paused and rubbed at his chin. "It asks more questions than it answers."

158

"Let me guess." Ulla pulled at the gold chain around her neck. "Did he ever paint it and if he did, where is it?"

"Right, if he did, was it destroyed and have there been others? The fresco by Juan de Borgoña he mentions is not where Francisco says it was. I've been all over the Chapterhouse and it's full of the Virgin Mary and scenes from the life of Christ, but there is no work showing Lazarus. There have been plenty of wars and uprisings, including the late Civil War. Has it been destroyed like the others that went before it?"

"If he did paint the event and it hasn't been destroyed, my bet is that it's in a church or a monastery around here. It has to be. The Condesa lives on the ruins of a disused monastery and the codex refers to two other monasteries, one in Segovia and the other in Valencia. If we can locate their vicinities, we might be able to find where those figures are pointing to in Raúl's paintings."

"They're clues of some sort. Doesn't it strike you also that one of his paintings is lodged in Valencia's Cathedral where the alleged Holy Chalice is kept?"

"You've been reading too many Templar novels, Brodie."

"I don't think so. Why don't we spend a few days in the Valencia area? Then, we can both check out the Valencia painting and try to locate those monasteries."

"Of course, and we let Evita know about this Lazarus connection?"

"Naturally."

— — —

Throgmorton's visit to England would be a day trip, and besides, prisons never failed to depress him. Long Cross was no different.

He drove through the massive open steel double doors bristling with security guards. A double entry system resembling a giant airlock allowed him to drive in before an equally mammoth set of doors opened up at the other end, as those behind him hummed to a menacing close.

I've sent scores of men to this place, he couldn't help thinking as he drove out to the secure parking area. *I hope De Witt's in a forgiving mood.*

Stefan De Witt, of Dutch origin, had about two weeks to go out of a seven year stretch, before early release for good behaviour. De Witt was a master forger. His crime was passing off fake paintings into the salerooms and to dealers who knew, or otherwise. His works had an added stamp of authenticity. He'd constructed elaborate provenances that had been almost impossible to disentangle. His speciality was medieval works. He'd maintained that his signature artist was El Greco. After his conviction, his bank account had been sequestered and two million pounds had been repaid to a handful of anonymous victims. At one point, the Russian Mafia had threatened to execute him if he revealed what paintings he had faked. Nobody, especially criminals, wants to admit to the mistake of buying a fake.

At his trial, he had demonstrated his skills by painting, from the dock, an El Greco work in less than an hour.

Experts had found it almost impossible to decipher it from an original.

Throgmorton, as the sentencing judge, remembered being impressed and somewhat amused by De Witt's uncanny talent.

Walking down the green and cream painted corridor, he approached the visiting area with a sense of caution. He knew enough about the system to know that he'd be targeted unless he remained undetected. He did not want his presence to be general knowledge. De Witt knew he was on his way, but a message had been sent to him to keep his mouth shut or he might end up the loser. Throgmorton needed De Witt's cooperation to put his plans into motion and extract a fortune from the idiotic Condesa. Afterwards, he planned to vanish from the world into a life of luxury.

Being a criminal had undeniable attractions.

Once in the main area, he did a quick survey and saw De Witt sitting alone at a corner table. Two warders stood back at a discreet but watchful distance. A few years in jail hadn't changed him. He looked unassuming. A squat man in his mid-forties with white hair cut in an abrupt but vigorous one-inch crew cut. There was a suppressed nervousness about him. It was a condition he intended to maintain between them.

"Mr. De Witt" Throgmorton extended his hand.

De Witt remained seated and ignored it. "Judge Throgmorton, this is hard to believe. What do you want to see me for? I don't think it's to offer friendly advice." His top lip curled.

The judge knew this wasn't going to be easy. He pulled out a chair and sat opposite him. "You're right on that point, De Witt. You're not getting friendly advice. I'm not wasting time on small talk, so I'll get to the point. When you get out of here, you'll have nothing. You've been cleaned out. You're broke. The best you can hope for is living in a halfway house and you'll barely able to afford a piss at Waterloo station. Looking forward to that, are you?"

"You haven't come all this way to tell me what I already know."

"True. We may be able to help each other."

"How's that?"

Throgmorton saw his eyes narrow. *Once a villain always a villain.* From his case, he pulled out the three enlarged photographs of Francisco Cortez's known paintings, and pushed them across to him.

De Witt scrutinised them. "I didn't do these." His face glowered.

Throgmorton couldn't resist a smirk. "I know you didn't. Two are in the El Prado and the other is in Valencia Cathedral. The artist was Francisco Cortez, a little-known sixteenth-century painter. Experts rate him more highly than your pet baby, El Greco. What do you think?" He handed him a magnifying lens.

De Witt picked up each one and subjected them to an in-depth examination. He then sat back, took a deep breath and lifted his chin. "Masterly, without a doubt. Whether they are better than Greco is a matter of opinion. Why are you showing me these?"

Throgmorton paused. Raúl's recent information had been most useful. "He painted religious scenes, mainly, as you can see from these examples, the miracles of Christ. If asked, would it be possible, for example, to do a sixteenth-century Cortez showing Christ raising Lazarus from the dead?"

The prisoner leaned forward. "If asked, the answer would be yes."

"I'm asking."

"I'd need to see originals, make sketches and notes, plus photographs. There is one other important factor to consider."

"Let me guess. Price?"

"Exactly. An authentic work is not cheap."

Criminals never learned. Even after experiencing imprisonment, this man was willing to walk down the same path that had sent him here in the first place. For the same reason. Money.

"Five grand."

"Ten."

"Seven-fifty."

"You're on. Where do we go from here?"

"The day you are released, you will be met outside the gates and from there you'll be taken to Heathrow with a ticket to Madrid. When you arrive, someone will meet you and you will get full instructions. Okay?"

"No tricks?"

"No tricks. I promise."

CHAPTER 26

T ravelling by air, he found boring. The flight back to Madrid was no different although it gave Throgmorton time for reflection. Gazing out into the tumbling cumulus, he thought about his life. He'd gone a long way in five years from the safe and respected world of the legal profession. Under a dark and heavy cloud, he'd only just avoided the fate of criminals like De Witt. He'd travelled into a world of shadows. They were now to be his home and he had no illusions. It was as if he had been born to it. The thrill and excitement it created amazed him. It was a million miles away from the dreariness of the Inns of Court. He rationalised that if he could have his life all over again, this would be his chosen path.

Murder, violence, robbery and extortion, he'd begun to know them well, like long lost friends.

The vibration of his mobile caused him to check. It was López. He'd paid him, together with his accomplice, Copin, to follow Ladro and Stuart and report back to him on their movements.

"They are on their way to Valencia."

"Stay with them and report back," he said, and switched off the phone. *Interesting. Valencia Cathedral without a doubt. Cortez's painting in the Chapel has to be on their visit list. Why?* He thought De Witt was the key. Ladro and his woman's fate would be determined by what he could produce.

— — —

The Condesa's countenance was grim as she walked into the study, her thoughts contemplating Throgmorton's death threat.

Pausing, she gazed around the room before moving to the furthest fan vaulted pillar. What she was about to do had not been done or known for centuries. Her father, the former Duke, had revealed it to her as a drastic resource for self-protection. He had shown her how the former monks of the Abbey, facing increasing attacks not only from the Moors but later from the Archbishop's army, had constructed a final way of protecting their holy prize, *The Eyes of Christ.*

Reaching into a slot concealed next to a wall-mounted crucifix, she extracted a thin leather wallet tied with a thick black thong. Untying the knot, she opened the covering flap and with great care, unfolded it before reading its contents.

The chest containing the tabard stood at the far end of the room. She removed it and draped it gently across the closed lid so that the black cross was in full view.

Holding the wallet, she headed for the door. Before she reached it, she removed a small silver pistol from her desk drawer and placed it in her pocket. Then, reaching out, she pulled hard on the crucifix, letting it move downwards before releasing it and allowing it to spring back into position. There was a sound of gears and metal moving from beneath the room. She stepped out of the room and shut the door.

CHAPTER 27

L adro pulled the car over, bringing it to a stop by the roadside. They were taking the scenic route and were about forty kilometres from Valencia.

"They're still behind us."

Ulla stretched her neck to look behind. "They've stopped, too. What do you think they're going to do?"

"Nothing. They're on an observational exercise and not on behalf of the Condesa."

"I'm pissed off about this. Brodie, reverse towards them, will you?"

He raised an eyebrow but did as she asked. "What are you planning do?"

"Stop the car and watch."

They were about fifty metres away. Without a word, Ulla stepped out of the car and walked towards the parked vehicle.

"Ulla! What are you doing?"

She didn't answer. At about thirty metres away, she reached behind her jacket and produced the Glock. Safety catch off, arms extended, she fired three shots in quick succession. All three thudded through the front grille. The car was disabled.

With a smile, she got back in the car. "Valencia please, James."

— — —

"I learnt more by looking at Raúl's paintings yesterday than several hours trawling the Internet."

"What did you find?" asked Ulla.

"I don't quite know yet. They're full of clues to something, and it seems they were painted before the work we are looking for. The background hills are the same and the pointing figures are all looking in the same direction, at what looks like a church of some sort in the distance. What are they trying to say? It doesn't fit the historical scene and as you said before, it's out of context."

"The story as we've heard it says he committed suicide after his last work, if he ever painted one. That wouldn't fit in with the paintings we've been looking at. They suggest a later date."

"And we know the black cross and the lettering refer to the Knights of the Risen Lazarus."

"When we examine the third painting in the Cathedral, we might get more answers. Otherwise, the codex and the diaries are all we have to go on. We're almost there." He pointed to a road sign, *Valencia 5 km.*

The third largest Spanish city was saturated with tourists. The Cathedral, layered in early medieval history and the resting place of what is claimed to be the Holy Grail, worked like a magnet for believers and non-believers alike. The story goes, that the persecuted Roman Catholic Church gave the Holy Chalice to Saint Lawrence for safekeeping. He sent it to his parents in Spain before the Romans roasted him alive on a gridiron.

"Where are we going?" Ulla asked.

"Follow me. Remember, we're not tourists."

Ladro strode into the main entrance and in spite of the number of people moving around, the coolness of the air surprised him. Frankincense wove it all together.

Passing by Corinthian pillars, numerous arches, and a wealth of famous art, he made his way to the small chapel of The Blessed Saint Lazarus of Bethany.

"We're here."

They were alone.

"What are we looking for?" Ulla ignored the pews and homed in on *Christ Crucified and the Mother Mary* behind the altar.

"I told you the other two paintings showed a figure of a man pointing, but this one shows a woman."

Ulla moved to within inches of the painting. Using the lens, she began concentrating on the forlorn figure of the pointing woman. She said nothing. Following the outstretched arm, she moved up to the line of broken hills and the vague outlines of the building. She began squinting and then snapped her fingers.

"Brodie, notebook and pen."

He knew her well enough not to interrupt. He handed her what she wanted, and sat down in a pew. She scoured every inch of the painting. At times, she would pause to write notes. Ten minutes passed. She snapped the notebook shut, took a deep breath, and sat next to him.

"Well?"

She leant against him. He saw the disbelieving shake of the head and the gleam in her eyes. Her hushed voice matched those of the pilgrims and tourists queuing to see the Holy Chalice.

"It seems that this place has got more than its fair share of sacred mysteries." She lifted her hand, placing a finger on her lips to signal no interruptions. "Cortez has to be an amazing artist. The preliminary sketch that Evita had of the Abbot praying to the Virgin Mary, and the other drawing of the young woman, remember?"

Brodie remembered, nodded, but said nothing.

"She has the same face of the Virgin Mary in this work. It's the same woman. Whoever she was, she played an important part in his life. Artists in those days rarely used a model more than once.

The painting of the Abbot and possibly of the woman, may also still be in existence. Now, here's another clue. Make out from it what you will. Hold your breath, Brodie."

"Just get to the point."

Ulla pulled him up towards the painting. "Look very closely." She handed him the magnifying glass. "That lone figure of the pointing woman, who d'you think it is?"

"My God, Ulla! It's the same woman again."

"What else can you see? Just look at her."

Ladro stared hard. It was not easy to spot but then it dawned on him. "She's pregnant! That's why she looks unhappy."

"Exactly. There's more to come. What do you think she's doing?"

"Pointing upwards?"

"More. Look at her other hand. It's turned with the palm upwards."

"What does that tell you?"

"She's asking for help from that odd building in the distance; a church, a monastery or a convent?"

"That's what I think."

He could see she still had the gleam in her eye.

"Tell me," she asked him, "what's the short form of Francisco?"

"It's Cisco. Why?"

"I might be reaching but look, let me explain. The central construction here is the figure of the Virgin Mary, the Cross, and the dead Christ. Look at the body postures. Cortez had used a palette knife in certain places. The way Mary is leaning over, the palette knife clearly marks out in her shape the letter C. Agreed?"

"Agreed."

"The base of the cross stands almost between them, but towers upwards and out of sight. So, you could say we have the letters CI?"

"Okay. What next?"

"Cortez, using his palette knife, has given Christ's bent body from one side--the letter S. Can you see that?"

"Yes, I can see that. So, we have CIS."

"We now need a C. Easy, look." Ulla traced her finger along the drape of a large white mantle of cloth lying next to Christ. "The letter C. CISC --- the letter O is trickier, but watch. The shape and bend in Christ's arm from his body form the Greek letter Ω --- Omega. O is the last letter, literally the end, and his fingers extend out towards our pointing woman. So, we have CISCO."

Silence.

Ladro became analytical. "An interesting interpretation. A first-year student could pick a dozen holes in it. What's it got to do with our search for a speculative painting? It tells us nothing."

Ulla placed her arms across her chest and with a pinched expression stared back at him.

"You can be an arrogant shit at times. It has everything to do with it. This woman is central to what we are looking for. Here, she is pregnant. He spells out his name and points at her, and she looks unhappy while pointing to a church of some sort. He's painted her at least three times. Doesn't that suggest something to you? Why did he paint her? Is she unmarried? Is he the father? The records suggest he vanished. When was this painted? It would have to be before his alleged disappearance. Why paint it at all? C'mon Brodie, you can do better than that." She turned her back on him.

"Ulla, it's too simplistic. If he was the father of the woman's child, he could have added her in at a later date, after he signed it. Didn't you say a while back that answers often stared you in the face? Where's the best place to hide a stone? The most obvious is a pebble beach."

"I take your point. So, you're suggesting what we are looking for is under our noses?"

"I am. That line of hills must be around here somewhere, and the place where that building stood, or stands."

"So, let's get this straight. We need a historical record of this area; buildings, people, events, and the social order. We also need to find out about the pregnant woman. There must be something in those diaries … listen."

Ulla turned around. From outside in the central pews, about sixty people were kneeling as a service started, complete with a choir and organ music. She saw a figure dart behind a pillar.

An uncanny mixture of sound and silence.

"Something's not right here. Hey! He's got a gun!"

Ladro flung Ulla to the floor.

Three bullets from a silenced weapon thudded into the oak woodwork above him.

Nobody seemed to have heard anything. The congregation was still singing. Three more shots splattered into the plaster and one thumped into a pew next to Ulla. He saw three men, one wearing a yachting cap, running towards the west entrance at the far end of the side walls.

"Let's get out of here before any questions get asked."

Ulla ignored him. She was already in a firing stance.

"Ulla! No!"

There was clear daylight between her and the escaping figures. She pumped off three shots in quick succession. One of the figures staggered, but the hit didn't stop him as he vanished with the others out of the door.

"You stupid bitch." Ladro pushed her arm down hard and propelled her in the same direction as the men had taken. "Put that gun away and just follow me. If we're caught, we're finished … in more ways than one."

As they exited, he saw the main doors swing open and a swarm of uniformed police rushed in.

"I don't think we've been spotted."

Ulla looked angry. "Hell! What was that all about? Someone's trying to kill us and you tell me not to fire back. I don't believe it!"

"Throgmorton's giving us a warning. He's obviously well pissed off. What's got into you? You've raised the stakes. First his car, and now you've just hit one of his men. He only needs to be lucky once and our research days are over."

She gave a grim smile. "At least it's not boring."

Their quick footsteps clattered across the flagstone flooring. "Quick, what do you want to do?"

"We carry on, and from now on, I'll also be carrying a gun." He pushed the door open and stepped out into the sunlight.

CHAPTER 28

S hielded from view, the Judge stood in the shadow of the Cathedral, hidden by one of the small statues around the Almonina entrance.

It hadn't gone quite to plan, but close. He stood in the circle of onlookers before his men approached him. He'd seen them emerge from the Cathedral and Copin looked as if he'd taken a hit. The arrival of the police had drawn the crowd's attention, as some of them were armed with more than handguns. People had seen the gunfire and were streaming out. It was becoming chaotic. The entire approach was flooded with police and flashing lights.

His earlier phone call had almost worked. He'd wanted Stuart and Ladro to be caught by the police, carrying weapons. That would have removed them in the gentlest manner possible. Their removal hadn't happened, but they must have got the message. Nobody messes with him and gets away with it.

It would be a while before any witnesses would be able to describe the men who had fired the guns. The situation had become more physical. But as always, he told himself to relax. He was enjoying it. More police were arriving and barrier tape was going up like bunting.

His men sidled up to him pretending to be innocent bystanders.

"Were you hit?" Throgmorton demanded.

Copin grabbed his hand. "Feel this."

Throgmorton felt the rigidity of body armour.

"Good thinking." Ladro and Stuart were not easy meat. Far from it. Even with the odds stacked against them, they were dangerous, resourceful, and had nerve. His initial checks on them hadn't mentioned that, but he was beginning to understand why they were successful.

He turned to his associate. "Next time make sure they're the target, not the woodwork."

His phone rang, it was De Witt.

"I'm out tomorrow," the voice growled in his ear.

"Good. I trust you have some ideas?"

"I think you'll be pleased."

"You remembered my instructions?"

"I have."

"Then we'll meet in Madrid in a few days' time.

The judge switched off the phone. What De Witt could come up with would be interesting. Enough, he hoped, to fool any researchers ... or a Condesa.

— — —

Ladro gunned the rented car out of Valencia, in the direction of Toledo. The shootings in the Cathedral had unsettled him more than he had anticipated. They had been lucky to get out unscathed. They could have been killed or imprisoned. Luckily, the ensuing chaos had enabled them to slip out without being detained. He had powered the car past a police patrol setting up a road block. After years of precise planning on each and every mission, he felt they were being out-manoeuvred.

Ulla said nothing but wore a tight-lipped expression. He

hadn't expected her to get involved in two bouts of shooting, but again, she was proving as unpredictable as ever. The thought of it kept his foot hard pressed on the pedal. He'd always been a prudent driver, but now the needle was clocking 145 km per hour and moving upwards.

"Brodie, slow down, will you?" Her voice had to compete with the engine noise.

"There are times, not often, when I feel like driving fast. This is one of them," he snarled at her.

"We've just avoided a load of police. The way you're driving will draw them to us like flies around shit."

Ladro refused to answer but he decreased the pressure on the pedal.

An uneasy silence ensued as he slowed the car. Ulla peered against the sunlight with her hand over the top of her eyes.

"Brodie, stop please. I saw something."

"What?" He couldn't disguise his irritation as he pulled the car over.

"That line of hills over there." She pointed to the distant skyline. "Do they remind you of anything?"

He braked, switched off the engine, and stepped out. He squinted into the direction of the dipping sun. At first, the glare blinded him. Then, he began to understand what Ulla had seen. The hills stood part in sunlight and part in silhouette. He let his eye wander across the undulating range that ascended sharply in one part, before dipping down to two smaller summits. He paused and repeated the exercise.

"I see what you mean. They look as if they were lifted straight from Cortez's paintings. I think we need to go up there. Okay with you?"

"That's what we're here for. Let's go."

Ladro soon found a turnoff, a dusty side road that led in the direction of the hills. His imagination heightened as they drove down into a small valley, before climbing upwards and passing what had once been a remote hamlet.

Staring up the twisty road, he couldn't help thinking that if there had been a religious community in the area, plus the Holy Grail in Valencia, the place was an ideal setting for a religious mystery. It wasn't hard to imagine monks, knights, and pilgrims inhabiting the place.

More twists and turns and the road began to disappear. The summit came into view. He slowed and passed through a crop of dilapidated stone pillars and arches. Sagging black and yellow safety tape barred further progress.

Ulla climbed out and gazed at the ruins. "It looks ancient. What do you think?"

"Some sort of church or monastery. It matches the structure shown on Cortez's painting." He pointed to the roof, once fan vaulted and supported by a crumbling pillar.

"By the sheer size, it looks more than a church. It's remote enough to warrant it being a monastery. That ruined hamlet back there was typical of such places springing up close to a community of monks. We can check that out later when we get back."

"There's no cross here that's shown on the painting."

"That must have long gone."

"Hey, we're not alone here. Look." Ladro pointed up a narrow flint strewn track. Three people, in single file, laden with backpacks and wearing chunky walking boots, were heading towards them. "Let's ask them, they might know."

They knew. They told Ulla it was a monastery built in the fourteenth century, before it was burnt down later in the seventeenth-century.

"What was it called? She asked.

"Monasterio de San Vicente de Valencia," came the reply.

"Thanks. That's very helpful," he paused, "and we can check that out when we get back home."

A wind had sprung up. Ladro turned to his left and peered down a vista of fields, wooded slopes, valleys and rocky boulders that stretched out endlessly. More ruins. Just below him stood the remains of an old tower showing the semblance of turrets, the structure surrounded by a cluster of old granite and limestone walls.

Crash.

Shouts, screams, blood, and the sounds of steel and war, smashed through his consciousness without warning.

"Muerte a los Invasores!" Death to the Invaders! His voice rang down through the valley. "Ulla, help!" The veins in his neck bulged as he threw back his head. "Ulla! Ulla! It's happening again." His eyes squeezed shut and a violent pain wrung every nerve end in his head. Her arms were around him.

"Brodie. What is it? Speak to me." She began shaking his shoulders.

For a moment, his head flopped but he was aware of full consciousness returning. One mammoth deep breath and stability resumed. He held his arms around his chest.

"Again ... Oh my God ... The same sort of thing happened at Maria's place. What the hell's happening to me?"

"I've no idea, but if you're okay now, let's get out of here. It's getting too spooky."

They headed back to the car and Ulla elected to drive. As they got in, Ladro looked back at the scene. It looked quiet and peaceful, yet he couldn't dismiss the thoughts that he once knew the place and the people involved.

CHAPTER 29

F rancisco Cortez. There wasn't much to go on.

De Witt, installed in a small downtown hotel situated in the Malascaña suburbs of Madrid, attempted to piece together what he could find out about the artist. It was essential to his approach that he gathered as much knowledge as he could about the man. Information enabled him to get inside the artist's mind and access his emotions; the way he regarded things, the way he observed life. These would give him insight into the artist's heart ... his soul.

With only three known works to guide him, anything decent was asking a lot. *What does Throgmorton think I am? A miracle worker?*

On the Internet, he'd found a collection of learned papers from a retinue of art historians and professors. To a man, they upheld the viewpoint that Cortez's works were important, but there needed to be more of them to cement that belief and place Cortez up there with the established masters. De Witt needed to look at the known works up close.

He gave a small smirk. Another masterpiece could just about shift Cortez up the rankings chart.

There was a loud rap at the door and he knew it would be

Throgmorton. He had no love for the man. He loathed him, but money was scarce so he was happy to take the judge's. Whatever Throgmorton planned to do with the finished work, would be his own business.

"How's it going, De Witt?"

"Well enough." He sensed his dislike of the man was reciprocated.

"Anything to show me?"

"Preliminary sketches I've worked on from a few of Christ's miracles. For reasons you wouldn't understand, I need to see Cortez's actual paintings. Can you arrange that?" If his jibe had registered, it didn't show.

Throgmorton picked up the preliminaries. Going from one to the other, he looked through them several times without comment. "They look good." He pointed to a sketch of Christ standing outside a rocky outcrop with a large stone rolled to one side. "This one I like." Emerging from it was the figure of the risen man, Lazarus. "You've left the faces blank. Why?"

"If I thought you would understand, I'd tell you. That is why I asked you to arrange for me to see originals."

A flash of annoyance crossed Throgmorton's face. "It's done, and arranged for tomorrow. Looking at these, I like the Lazarus idea. Let me have three suggestions on that before you start?"

"I'm not painting anything until I've looked more closely at Cortez's paintings; the way he worked, his brushwork technique, style and structure. I'll also need to know the type of paints and hand-ground pigments he used. Did he use egg tempera or did he use glue, honey, milk or water? Did he mix them with a percentage of oil? He may have used specific ingredients, and paints like that must be made since they are not available today. But that's a bridge to be crossed when I get there. These are things you know nothing of. There are other issues too, but they're not your concern."

De Witt felt an old, familiar emotion take hold of him. He had always likened it to a monk finding God. He felt imbued with the spirit and character of the man he was copying. It was vital to his own work.

He could see Throgmorton looked out of his depth. He was happy for him to stay that way.

"You'll be picked up in the morning at ten and taken to El Prado. I've arranged for you to have a private viewing. After one hour there, you'll be escorted to Valencia to see the third painting in the Cathedral. Please, don't be late."

Throgmorton turned and without another word, walked out. His expression, thought De Witt, looked sour.

CHAPTER 30

Evita sat close to Ulla making careful notes of what she was telling her. It was information she knew Raúl, her father, would pass on to Throgmorton. Ulla had discussed this with Brodie and there was to be no mention of visions. The information would be about shootings, similarities in the paintings to the local geography, disused monasteries, and a suggestion that the elusive painting could be close at hand.

Enough, they had agreed, to whet his appetite.

At the far end of the Bodega's library, Brodie had surrounded himself with Cortez's drawings, manuals and diaries. Lifting his head, he watched Ulla talking to Evita. What struck him was Ulla's flat response to what had happened to him, not once, but three times. He couldn't understand that.

The forlorn monk, the weeping woman, and the lost child.

He couldn't tell her. That vision had become like an irritating sore.

He knew he was far more involved in this affair than he could ever imagine. It had become personal and very strange.

He glanced at his watch. A little after nine-thirty and Evita had left, leaving Ulla alone, working on the codex. He looked at her ...

practical, hard-nosed and fearless. She didn't like making mistakes and she loathed anyone who pointed them out to her, including him. The recent shootings had unravelled another facet of her complex makeup. She had many talents that shone when analysing or planning a project that required stealth and cunning. He'd watched her many times make tough and perilous decisions in a variety of situations, and admired her coolness. Now, he wondered about her present frame of mind, their objective, and the strange effect it was having on her usually sound judgement. The project was not going to plan, and his intuition, which had never failed him over the last fifteen years, said he was going to need her. *I'm going to have to tell her all the details of those visions, every detail. Whether she believes it or not doesn't matter. It's unsettling me.*

Absorbed in his investigations, Brodie had spent most of his time placing and shuffling piles of pages and notes into a semblance of order. Dates and locations appeared to be random, thrust into the chest and boxes that had been left abandoned without care or feeling. Much of the material related to the running and organisation of the vineyard. Delving deeper he hoped to find a name or reference for the woman who had modelled for the Virgin Mary. There didn't appear to be any. He turned back to his original pile of documents and received a clue. In the form of a small booklet or diary, it was bound with board, decorated with gold and red inks or paints, and held together with a faded black ribbon.

He untied it. It was headed, *Valencia, Junio MDLV* (1555).

The writing, in strong black ink, was in the style and practice of the times. The letters were small and embellished with innumerable long flourishes and swirls. Ladro stared hard at the pages. It was set out in a precise and structured fashion. The margins were decorated with scenes and faces as were the gaps between paragraphs. Even without checking, he knew it had been written by Francisco Cortez. He counted the pages. They amounted to twelve and covered the months of June and July. Ladro read them through several times. An element of sadness ran through it—

the sadness of a young boy who was missing home...

Friday, 3rd June 1555

Another hot day here and the hills are no longer green, they have turned to brown. Today is my fourteenth birthday and I have received from Señor Méndez a letter from my parents, wishing me an auspicious day. Since papá sent me here, it is hard to believe I have been in Valencia for almost two years. I miss Toledo and my dear mamá and papá. It is worrying that they are both unwell and papá can no longer walk well. I am praying to God to keep them safe.

Papá's ring now fits me and I shall be wearing it soon. I have seen Señor Méndez with his and I'm afraid to ask him its meaning, as he had forbidden me to speak of it.

Life here in Valencia is not bad but it is not home, and I am counting the days to Christmas when I can return home for a while...

That confirms his birth date at 1541, and the black pattée is linked to all this, Brodie thought. What is Cortez doing in Valencia and who is Méndez? Several pages later, he saw what he was looking for.

Thursday, 9th June

Salvador Méndez's studio has been busy and he has had many new clients who want portraits. He has asked me to watch him and I am to be allowed to finish a small section of a work on the city tailor, Miguel Ribera. It is a high honour. I hope one day I can be allowed to assist on his more important works.

Here, Brodie struggled to read the writing that tapered off the end of the page.

Well, he thought to himself. He's apprenticed in the studio of Salvador Mendez, he misses home, his parents are unwell and he has ambitions. The next entry transfixed him.

Sunday, 19th June 1555

...and prayed in my favourite small chapel in the west wing of the Cathedral. What has happened, I cannot speak of to anyone!

At first, God was not with me, and then He came to me. I saw Juan de Borgoña and he was looking into my head and pointing to his fresco, The Raising of Lazarus at Toledo's Cathedral. A terrible heat seized me. I dared not open my eyes and my body trembled. I heard the voice of God or was it Borgoña? It said, "Francisco, do not be afraid. You know of me. You shall be the heir to Lazarus. When, it cannot be said, but be prepared."

I saw the fresco clearly and then the vision vanished. I opened my eyes and it was as if nothing had happened. I was still there in the chapel. Inwardly, I am joyous but nervous ... because I believe all this. O Joy. My vision remains alive. I can speak to no one.

I was preparing dishes for evening supper when Señor Méndez returned from Toledo. He had been to see the Duke of Alba for a commission. He looked tired. He gave me instructions concerning what items I was to collect from our suppliers tomorrow. He sat down to eat and told me something most strange had happened at the Cathedral.

"A wall in the Sala Capitular had collapsed. One of Borgoña's frescos was destroyed."

"Which one?" I asked. I confess to feeling startled.

"The Raising of Lazarus. Unless a miracle occurs, it's irreplaceable." He looked at me in a very odd way.

"It fell down?"

"Yes, it collapsed in an instant." Without another word, Méndez kissed the black cross of his ring and walked out, not finishing his supper.

I feel no shock or surprise. How could I?

CHAPTER 31

T wo monasteries, one in ruins outside Valencia, and the other sited at Guadamur, now the home of the Condesa, matched the dates mentioned in the Bodega's archives. Ladro was pleased at their progress and suggested they eat out at a restaurant that evening. Additionally, he had discovered the rough date that Borgoña's fresco of Lazarus had met its fate. The information was exciting and needed to be discussed away from their usual rooms. Scientific proof didn't exist, but he was convinced that another painting existed.

At a restaurant in the older part of town, they shared a large plate of paella with two glasses of white Rioja. Ulla leant forward.

"I'm beginning to believe this fable. There seem to be too many things that are starting to link up."

"True. We need to discover the events surrounding the pregnant woman." Ladro paused, pushing a piece of squid to one side of the plate. "There's something I haven't told you."

Her eyes narrowed. "What?"

"That ruined monastery ... I saw and heard something else."

Ulla stared into him. "What was that?"

He shivered. "I saw the pregnant woman, and a man dressed

as a monk wearing a tabard with a black cross. They were crying and reaching out for each other. There was an abandoned child on the ground. A building was on fire. It was the monastery we saw."

"Carry on." Ulla sounded uncertain.

Ladro stared down at the tabletop. "There was a voice."

"A voice?"

"Yes, it was a woman's. She told me I had the key to this. Please don't ask me what because I haven't a clue what's going on here."

She placed her hand on his. "Brodie, anybody else telling me this and I would have asked them to get their head examined. I believe you. I shouldn't, but I do. I think something is staring us in the face and we just aren't seeing it."

"Thanks, I think the same. Let's get back to the hotel and sort out what to do next."

— — —

They left the restaurant as that part of Toledo was shutting up for the night. Doors and shutters were being bolted. Darkness encompassed the narrow, cobbled lane that led back in the direction of the hotel. Nothing stirred.

In front of them rose an incline where a church had been built to serve the needs of the Cathedral many years ago. It was closed tight but the gardens remained open, offering a route directly towards the hotel. Ladro propelled Ulla in through the gateway, as a small moon broke through dark scudding clouds to illuminate the walkway.

Ulla whispered. "You know we're being followed?"

"Of course. That's why we're going through here." He half turned and saw a figure duck behind a large tree. "Through here and keep walking. Don't wait for me." He slid behind a large broken headstone shielded by a mass of dripping moss, and waited.

The man passed the covered headstone and Ladro leapt forward and jammed his fist hard into his soft stomach. He sent another blow to the man's jaw, crashing him to the ground and sending a pistol spinning across the pathway.

Ulla came running towards them.

He hauled the man up and inspected him. He was short, with a dark stubble and a shaven head. At the same time, he booted the weapon out of sight. Ulla didn't hesitate. Her Glock was in her hand and she pressed it hard against the man's temple. He looked dazed and Ladro patted him down for any other hidden weapon. He removed a flick-knife that had been secreted beneath his jacket. Ulla shoved him hard and he doubled over the headstone.

"Who are you working for?"

No reply.

"You speak English?"

The man shook his head, gasping for breath.

"Ulla, make him understand."

She cocked the hammer on the Glock.

Ladro saw the man tense as the message registered. "Throgmorton?" he demanded.

The man's voice quavered. "Si, Señor, Si. Throgmorton."

"Where can I find him?"

Ulla pushed harder with the barrel of the gun.

His reply was quick. "Madrid. Hotel Bella Vista."

A gunshot sent them ducking as a bullet thudded into the trunk of the tree in front of them. Both Ladro and Ulla dived. Ladro saw a darkened figure standing forty metres away, half leaning against the arched porch behind them. Another shot whistled off the headstone just above their prisoner's head. Ulla jumped to one side and released her hold on him.

The next bullet cracked into the headstone. This time the man got to his feet and bolted into the darkness. That had the desired result as Ulla took aim and cracked off two rapid rounds in the direction of the assailant. The shooter didn't wait. Ladro grabbed the Glock from Ulla and moved in the direction of the fleeing figure when he saw him jump over a small supporting wall and head in the direction of the exit. There was a six-foot wall with a matching drop that led into the car park.

Ladro didn't stop to think. He paused and pumped off three more shots that he heard slice into woodwork and knew he'd missed his target. The man was still running. He saw him vault the wall and drop down on the other side, and heard the revving of a motorbike a second after. Their prisoner was on it. He skidded it around in a furious circle of white dust as the shooter sprang onto the back.

Another shot sent up a burst of sparks ricocheting off a nearby metal post.

The bike roared off avoiding the narrow entrance and zigzagged down another narrow street and into the darkness.

If the roar of a motorcycle and gunshots were unfamiliar in this part of Toledo it didn't show. Not a light came on. Ladro was in no mood to wait around. Ulla was right beside him.

"I wouldn't have missed" she said.

"That was what I was worried about. Then we'd have some explaining to do."

"So now we know where we're at with Sir Max."

"Too right. The stakes are raised. I don't think he wanted them to shoot at us, but meat heads are the same the world over. We could go after him"

"Perhaps we should?"

"Let's discuss that at the hotel. C'mon, let's get out of here."

Their footsteps echoed across the loneliness of the burial ground.

CHAPTER 32

S tephan De Witt stepped back from his easel and was less than happy with his progress. He'd seen all three of Cortez's paintings over the last few days and had extracted as much information as he could from both the curator and from his own drawings and photographs. With the camera, he had zoomed in on every corner and part of the paintings. Working on an artist he'd not done before required a special degree of attention.

He'd established that Cortez had painted on both canvas and board. For stability, he'd used an egg tempera *grassa* mixture. Oil was used in a strict ratio to produce water soluble paint, but which could resemble oils. It dried fast but could only be applied in thin layers. To achieve any suggestion of depth, numerous coats and small strokes had been used.

De Witt found himself admiring the skill of Cortez. He was proving to be an unprecedented discovery. Examining the works through a powerful lens, he was convinced the paints Cortez used were hand-ground pigments consisting, as was common for the age, of cinnabar, containing mercury; the arsenic based orpiment with its rich lemony colour and varied lead whites. Replicating these substances had become easier as several modern painters were experimenting with medieval and contemporary techniques and processes.

Of the three works he had examined, *Christ Crucified and the Mother Mary* excited his attention the most. It revealed a maturity that made use of every component of the medieval painter. It was awash with symbols. He wasn't being paid to investigate hidden meanings, but Cortez's work was full of them. For a reason that Throgmorton wouldn't divulge, he'd taken an unusual interest in Cortez.

Why does he want a fake Cortez showing Lazarus being raised from the dead? Whatever reason, he's not doing it for the love of painting. There has to be big bucks in this. It's going to cost him more than he thought.

Something was not going right. In front of him and to one side stood his sketches and a rough draft. First, he examined several works of the masters of the period and how they approached the subject. Rembrandt, he considered too ghostly, morgue like. Caravaggio missed the point in his usual over dramatisations. He preferred Salviati's approach that embodied and captured the human qualities he thought would be present at such an event. He stared long and hard at Cortez's works, wondering how he might have approached the subject .... the number of people present, foreground, background, expressions and postures; the colours employed, light and shadow, and the drapes and folds and the state of their clothing.

De Witt used the medieval religious practice of *Lectio Divina* to imagine he was Cortez participating at the event itself, to experience the emotions that would have been present there. He mumbled to himself in gibberish, waiting for a spark to illuminate his consciousness and guide his hand in the mysterious way it had done so often in the past. He closed his eyes and transported himself back to a Spain drenched in the sun of the mid-late sixteenth century. He reached out for Cortez. Stretching out his arms he called out his name, "Francisco Cortez, I pay you tribute. Please come to me, enter my body and soul and let me paint as you may have wished."

Nothing.

De Witt was a patient man. It took time to be taken over and for him to absorb the essence of the chosen painter. He had agreed in his mind how he would scan out the composition and it came to him how he would place the figures and their number into the geography and landscape. Between them all, he formulated an idea for a structure.

He would depict a multi-figured scene from inside the tomb with the guarding rock rolled away, revealing unusual configurations of light from outside and faces peering in. It would be expressionistic, with figures and faces looking elongated with agonised curiosity. The inside light would be of muted yellows and greens breaking up shards of blackness. Some onlookers would be masking their faces to protect against the stench of death. They would be wide-eyed and clothed in simple robes. The major proportion would be in a tempera and gold combination around Christ.

Two things eluded him. The figures and placement of both Lazarus and Christ did not fit into his idea. He could place them anywhere, but it wasn't right, and it wouldn't have been what Cortez would have done.

The spirit of Cortez was not forthcoming. He knew he could paint a passable and accurate 'Cortez' but that alone was not enough. He felt offended at being ignored. There was more to his skills than copying techniques and processes. As with the other masterpieces he had painted, he needed to be possessed by the artist and this was not happening. The expressions of the two main characters eluded him.

He paced the studio. "I've tried wonderment, solemnity, incredulity and weeping gratitude ... but nothing looks right. The expressions and the eyes, I cannot get what I want ... from either of them."

He slammed his brushes down hard into his brush holder.

"Rembrandt would have been easier than this!" He decided that unless he could get it right, he would do an amalgamation of the expressions in all three paintings and hope it would somehow look correct. Throgmorton wouldn't notice. Yet, that wasn't the point. He was more than a mere copyist ... he was the embodiment and upholder of a golden lost age. Professionally, for the first time, he was aware of an inadequacy.

Maybe I've been away from this too long?

But he knew it couldn't be the case. It was like riding a bike. Once mastered, never forgotten. Cortez would not let him come close. He decided to make the best of something he knew he was not truly capable of producing. Around him, he lined up the enlarged shots and sketches he'd made from the other three paintings. He leant back, took in a large lungful of cigarette smoke and studied Cortez's works. He didn't know if he should curse or praise him. A cold shiver rippled through him. He looked around and had a distinct feeling of being watched.

CHAPTER 33

E arly the following day, the Condesa rang and asked them if they could pay her a visit. There were several things she wished to discuss and preferred not to talk about them over the phone. They agreed. It was a wiser move than going up to Madrid to pay Throgmorton a visit.

Ladro slid into the driving seat.

"Do you see what I see?" she asked.

"Our two amigos are back again. This time it's a car." He indicated the grey coloured BMW parked beyond the approach to the hotel. "They don't give up, do they?"

"The pay must be good."

"Let's pretend we haven't seen them."

Ladro adjusted the wing mirrors so they both had a clear view of the BMW. Tourists were arriving in buses and cars and the car park was filling. The fine weather of yesterday had vanished and metallic clouds rolled with menace above. Rain was on its way. Guadamur wasn't far but Ulla wanted to lose their tail.

"If we run north of the place and then double back through the hills and across country, we could lose them. We don't want to put Maria in any more danger than she is already."

"Agreed. Let's go." Ladro cruised out of the hotel area and through the stone arches that once guarded the city. Clear of the outskirts, he checked his mirrors. The BMW was still there and keeping a discreet distance.

"You reckon you can lose them?"

"Yep. I'm going to do it as they do in the movies."

"What's that?"

"You'll see."

A short time later, Ladro swung the car into a sharp turn and began heading north away from Guadamur. Ten kilometres ahead, the road forked. One went direct to Guadamur and the other skirted up into the hills toward Valencia. He decided that was the route to take. The BMW continued to follow. Since they were exposed in the emptiness of the terrain, any pretence was abandoned.

Another roll of thunder and a flash of lightning signalled a deluge of heavy rain.

"Damn." Ladro flicked on the wipers and switched on the lights. He was forced to slow down. The road was empty and in his mirror, he could see the BMW closing on them and it was drawing level. The passenger window began to slide open and a gun appeared, pointing in their direction.

"Hit the deck!" he shouted at Ulla who needed no second command. "Change of plans!"

He floored the pedal. Turning the wheel hard right, he skidded into a tight bend sending up a volume of spray and fine mud. Without firing a shot, the BMW spun left and right and lost ground.

"This is getting nasty. You okay down there?"

"Fine. Just get us out of here."

He avoided aquaplaning around the next bend as his pursuers closed the gap between them. Keeping the car steady was getting tough as the tarmac took on the consistency of an off-road event. It was getting difficult to know where the edge of the road began and finished. The rain got harder.

A bullet smashed through the rear window and passed with a neat hole through the front, but without causing the glass to shatter. Another one and it would explode. The rain made it hazardous to maintain the zigzagging course through straight stretches and bends in the road. Only when a crunching sound arose did he know he was on the edge of the road. In front of him, he spotted a car approaching in the opposite direction, causing him to wrestle with the wheel and swing the complaining vehicle back into his own lane.

"Ulla! For God's sake! Use the Glock!" he shouted over the noise of the screaming engine, his head bent low. "It's got a full clip and there's another under my seat! Don't miss."

From the corner of his eye he saw her find the pistol, lower her window before extending her arm out and take aim.

"Make them count!" In a blink, he heard her blast off three rounds.

They had the desired effect. The pursuing car dropped back with a shattered headlamp and another hole through the windscreen. Brodie swung the car to the left as he lurched around the next bend, his foot spread across both accelerator and brake, alternating both in a crazy unison. His racing car days hadn't been forgotten.

It was time to reveal some hidden skills.

An approaching vehicle passed by in a blur.

A brief glimpse of a startled driver.

Brodie shouted out. "Hang on!" He slammed on the brakes. The car struggled for grip as it wriggled and shook to a slippery halt. The BMW overshot. At once, Ladro let off the brake, moved up to second and hit down on the accelerator hard, using a rapid heel and toe technique.

Struggling to grip, the tyres faltered for a microsecond before the car sprinted forward. The seatbelt caused his body to lurch and jerk his head back. He screamed the car to maximum revs in all gears.

The BMW was now in front of him.

"Come on, car! Come on!" The needle of the speedo moved up to seventy. On the twisty route, his heart began to pound. "Ulla, get ready."

The road straightened and he moved the car up to almost alongside the BMW as they crested a short incline surrounded by fields of yellow sunflowers and bright red poppies.

Looking across, Ladro recognised one as the man he had grabbed the other night. He was crouching low and preparing for a shot. He was too slow.

Ulla let off three rapid rounds that sent the man's weapon spinning into the air and out of sight, into the slushy roadside mud. Ladro heard his yell echoing above all else just as he confronted the back of a lumbering farm lorry laden with tomatoes and well over its safety limits. It was what he had been hoping for. If he kept his course running in tandem with the BMW, there would be no way out for it. Its only escape would be to stop ... unlikely at this speed. He would have two options ... crash into the back of the lorry or veer into the wire fence and into a mud soaked field.

Ladro hugged in tight, sped alongside the truck and passed it. Looking in the mirror, his guess was correct. The BMW had swung into the mud in a cloud of spray and steam.

"Wow!" Ulla shouted. "Amazing!"

"I told you to wait and see. I enjoyed that." With a broad smile, Ladro slackened the speed a fraction before he picked up another auxiliary route back in the direction of Guadamur.

— — —

Ulla noticed Brodie's triumphant mood changing the closer they got to the town. He'd gone quiet.

They arrived in forty minutes. The rain had stopped and now the sun shone, sending up wafts of steam from the nearby road, surrounding hills and countryside. A rainbow struggled to make an appearance.

They got out of the car and strolled up to the main entrance. She thought Brodie looked nervous. The walls looked bigger, and there were suggestions of arches and steps leading to forgotten areas that had been turned into gardens and what looked like places of sanctuary. Brodie looked only at the ground in front of them.

"Something wrong?" she asked.

"I don't know. Something about this place gets to me."

Without warning Maria appeared from behind a bower. She was dressed in a lightweight black trouser suit, topped with a flimsy chiffon neck scarf. Everything that she wore, Ulla, thought, accentuated her illness. She looked ashen, thin and drawn. One hand gripped a silver mounted walking cane and in the other she held a small volume. Ulla noticed the title: *Nothing Lasts: How to Beat Pain.*

Ulla gave a questioning look. *Clearly it isn't working.*

The Condesa put down her book and extended a knobbly hand. "Ulla and Brodie, I'm glad you could get here."

"We came through the scenic route." Ladro shook her hand and gave Ulla a sidelong glance.

"I hope the rain didn't spoil it for you. Please sit, I have something to tell you." She indicated a long-cushioned bench beneath a protective blue striped awning. She patted the seat, sat down and let out a deep sigh.

Ulla wasn't sure if the sigh was from pain, tiredness or both. For a moment, there was silence as if the Condesa wanted to imbue them both with the mystery that draped itself around the place.

Ladro broke the spell and spoke first. "Before you speak, we have something to tell you."

She lifted her chin.

Ladro, without missing any detail, told her about their visit to the Cathedral in Valencia. He explained what Ulla had seen in the painting, the clues and symbols and the pregnant woman crying out for help.

"It was then we were shot at," interrupted Ulla. She avoided mentioning returning fire. "To cut a long story short, on the way back, Ulla spotted a hillside that looked the same as in Cortez's paintings. We drove up there and discovered very old ruins of a monastery we now know as San Vicente de Valencia."

The Condesa's alert expression did not change. She leant forward as if devouring a plate of her favourite food.

"He got taken over again." Ulla found herself laughing as she explained the event, omitting some details.

The Condesa closed her eyes. Ulla noticed her lids had begun to flutter, slowly at first, before a short burst of rapid movement bought them to a halt. She opened them again like a drawbridge reluctant to complete its movement. She spoke, her voice sounding lower than before.

"You are getting close. I sense it. Lean nearer and listen to what I am going to tell you."

She paused and spoke with effort. "I was told that the monastery that stood here often got caught up in the fighting and harboured battle worn and injured Crusader knights in the early centuries. Somewhere in the codex, you will find a list of names of many of the knights who took part in the wars. Amongst them is the name of one, Custodio Baez. He was an artist and slain in battle, but not before he had finished his work which he intended for the monastery. It was said he was exceptionally handsome, but loved no one as he did Christ. Every moment and action was devoted to him. He was known as the Guardian, from our word, *custodio*.

Ulla interjected. "That painting would be *The Eyes of Christ*?"

"Exactly. I was told that when he died, the work was discovered, and it was wrapped in his blood-soaked tabard and taken to the monastery. The painting was said to have possessed miraculous powers."

"In what way?"

"Both grandfather and my father said they had heard stories

passed down since the last days of Christ, of devout people being cured of their affliction by gazing into the eyes of Christ."

"That would explain the frequent attempts to steal it."

"As prophesy predicted, it was lost, destroyed when the monastery was razed to the ground. Somewhere and somehow, it was said there would be a new work to replace it. I believe that Borgoña and possibly Cortez were part of that holy lineage."

Ulla looked at the Condesa and knew with certainty what was behind her drive. "Maria, there are a few things we haven't told you."

"We *think* he was a successor. Cortez's diary tells of Juan Borgoña's fresco *The Raising of Lazarus*. It makes a significant reference to what happened to him back in 1553 and the miraculous effect it had. It also mentions what had happened to the fresco. His tutor, Señor Méndez, saw the event. The wall on which it was painted, collapsed."

Ulla noticed the Condesa's excitement as she blurted out, "I know I'm right. What else have you managed to find out?"

"We suspect what we are trying to find is not far from this area, possibly guarded and protected in some way. What it is, we have no idea ... Brodie, how's that antenna you've developed of late?"

Ladro looked grim. "Who knows? I have no control over it. A month ago, I would have denounced such things as a heap of deluded rubbish. What I've seen and heard, plus the frantic attention of Throgmorton, leads me to believe otherwise."

"You are blessed." Maria laid her hands on his arm.

"Not so, after the attacks we've experienced. The answer, I'm certain, is in the records of the Bodega Cortez. On top of that, Raúl Cortez is feeding the information we give him directly to Throgmorton, for money to help cover his debts."

"And we've decided to go after him, haven't we?" Ulla nudged Brodie and at the same time patted the gun hidden at the back of her jacket.

Ladro said nothing, his face expressionless.

CHAPTER 34

El Desierto de Tabernas
30 Kilometres North of Almeria
Spain, 1562 A.D.

T ight leather thongs securing his wrists to the saddle cut into his flesh as the mule the monks led behind them swayed across the rock-strewn terrain. For two days and nights, Francisco, Brother Francis, had silently endured the chaffing torment as blood seeped from beneath his restraints.

Blood of Christ, cleanse me.

Not a morsel of food, but only a sip or two of water had passed his lips since leaving the monastery. Not a word had been spoken. His penance, forty silent days and nights in the Tabernas Desert had begun.

The heat's shimmer distorted the distant hills, and blackened shrubs bent low in despair towards the barren sand.

Without a sound, the three monks came to a halt and one stepped forward, and with a few slices of a large knife, cut the thongs that held him to the mule. Francisco slid to the ground and collapsed, his fingers digging into the sand and grit. Three brown bundles held together with drawstrings were thrown in front of him, together with two large gourds of water.

"God save you," whispered the man who had cut the thongs. He crossed himself, turned, and with the other two, set off in the direction they had come.

Francisco clutched the crucifix on his rosary and muttered three *Ave Marias*. Not a cloud could be seen. It was high noon and in all directions, life wilted in a shimmering heat. Any sensible living creature hid in their burrows or sheltered beneath rocks. His sandaled feet scuffed into the reddish dirt, careful to avoid the numerous razor sharp flint stones that stretched out forever. He began moving toward an overhanging outcrop of rocks.

His bundles contained a few small loaves to be used only at his personal mass, a crucifix, a stout leather whip embossed with metal studs for self-flagellation, and an illustrated text on repentance taken from the *Book of Ezekiel*. The largest bundle held canvases, brushes and paints. The Abbot had made it clear that as part of his penance and to avoid eternal damnation and excommunication, Francisco was to paint a work worthy of God that would form part of the monastery for time immemorial.

Francisco was under no illusions. His chances of survival were minimal. Both the loaves and the water would soon be gone and what he would do then, he had no idea. Certain death faced him. The desert's hardships were all engulfing, merciless, and excommunication was but a step away.

The total quietness heightened the shifting waves of blistering heat. He reached the coolness of the rocky outcrop, a small cave structure, and dropped his bundles to the ground. He sat on a large flat rock. He would stay here and work out how to get food to live and where he might find water. He also knew that he had to get a fire going. With that, his chances of survival would be greater. Making a fire was not one of his skills. He'd been given a fire steel and he needed to collect flint stones and there were plenty around the rocks. Thoughts of Paloma and what had become of her added to his torment.

"Paloma! Paloma!" His voice echoed around the rocks as he fell to his knees and tore off his robe, and reached for the whip.

"Paloma, forgive me. I beseech all the Saints, the Holy Mother of God and Christ himself for your forgiveness. Do not abandon me in my hour of need."

He swung the whip high in the air and back down as hard as he could across his back.

Crack.

"Paloma!"

Crack.

"Paloma!"

The whip struck thirty times and thirty times he cried out. Paloma answered him.

He heard her voice. It echoed in his head and around the craggy walls of the small cave.

"Francisco … Francisco, I am here and I hear you."

Francisco stopped the whip in mid-air and his eyes widened. His head swung left and right but there was nobody to be seen.

"Paloma?" his voice rose in an urgent, disbelieving whisper. "Paloma?"

"Beloved, put down the whip and listen to me." Her voice filled the cave.

Francisco lowered the whip to the ground. His jaw had dropped and his eyes looked wild. Blood trickled down his back as he struggled to speak. "I am listening, Beloved." He bent his head low and covered his face with his hands.

"Francisco, I feel your sorrow and your pain and you have been forgiven. You must now paint … paint as you have never done before and as you do, think only of me and of the power of Christ. If you do, I promise you your work will be blessed. When it is finished, we shall be together once more."

His agonised howl filled the confined space. "Paloma! Paloma!

I promise." He sensed her leaving him. "Don't go! Don't leave me, Paloma, please!"

There was no response and she was gone as quietly as she had appeared.

Silence.

Naked, with his back and shoulders a patchwork of bloody welts, he used his tabard to clean off the crimson stains. Francisco bent in fervent prayer. His love of God mingled with his everlasting shame. His mind overflowed with visions of Paloma ... her child, he neither knew was alive or dead. His torment mingled and shifted with her and increasing visions, memories of Borgoña's fresco ... Lazarus ... Christ ... the shifting shroud ... that stare. The hours of day passed into the darkness of night. He knew what he had to do, what he had been singled out to do from the day he was born.

— — —

He ignored the hunger and the thirst that had caused his mouth to swell and blister, and agonised him at every swallow. The shadow of the overhang gave Francisco the quality of light he needed and protected him from the burning sun. As if in a trance, he laid out his paints, brushes, boards, canvasses and palette. He had no plan ... but God would guide him. There was no hesitation. He became the paint ... became the brush and the colours.

There was nothing to think about. Francisco painted at speed, shaped and formed wet oils into tangible effortless creation ... total flow, harmony and grace.

Before the sun began its final downward dip, Francisco knew it was finished. He could not look at it although he knew he had never painted anything finer, having poured into it his total sorrowful being, body and soul.

Contrition.

After covering his work with his blood-stained tabard, he

prostrated himself fully on the ground, naked, in front of his creation. *Lazarus ... Lazarus ... Lazarus.* He repeated the name over and over.

Absorption.

He knew the time had come. Francisco, Brother Francis, rose to his knees and bent his head, not daring to gaze upon the soft gold light that now emanated from beneath the tabard ... reaching out for him. He lifted his head, spreading his arms wide.

I can see you! Paloma, I am coming!

Then he vanished from the earth forever.

Redemption.

CHAPTER 35

"**D**amn it!" De Witt cursed as he wiped away the paint from his canvas. The eyes did not look as he imagined they should. The expression he sought eluded him.

In his mind, he could see it … clearly … but his hand and fingers could not capture it. The seventh attempt, even after a large whisky, was as off the mark as the other six. He stood back and looked hard at what he had achieved. All the components were in place and the colours matched those that Cortez would have used. It all seemed correct, the rocky tomb, Lazarus emerging from his shroud, the gawping onlookers and before them all, the figure of Christ in a tattered white robe with his hand outstretched. It was all very much as Cortez would have painted. The almost surreal interpretation, the merging of dark greens and blues, the right pigments, the aged canvas, the suggestion of cracking here and there all amounted to a genuine Cortez and only the highest handful of experts might be able to cast a doubt or two on its authenticity … if they looked hard at the problem of the eyes.

He tried all he knew. There was an essence, a quality that eluded him … and his result, whilst passable for most, was not one from the deepest part of his being, not one he was happy with. He could not do better. Throgmorton and whoever his client was would never know the difference. He would be paid and at that moment, that was his only concern. But his professionalism was rattled. He had always strived for perfection and that hadn't happened. He remained dissatisfied. Reaching for the dust sheet, he covered the work. It was time to let Throgmorton know the work was finished, collect his fee, and then get the hell out of Spain.

— — —

Throgmorton enjoyed a flush of pleasure from De Witt's news that the project was complete. He plotted his next move. First, he needed to see the finished piece. If the work came up to standard, he could make his move on the Condesa. She was a desperate, dying woman willing to believe anything. He would extract every possible cent out of her. From that point, it wouldn't be difficult to dispose of her, retrieve the work, and begin the task of presenting to the world the miraculous moneymaking equivalent of *The Shroud of Turin.* At the least, it could be presented as a masterpiece worth millions. There was, however, one major problem; Ladro and Stuart.

He poured another flute of Dom Perignon, twirling the glass with grace around his fingers. He thought hard, and knew there could be only one outcome. Threats and warning encounters had had no satisfactory result. Their presence had to be eliminated once and for all.

The entire business had become a revelation to him as he realised how much he was enjoying the danger. Every twist and turn had become so much more rewarding to the spirit than the world of the judiciary. How tragic it was that what he had always suspected in himself had begun its blossoming so late in life.

— — —

With a theatrical flourish, De Witt snatched off the white covering sheet, stepped back and executed a sweeping bow.

"Behold."

Throgmorton, accompanied by his guard, Copin, surveyed the work. With a flat tone of voice, he prevented any emotion from expressing itself. "You're an idiot, De Witt." He stared at the fake Cortez shimmering at him from the easel. "It's quite dreadful. Who in their right mind would want to buy a thing like that?"

"From the fuss you're making over it, someone obviously," retorted De Witt.

"Let me see the photographs of his other works."

De Witt extracted from a large buff envelope dozens of blow-ups and angle shots he'd taken of Cortez's paintings. He handed them over to Throgmorton.

He looked continually from one to another and back at De Witt's painting. He might not have liked what De Witt had accomplished, but he knew he couldn't fault it. *Will it fool the Condesa?*

"I don't like them at all, they are dreadful, but I couldn't tell that what you've painted isn't by Cortez. It's uncanny what you've achieved. It even looks centuries old. I congratulate you."

"It's what I do. There's nobody better."

"I hope not. There's a lot depending on this. I want it packed with great care and delivered to me at my hotel. Please see to it. When it arrives and my deal is completed you will be paid."

He could see from the expression on De Witt's face he wasn't happy with that. "You don't look too pleased. I'll tell you what, I'll make it easier for you, three thousand now, the rest as I said."

De Witt's face hardened. "I'm not falling for that. You're as big a crook as any I met in prison except you hide behind a show of crap respectability. I'll tell *you* what, Judge, it's all now or nothing. No cash, no painting. If not, I'll destroy it before you get out of the door." De Witt moved across to the work. In his hand, he held a tin of lighter fuel and a Zippo. "What's it to be, Judge?"

Throgmorton remained expressionless but he was startled. Face to face with a criminal dilemma was different from a courtroom ... very different, and one requiring a sharp decision. He'd often wondered how he would react in a situation like this, and now he knew. For a moment, he savoured the flavour of a man stepping onto the gallows.

De Witt unscrewed the cap. "Judge, I'm waiting." He held the bottle closer to the painting and the lighter at ready.

"I'll pay you in full and what you deserve." Throgmorton turned and nodded at his man.

Copin's top lip curled as he reached into his jacket and pulled out a small suppressed pistol. He fired once. The shot went neatly through De Witt's temple, dropping him to the floor before he could say a word. The lighter fuel spread out around his body marbling with blood.

The Judge had never seen a man killed before and he was surprised at how little he reacted. It was the same as the feeling of satisfaction he got when sentencing a man to a long period in jail. It wasn't personal, and something he could tolerate with ease. Stepping over the body, he picked up several large sheets and covered the painting.

"Copin, grab that painting and bring it to the car."

Locking the door quietly behind them, unnoticed, they exited the building.

— — —

Pain continued to wrack her and cold sweat trickled from her forehead. The Condesa leant forward, baring her teeth, her face warped into a symphony of creases. She wrapped her arms across her stomach not knowing the exact area of pain. It oozed from every pore of her body. She'd had attacks in the past but they were becoming more frequent and more painful. This one was exceptional in its severity. Her prayers to God were intermingled with increasing doses of a bitter tasting opium mixture of laudanum and cannabis. She gulped a mouthful straight from the bottle. It was illegal but its relief was rapid ... much faster than the prescribed doses of morphine. Salvation, she prayed, would be in the hands of Ladro and Stuart and how quickly they could find the hoped-for miracle work by Cortez. She would then be rid of disease and her creeping dependence. Of that she was certain.

Relief wafted through her in spasms, its potency increasing by the minute. As the pain lessened, she managed to ease herself into an upright position. "Thank God," she muttered and followed her exclamation with three Hail Marys. She took several deep breaths. *I can't take much more of this. I'd rather be dead. God is asking more than I can cope with. Lord have mercy, I beg you.*

From another room, she heard the phone ringing. The door opened and Donna announced she had an urgent call from Sir Maxwell Throgmorton.

Maria forgot her pain. "What the hell does he want?" She snatched the phone away from her, sending Donna scuttling from the room.

"Throgmorton, our business has finished. What can you possibly want?" His voice and what he said next unnerved her.

"Listen to me Condesa and don't interrupt. I want what you want and that is for you to become well once more. I have found what you have been looking for."

There was a pause and before she could speak, he continued.

"Yes, the long-lost painting by Francisco Cortez ... I have it."

Silence.

Maria grabbed at the chair to prevent herself from falling as blood rushed to her head. "That's impossible," she gasped. "Ladro and Stuart."

"Forget those two. They're history and not the only people able to do research. It's a long story but I think we need to talk. Those two are not what they pretend to be."

She fought for control but couldn't prevent the questions

rattling out. "Where are you? Where is the painting? Where did you find it?"

"That's my business. I have several photographs of the work and believe me the painting is genuine, one hundred per cent."

"I need to know more."

"Of course, you do. You shall see it soon, but you need to promise me something."

"What?" She knew what he was about to ask.

"You tell nobody, especially our two friends."

"I promise."

The phone went dead. It was a promise she had no intention of keeping.

CHAPTER 36

L adro's raised eyebrows said it all. He thought he must be hearing things, but what the Condesa had said was true. Throgmorton had claimed to have found the painting by Cortez and was meeting with her the next morning.

"It's a scam." Ulla sounded incredulous.

"Too right, it is. We know for certain that if the painting exists it's somewhere secure in this area, and he, by some miracle, claims to have located it. Total rubbish."

"We could go there and confront him. Why not?"

"It places her in an awkward position and she's not strong enough to handle any rough stuff. Besides, she'll let us know everything." Ladro didn't say, but he was wary of Ulla's tendency to fire from the hip.

"Will she fall for it?" Ulla tapped the pistol across her hand.

"Definitely not, no matter how convincing he tries to be."

"Then, why see him at all? Will she be safe?"

"Because she lives in hope that there could be a thread of truth in it, and as long as she has money, he won't harm her."

Ulla's looked cynical. "Well, where could it be, this sacred painting?"

"Evita gave me a list of three monasteries around the Valencia area and two, at least have stood there for centuries. Once we've ploughed through the codex and the diaries, we should have a clue which one to visit."

"The Condesa?"

"She promised us she wouldn't be buying anything. She intends to string him along and feed us with information."

"What about Evita and her father Raúl?" Ulla looked puzzled.

"All as usual. We're due there in the morning and we'll tell her anything that her father will pass on to Throgmorton. That way, we'll know what he'll be doing."

Ulla nodded and attempted to pour another glass of wine. The bottle was empty. "We're out. I fancy another. How about you?"

"Yep. You going to get some?"

"I'll be ten minutes at most." Ulla stood, shouldered her bag and headed out into the darkened streets.

— — —

She could see the shop's glowing red sign, *Vinos y Cervezas*, 100 metres ahead, lighting up the dark and deserted cobbled street. Buying wine there was less expensive than hotel prices per bottle. She pushed open the door that was connected to a tinkling bell, a sound she hadn't heard since she was a child. For five minutes, she became lost in an atmosphere heightened by aromas of wax polish and fruity wines, before emerging with a stout brown carrier bag and four bottles of fine Rioja. In that brief span of time, all thoughts of Cortez and Throgmorton disappeared.

Absorbed in nostalgia, she passed by an alleyway and never heard the soft footsteps behind her.

She began falling as consciousness left her, aware only of the sound of bottles breaking and a blaze of pain tearing into her skull.

— — —

Throgmorton looked down at the crumpled body of Ulla Stuart. She was covered by a thick array of sheeting. The dank, cobbled cellar was lit by three tripods of powerful halogen strips, which in turn were connected to a junction box leading to a large generator. Copin and López stood there dressed in long black coats, with woollen hats pulled down low on their heads.

All that could be heard was the hum of the generator. The lighting did little to disguise the dampness that clung with a slimy grip to the walls and the curvature of the roof.

"What do we do with her, Boss?" Copin asked in a whisper.

"Nothing yet. She's a bargaining chip and bait material. She's to be kept alive until I get what I want." He indicated to Lopez. "See if she's awake."

Lopez poked at her with his foot and then again, but harder. All that happened was a slight stirring followed by a low moan. "She'll be out for some time yet."

"You shouldn't have hit her so hard. But she's tough and it won't be long before she comes to." He turned to them both. "I have to leave now and won't be back until later. Don't leave her alone too long and you are not to touch or harm her in any way. We need her intact. Understood?"

"Understood." Both men nodded in unison.

"Good. I'll see you later." Throgmorton moved to the ladder and climbed the metal rungs leading up the shaft and into the central area of the ruined monastery.

The shaft was sunk to a depth of twenty metres and was the only way in or out of the cellar area. He climbed with care as the ladder swayed bearing his weight. He congratulated himself on the choice of location. It was what Ladro would least suspect and the location had a certain irony about it. A wooden door shielded the entrance, and the authorities had wrapped it with a double row of NO ENTRY tape. He ducked under it, smiled up at the stars, and decided to contact Ladro after he'd seen the Condesa.

Let him stew. I now hold all the aces. Six months from now, I'll be able to do whatever and go wherever I want, and the likes of Ladro and Stuart are not going to stop me.

He marvelled at his new life. Not long ago he was a former High Court judge vegetating in Vienna and now he was committing serious crimes, robbery, fraud, murder and now kidnapping. He looked up at the sky and the myriad stars shining down. He'd never felt so alive ... *extraordinary!*

— — —

Ladro looked at his watch for the umpteenth time. Ulla had been gone for over an hour. Something was wrong. She never failed to communicate about any delays. Five minutes later, he stormed out of the building and strode at speed towards the wine shop. Within minutes, he burst through the door and into a shop with no customers.

"Señor ¿qué puedo conseguirte," the startled shopkeeper asked.

"Nothing. I'm looking for a woman who should have been here a short while ago to buy wine. Medium height, blue eyes, blond hair. Did she come in here?"

"Si, Señor, si. A woman like that left here a while ago and bought four bottles of Rioja."

Ladro didn't wait for him to finish and headed out of the store. Halfway up the cobbled street, alongside a passageway, he trod on a quantity of broken glass.

"Shit!"

He bent down to look. The labels were clear on the shattered bottles ... Rioja. His fears multiplied as alongside lay a shoe he knew to be hers.

"Throgmorton!"

His shout, unanswered, echoed down the passageway.

CHAPTER 37

S truggling for clarity, Ulla's senses surfaced as consciousness resumed. Her eyelids fluttered against the brightness of the halogen lighting. Something was covering her mouth. She couldn't move her hands to touch her face and realised she was bound, but she could see. Looking down, she saw the duct tape around her wrists which limited her movement. The same tape was across her mouth. She tested her feet and legs and they had received similar treatment.

She had a momentary flash of crashing down and the sound of breaking bottles.

Oh God! This has to be Throgmorton.

She managed to turn over and saw she was in some kind of subterranean vault. The area looked large and empty apart from an enormous old wooden vat and the rotting remains of long wooden shelves, most of which had crumbled away.

Not a place she recognised.

No sign of anybody and nothing of Throgmorton.

This must be some sort of storage room. *But where?* The only way out looks like up. *What's happened to Ladro?*

She wriggled her fingers and attempted to increase the blood circulation to relieve the numbness. At that point, she began to panic, which made her breathing difficult. Nothing positive was going to come from being terrified. She had to remain focused. *Calm and relaxed.* She began repeating this over and over as if it were a mantra ... *Remember your training!*

She placed all her attention into the pit of her stomach and soon the tension began easing and muscles relaxed. She regained composure. Yet, this wasn't a movie and she had no hidden blades, nail files or a lighter that would help her escape. This was a different script. She was the wrong heroine and long fingernails were non-existent.

Helpless and hopeless.

She began sweating as she wriggled to loosen the tape. It didn't budge. Then, she noticed something in the corner. There were half a dozen mugs and containers and packages she could read as coffee and tea. Next to them were several plates and two large insulated bags. Someone was expecting to be around for a while.

The pulsating at the back of her head hurt like hell. Whatever she had been hit with, she reckoned, had come within an inch of fracturing her skull. A wave of nausea threatened, but she suppressed it. Sounds came from the top of the shaft and she heard a door opening. It was followed by the sounds of two men talking and the dull clunk of shoes moving down the ladder rungs.

— — —

Once inside the hotel, Ladro strode to their room half expecting to find Ulla sitting there. She was not. Reaching for a bottle of vodka, he poured himself a large drink and forgot about a mixer. His mind began reeling with a range of dilemmas and options. He had no doubt that Throgmorton was behind this.

Shall I call the police? No! That could seal her fate. He didn't know where Throgmorton was or where to start looking. There was nothing he could do until he was contacted.

He imagined how she must be feeling. Ulla was a feisty, tough and resourceful woman, who would be working on some sort of solution. She had the gun concealed on her and if they hadn't found it yet, she would use it at the first opportunity. *All I can do is wait. Should I ring the Condesa? She's meeting him tomorrow. No, Ladro, wait!*

He knew sitting alone and drinking too much wasn't going to be helpful, but there was no way he would be able to sleep. It took a traumatic event to highlight his feelings for her.

The night and early hours passed at the speed of a tortoise crawling uphill. Sleep came in fits and starts. He thought of Throgmorton and knew he would kill him.

"I must have dozed," he muttered aloud as he saw the early morning sun glistening in the horizon. He looked at his watch. It was six-thirty and sounds from the street told him the city was awake. For a fraction, he'd forgotten his predicament, but it came flooding in. *I need a shower.* Before he reached the bathroom, he saw the morning paper had been thrust under the door. He didn't normally read it first thing, but he had an inner compulsion to do so. There might just be some news.

There was nothing in there that could be connected to Ulla. It was the usual newspaper fare; scandals, corruption and alarmist reports. He began skipping over one murder, but bells rang loud inside his head and he found himself re-reading the article. It was hard to believe what he was reading. It was too much of a coincidence.

INTERNATIONAL ART FORGER FOUND MURDERED

Stephan De Witt, well known criminal art forger, was found dead in his room this morning. He had been shot. De Witt had just completed a long jail sentence in the UK for fraud and deception. His forgeries were regarded as exceptional and almost beyond detection.

Ladro froze. His head reeled and he was coming up with

answers. He didn't have to read any more. *He knew.*

Throgmorton, the 'discovered Cortez painting,' De Witt. It couldn't be a coincidence. He was in the same city. Somehow, Throgmorton had persuaded him to paint a Cortez and the man had got himself murdered in the process. The Condesa's about to be asked to part with a large sum of money for a fake.

If Throgmorton was capable of murder, it placed Ulla in great danger. Why kidnap her? *Where is she?*

CHAPTER 38

etending to be unconscious was pointless. Ulla struggled into an upright position and made muffled sounds from behind the duct tape. It wasn't until then that she knew her kidnappers had made a fatal mistake. They hadn't done a thorough body search. She could feel the pistol pressing low down the small of her back, hidden under her shirt and covered by her bulky duvet jacket.

One man drew up a chair, straddled it, then leaned forward and looked at her. His face was expressionless. He was dark, short, and muscular, with a crumpled face dominated by a crooked nose that looked like it'd been hit too many times.

"My name is Lopez." His voice matched his expression. "This is Copin." He nodded towards the one leaning up against the wall. "We've been instructed to look after you. Do you need anything?" He added as an afterthought, "The toilet perhaps?" His leer was unmistakeable as he looked back at Copin who returned the smirk.

Ulla nodded and attempted to move her legs to indicate urgency. She had no desire for the toilet. All she wanted was a free hand to reach for her gun, get it all over with and get back to Brodie. She'd do whatever they wanted as long as it gave her the chance she needed. She tried moving her legs faster.

Copin moved across to her. "We'd better help her or the boss won't be too pleased."

Ulla sensed he was the more dangerous of the two. His black trench coat failed to disguise his lean and angular frame from which she spotted the tell-tale bulge of a holster strapped to his right side.

Lopez stood. "Watch her, she can be dangerous. We've seen what she's capable of, so take it easy."

"Pissing in a bucket should quieten her down. Over there." He indicated a large metal bucket standing in a corner. He began zipping off the tape from her legs.

Her toes began to tingle.

He hauled her up but left the tape over her mouth and wrists, and began pushing her towards the bucket.

Ulla knew it was vital to get her hands free. She didn't want their assistance in getting her trousers or underwear down—not that she intended to get that far. She had to think fast. With a sudden jolt of her body, she came to a dead stop. She closed her eyes, lifted her head, shaking it from side to side, and jumped up and down on the spot. She gurgled muffled shrieks from behind the tape. She widened her eyes and shook her two bound arms up and down. *If this doesn't work, I don't know what else I could do...*

"I think she's shy," Copin said to Lopez.

"The boss told us not to touch her in any way, didn't he? That didn't mean we couldn't watch, did it?"

She looked at his face and saw the perverse excitement.

Copin shifted around to her side and whispered into her ear. "You're an interesting woman and I think you are about to make it more interesting. Make no sounds apart from what I tell you. Do you understand?"

Ulla guessed what was on the menu, but nodded furiously as if in agreement.

With one sharp but painful tug, Copin ripped off the tape

around her wrists, and manoeuvred her across to the bucket. She pointed to her mouth.

"No, that stays put."

She watched him studying her. Mentally, she counted the number of strides to Lopez, who was sitting in front of the bucket, with an inane grin across his face. She counted four.

Ulla decided to play for time and as stupidly as she could. She rolled her eyes and gestured to a large tarpaulin sheet, hoping they would understand a request for privacy.

"No curtain." Copin moved her backwards to the bucket.

Ulla promptly turned her back on him and faced the wall. She knew he wouldn't want that and his hard grip on her shoulder spun her back around again.

"You filthy bastards." The words only came as a muffled indignation.

"Look at us, sit and piss ... now!" Copin had clenched his fist.

Ulla paused to gather her emotions. She began to unbuckle her trousers and kept any expression from her face.

He moved to one side so as not to obstruct Lopez's view, and leaned forward further, anticipating the show. "Lift your head and look at us." Copin sounded breathless.

Exactly what I want to do. She raised her head and did as he asked.

She pretended to fumble with the fastenings, put one hand on her zipper, and moved the other behind her, beneath the jacket, until she located the reassuring butt of the Glock nestled against the small of her back. She wriggled her hips and the gun was free. A small flicker of her eyes, a play with the zip, and she saw their transformation into eager lustfulness. Inch by inch she lowered her trousers, keeping one hand behind her back.

She had to be fast.

In one movement, she had refastened her belt and her other arm swung around, fully extended and aiming at them. There was a momentary look of disbelief on their faces as they attempted to react.

Too slow.

Lopez jumped to his feet, kicking the chair at her as his hand reached for his gun. It was as if he'd forgotten where it was. She fired at him. He dropped to the floor without a sound, a single bullet had gone through his chest. Her next worry was Copin. He attempted to dive behind a pillar and fired at the halogen lighting. He missed. Ulla didn't. She crouched low and her first shot struck his outstretched leg. She heard him groan but didn't wait to for him to recover. On autopilot and with an unemotional focus, she moved behind him and her second shot went through the base of his neck.

She stopped, gulped in air, ripped the tape from her mouth, and became aware of an overpowering silence. She replaced the Glock behind her back and began climbing the ladder. The top door opened with ease and she stepped out into a cool starry night.

For a moment, she had no idea where she was.

CHAPTER 39

Monasterio de San José de Nazaret
Nr. Segovia, Spain
1604 A.D.

B rother Alfonso's initiation was not over. For seven days and nights, he was to be the lone sentinel — *The Guardian*. His mission: to protect the monastery's legacy from robbers, damage and unwanted curiosity. No person, not even a monk, would be allowed to pass into the caves. Guardians of the past had been attacked, even wounded by those who had heard rumours of a priceless relic and had attempted to steal it. Not one had passed into the caves. His other mission was sacred. He was to contemplate the mystery and grace of what he had witnessed.

Over his robe, he wore the Order's tabard embellished with a black cross. He also carried a large two-handed sword.

A monk, early each morning, would bring him his one meal a day, plus wine mixed with water and herbs. The remaining time, Alfonso spent in prayer, contemplation, reflection, and twice daily flagellation. One scourging was performed upon waking, to purge

222

the body of evil dreams and desires, and the other before bed for any lapses during the day.

The flesh on his back seeped blood and pus that soaked his robes. The pain was constant. He thanked God for allowing him to be so blessed in receiving the sacrament of Holy Punishment.

Looking up to the hills, he could make out the silhouette of the monastery and its jutting buttresses. Alone and in silence, Brother Alfonso was unable to resist the flood of memories that hauled his mind back in time, when as a young boy, he realised he had neither mother nor father. The recollections came as they always did, like a whiplash striking at every sense and emotion ... the Institution, the blows and the taunts, the relentless labour. He worked harder and received more blows than the Institute's donkey. He was unloved. They said his mother was a whore and his father a worthless artist.

They called him *El Hijo de Puta.* The Bastard.

As he grew older, he took to stealing and drinking wine, brandy, and anything he could find. He endured his rough existence but thought there had to be something more in life than the one he was living. One evening, after a day of taunts and blows, he decided he had had enough. Wasn't he good at stealing? He could run, he could hide, and he didn't need the Institute. They needed him more than he wanted them. It was time to leave.

In the early hours, he loaded their donkey with wine, bread and rice ... and escaped.

He was twelve years old.

At seventeen, he looked rough and menacing and he knew people were wary of him. He saw their sidelong glances and heard their whisperings whenever he passed by. Unwashed and dressed in tatters, his mouth and skin infections smelt and most people stepped away from him. But he had grown into a strong young man and he knew how to survive. He had no friends and was forever on the move. Casual work and thieving kept him alive. Of late, his way of life had begun to disturb him, but he didn't know how to stop it.

KEN FRY

He could see no escape.

That afternoon, scratching at his sores, a gripping hunger had overwhelmed him. He hadn't eaten in forty-eight hours. A butcher's shop looked inviting. Meats and fly-blown carcasses hung from hooks around the premises. Nobody was around, apart from the serving girl. She was no problem and with a swift blow he sent her spinning to the floor. He reached up to lift a cured ham from a hook. Before he could run, two enormous blows struck him on the back of his head. The last thing he saw before he lost consciousness was an angry looking butcher holding a mallet, glaring at him.

How long he'd been out, he couldn't tell. At first, he thought he was dead. He struggled on the edge of full consciousness and knew he wasn't in the butcher's shop. It didn't smell of blood and flesh ... he smelled incense. He was on a bed, and through half open eyelids, he could see the flicker of candles. A bright white light bore down from unknown eyes into his ... there was a voice in his head ... *Rest, you are home.*

The Bastard cried out, raised both arms and fell back again into a deep sleep.

When he next awoke, he could see a serious face staring down on him, but with a welcoming smile.

"My name is Brother James, and you are at our monastery. Who are you?"

The boy shook his head with a puzzled look. "I am called The Bastard. How did I get here and where am I? How long?"

James laughed. "Well, we can't be calling you that. This monastery is close to Segovia. You were brought here by two of my brother monks, who rescued you from a certain beating and being thrown into jail. You've been here four nights. You may stay here as long as you wish, and if you do, we shall give you a new name."

The Bastard rubbed the back of his painful head and looked at his rescuer with interest. Food and drink had been set out alongside his bed. He couldn't remember the last time anybody had shown

224

him kindness. Another dazzling but overriding image reverberated in his mind. His eyes widened. *Christ spoke to me. He said I was home.*

James smiled. "These are my brothers." He indicated several other monks who had come into the room. Without exception, they all spoke kindly to him and invited him to stay.

For the first time since he was born, The Bastard felt welcomed, and wanted … a deep peace engulfed him … a peace he'd never known. His lips quivered. *Why me?* His entire mind and body filled with remorse, shame, and guilt at his past misdeeds. He looked up at Xavier.

"I can stay?"

He was renamed Alfonso. That was twenty-five years ago.

Now, as a warrior monk, he knelt in humility and performed his prayers — twenty decades of the Holy Rosary. The weeping sores of his skin disease remained as they were from the day he was born. He was born in sin, so after each decade, he beat himself with his knitted cord whip. This time, he hit harder than before, and twice as often.

It was the third night of his guardianship.

His true anguish came from within.

At first, he ignored it — but it grew louder. Alfonso could not stop the loud pounding of his heart or the voice in his head. He knelt and placed his head between his hands. The voice persisted.

"Brother Alfonso. Your father painted me well. He was devoted until the day he came to me. Twenty-five years ago, you became as Lazarus. You found me, as have your Brothers. The faithful are few. Not many find me nor can all gaze freely upon me. Those that do can be healed. Your time is here. Before your watch is over, you will hear my call. Do not be afraid."

"I promise. I promise with every last drop of my blood." Alfonso's voice shook and he sank to his knees, eyes raised to the darkening sky, his voice loud and ecstatic, booming upwards into the gathering night mists.

It was then he saw that his sores had gone. What remained was whole plump skin and all blemishes and scars had vanished. His arms, his fingers, legs and toes, glistened with radiant newness ... and his back was free from the marks of lashing.

"God in Heaven be praised!" Alfonso raised both arms skywards and fell to his knees with tears cascading down his face. He repeated it over and over. Above, the night grew darker and thunder rolled through the clouds. He became oblivious to the rain splattering onto the rocks and sandy soil. Two colossal lightning strikes struck the mouth of the cave with a tumultuous splintering of rock and granite. He was forced to look up from his drenched praises. The giant boulder that secured and concealed the entrance had taken three men to roll it into place. The lightning had moved it wide open in seconds.

Alfonso forgot both his joy and discomfort. It was replaced by astonishment. Emanating from the depths of the interior, he could see a soft golden glow that lit up the walls and roof.

"Holy Mother of God! What is that?"

He gripped his sword with intensity, raised it to his shoulder, forgot his fears, and moved inside the entrance.

Robbers. Intruders.

His duty was clear. In accordance with his Holy Vows, they would not be allowed to escape or survive. The light on the walls and passageways increased in brilliancy the closer he got to the central chamber, where the Holy Artefact stood shielded in its gold mantle. For this cause, he would sacrifice his life.

The light intensified as he moved into the central area, causing him to shield his eyes. It was coming from beneath the shrouded painting. There was no one there. His steps began to falter the closer he got.

It was then he saw them.

Silhouetted in the radiance of the gold mantle, two figures approached him. Alfonso went dizzy and dropped his sword. All fear left him, replaced by an overwhelming joy. He knew who they were.

Their arms were outstretched towards him and he could hear

their voices inside his head. He knew his time had come. He opened his arms.

"My father, my mother, I am ready. Take me."

Francisco and Paloma took him in their arms and he held them tight, feeling the warmth and joy of their embrace. He turned his head to the Holy Artefact, gave thanks and praise, before they vanished together … their three bodies disappearing forever from earthly sight.

The light faded and the gold mantle fell to the ground to reveal an empty frame.

Outside, the ground shook and trees swayed before being uprooted, and the boulder rolled back into place.

CHAPTER 40

Before he left, Throgmorton took a long look at himself in the mirror. He had made a calculated decision to abandon his normal suave attire and switch to a mode he considered more in keeping with his role as an international criminal. Gone were the Saville Row suits, handmade shirts, brogues, and old school ties. He had replaced them with comfortable simplicity, a black soft fedora hat, dark glasses, black fitted leather jacket, polo shirt, minus the logos ... always a tad too vulgar, moleskin shooting trousers and elasticated boots.

He decided that he looked the part and he felt comfortable. Now he was ready to deal with the Stuart woman. She was a prize. With her, he could begin his plans to remove both her and Ladro. With them out of the way, the Condesa and her money shouldn't be a problem. Raúl Cortez's contribution had been useful, but that had to come to an end. De Witt's work had given everything a new dimension. If Ladro found the missing work, it wouldn't do him any good because he had Stuart ... plus an exceptional fake. He held all the aces. It was time to visit his prisoner.

An hour later, the hired car made its way across the hills that led to the narrow track heading up to the monastery ruins.

▬ ▬ ▬

Ulla crouched low in the trench hidden behind a wall of bushes. She realised where she was … the ruins of the Monasterio de Sant Vicente de Valencia. Her heart pounded against her chest as she took on the enormity of what she had just done. She was flooded with a mixture of emotions … of exhilaration mixed with horror and disgust of her ability to dispose of two lives. A process of rationalisation took over.

They deserved it. Sooner or later the result would have been the same. A pity it wasn't Throgmorton. If anybody deserved to be dead, it was him.

A flash of lights approaching up the narrow track alerted her to a car making its way in her direction. She crouched lower. It passed her by, crunching and disturbing the ancient pebbles and rocks. She knew it could only be going to the ruins she had just escaped from. There was nowhere else a car could go.

Throgmorton. It could be no one else.

The brake lights flashed on and the car came to a stop. She had no idea what she was about to do, but without thinking, she reached behind her jacket and gripped her pistol.

The door opened, and Throgmorton stepped out looking neither to the left or right. He headed straight for the hidden door. The engine remained running and the lights dimmed. It didn't look as if he was going to stay long. She didn't hesitate. Crouching low, she began moving towards the car and waited for him to disappear. She watched him duck under the tape and vanish into the entrance. She counted to twenty and before she had reached the final number, she sprinted to the car, flung open the door, jumped in, put it into gear, reversed, and put her foot down hard on the pedal before scrabbling off in a plume of dust and debris.

The headlights flashed their beams through the unlit track as she swerved from side to side at speed, desperate to put distance between herself and Throgmorton. Her next hope was that Brodie would be at the hotel when she got there. Her mobile had been taken by the two guards and smashed. She gripped the wheel harder and pushed the car's speed until she hit the main road. She relaxed only as she swung left onto the deserted tarmac that would take her back to Toledo.

— — —

Throgmorton stood at the top of the ladder and listened.

Nothing. Not a sound.

"Hola! Hello!" His shout bounced around the damp walls and received no reply. He tried again, and with the same result.

"Copin, Lopez, are you there?" A pang of alarm shot through him.

He clattered down the remaining steps of the ladder and wasn't prepared for what he saw. Lopez was on his side and bleeding profusely— behind a small pillar, Copin lay sprawled across the floor and from the astonished wide eyed expression on his face, was very dead.

Worse.

Ulla Stuart was gone.

He turned and hurtled up the ladder, and burst back out of the door. A quick glance confirmed his car was gone.

He held his head in his hands and then raised them to the black sky and shouted out at the stars. "The Stuart woman! I'll kill her if it's the last thing I do!"

CHAPTER 41

Nursing a stiff scotch, Brodie simmered with rage. Ulla sat in front of him. The car had been dumped in a backstreet away from the hotel area. She had not been able to stop shaking and she too held a large drink as she explained what had happened.

"I shot two men, Brodie, and probably both are dead. What am I going to do?"

"Nothing," he said. "There's nothing you can do and that's now his problem. How he explains away what he was doing in an underground cellar of a ruined monastery with the bodies of two known criminals, I'd like to hear. It'd be more than he dared involve us in, and that's if the victims ever gets found."

"What do we do now?"

"We carry on. What we are looking for has to be here somewhere."

"What about Throgmorton and the Condesa?"

"We haven't heard the last of him and nor has the Condesa. She's about to be presented with a fake and that's for sure."

Ladro looked at his watch. "It's two-thirty. I'll call her first thing and then we make a big push on the research. I don't think

Throgmorton's going to be keen on contacting us again." He looked at Ulla and could see she looked drained.

"Fancy some sleep?"

He needn't have spoken. Her head had dropped to her chest and she had plunged into a deep sleep.

— — —

Throgmorton wasted no time. The car lights vanished and he spun around and descended back into the cellar. A quick check on Lopez showed he wouldn't last much longer. He turned the semi-conscious body over, rummaged through the pockets, and found the two items he was looking for; a gun and the car keys. He ignored Lopez's last feeble groans, pushed him to one side, and headed back to find their car.

Minutes later, he was on the main highway heading back to Toledo.

Raúl Cortez's last message had stated that the research had deciphered a number of hidden clues in the paintings, and he thought they were close to discovering what they were looking for. That was helpful. All he needed to do was convince the Condesa of the originality of De Witt's work. Take her money, and hope she died soon, one way or another. By the look of her, that wouldn't be long in happening. Next, he had to acquire whatever Ladro came up with and then he could go global.

The car lights cut through the trees throwing up shadowy apparitions that flickered at speed and menace across the tarmac. An owl, startled by the lights, dived across the beams and twisted in the air to avoid a collision. Throgmorton ignored it. His foot pressed harder on the pedal. He had others who could deal with Ladro and Stuart. His priority now lay with De Witt's interpretation and how to convince the Condesa part with a large sum of cash. He had no doubts he would be highly persuasive.

CHAPTER 42

Nine-thirty and Brodie had been up for two hours. He hadn't slept. His head had been full of strategies and scenarios. Ulla lay in the position she had started off in and he didn't want to wake her. It looked as if she had several hours sleep left yet.

He had two tasks. The first was to finish his research at the archives in the Bodega, and the other to contact the Condesa. He checked the phone directory and highlighted her number. He let it ring for thirty seconds. There was no reply and he decided to call her later.

He left Ulla sleeping and placed a note by her bed.

The drive to the Bodega was uneventful although he kept a constant check on his mirror. He knew Throgmorton wouldn't scare easily and would be pursuing them both until he got what he wanted.

The car crunched across the gravel parking area of the winery which looked deserted. There was nobody about. He had expected to see workers, tractors and machinery on the move, but the place appeared empty. Switching off the engine, Ladro, clutching a bulging briefcase, got out and headed for the office and the library.

Before he got there, Evita ran towards him. She looked drawn and worried.

"Hey, what's wrong, Evita?" Ladro put his arm around her.

"It is my father," Evita replied. "He has had a heart attack and is now in hospital."

"What! Evita, I'm so sorry. When? Is he okay?"

"Yesterday, he admitted our financial problems and that he had done things he wished he hadn't and was asking to be forgiven. It was then he collapsed, and if the medics hadn't arrived in time, he'd be dead."

"Was it about Throgmorton?"

"Yes. My father said he put your lives at risk."

"He did, but he couldn't have known that. Look, don't worry, he'll be okay in the hospital and if we find what we think we are about to, your money troubles could be over."

"You're kind, Brodie, and thank you. Would you like your usual material this morning?"

"That'll be good. The sooner we crack this, the sooner both our worries will be over."

Over the next hours, Brodie immersed himself in the history of the surrounding area. Catalogued were the lives of the local communities, and battles and conflicts that affected their lives. He began cross-referencing with Francisco's own diaries and records. The more he read through it, the more recognisable it seemed.

What he read began to both mystify and excite him. The familiarity was baffling. There were passages he knew word by word or what was going to be written next. He ignored the sensation, putting it down to knowledge gained from his years of study.

The ruined monastery had to be where Francisco had lived as a monk. His diaries appeared to have come to a stop, and yet somehow, material by someone unknown had described the monastery's demise. If they had survived, so could the painting.

But where?

The final date of the writings was Friday, 12th June, 1562. Ladro paused, something rang a bell.

He reached over for the codex and began turning over the pages, scanning for the event he suspected. At one page, he stopped and read it through, going back several times to three lines towards the end of the page.

"I wonder? Evita, are you there?" he shouted through the open door.

"Brodie, what is it?" She appeared from her father's office.

"Read this." He poked his finger at the page. "What does it suggest?"

The earth shook ... the houses fell and bells rang with no one ringing them...

"Evita, that has to be an earthquake, doesn't it? And all at about the time these records stopped. And that appears later in the year. If so, that may explain what happened to the monastery back then. At some time, it was wrecked during an earthquake. The records we have here somehow survived, but it doesn't say where the rest went and the monks."

"Did you know we're in an area known for earthquakes?"

"No, I didn't. Tell me."

Evita pointed to a large wall map and drew an imaginary line through it. "This region is what the locals know as the Toledo Triangle. From here in Toledo, across to Valencia, and all the way down to Malaga, particularly the Murcia region, there have always been earthquakes. The last was in Lorca a few years back, and 20,000 buildings were damaged. So, we could be in line for another event. It is likely the monastery was destroyed because back in the late sixteenth century, there was a series of earthquakes accompanied by severe hurricanes."

"So, if the monastery was wrecked and burnt, isn't it possible that the monks could have taken what valuables they could carry and gone elsewhere?"

"But where? There were many monasteries in those days although few still survive."

"Evita, could you research what places existed back then and what few remain to this day?"

"Yes, of course. There are several; give me twenty-four hours."

— — —

Ulla struggled to wake.

From outside, she could hear the muffled noises of the street traffic. She shook her head in an attempt to rid herself of the dull ache banging inside. She'd had dreams, dreams of killing men.

"Brodie, where are you?"

It was then that she saw his note. She wasn't surprised to see he'd gone to the vineyard. Her next thought concerned Throgmorton. What would she do if she were him? She couldn't see him walking away with his tail tucked between his legs. They hadn't seen the last of him. The chain of events had gone a long way to convince her there could be some truth in the Condesa's belief in the existence of a miraculous work of art.

A knock at the door startled her.

"Who is it?" She gripped the butt of her concealed pistol.

The reply threw Ulla into confusion. "Sister Agnes de León. I am the Abbess of the Monastery of Our Lady of Olives in Valencia. Please, Miss Stuart, I need to speak with you."

Ulla gasped. *Who on earth ... what?* She kept the door on the security chain and eased it open, keeping one hand behind her on the gun butt. The person she saw standing there was not what she expected. She found herself staring into the smiling green eyes of a diminutive woman who wore the simple black pinafore dress and headwear of a modern-day nun. Around her waist hung a heavy black rosary, and in her hands, she carried a small black bag. Her face looked ageless.

Without thinking, Ulla drew back the door bolt, and stood back to allow her in.

"Sister?" She didn't know how to address her but gestured for her to step inside.

She strode in as if on a mission.

"Miss Stuart." She turned to face her. Her soft voice was clear but with an edge. "I'm sorry to startle you and I won't waste your time. I'll get straight to the point as to why I'm here."

Ulla found herself recovering. "Well I can see you're not here to collect money for starving orphans. Take a seat. What can I do for you?"

The Abbess sat but remained bolt upright. "Miss Stuart, you and Señor Ladro are looking for a painting by Francisco Cortez. Am I correct?"

"*What* ... but how do you know that?"

She ignored the question. "I will tell you in a moment. The painting by Cortez is a monastic legend, which I believe in. So must you or you wouldn't be looking so hard."

"So, why are you here and how do I know you are who you say you are?"

"You must trust me. What I say is true and I can help you. Before Cortez was banished into the Tabernas desert, he made certain alterations to several of his finished works. He was being punished. That much is known and he was rumoured to have painted a picture that I believe is the one you seek. He was never seen again and no proof exists that he committed suicide. What he painted was the only thing the monks found, together with his paints and brushes."

Ulla hesitated. She had a whole clutch of questions she wanted to ask. "Sister, you don't beat about the bush, do you? Where did those monks come from and where is the painting?"

The Abbess sat still with her hands resting on her lap. "The monks came from the Monasterio de San Vicente de Valencia."

"What! We've been there. It's a ruin." Ulla's voice rose but she refrained from telling the nun she'd been held there as

Throgmorton's prisoner.

"Yes, it's a ruin and was destroyed in an earthquake in the sixteenth-century."

"So, are you telling me, Sister, that we're on a wild goose chase and the painting doesn't exist?"

"Far from it, Señorita. There is much to suggest that it survived or its spirit survives ... waiting to be resurrected by the right person."

"I don't understand what you're saying. You'll have to explain more."

"At about the time Cortez was being punished for a non-discloser in his first confession, a fresco in the Toledo Cathedral, *The Raising of Lazarus* by Juan de Borgoña, disintegrated without warning. That fresco was reputed to be powerful and many witnesses reported seeing it move on certain occasions. The monks who went to bring back Cortez from his ordeal in the desert found not only what I've just told you, but also notes referring to an experience he had while looking at that fresco when he was a young boy. Cortez's painting was taken back to the monastery and in the same year, the earthquake destroyed the building. The painting had been kept in secret, but it has never been found and no one had a clue as to where it went. All that was discovered were Cortez's old brushes. We know they were his because the monks had mounted them in a glass case with his name on it. Those who know the story regard them as a sacred relic, as do I."

A cold shiver went down Ulla's neck. She exhaled slowly. The Cortez story had gained some flesh on its bones. She emptied the dregs of last night's scotch into a heavy tumbler.

"So, where are these brushes, Sister?"

The Abbess relaxed and now leant back a little into the chair. "We have them at our Abbey. They are not on view."

"Can we see them?" Ulla stood staring down at the frail figure of Sister Agnes. "And why are you doing this? How did you know about us?"

"Yes, I can arrange for you to see them. Why am I doing this? That's a long story. When I was a child, I lived in shame and degradation, forced to steal and perform sexual favours for anyone who asked. My mother had died when I was born and my father was a drunken degenerate who continued to hire me to anyone who wanted me. One day, as I sat half naked in the street, a woman passed by. My father sold me to her. The woman wanted nothing from me. She took me to her home and became my stepmother. She gave me a kindly life; one I didn't deserve. Without her, I would not be where I am today. You know her as the Condesa Maria Francisca de Toledo."

Ulla's hand covered her mouth as for a few moments her body went cold. "Oh my!"

The Abbess continued, "When she told me of her illness and the story of Cortez, I thought of the brushes we have, although, bound to secrecy, I could not tell her. But, I resolved that if they could help her in any way, I swore I would break my oath. She has told me of your involvement and that is why I am telling you. If she can be helped in some way, I will do it."

Ulla couldn't remember the last time she was rendered speechless. "Give me a moment, please." She bent her head, and took a deep breath before looking back up at the Abbess, who was smiling at her.

"Oh wow! I'm honoured." Ulla struggled, paused, composed herself, then spoke, "Tell me, Sister, do you have any idea where the painting could have gone to?"

Sister Agnes shook her head. "No, but there are monasteries in this region that were built during the middle ages, any of which could be harbouring the work."

"I'm sure my partner Brodie can find them."

"With God, all things are possible, Señorita Stuart. If you can believe the universe came from nothing, then what's so odd about paintings that have an ability to heal?" Sister Agnes stood. "My time is over. Please call me to arrange a viewing with Señor Ladro,

but don't leave it too long. I suspect my mother has not much time."
She moved to the door.

Ulla had a desire to hug her.

"God bless you both and bring you success." She hesitated a moment, gave a small smile, bent her head and walked from the room.

The small tear in her eye did not escape Ulla's notice.

CHAPTER 43

Throgmorton thought her voice sounded peculiar, almost as if she was drunk, but he doubted that. Medication, he concluded, produced similar symptoms.

He dispensed with etiquette. "I'm going to show you what I've found and you will see that it's genuine. Bring any expert over to examine them and I'm certain they'll agree to its authenticity. I'll also bring over some photographs. When would be convenient?"

She paused. He let it hang.

After what seemed an age, she finally spoke. "It seems hard to believe, but yes, I would like to see the painting and its provenance, but you need to give me a few days. There are some matters I've to attend to."

He sensed reluctance. "I thought you were desperate? But I'll give you forty-eight hours. That's all the time I can give you as I have another interested party. And remember, this is strictly between us."

Something didn't seem quite right. *Why, if she's so ill, isn't she jumping at the opportunity?*

Brodie's head ached. He'd been working for several hours going through community records and the archives, trying to bring some coherence between them. Perhaps the whole thing about a miraculous painting was a hoax, a local legend, an invention, a potential money maker. But for what purpose? He recognised something in himself that connected with the story and that he'd gone beyond the point of speculation. The Condesa believed it, she had to, for without it, all she could do was curl up and die. If the work was found, then only Evita and her father had a genuine claim to it.

What do I think? I started off disbelieving, but now ... too much has happened to me and I have to believe it whether I like it or not. It's like tracing your ancestors; the more you get into it, the more you sense them and know them. You feel as if you are part of them. I sense that I fit into this story ... played a part somehow. I've researched one-hundred-and-one stories and have never felt like this. How is it I seem to know what's coming next and know where places mentioned are? Why do the characters seem familiar? I do believe this story has truth.

He was past jumping to conclusions. The records mentioned the same monastery where he'd had the vision. They also mentioned the former Guadamur monastery, now part ruin, where the Condesa lived. Evita had given him a short list of monasteries which remained standing, that had their roots in the fifteenth and sixteenth centuries. There were four and he wasn't going to make predictions. His phone began ringing. It was Ulla.

"Brodie, you're not going to believe what I'm going to tell you."

"What?"

"The Condesa has a daughter."

"Should that surprise me?"

"It will. Listen, she's a stepdaughter and it gets weirder. She's a nun. More than a nun, she's the Abbess, the hotshot of the Convent of Our Lady of Olives outside Valencia. I've just been speaking with her."

"I'm listening."

"What is going on here, dear Brodie, is that the Abbess knows what we are doing and has been informed of our work by the Condesa."

"I can't see why that's anything to get excited about."

"You will when I tell you that in her monastery are kept the actual brushes that Francisco Cortez used on his last painting.

"She has what!"

"You heard. Stay right where you are. I'm on my way over."

The phone switched off and Brodie's skin began to itch.

CHAPTER 44

Throgmorton licked his lips. He now knew there was little he would stop at. Finding a replacement for his dead men had not been difficult. The new man was to do nothing until something significant occurred or if instructed otherwise. Of one thing, he was certain. The meddling duo, when the painting was found, would not be allowed to live. His plans for the Condesa were no less destructive.

He began part one of his plan.

The Condesa wanted provenance. He'd anticipated that and had found a fifteenth century chest, battered, worn, and hanging together on ancient rivets and discoloured nails. Using the National Library of Spain in Madrid, he gained access to monastic hymnals going back to the thirteenth century. Pretending to study them and to write notes, he managed to remove several vellum pages and later paper examples of monastic rituals and Gregorian chants. The desecration went unnoticed, as he knew it would. Then, feigning a fit of coughing, he replaced one small volume with a similar but modern facsimile, picking up the genuine article and placing it in his bag. Fake authentication by one of Spain's leading art historians was just as easy. Large amounts of cash had always been persuasive. An hour later, he began heading back to his hotel.

It was time for part two.

— — —

The following morning, the sun refused to appear. Black clouds scudded across an unwelcoming panorama of shrubs and barren ground that led to a small track into the Condesa's grounds.

Throgmorton eased the 4x4 into the crunchy driveway of her home, following the large circular turnaround before he brought it to a stop outside the main entrance. Stepping outside he found himself engulfed in a silence that filled the entire complex. He didn't have to wait long.

The door was opened by the maid. "Señor Throgmorton, I am to show you to the waiting room. The Condesa will not be long." She stood back and gestured him in.

Being kept waiting was one of many things he hated. He ran his hands with obvious irritation through his silver hair and, without looking at the maid said, "I'm not used to being kept waiting. Tell her she's got a maximum of seven minutes."

The maid's expression didn't alter as she turned and walked off without answering, her sensible shoes clattering across the giant flagstones. With thirty-seconds remaining, the Condesa appeared. He could see her face was expressionless. She'd deteriorated since they had last met. She looked years older.

Her tone was hostile.

"Throgmorton, frankly, I suspect you are wasting my time. But, I examine everything. You say you have the missing painting by Cortez. I doubt that. How on earth someone like you with no professional experience could find it when experts have struggled in vain is beyond me. So, before I ask you to leave, show me."

She was, as ever, arrogant, brittle and overflowing with suspicion. He remained confident. "It took me a lot of time and money to achieve that. The work is genuine and authenticated by Professor Miguel Garcia, one of your chief art historians and an expert in medieval and Spanish art up to the eighteenth century.

He saw her hesitation.

"Experts are no guarantee and they've often been wrong. Where did you find it?"

"That's my business." He began buttoning up his coat. "If you want to see it, it's in the car."

He could see the hopeful desperation that she was trying hard to conceal.

"It's not too much to ask where it was found, is it?"

He ignored her request and made his way towards the door. Shaking his head, he adopted an expression of injured innocence, but knew she wouldn't let him go. She was hooked.

With surprising swiftness, she had turned and blocked the doorway. She raised an arm. "Stop."

Feigning an air of exasperation, he halted. "Look, you fired me and now when I independently find what you wanted, you don't believe me. I'm wasting my time here. Let me pass."

"I'm not saying that. I may have been hasty. I admit I could be wrong."

Music to his ears.

He wasn't going to make it easy for her. "No, sorry Condesa, I've somebody else who is more than interested." He made a half-hearted attempt to manoeuvre around her. Her resistance surprised him and her eyes glowered with a tenacity he hadn't thought possible.

He stood back, and stared into her fierce expression.

He refused to speak. The game was enjoyable.

Checkmate.

"Please, Sir Max," she pleaded.

She's more desperate than I thought. "It's Max now, is it? Well, I'm not the bastard everyone thinks I am. Let's start afresh, shall we? All you have to do is say, 'Sorry, Max' and I'll show you the painting and tell you how I found it, together with the authentication.

"Sorry, Max." Her reply was immediate.

"Follow me." He strode out to the car and Maria struggled to follow him. He swung open the boot lid to reveal the distressed antique chest. "I checked the monastic records at the National Library. There was only one place it could have been and that's my secret. This is what I found it sitting in.

She attempted to open the chest but Throgmorton pushed her arm down. "Don't you want to see the authentication documents first?"

"Later, the painting first. I'll know if it's genuine or not."

"You're an expert, are you? Well, let's assume it is genuine. That brings into question a matter of my revised fees and costs." A sardonic sneer curled across his lips.

Her head tilted to meet his expression "If it's real, I'll pay you what we originally agreed."

"But Your Grace, that was yesteryear. Times and situations have changed dramatically and so have costs."

"How much?"

Throgmorton puckered his lips. He knew her situation was critical so he decided to milk it. "Five million sterling, paid on your receipt by banker's draft."

If she was startled, she failed to show it. She nodded. "Open it."

He noticed a hint of tension. Her knuckles whitened as she gripped harder on her walking cane.

He hauled open the chest as the vibration of his mobile jangled against his waist.

CHAPTER 45

J ourneying to the Convent of Our Lady of Olives was taking longer than expected. Ulla was driving and that gave Brodie time to consider what he'd found out from the archives, Cortez's diaries, and the additional material that Evita had supplied.

It was tantalising and there were lots of it.

He read aloud from his scanned copies and notes. "Listen, from what it says here, the original monastic archives were once kept in Jerusalem as part of one of the first Christian orders who established a settlement in the Holy City. The records stretch back until the eleventh century. There is a small black pattée drawn at the head of the document, followed by the inscription 𝕂𝕆ℝℤ. They were taken to Spain in the thirteenth century by Alphonse of Poitiers, after the Order collapsed and the monks fled under persistent attacks from the Muslim Saracens.

"The Order folded and was later resurrected?" Ulla asked.

"Alphonse lost no time in re-establishing it, and a new Abbot was appointed, Fr. Salvador Ruiz. There appears to be, would you believe it, a faded note, presumably from either a scribe or even Alphonse. It is dated 1249 A.D. The gist of it states…"

He is our fourth Abbot and is possessed of much energy. He knows our Order and its history and will avoid future mistakes. Our isolation is guaranteed and so with it, our secret is safe from the hands of murderous Islam and our own brothers, many who know not our holy secret or of our hidden Order. There has been no successor and we know that if there is, our blessed Abbot will reveal it when ready. Fr. Nicolás's work waits for a man worthy to carry our mantle. God bless his soul. God bless Alphonse, Abbot Ruiz and the Blessed Saint Lazarus, in whose hands our sacred secret remains safe.

"So," said Ulla as she swerved to avoid a horse drawn cart, "an Order existed within an Order."

"It looks that way from just one small note. It was sublime. Who would think of looking for another Order or guardians existing within another? The treasure has to be a painting or *the* painting the Condesa is seeking."

"Who was Nicolás, another painter?"

"At the moment, no idea."

"What order was Cortez in?"

"Cistercian, but he would have belonged to this other order secretly. The Order all but collapsed and their connection with the historical Lazarus was the only thing that kept the flame alive. But how does all this information help?"

"I can't say. It sounds like a secret society, but if it was, why advertise it with initials?"

Ladro went quiet and Ulla looked across at him. He carried on reading. Thirty minutes passed by.

"Oh, my God!" he muttered aloud. Then he shouted, "Ulla, stop the bloody car. Pull over. Stop it!"

"What on earth!" Ulla swung the car into a lay-by. "What's got into you?"

Brodie didn't look at her. Instead, he stared intently at a sheaf of papers. "This explains a lot." He rapped the papers with the back of his hand. "Unbelievable. Read this."

She took them from him and read it in English:

Fr. Covas, Abbot of the Monastery of San Vicente of Valencia
September 1562

We live in troubled times. I fear our sacred trusteeship has run its course. I chose badly. Francisco Cortez, it appears, was chosen by Satan who blinded both my eyes and those of Cortez and of Mendez.

To think our role was passed onto us through generations by the personage no less than the Blessed Saint Lazarus himself. Glória in Excélsis!

Alphonse delivered to Spain this most sacred of relics. Protected and guarded by the Knights of the Resurrected Lazarus, its safety was threatened by the Muslims overrunning our sacred city of Jerusalem. Albeit the image is known to change for those blessed to receive its wondrous powers. Cortez, I know not where he vanished, or if what he painted was given by God. It was God who spoke to me in a dream telling me a painter was soon to come. It was Méndez who brought him to our secret Order, and from this, I believed my dream was fulfilled.

Cortez's paintings were strange and beautiful, revealing thought I, that God worked through him. The previous work, like its forebears, had vanished ... and we were to expect a new vision. I was in error to think Cortez was the appointed one. It was Satan's doing. For it was only when Méndez revealed to me that Cortez had fathered a child and the mother had died, did I understand that Cortez had not revealed all in his confession to our most sacred portals. He deceived us. A mortal sin. When confronted, he did make full confession and was stricken by grievous remorse. Knowing that God moves in ways too mysterious for us to understand, and remembering the power of the dream he gave to me, in my sorrow, I banished Cortez to the desert for forty days and nights. All sin is forgivable, but once the Holy Father in Rome hears of this affair, he should expect the punishment of excommunication, and burn forever in the fires of Hell.

I sent him out to redeem himself and to fulfil what I know God revealed to me. It is God's mysteries that draw men to him. Cortez disappeared and was never seen again. The painting he left was covered in his tabard and was brought back, together with his brushes. When first I saw it, I knew God had forgiven him. The work was almost too painful in its intensity to look upon. Indeed, it was alive with goodness. Of that I had no doubt. It will remain here, concealed from all until God deems otherwise.

Post Scriptum: *It has now been two years since the events I wrote of above and they are as clear today as ever. My monastery has been destroyed by God's wrath and my days here at San Jose are now numbered in weeks alone. I am ill, old and dying. Far too old, and I now look forward to joining my beloved Saviour with his Father in Heaven. Our secret guardianship is safe and awaits its next miracle.*

Glória Patri, et Filio, et Spiritui Sancto.

Nothing was said.

Ulla swallowed hard and spoke in a whisper. "So, it is true and it's written down by his Abbot."

"Now we know. But where is or was that monastery? It's not on Evita's list."

"Well, our local Abbess should know. You know what, Brodie?"

"What?"

"I'm getting to enjoy this."

CHAPTER 46

O ne moment." Throgmorton snapped the lid shut. He turned away from her and answered his phone. "What is it?"

The voice of his new hit man, known simply as Ox, spoke. Ox was an American, real name, Frankie Oxendale, who specialised in assassinations. He'd only been caught once and that was in the UK but the evidence to convict him was inconclusive. The judge at the trial was Sir Maxwell Throgmorton.

"They are leaving and in a hurry."

Throgmorton winced. He never cared much for American accents and those from New York emphasised his reason why.

"Just stay close but don't be obvious. Do nothing, just observe and report back. The woman is dangerous so be careful of her." He switched off the phone and turned to the Condesa who was leaning for support against the car. "Where were we? Oh yes." He pulled back the lid.

He watched her as she lifted out all the documentation and the stolen materials from the library. She didn't even glance at them. The painting was wrapped in a heavy brocaded purple silk covering. She started to unravel it.

"Not out here if you don't mind." Throgmorton grabbed her wrist and pulled her away. "I'll take it inside."

Minutes later he stood the painting up against a wall and positioned her a suitable distance from it, walked over and in a dramatic sweep of his arm exposed the work. "Magnificent beyond belief, isn't it!" He saw her head start back.

A thin beam of sunlight filtered across the room and shone straight in to the face of Christ who was gesturing to Lazarus as he unravelled from a heavy shroud.

That ray of light gave her time to check her emotions and reactions. She placed a hand to her mouth suppressing a gasp. She moved in closer. Her skills obtained from a Master's degree in Fine Art History surfaced . . . *composition, placement, perspective, angle, colours, brushwork, genre and structure.* In a moment, she should be able to make a preliminary assessment of the work, based on that knowledge and what she knew of Francisco Cortez's other works.

It was all there. It shouted out ... *Cortez.*

But not loud enough.

Something was missing. All she could sense was a deadness. She stared into the eyes of Christ and then into those of the rising Lazarus, and then back again.

Nothing.

This wasn't right. It lacked an insignia, a miniature back pattée, the eyes were dull like a fish on a monger's slab, but above all it lacked what she had dearly hoped it would have ... a miraculous soul. Then came the warning bell. Throgmorton was an unconvicted criminal of whom *anything* was possible, even murder. The wrong reaction could activate God knows what from him. She made a calculation based on her emotional insight and religious feelings that this so clever, but preposterous work was not Cortez. It was a phenomenal, uncanny fake. Making an interested show she peered at it, stood closer, stood further away, and bent herself lower as if to inspect parts of it.

She walked around it, sniffed the canvas, tapped the side of the frame with her folded glasses. "I congratulate you, Sir Maxwell. A remarkable find. Where was it you said you found it?"

"I didn't. That monastery is extinct. It's all in the paperwork.

He's bluffing. "I'm surprised it was never found having been lying somewhere for centuries, Sir Maxwell. An extraordinary find. Let's say I'm interested, more than interested. You will of course give me a few days to make a more detailed consideration." She saw Throgmorton's cautious look give way to one of unrestrained greed.

"Five million, Condesa. How much is life worth, eh?"

He stood smoking his cigarette, looking outwardly calm and assured. One, she surmised, that one would not, for all the oranges in Seville ever expect him, a former High Court judge to be a major criminal. Her lips puckered. "Well, it's not everyone who can say they own a Francisco Cortez even at that ridiculous price."

He said nothing but tilted back his head and blew an elegant smoke ring.

It was a game of bluff and for a moment, she wondered if the work was genuine. She dismissed it. "For the money you're asking, you will at least allow me to retain the work for a few days?"

"Of course not. It's far too valuable. If something happened to it there would be too many issues to deal with."

"All I can say is, if you continue to refuse, then good afternoon, Sir Maxwell."

She saw his fist tighten as he fought to control his inner rage. Even at her age, she could play a close game, but she feared what he would do next.

"You really don't understand, do you? You stupid old cow. Sit down now and shut up."

He grabbed her thin wrist and twisted her arm up around her back and at the same time pushing her forcibly into the sofa. Her voice froze at the back of her throat as she found herself staring into the barrel of a large pistol. An unexpected calmness descended on her as she thought for an instant what it might be like to be shot.

"Do what you may, but you'll not get a penny from me. I suspected that your picture would be a fake, as clever as it is, although I admit part of me wanted to believe."

"There are ways and means, you pathetic bitch..." His voice stopped. There were footsteps approaching. It was her maid.

"Donna, I don't need you. Go home." She managed to shout again, "Look out!" But it was too late. The door swung open and before she could warn her again, Throgmorton had swung in behind her, grabbed her around the neck and had the gun pressed against the side of her head.

Donna's eyes widened in panic.

"Don't move." He pushed her down to the floor with the gun, his eyes fixed on the appalled face of the Condesa. "Now, you skinny wretch, how much is a life worth? Five million seems a fair price."

Donna began whimpering. Throgmorton's foot remained firmly pressed into her back.

"I'll count to five. The money or she's dead." He began counting. One ... two ... three ..."

The Condesa heard the safety catch release.

"Stop! Don't harm her." Her voice croaked. "Stop. I'll get the money."

"Where is it? I need it now.

I have it. It's in Bearer Bonds. Now let her go please."

"Where is it?

"My strong room."

He hauled the terrified maid up by her hair with the gun pressed hard to her head. Her glasses were falling from her head at a bizarre angle. "Lead on, Condesa and remember her life depends on you."

Maria picked herself up and now she was shaking. Donna had been with her for over ten years and regarded her as a friend and confidant. Staring hard at Throgmorton her look registered all the disdain and contempt she could put into one look. "Follow me,

Donna, I'm so sorry!"

Donna stared at the floor and shook her head, causing her glasses to fall to the floor. Throgmorton propelled her along in front of him with the Condesa leading the way to the strong room.

Her heart raced. *What can I do?* She realised there was nothing she could do.

Nothing.

The safe was located behind a large array of medieval pottery. The thought occurred to her of throwing them at him but that was out of the question. *Too heavy.* She exposed the lock and dialled the combination of numbers and letters and the metal door swung open with a loud click.

"Do it slowly and I want to see your hands at all times."

She reached inside. It wasn't the movies. There was no hidden gun to grab hold of or a pile of blank papers to deceive the robber, only what she had said, Bearer Bonds. Her fingers counted out ten. She knew they were in denominations of half a million each. She turned and faced Throgmorton who still had hold of a petrified Donna. With his free arm, he extended his hand. She began handing the bonds to him as if in slow motion. *This cannot be happening!*

It was then she passed out with the softest of groans.

The bonds flew into the air.

Donna's scream was the last sound she ever made as the bullet passed through her brain, exiting unseen somewhere into the room.

CHAPTER 47

O ur Lady of Olives lay in the rocky embrace of low lying brown and gorse covered hills as it had done for centuries.

Brodie stepped from the car and looked down on the ancient convent. For a moment, he wished he had paints and canvas with him. It screamed to be painted. He scanned the area and it was as he knew it would be. Its grey stone walls and red roof tiles whispered to him, welcoming him back.

The silence was all engulfing. *I know this place.*

Only Ulla's gentle shaking of his arm broke the reverie. "Have you gone deaf? I said it looks like the kind of place that contains a mystery, like how did Cortez's brushes get here and are they really his? What do you think?"

"It contains a mystery all right, trust me. So, let's get down there."

Ulla raised an eyebrow.

Twenty minutes later they were in the main courtyard. It was surrounded by whitewashed walls, their symmetry interrupted by numerous arches and small windows overlooking a simple cloister that ran the entire circumference of the courtyard. It was broken by various exit routes. A sweet smell of roses intermingled with lavender hung in the air. Sister Agnes was waiting for them in the main courtyard. She was dressed exactly as when Ulla had first met her. She stepped forward and opened her arms and gave the broadest of smiles that surprised Brodie. She gave Ulla a large hug and a kiss on both cheeks, then stepped back to appraise Brodie.

"Señor Ladro, I know much of you." She shook his extended hand.

"You do?"

"Yes, my mother, the Condesa, remember her?" She accompanied her reply with a mischievous grin.

"I told him," said Ulla. "He was even more surprised when he heard about the brushes."

"Yes, I expect you want to know all about them but first follow me to my room and let me offer you some refreshments. When I have told you all I know, we can look around."

Brodie nodded. "Lead on, Sister."

Drifting through the air he could hear the melodic chant of nuns singing the Marian Canticle. He didn't understand how he knew that but let it go.

Her room was simple. In the air hung a faint aroma of incense, otherwise, there were just the bare essentials; whitewashed walls, an icon of Madonna and Child dwarfed by a large mounted crucifix. The only submission to modernity sat on the desk, a cordless telephone and a laptop computer.

"Sit down, please." The Abbess indicated two easy chairs placed by the desk. A side door opened and a nervous looking nun scuttled in, bent low with a tray of three tall glasses of iced tea. She placed them down on the desk. "Thank you, Sister, you may go." She pushed the tray towards them. "Please." She picked up one and sipped at it. "I expect you are itching to know the story of how we obtained the brushes that I'll show you later."

Ulla nodded. "Before you start Sister there are some things you should know." She told her the information they had discovered and the strange things that had been happening to Brodie. She said nothing of the threat from Throgmorton.

Ladro said nothing but his psoriasis sent out painful messages that refused to be ignored. When a crisis loomed, it got worse.

Sister Agnes looked at him with an odd expression. She began speaking in hushed tones as if she was speaking of some unmentionable secret. "You know much and I congratulate you. There is a mystery here and where the painting went has never been discovered. There are those who say it never existed but we know from our archives that something did. Before Borgoña, it was said a painting of Lazarus by Fr. Nicolás existed and was greatly revered. It was his major work and like all others, including Borgoña and Cortez, no traces remained. Borgoña's work succeeded the legend of Nicolas's work. Whilst on public view, its power remained a secret that only—"

Brodie interrupted her, "—the Knights of The Resurrected Lazarus knew of." He continued to speak as if he were her.

Sister Agnes and Ulla stared at each other with astonishment as Brodie continued. His head had tilted upwards and his eyes closed.

"The brothers had decided that as times were precarious and rumours rife, the best way to hide a pebble was to leave it on a beach. Only one person had the privilege of truly discovering its secret. It is said that Francisco Cortez was that person although this cannot be proven nor can any of the other stories that surround other paintings of Lazarus that they guarded so jealously. Borgoña's work mysteriously disintegrated in a pile of fine rubble. Señor Méndez, Cortez's tutor and known to be a lay member of the Order, witnessed that very event."

Brodie stopped talking and his breathing came in shallow spurts. His eyes opened and he lowered his head.

Total silence.

The agitation of his skin lessened. He looked first at Ulla and then Sister Agnes. "What happened?"

KEN FRY

"You don't know?" asked Ulla.

"Did I black out?"

Sister Agnes made the sign of the cross. "God be praised. You spoke every word I was about to say. In fact, as you spoke, I was repeating what you said in my mind, and no, you were fully conscious. I swear I believe you have been sent to us." She crossed herself again. "My mother told me what happened to you, and now I have seen it myself. There is something very strange happening around you. For my mother's sake, I want you to find this painting."

"Hey, are you okay?" Ulla reached out to him.

He didn't answer. He placed his head in his hands and shook it to and fro. "We're close. We're close." He couldn't say anymore. His head became full of a kaleidoscope of whirling colours moving first one way and then another then intermingling with an array of images and suggestions of a million faces moving up and towards him first slowly and then at speed … faces he thought he knew but changing into a ghastly broken diseased ugliness. Then they ceased, replaced by a golden aura of immense calm and peace that descended and filled him.

"Stop! Stop!"

It finished as fast as it had started.

He sensed Ulla's worry and Sister Agnes's mounting expectancy that his behaviour was causing. "Don't ask me, I don't know," he shouted, not knowing what else to say.

There was a long pause. Sister Agnes broke the silence. "It's time I showed you the brushes, do you agree?"

Ulla stood. "That's a good idea, Sister." She hauled Brodie to his feet. As he stood the colour came back into his face.

"Let's go. I can't wait." In his mind played an image of what they would look like and couldn't wait to see how accurate he was. "And Ulla, stop looking at me as if I was some sort of circus freak."

Sister Agnes led them through a series of heavy doors that descended to progressively lower levels. The route became more twisty and the space between the walls narrower. The way was lit by what Brodie thought looked like emergency lighting with bulbs strung every twenty feet from an endless cable fixed to the walls. The air became dry and colder. He could see their breath had become visible.

The Sister called out. "Mind the steps."

The passageway took a sharp turn up some well-worn stone steps that broke into a small semi-circular room with a low vaulted ceiling. The lighting gave an occasional flicker. Brodie could see they had reached the end of the route. In front of him he could see a small altar adorned with one simple crucifix, and in front of this, mounted to the floor was a prayer stool with a small balustrade.

Sister Agnes bent one knee and made the Sign of the Cross. "This is where Sisters who transgressed in some way were sent or others wanting solitude came; to reflect on the reason they were here. Sadly, those days have passed and this sanctuary is now rarely used. Let me show you the brushes." She moved across to the side wall and pulled back a heavy, purple brocaded curtain.

Ladro gasped. "Wow." He looked at an oblong glass case in which had been mounted a velvet support and a gold bracket. Resting on this was a series of brushes in differing lengths and thicknesses plus what looked like a palette knife. "Oh my, are these really them?" Brodie pressed his face close to the glass and ran his hand across the top. The feeling he was getting, he reckoned, had to be like an archaeologist making an unprecedented discovery.

"Wonderful, aren't they? They were received by this monastery not long after an earthquake that destroyed many buildings and homes in this region. Fortunately, we survived. With the brushes came the story of Cortez and Lazarus."

"Yes, it is true. Ulla and I've read Cortez's diary that gives an account of his original vision in Toledo's Cathedral plus the date. We know of Abbot Covas, Salvador Mendez his tutor, Paloma his lover and of his banishment but beyond that we have come to a dead end."

Ulla nudged Brodie. He looked up and saw that Sister Agnes was on her knees at the altar. Ulla held onto his hand. "Sssh! Wait until she's finished."

The wait was short. She rose and turned to them. "Ulla and Brodie, while we talk and discuss these remarkable events, my mother is dying. I believe she can be saved. You also believe that a painting may exist that can save her and I believe you have been sent to find it. What happened to you back there gave me the evidence I needed. I am breaking my oath by showing you the brushes and I am now going to go further." She took a deep breath and stared at Brodie. "God forgive me, but I do this to save a life. Brodie I want you to lift out the brushes."

He gave Ulla, a querying look before nodding to Sister Agnes. "Okay, but in structure they don't look a lot different from my own."

With a petite key that hung behind her personal crucifix she located the small brass lock and lifted open the glass lid. She pointed, "Brodie, please."

He hesitated. It seemed extraordinary and he didn't know how he should touch them. The brushes were of hair, he guessed at miniver, derived from stoats, but he couldn't tell. The heads varied in shape and thickness and were bound together with a discoloured wax thread. Each performed a separate function just as his own brushes did at home. The palette knife, made from horn, looked discoloured from age. Otherwise, it had been cleaned.

He reached in and grasped the handles with both hands.

CHAPTER 48

Unbelievable! He had blown out an innocent woman's brains all because the stupid Condesa had for some reason crashed to the floor.

For the first time in his life, he experienced panic. This was not what he had planned. The bonds lay scattered around the room and the Condesa looked unconscious, sprawled out on the floor. He picked up the bonds and counted them out. There were five million pounds worth. Next, he placed the painting back in its chest together with the bonds.

What am I going to do with her?

He nudged the Condesa with his foot but she didn't move. *I could kill her now.* He looked at the gun and then back at the Condesa and pointed it at her. Yet he couldn't bring his finger to squeeze the trigger. *One's enough and that's too much! It doesn't look like she's got much longer anyway.*

He reasoned she wouldn't go to the police and there wasn't going to be a body to be found. Calling in the police would get Ladro and the woman arrested ... more delay in finding her painting and she couldn't spare the time. *I could get up and vanish with the money.* For just a fraction, he paused. The vista was tempting. Another form of excitement struck him; it was the excitement of danger, a challenge he needed to experience.

If that painting exists, I want it. Whether it's true or not there's a fortune here and there has to be a story to tell. The gullible will flock to it in droves and pay good money. It could take over from Lourdes and with a few decent bribes I'll have a whole host of those attesting to a miracle. De Witt's painting as good as it is, could be discovered for what it is, a fake. No I need the real thing. Once those two meddlers have found it I'll take it from them one way or another.

An hour later, he drove deep off road into the desert wastes. What impacted on him was how little he felt ... a small panic maybe, but that was to be expected ... to be forgiven even ... a small weakness that would diminish in time.

Donna's body, wrapped and tied inside several thick sheets and rolled up carpeting, was bundled into the back. He'd stripped it of clothes, identity marks, rings, ear rings and all jewellery. Coming to a halt, in front of him laid a narrow but almost bottomless gulley, impossible to climb either into or out of. He pulled out her lifeless body and dropped it to the ground. Minutes later, he'd dragged it to the edge and with one last heave propelled it into the shaft.

He never heard it hit the bottom.

— — —

She took stock of herself and had no idea how she came to be on the floor. The coolness of the flagstones connected with her hands, letting her know she was alive. She couldn't be certain, but had she heard a shot? The pain stabbing at the back of her neck caused her to raise her head with caution. She turned her gaze left and right.

"Throgmorton, you bastard, where are you? Donna! Damn it, where are you?" She pushed herself into a sitting position and saw the room was empty. No painting, Donna or Throgmorton. *There was a shot, I know I heard it.*

"Donna! Donna!" Her cry was feeble but Donna had always answered it wherever she was.

Silence.

The shocking realisation that she was gone, hit her. No, he hadn't abducted her. That shot meant he had wounded or killed her.

She got to her feet and ran as fast as she could to the telephone.

— — —

The old wooden handles had remained untouched across the centuries. They felt little different from what he was used to. He held up the brushes in both hands.

Sister Agnes and Ulla watched him.

"If you two are expecting a miracle or some bizarre event, I'm going to have to disappoint you." He waved at them with the brushes. "I've had some strange experiences getting to this point, but this is not going to be one of them. What did you expect or want to happen— a revelation? The brushes are hardly Holy Relics, are they?" He put the brushes back.

Sister Agnes looked disappointed, and chewed on her bottom lip. "From what my mother told me, I confess, I was hoping."

Ulla gave a wry smile. "I'm sorry too, Sister."

"Where to now?" Brodie looked thoughtful." If the brushes were given to your Abbey and they came from that ruined monastery, either the painting was destroyed or it's hidden hereabouts. We know the year Cortez vanished and we know the date of the earthquake and of the collapse of the monastery where the Condesa has built her home. We've got Evita's shortlist. Ulla, show Sister Agnes."

Ulla handed her the list.

The Sister studied it. She looked thoughtful. "These names have to be strong possibilities."

Ladro moved back to the brushes. "It would have saved a lot

265

of time if these bad boys could have short-circuited up an answer. Nothing happens as you would like it to, does it?" He reached out to pick up the palette knife.

Firm and tactile, it fitted his hand like a glove. He passed it across in the air as if he was at home painting.

He couldn't prevent the colours from invading his mind. They were unstoppable.

Beginning at a slow pace, his pace quickly picked up as the greens, greys, blacks, browns, red, yellows and dark blues overwhelmed him. They danced in an array of motions that circled and whirled faster and faster, interweaving and plaiting strands that formed visions he couldn't grasp ... faces arose and vanished at speed, animals, scenery, towns and villages. His arms and hands began to move as if he had a canvas in front of him.

Using the palette knife, he made fast bold strokes, first one way and then other, adding delicate touches to counterbalance the dramatic thickness of colour that rushed by.

Brodie finally stopped, gasping for breath. It was finished.

He *knew* who it was. He knew *where* to go.

His knees hit the floor with a thud. The palette knife fell to the floor with a clatter that was too loud. His head tilted back to reveal the whites of his eyes. The skin around his mouth stretched wide to expose his teeth. Bolts of a sensation, nothing less than ecstasy, climaxed and blasted through the marrow and sinews of his mind and body.

It ended like a flashlight beam switching off.

He bent his head low as if he were hearing somebody. Inside of him was clarity and resolution. It had become so clear.

Breaking the stunned silence, he heard the piercing tones of a phone ringing.

— — —

Ulla glanced at Sister Agnes who looked confused.

"Sister, answer your phone. Brodie's not harmed. This has been happening ever since we arrived in this area. He'll be fine, I promise." She nodded rapidly at her. Sister Agnes appeared more confused, uttered 'thanks to God,' turned and headed in the direction of the phone.

Once the Sister was out of earshot, she asked, "Brodie, what on earth was that? What's happening to you?" Her voice was urgent. "Are you okay?"

He didn't look at her. "I wish I knew. Ulla, I saw him."

"You saw him, who?" She knelt beside him. "Who did you see, Brodie?" She watched him take in a lungful of air before letting it out between pursed lips.

"I saw Cortez, Ulla. I saw Francisco Cortez."

Her arm went around his shoulders. "I believe you," she whispered as colour returned to his cheeks.

"Ulla, I saw him as clear as you are sitting here. I could have counted the hairs on his head. I saw where he lived, the countryside, the buildings and Toledo Cathedral as it was. I saw Paloma, his lover, There was another, and I *knew* he was their son. He looked like a monk and wore a tabard with that black cross on it. They were smiling at me. Everything Cortez had ever drawn or painted was running through my arms and fingertips. Then, two other men appeared. One was his tutor and the other was a monk, his Abbot, the one we saw the rough drawings of. Other faces passed by, and again, I knew who they were, starting with Borgoña, the artist responsible for Cortez's transformation. Ulla, I saw him, that's unbelievable! The others were former painters. They had all painted Lazarus being raised from the dead and they all belonged to the Knights of the Order of the Resurrected Lazarus. I know the history of how it began. I am astonished, Ulla. It's unbelievable."

"I think you'd better start from the beginning, slow down some and we might discover where we should go from here."

"How long did it go on?"

"Several minutes."

"It seemed like hours."

"Spit it out, Broderick Ladro. This involves me as well and I can't wait to hear it."

"It began with Lazarus."

"What … *the* Lazarus?"

"It began with a man named Zevi, who painted the first ever work. He lived in Bethany and worked as an artist and potter. He had even done work for the Romans and for the governor, Pontius Pilate."

"What!" Ulla blurted out.

"Zevi witnessed Lazarus's resurrection and when the people had departed, he went inside the tomb. Inside, he picked up the wraps of cloth that had been around Lazarus. He knew it was important and when he returned home, he was compelled to paint the event, to record it. Cortez said Zevi had painted like never before. When he had finished the work, he covered it with the winding sheet that he had brought from the tomb. It must have contained the power of Christ. From then on, believers who were sick or ill could look into the eyes of Christ, and be healed. That tradition has carried on to the present day, although the painting changes, as does its covering."

Ulla began to interrupt. "But..." That was as far as she got.

Brodie stood. A wave of his hand indicated her to shut up

"That inheritance was broken at the time of the First Crusade, in its attempt to recapture Jerusalem under Pope Urban II. Nothing was known of the painting. It was discovered by accident as the Crusaders rampaged across the lands leading to Jerusalem. Spanish involvement was under Prince Sancho of Spain who later became King but died in 1072. He had one devoted follower, known by all as El Cid, famous for his heroic battles. Amongst his men was a poor soldier named Gil Diaz, devout in restoring the city back to God, but suffering and dying with dysentery and scurvy."

Ulla listened and watched Brodie. It wasn't him speaking. The voice was disembodied and he seemed to be staring at some non-detectable object in the far distance.

"Brodie?"

He carried on. "Diaz, determined to live and die by his sacred oath, found the work in a small alcove in the abandoned ruins of a long disused church on Jerusalem's outskirts. Bodies were strewn everywhere. He had no idea who owned the painting. He removed the covering and immediately was overcome by what he saw. When he regained consciousness, he had become whole and well with no trace of disease. In great joy, he took the painting back to his master, El Cid, who promptly made him his personal servant."

"Brodie ... please."

He paid no attention.

"After Sancho died, Alfonso the Brave conquered Toledo and proclaimed himself Emperor of Spain and El Cid presented him with the Holy Painting. The painting vanished during the Valencia wars and only when Peter the Holy was about to be executed did he reveal he knew of its whereabouts and that he was the artist; one of a sacred succession. His biggest secret, he declared, was that the painting never remained the same. It was periodically and mysteriously destroyed when a new era dawned. He never disclosed its situation and was killed and his secret died with him. There was no one who remembered what it looked like but the next artist must have gazed upon it. This may sound crazy but I was told that Cortez was the successor to Borgoña's healing work hidden in full view of all. His work has reached its time. A new painting was imminent to usher in the next epoch. Each work draws closer to the end of all things. Those who gaze upon it, believe in it, will not only be healed of their sickness but will not perish when the world as we know it comes to an end. The painting is..."

His words were cut short. The door flung open and Sister Agnes rushed in.

Something was wrong, very wrong.

CHAPTER 49

T hey left in a hurry, you say?" Throgmorton spoke to Ox
who sat leaning his ponderous bulk frontwards on the
back of the chair and staring at an unseen panorama of
violence in the depths of his fingernails.

"Yeah." He cracked his knuckles and spoke in low thick tones.
"They went back to the place you left and as far as I know, they are
still there. There's a tracker device on their car that they'll never
find and the car hasn't moved since they got there."

"Excellent. I need to know where they are going. I don't want
you killing anyone until I get what I'm after and I say so.
Understood?"

If his remarks irked Ox's natural inclination to destroy
anything that got in his way, he showed no indication of it. "I can
wait."

Throgmorton grimaced. The entire enterprise had fouled up
thanks to the meddling twosome. It was also costing more than he
had envisaged. His major consolation rested in the Bearer Bonds.
They had to be liquefied and the money transferred immediately to
his Cayman Islands account. Although bonds were now a rarity
and not much used because of the risk factors, there was no way
the Condesa could prevent their utilisation or recoup her losses.

"Sooner or later I'll know whether this painting exists or not. We do nothing and even if it doesn't exist, the end result for those two remains the same."

"Leave it to me, boss." He patted the tell-tale bulge under his left shoulder.

"We sit and wait."

— — —

Sister Agnes's twenty-year training in restraint evaporated. Brodie looked at Ulla as Sister Agnes gathered up her habit and ran with unexpected speed into the Condesa's home.

"Brodie, take this." Ulla handed him the Glock and sprinted after the Sister.

He stuffed it in his belt and followed the two women.

He wasn't expecting to see the sight in front of him. Spread out across the floor like an upended starfish lay the Condesa. Dressed in black, her clothes were in acute contrast to the whiteness of her face. Her terrified eyes were open wide, displaying the yellow stain of creeping jaundice. Bony fingers revealing lines of age and liver spots clawed at the floor. The only sound came from the terrible gasps from her attempts to breathe.

"Mother of God," whispered Sister Agnes as she knelt beside her mother.

Ulla got in behind her and cradled her head. "She looks as if she's about to or has had a seizure. What should we do.?" She looked up at Brodie and Sister Agnes.

"Nothing." Brodie stared down at her. "She's had a severe shock. Give her some brandy and in a few minutes, she'll come around. Trust me."

Sister Agnes crossed herself and began muttering prayers.

"Not prayers Sister, brandy. Give her some of this." He unscrewed a bottle from the display cabinet. "Small sips only. Can you manage that?"

"Throgmorton's raised the stakes and none of us can be safe. I've seen what his men are capable of." Ulla propped up the reviving Condesa.

"Nothing that you're not capable of either, Ulla."

Ulla winced. "What now?"

"My mother has not long to live, two months at the most. Medicines and drugs have prolonged her life but I have lived with life and death for years. I know the signs. She wants to look on the painting. She believes it can save her and so do I. Will you find it Señor Ladro?"

"I've a clue or two. That last performance gave me some direction." He paused.

"Well, are you going to let us know or not?"

"I can't because I don't know—yet."

A low moan escaped the Condesa as she attempted to sit up. Her face contorted and she clasped her hands to her chest.

Sister Agnes held her close. "Mamma, Mamma," she whispered into her ear.

Brodie looked at the Condesa. His face remained expressionless. He couldn't deny that this broken woman had been instrumental in bringing him to this point. There was one thing he knew that the others didn't. The Condesa somehow held the final key to this mystery. She, through her bloodline, was linked to the earliest of those who knew of the Lazarus painting and its mystery. The Dukes of Alba themselves had passed down enough tantalising clues to get any historical investigator twitchy.

"Sister, can you and Ulla find your mother's medication and if possible stay with her or take her back to the monastery. She's in no fit state to be on her own."

"She shouldn't be moved. She's had an enormous shock and is very concerned about Donna her maid. We must call the police."

"That's the last thing we do, Sister. Don't even think of it, it's far too complicated. Can you both stay here? There's somewhere I need to go."

"You're not going anywhere without me," Ulla retorted.

"This time you do as I tell you Ulla. Take this and guard these two with your life." He held out the Glock. The look on her face told him she wasn't happy about it.

"What about you then?" She took the gun from him.

"I'm okay. The backup's in the car. I'm going back to Valencia, to the Cathedral."

"The Holy Chalice?"

"The very one."

Sister Agnes looked startled. "Holy Mother of God." She made the sign of the cross. "Are you going to tell us why?"

"As best as I can. Remember, all that I tell you may or may not be true. It all happened in my head and it could all be very wrong. Understood?"

They nodded and as they did the Condesa managed to haul herself upright. "Donna, where is she?"

"We don't know, Maria." Brodie knelt beside her. "Only Throgmorton can tell us that.

"It can't get worse." She struggled to speak and spluttered into a handkerchief. "Forgive me, all of you. This was never meant to happen."

"There's nothing to forgive." Her daughter leant forward and kissed her head.

Ladro continued. "How true what I saw and heard was, I can't say. The clue lies in the Cathedral. Why it should be in the same location as the Holy Chalice, I can only guess at. There appears to be a connection and what that is I've no idea. The Cortez painting in the chapel, I believe holds information we've missed, Ulla. It was almost the last he painted."

"Almost, what does that mean?"

"I suspect it was the one before Lazarus."

"Wait." The Condesa pulled herself into a standing position. "Before you leave there are some things you should know." She held on to the two women. "Throgmorton has a painting, a fake I believe, that he is attempting to pass off as the real thing. I've seen it and it has no miraculous powers, believe me. He has also stolen five million pounds of irretrievable bearer bonds from me and intends to make more from his fake. Poor Donna came in at the wrong moment. I was so confused." She faltered and clung to her daughter. "Brodie, do what you have to. Go to Valencia and where else you have to. Believe me, the legend is true ... it is all true, and you know it is. One thing I do know is that it will end here amongst these old walls. Now go and leave me to pray for Donna."

He looked at Ulla.

"Get going, Ladro. We'll be okay, but keep in touch and take care." Ulla kissed him.

CHAPTER 50

"Y ou drive like an old woman," said Throgmorton to Ox as they passed the Shell station outside Toledo. He put his hand to his forehead and stared at the road in front of them, willing it to pass faster beneath the wheels of the Suzuki.

"I'm driving as fast as it's possible. We know where his car is heading so stop worrying."

Throgmorton took a blue-tinted bottle of Solan mineral water from under the seat and took a long drink without offering any to Ox. The radio announcement that police investigating the murder of international art forger De Witt had found a diary and records giving them significant new information on a possible suspect caused him to drop the bottle and swallow the water the wrong way down.

Suppressing the coughing spasm, he attempted to regain composure.

A moment of calm before his bowels began churning as he guessed at what De Witt may have written. There was a new element to consider. The police would be looking for him and getting out of the country could be expensive.

"You okay there, boss?"

KEN FRY

"For fuck's sake, shut up and drive faster will you. "

— — —

Standing in the Holy Chalice Chapel, Ladro stared at the cup. The additions seemed unnecessary. They didn't look right. The precious stones, the stem and handles and the gold had been added later. The cup was a different matter. Its symmetry was simple but stunning. The history surrounding this Holy Chalice was more convincing than others. He thought of the Chalice and its provenance. His research showed it had been handed down through Saint Peter and various Popes until it reached Pope Sixtus. The Roman Emperor of that time, Valerian, was persecuting Christians. To avoid the inevitable pillage, Sixtus handed down the Chalice and various treasures to his Deacon, now Saint Lawrence. These had been listed in a velum parchment dated A.D. 262. Valerian never got the treasures as they were spirited away to Huesca in Spain. Saint Lawrence was allegedly roasted alive for this act. The Cup and the treasures found their way through various Kings and monasteries until it found its way to its current resting place in Valencia. What happened to the treasures was not known.

Is there a link between the Holy Chalice and the Lazarus paintings? The original painting was done whilst Christ was alive and this cup was used before he was crucified. Could there be a connection? The painting is believed to change through time but there is no way of telling how and when. If found, it could surpass in significance all known Christ style relics put together. I was given a clue at the monastery. The Chalice was one of them the other, Cortez's painting, in the Saint Lazarus Chapel.

Ladro stood back and in the background, he could hear the assorted voices and hushed whispers of the tourists and pilgrims as they gazed on the Chalice. Cutting through this, he could hear the soft harmony of the choir performing a religious chant that overloaded an atmosphere struggling to cope with a mixture of fervour and incense. He turned and began walking in the direction

276

of the Saint Lazarus Chapel, glad to escape the throng. His mind turned over the events and the mystery of Cortez and his works. A thought began to dominate his mind.

Why is a painting showing a grieving Virgin Mary and a crucified Christ displayed in a chapel dedicated to Lazarus, who is clearly absent from the work? It doesn't make sense.

He bent his head and ignored the mixture of Gothic and Baroque decor that festooned every inch of the building and let his feet walk their own way to the Chapel. Without looking up he knew he'd reached the entrance. It was deserted. Stepping inside it looked no different from the last time he'd stood there. Cortez's painting looked the same and there was nothing to indicate why this painting should be in a chapel dedicated to Lazarus. Ladro sat in a small pew, ignored the crucifix and the altar and stared rigidly at the painting. Ulla's deciphering of the coded body postures made so much sense.

The more he stared at the work the more it drew him in to feel part of the drama. The composition, the colours and the topography danced and wove around him.

It was then he saw it.

The dark red agate of the distant hills and the valley contours matched those of both colours and shape of the Chalice.

My God it's so clear. I've seen copies of that parchment ... it's there for all to see. How could we have missed it? Cortez must have known more than he ever revealed or he was guided without knowing to paint what he did. The original Lazarus work must have been listed on that document. There was only one painting listed amongst a collection of precious stones, the Holy Chalice and other relics. For protection, it was made to look obscure and of little value. In Aramaic, it's listed as 'Elazar—Qûm'— Lazarus Rises. Apart from the Chalice, every item on that list has vanished. Cortez is showing us where it or the next painting could possibly be found. The clue was in the Chalice. Its shape and colour Cortez has duplicated in the hills.

"I know where it could be!" His loud voice startled two

visitors who backed away from him.

— — —

Ox tapped the slow red dot moving across the screen. "He's on the move and he's heading in this direction."

"Turn around and pull over. When he passes, follow him at a safe distance." Throgmorton craned his neck forward. "How long?"

"Less than eight minutes and he's moving at speed."

Close to eight minutes Throgmorton spotted his car. It was the only one on the highway. "There he is." He pointed at the approaching car. "Just where, oh where, is he going and what has he discovered?"

— — —

Ladro glanced in his mirror. Every car was a potential tail. The speed-dial connected with Ulla's number at six minute intervals. She didn't answer. She and Sister Agnes must have a problem with the Condesa. *Answer please.* He slapped the mobile against the steering wheel in frustration. *C'mon Ulla, I really need you to answer ... please!* No response. He yelled into the voicemail as if it would conjure a reply. *Nothing.* He threw the phone into the passenger seat and drove on.

Large raindrops began drumming on the windscreen. He leaned forward attempting to see further through the relentless spray. *Slow down ... slow down* What was daylight had turned to night. Red brake lights came on and off all around him. *If Throgmorton or his men are following me, I've no idea in this shit.* He felt the back wheels slip and slide as the car began a slow drift into the hard shoulder. It came to nothing. Resounding in his head, the name of *Bethany*, used in the Chapel of the Blessed Saint Lazarus of Bethany, could in Aramaic also be translated as the House of the

Poor or of Misery. Ulla, Sister Agnes and those brushes, who could explain that? The three people he had seen, he could see them as clear as day. A violent judder at the back end of the car snapped him back to attention as it attempted to slide off the road. He brought it back under control and glanced in his mirror. It was too confusing to give an indication he was being followed or not. A quick look at the dashboard clock showed it was almost seven-thirty. His mobile erupted into life. He grabbed at it and pulled off the road onto the hard shoulder.

"Ulla at last. Just listen and don't say anything."

"Brodie..."

"Ulla, Shut up. I'm not certain if I'm being tailed or not but I'm going to assume that I am. Are you three safe?"

"Yes..."

"Then do as I say. Let no one in, whoever they are. Do you still have Evita's list of monasteries?"

"Yes, it's with me now."

"Is the Monasterio de San José de Nazaret listed?"

"Yes, it's top of the list."

"Excellent. That's where I'm going."

"But Brodie, it's miles away to the north. Why there?"

"Let's say a penniless artist told me. If there's anything to be found, it will be there. The past Kings of Spain and the Dukes originally hid Valencia's Holy Chalice there together with an obscure painting they titled *Lazarus Lives*. I believe its real title was *The Eyes of Christ*, the forerunner of a series of miraculous Lazarus works across the centuries that have all vanished, and of which Cortez was the last heir apparent. When we find it, and if it does what it says on the tin, then we have a religious bombshell. No wonder Throgmorton wants to get hold of it."

"Brodie, I need to come with you."

"No chance. Those two need your protection. Stay put, be on your guard and I'll call you when I know more." He switched off. He didn't want Ulla pressurising him. In the depths of his being, there was something calling him. He didn't know what but he knew it had to be answered and answered alone. Checking his mirrors, he pulled out onto the highway and began accelerating towards Segovia. No one followed.

— — —

"Don't follow him!" Throgmorton's bony hand slapped the dashboard with a sharp crack.

Ox came to a screeching stop. "Why? He's getting away."

"We only need what he's going to find. If he does, he will take it back to the Condesa and submit it to its true test. We have to be there for that event and then my friend, we shall be masters with unbelievable wealth. I think it's time we set our trap. We're heading back to her place so drive slow. I need time to think and put together a plan of action. Just do as I tell you."

Ox grunted and turned the car around, and began the drive to Guadamur.

CHAPTER 51

Mile after mile of uneventful terrain gave way to steep climbs and hills as the road to the monastery led through dipping and twisting roads. Ladro piloted the car off the main highways and along narrow tracks that climbed ever upwards. The weather had cleared and the air smelled sweet and moist. Olive and orange trees grew at random amidst rocks and sun baked earth.

He knew he was close and he didn't stop to ask himself how he knew that. He just did. It was if he was being pulled by giant magnets. He couldn't resist the force. He carried on until he could drive no further. A firmly mounted signpost prevented that. It stated all vehicles prohibited bar essential deliveries. The engine sighed as he cut it. He checked once more and there was no sign of anybody following him. His objective was beyond the brow of the rocky outcrop and hidden from view. Slinging his small rucksack across his shoulder he began the grinding trek upwards. He stopped and listened to the majestic silence.

For a moment, he heard something to fracture the magic. Whatever it was, it stopped as soon as he heard it. He thought it could be distant thunder, but there wasn't a cloud in the sky. He ignored it. With a few more strides, he was at the top and gazing down a long undulating and winding track leading down into the monastery. It was a large stone coloured structure. Around it was a small lake bordered with several outhouses and low buildings. The centre was dominated by a red earth courtyard, and on all sides ran a cloister. A large encompassing perimeter wall encompassed the entire structure. Outside the main building, he could make out the straight rows of planted vines and other crops being attended to by figures wearing the brown and white robes of monks. The grip of medieval antiquity had not diminished.

It was identical to what he had seen in his vision.

Another rumble, but closer this time, broke his concentration as he began the slow descent to what, he had no idea, but was full of hope.

A sweaty weather-beaten monk stood resting on a hoe close to the gates and gave Brodie a broad grin. "Come to join us, brother?"

"Not if I can help it, brother." He returned the smile and read the inscription on the large gated entrance, *Pax Intrantibus* --- Peace to Those Entering. He somehow doubted that. He struck the large bronze bell three times for admittance. It was a few minutes before the gate swung wide and a stooped old monk ushered him in.

His voice croaked like a rusty hinge. "The Abbot is expecting you. Follow me, Señor." He lurched forward with a pronounced limp.

Brodie jolted at the monk's words. So many strange things had been happening around him that he shouldn't have been surprised. The route to the Abbot's chambers took them across the central courtyard and then up a narrow spiralling and worn stone staircase before crossing a small corridor lit by meagre strip lighting. It was then he noticed that hung around the walls were numerous religious paintings, including portraits of monastic dignitaries. One work caused him to come to an abrupt halt and at the same time gasp for breath. He recognised the exquisite hands, the solemn face of a man praying and the rapt expression of the Virgin Mary.

It was Abbot Covas. The girl must have been Paloma! It was the culmination of Cortez's sketches and rough drafts he had seen at the Bodega.

"Wait.," he shouted at the monk. The monk showed no sign of having heard him and continued shuffling forward. "Damn it," Brodie cursed the hunched shape of the monk.

How did that get there? The rumours that there was no trace of Cortez's former works in existence had just been proven wrong ... very wrong. *How many more are there?*

The monk ignored all communication and came to a stop in front of a metal studded door. His rap on the door was performed as if part of a religious ceremony by bowing his tonsured head at it. He stepped back when it opened without a sound to reveal a small man with youngish looks and a beaming smile.

He was dressed as the other monks apart from an extra wide cord around his waist and a large gold crucifix hanging from his neck. He nodded at the other monk who bowed, turned and walked off. He gestured for Brodie to enter and extended his hand.

"Señor Ladro you are most welcome. I am Father Louis, the Abbot. Please, take a seat."

Ladro sensed himself disadvantaged. His arrival and name all known, and then the Cortez painting on the wall completed his disorientation. He gripped the extended hand, which had strength and vigour.

"Father, just what is going on here. How did you know about me?"

The Abbot's gaze was penetrating. His shaven head disguised his real age that was only to be guessed at by the small wrinkles around the eyes. He wore a pair of steel framed spectacles balanced on an aquiline nose. His lips were thin like a slit cut into a sheet of paper. Brodie put him in his late forties.

He spoke from behind steepled fingers, his voice sounded rich like a cello. "We are sorry, Señor, if we seem mysterious ... but it's all quite simple. We knew of you and your mission earlier today as we had a telephone call from Mother Agnes, who is with your friends, Senorita Stuart and the Condesa Maria. You were expected and here you are. What is mysterious is how you have known to come here."

Brodie relaxed as he realised the mystery didn't exist. Modern technology could explain much. Yet he knew he couldn't answer the Abbot's question. He didn't know how he'd got there. It all had something to do with his vision and that knowledge had been implanted into him.

"Father, I can't answer that because I have no idea. I'm attempting to trace a long-lost painting by Francisco Cortez and my research can't be far wrong as I've just seen what looks like one of his works hanging on your walls here."

"Ah ... Cortez. You are not mistaken; the work to which you refer is sixteenth century and of Abbot Covas who was local to these parts. We believe it could be valuable."

"You're right there, Father. I'd like to inspect it, if I may."

"Of course, but what makes you think more of his works should be here?"

"That's a long story. But if I say visions, ruins, a certain set of paint brushes and not least of all, a remarkable Condesa, would that help?" Ladro looked into the grey eyes of the impassive man opposite him, who said nothing before nodding.

"Señor, I would be guilty of a sin if I told you I have not known much of your activities. It is hard to keep secrets amongst monastics when God-given quests as yours are involved. You appear to be blessed. To help you, let me tell you of our secret."

Ladro's eyes widened. Discovering secrets in the field of research was not unwelcome but most revelations succumbed after scientific scrutiny. His instincts told him that this could be different. All he wanted was to look at the Cortez painting hanging in the corridor. He leant forward. "I'm all ears, Father."

"Before he died, Abbot Covas revealed to his Designate the true story concerning Francisco Cortez and the legend of the

Lazarus legacy."

"Legend? I hope it was more than that."

"My, you sound like a believer, Señor. Let me continue. A painting was found but Cortez was never seen again. It was said he made alterations to some works, although that is for historians to argue. Apart from the painting and his brushes, everything he ever had or owned was left to the mercy of the desert. Brushes and painting were brought back to his monastery. In time, the painting was revered as a Holy Relic, due to the number of sick and ailing monks, including the Abbot, who attested to its miraculous healing powers. To protect the painting, Covas, being a man of medieval values, ordered that any written records concerning Cortez and his work be destroyed, and forbade any monk from mentioning the painting under threat of excommunication. However, at that time in and around Europe, there were many disaffected and homeless knights from the Hospitaliers of Saint John and from the Holy League, dislodged after the Battle of Lepanto and the Ottoman Turks. All sought a home or how best they could serve God. To be brief, many came to monasteries in this area and became monks. It was said, by whom we do not know, that sick or injured monks and knights, if true in heart, had been healed simply by looking at the Lazarus painting of the time. I believe that there were several. Once cured, these warrior monks were sworn to protect the painting and its secret until death."

"If they didn't?"

"There were no reports of that. Excommunication is a powerful inducement."

A low rumble caused the floor to tremble and interrupt the Abbot's story.

"That happened earlier," Ladro half shouted.

"No need to be alarmed, Señor. It happens around here. We are in a triangle of tectonic plates that tend to move every so often."

The shifting stopped almost as soon as it had started.

"Okay Father, so where's the painting now?"

Father Louis's expression didn't alter. He said nothing but stared at Ladro who couldn't help thinking he was being evasive.

"You don't know, do you?"

"No, we don't. That's why you are here I believe, to help find it. What I can tell you is that it was here, guarded and protected in a secret location. The monastery was almost destroyed in a fire caused by a series of quakes that ravaged Toledo and Valencia. Cortez's monastery was reduced to rubble about that time. That is where the painting of Abbot Covas was found. Nothing is known since that date, as many died and no records were allowed to be kept.

Another tremor.

Ladro's eyes closed. He bent his head and his clenched fist rested between his eyes. A brief flash ... a dark place ... rocks ... candlelight ... noise ... shouts. It was clear. Too damn clear, but where was it? He'd got to the point of not being amazed or scared by his visions. He was beginning to look forward to them.

More ... more ... I know you are close, but where are you?

There was no reply and the vision faded. His skin irritation had become worse.

"Are you all right, Señor?" The concerned voice of the Abbot broke through his thoughts.

Ladro ignored the question. "Father, do you have any drawings, plans or that sort of thing as to how this place might have looked inside and out during the Middle Ages?"

"Of course, but most of today's building stands on what was the original construction. This very room has access to passageways and corridors that used to run the entire length of the monastery. Many of these are now blocked off and closed. Some, I believe, were to supply secret exit routes beyond the walls should an emergency arise. Times were very different then."

"Nothing has changed, Father. It's still the same old world out there, a hunt for power and wealth. When can I have a look at what lies beneath us? "

"First, let me show you what we have." He walked to a large wooden cupboard and slid open a retaining shutter. A row of ancient leather bound volumes stood in neat stacked rows an antiquarian would have died for. "These chronicles the monastery's existence, and so far, they have survived every disaster that has struck us through the ages." He scanned up and down the ranks before he pulled out a large brown and black volume and placed it with care on the study table. "I think this is the one we are looking for."

Abbot Louis's thin fingers, thought Ladro, looked like ivory spikes. He picked out a volume held together by a pitted metal clasp. Ladro experienced an overwhelming sensation of antiquity ... of things known and unknown. There was little dust as Abbot Louis flicked the vellum pages.

"Ah, this should be it." He began unravelling a gatefold section, handmade and stitched together by fine needlework that had survived the centuries. It contained an overall plan of the entire monastic structure drawn in black ink and inscribed in gold, blue and red letters. There was an exploded view of various rooms, which Ladro noticed drew the eye across the central courtyard and all converged to a central point outside the monastery walls. What was interesting, they were underground and not visible. He traced his finger along the lines. "So, Father, where would your room be on this plan?"

"Right there." The Abbot poked at a small ink square located at the centre of the complex.

"That's amazing, so if they all lead to one place outside the walls then that has to be an exit point."

"It would seem so, Señor, but since the building has been twice rebuilt I've not heard of any reports. I went down to have a look some five years ago, out of curiosity, but there is nothing there, just damp walls and dirt. They all look alike. It's the same story. A series of dead-ends."

"Father, I need to look. I may see things you wouldn't. You

can tell me as much as you like about God and I can tell you just as much about archaeological research, both practical and theoretical. So, I'm going to ask you a big favour. I need a flashlight or some sort of lighting. Can you do that for me?"

The other man's eyebrow lifted. There was a moment's silence before he nodded. "Of course, but should you discover anything, it automatically belongs to our monastery. Agreed?"

"Of course. Agreed."

Twenty minutes later the Abbot's desk was pushed aside to reveal a concealed trapdoor. Ladro hauled it up and was struck by a blast of cold air as the flashlight revealed a small spiral iron staircase leading down about twenty foot to the bottom. It looked uninviting and as soulless as the rocky walls that formed it.

He began the descent.

CHAPTER 52

L ooking from the window, Ulla saw the lights of an approaching car switch off. She needed no second thought. "Sister, turn off the lights!"

"What's wrong?"

"Just do as I say. It looks like we could be having visitors."

The lights went off, plunging the room into semi-darkness.

"It's Throgmorton, isn't it?" The Condesa's voice sounded croaky but calm.

Ulla's fingers closed around the butt of her pistol. "It's my bet whoever it is knows we're here and saw our lights switch off. I need to get you two out of here and fast. Maria, is there a way out of here without being spotted?"

"We could try the rear of the building and work our way to the front."

"Sister, can you drive?"

"Yes but..."

"No time for excuses, Sister. Grab these." She tossed the car keys to her. "You know where it is and if I'm not there in a few minutes just go without me. Understood?"

"But Ulla..."

Ulla cut her short. "Did you take Vows of Obedience, Sister? I'm sure you did. I'm in charge here and you will do as I say. Your mother's life depends on it. Now *do* it will you!"

Sister was left in no doubt. She put an arm around her mother and ducking low began to move out of the room. A loud banging on the front door froze her in her steps.

An unfamiliar male voice shouted out. "Hello, is somebody there?"

"Sister," Ulla hissed, "what are you waiting for? Go, will you?" She waved the gun barrel in the direction of the door.

Again, the voice shouted. "Hello there!"

Sister Agnes, leading her mother, crept towards the door and into the outside air. The banging stopped leaving the house in silence. Ulla's heart began to beat faster. She was tough, she knew that, but this was a different situation. There was somebody out there who could kill them all.

She flattened herself down as low as she could and pressed every inch of her body to the floor behind a long fat sofa. She pointed her gun at the door and waited. Her hands were sticky with perspiration. She had one advantage. Whoever it was didn't know where she was, and she could finish him with one shot.

There was an explosion of sound as a bullet burst the wooden door latch, sending splinters in all directions.

She gasped and pressed harder to the floor, her gun ready to blast at whoever it was. With a loud clatter the door swung open smashing into the wall behind but there was nobody to be seen. One hand held tightly on to her outstretched wrist as she let off a round in the direction of the door. There was a blur of movement as a man hurtled low through the doorway in a perfect shoulder roll and still clenching a large black pistol, came up to a firing stance. But he was pointing in the wrong direction.

Ulla enjoyed an unexpected calmness. "Drop it, arsehole or a bullet will go straight through your head." She watched as his fingers relaxed their grip on his gun before letting it clatter to the floor.

"Kick it over here nice and easy, if you please."

He did as he was told.

"I must be getting soft." Ulla found it hard to keep a note of triumph out of her voice. "I don't know who you are but I know who you're working for. We need to talk about that. Sit in that chair, will you" She gestured to a large wooden chair behind him.

Ox said nothing, turned his head towards the chair and moved to sit in it. She could see from his expression he was attempting to work a way out of the situation.

"If I have to I will disable you with a shot to the leg. If I'm terribly unlucky I'll miss your main artery. Do you understand?"

"I don't think that will be necessary, Miss Stuart." The voice from behind her was unmistakeable.

Keeping the gun trained on Ox, she swung her head around in confused disbelief. Throgmorton stood in the rear doorway with a smirk across his face. He held a pistol to Sister Agnes's head who looked terrified as she supported the Condesa.

His voice became guttural, coarse ... "Now drop the gun or this heavenly Sister will be getting there sooner than she had hoped for." He prodded the gun hard into the side of her head.

"Oh, my God." Ulla could see Sister Agnes's eyes were shut, her lips moving in prayer as she expected her head to be blown apart. Ulla let the gun drop but wasn't expecting Ox's huge bony fist to crash into her face. It spun her sideways. The second blow to her nose sent a spray of blood across her face as she crumpled to the floor in a haze of coloured lights.

CHAPTER 53

F linty pebbles, small rocks and stones crunched and shifted beneath his boots. Torchlight threw his shadow into immense proportions along the passageway. He could see his breath in the cool air billowing in small white puffs as he bent to avoid hitting his head on the low roof.

The Abbot's right so far, there's nothing to see at all.

Ladro let his finger run along the sides of the wall as if he expected to find something. Nothing. The structure was straight without a curve or a bend.

Whoever built this must have been a fan of the Romans.

At one point Ladro noticed a large indentation in the side of the wall, almost like an alcove. He stopped to examine it. He ran his finger across the pitted surface and brought the flashlight to bear in the recess. He could see what looked like the remnants of an old stone seat.

What point did that serve?

He sat on it and shone the torch all around the area. There wasn't anything to see.

Nothing but rocky wall. Others exploring must have sat here and if there was anything of significance they must have seen it.

He stood to move on but let his trained eyes survey the area inch by inch. It was then he noticed something. The wall opposite looked unnatural. He brought the light up closer. A small area had been smoothed off and the more he stared the more obvious it became. He leaned closer and ran his hand over the area. It was about A4 in size. The more he looked the more obvious it became. It was a face: the face of a woman cut with light relief directly into the exterior wall, and he knew who the face belonged to.

The face of Abbot Covas's Madonna, Francisco Cortez's lover, Paloma, gazed out with forlorn intensity.

"My God." His whisper filled the air. "It's identical to the sketches back at the Bodega and the one on Abbot Louis's wall." He scanned for more but she was the only clear evidence that Cortez must have passed this way some 450 years ago. There was nothing else to see. Using his phone and the lamp, he took several photographs from numerous angles.

Let's see what's at this supposed dead end.

The remainder of the passageway looked similar to the rest, but he now found himself bent low, scanning with increased intensity. After a further fifteen minutes of stopping and starting, Ladro calculated he must have passed beyond the walls of the overhead monastery, and open country lay above him. Finding the carved detail had given him extra impetus.

As Abbot Louis had said, he soon found himself confronting a blank wall of rock. He stood holding his breath. There was nowhere to go.

This is ridiculous. He didn't know what to expect. At that moment, he began wishing for another vision.

Nothing.

The only sound he could hear was the odd rock or pebble falling to the floor.

Is that noise increasing?

He listened harder and directed his lamp into the direction of the noise. Small rocks and chippings were being dislodged from both walls and roof. An intermittent, low cracking noise, like a frozen river breaking up, became louder. It was accompanied by an ominous rumble that made the ground quiver.

"Shit. I hope that's not what I think it is."

There followed an even louder noise and in front of and above him, a small section of the roof fell in with an enormous crash. Rocks and dust filled the air, billowing across the flashlight beam, and distorting into a pattern of weird shadows and shapes.

"Time to leave," Ladro shouted out loud as he tied his scarf across his mouth to stop the dust from getting in. The walls and ground continued to shimmy and shake. He turned in a rush and began to sprint back the way he came. There was another enormous succession of rumbles and the walls began to crumple and crack open, sending up sheets of flint and sandstone. He ducked his head and gulped in air through his scarf and found himself crashing into piles of loose stones and rubble.

"A fucking earthquake is all I need!"

It was then he smashed into a solid wall of rock. He fell to the ground and found himself spread-eagled across a pile of debris and damp earth.

A panorama of horror flashed through his mind as he panicked. *Entombed alive and a slow suffocating death. Ladro, get a grip or you will die!*

He forced himself to open his screwed-up eyes. The flashlight was still on, illuminating a million dust particles that swam and danced around in space. A faint tremor continued shaking the walls. With effort, he compelled himself into a standing position, keeping his arms over the top of his head to protect it from being struck by projecting rocks. A quick look in all directions and he knew there was no way forward. He was trapped.

CHAPTER 54

C onsciousness returned, accentuating the painful throb pounding in the bridge of Ulla's nose. Her eyelids fluttered.

What the hell?

Her first thoughts were for the Sister and the Condesa. *Have they been harmed in any way?* She attempted to sit up but couldn't. She was bound tight with duct tape. She kept silent, it was better not to attract attention. Throgmorton was a lunatic but something about him commanded respect. But if she had to, she would kill him and that included the animal he had as a partner. She turned her head and in the corner, saw Sister Agnes sitting on a hard wooden chair. She wasn't bound. Her head was bowed with her eyes closed and she appeared unharmed. Similarly, the Condesa was seated and overlooking them was the man who had broken her nose.

He stood motionless and expressionless with his arms folded. He looked as if he was from Central Casting, auditioning for a gangster movie. It was obvious they considered her the most dangerous. She could feel sticky blood on her upper lip and jaw line.

It was too early to assume the worst. Brodie was still out there and he could be ingenious in a tight corner. He had the capability of turning things around if he had to. That thought gave her comfort. It was then she saw Throgmorton, sitting with debonair ease on the sofa, holding a large drink; his feet perched on a stool.

He turned his head to look at her and spoke without emotion, as if passing sentence on a criminal in the dock.

"I'm beginning to believe there is truth in the rumours about this painting. It's a pity none of you will be here to enjoy it. It will be priceless and will make me a fortune. All I have to do now is sit and wait for your boyfriend to walk through that door with what belongs to me, without having to lift a finger to find it. And of course, I have De Witt's back up should all not go well. Who knows, two paintings could double my take." He sipped at his drink.

She began thinking through what could happen. Throgmorton held the trump cards. If the painting was found, then the Condesa would be needed to test its validity and Sister Agnes, herself and Brodie would be unnecessary. She forced herself to speak. "Let those two go. As long as you have me, they won't go to the police. You can take the painting, if there is one, and do what you like. We won't interfere, I promise you."

"After coming this far and doing the things I've had to do," he replied, "I will take no chances. Too many criminals have made that mistake. Risks and sentimentality are unacceptable. I'm sure you understand."

Sister Agnes looked up. "Use me, I beg you. Let me be a guinea pig, but let my mother and Ulla go. Harm me, cut me, injure me and I will willingly accept whatever should happen."

He walked over to her so that his nose almost touched hers. "Now why hadn't I thought of that before, but you're missing out one thing, two miracles are better than one, don't you think?"

The Condesa attempted to stand but he shoved her back down with a heavy push. "None of you is to move unless I say so. If you disobey, then my friend may be asked to remedy that situation. I'm sure you understand." He nodded at Ox who stood still and not a muscle moved on his face. "We may have a long wait, so make yourselves comfortable and think on what might happen to you later."

Ulla's sweaty clothes stuck to her and the tape held fast. She examined the room, staring hard at each aspect, looking for something that could help them out of the situation. There was nothing. A pair of scissors lay on the top shelf of a small bookcase close to the Abbess. It didn't look hopeful that the Sister could spring into action, and what chance would that frail woman have against the two men.

The clock ticking was the only sound breaking the silence. Ulla began willing Sister Agnes to look up at her by shaking her head at her but she wouldn't look her way. *Sister please look at me, please dear God, look at me!*

There was only one thing she could do. She screamed. She opened her mouth wide and screamed as loud as she could. It worked. Everybody jolted and all eyes swung in her direction. The two men moved with speed and stood in front of her. Ox backhanded her with a vicious swipe across the face.

Her head jolted to one side like an elastic band snapping and her bruised face spouted more blood. Ox then grabbed her hair, yanking her head back, ready to repeat the attack. A searing pain raged through her head causing another minor scream.

"Leave her," commanded Throgmorton. "Your screams are of little use now. Save them for what comes later."

Ox backed off. "I was enjoying that."

"You'll get your chance later."

Another voice spoke. "Let me help calm her down." Sister Agnes ignored the two men, and pushing Ox to one side, she knelt next to Ulla and began wiping the blood off her face with a small cloth.

Throgmorton returned to his drink and Ox gave a loud snort and repositioned himself by the door.

Ulla wasn't prepared for what she heard the Abbess whisper into her ear.

"Don't speak and keep your eyes closed. I know what you were trying to tell me. I have them here."

"How on earth...?" Ulla gasped.

With one hand, she wiped away the blood, and with the other, Ulla could feel her rummaging beneath her robe which she used to cover the scissors as they snipped through the tape. It was over quickly and Ulla was free.

"Moan louder, please," the Sister whispered urgently.

Ulla obliged and squeezed Agnes's hand with silent thanks. The scissors were thrust into her hands and covered with the sleeves of her jacket.

"Remember my child, I am with you. I don't know what you intend, but I will help you. Let us pray for Señor Brodie and wish him success, and for us to overcome the evil in this place, and for my mother's return to health. Let them see you pray and they won't know what I've done."

Ulla didn't question the order. She did as she was told and she knew she would look after the little nun to the end. She had no idea how to pray. She hadn't done that since she was twelve years old at her mother's funeral. She bent her head, clasped her hands that still looked bound together and mumbled meaningless words from her blood smeared lips.

"How very touching," remarked the judge, "you'll need prayers before this is finished. You there," he snapped at Sister Agnes. "You, get back to your seat and make sure your mother stays alive."

She moved back to the Condesa but managed a whisper to Ulla before she did. "I'll do anything needed. Believe me." She patted Ulla's shoulder.

Ulla, moved her fingers and her feet, flexing the muscles at the same time. *What am I going to do now?*

CHAPTER 55

Torchlight flickered and struggled to penetrate the dust vortices and minor debris that had choked the tunnel.

Holy shit! What now?

Ladro brushed the numerous particles from his eyes and face and thought that at least the Abbot knew he was down there, so some sort of rescue attempt would be underway. He attempted to peer through the swirl, but he could see nothing. He needed to conserve what battery life there was left, or he would be plunged into darkness. There was no way of telling how long he would be trapped. It was a miracle he had escaped injury.

He could just make out the piles of stone and rock that surrounded him. His first concern was how much air was there. He breathed in with care, holding his gloves over his mouth and realised he had no way of answering that question. The dust was settling down fast and he managed to stand. He stood still and listened … only the faint sound of falling debris. He appeared to be enclosed in a dome-like space that had somehow escaped the worst of the quake. He felt anxious. There was no point in trying his mobile, no signal could possibly escape from this depth. The route back was obscured by layers of impenetrable rock. He would have to wait to be rescued.

He struggled to maintain his optimism that there might possibly be a means of escape. That hope kept him from scouring the surface of the displaced debris, and trying to find something to indicate a way out. He walked up to it and ran his hands over every inch of the distorted wall. Claustrophobia had never been on his list of ailments, but now its clammy presence squeezed at his entrails. For a moment, he had a vision of himself dying in this hole, gasping for breath, and shrieking for water and food.

He suppressed the thought.

His lungs heaved with the effort and his breathing came in short bursts. Another noise that sounded like more rocks moving, ricocheted around the stony prison. The ground began to shake again. With increased vigour, Ladro threw himself under a projecting rock and curled himself into a small ball with his arms tight around his head. A splintering crash sent a full section of the remaining wall sliding and slipping in one whole piece, before collapsing into a pyramid pile of earth and rock off to his right. The overhang he was sheltering in remained unscathed, but showered him with clouds of dust and debris.

How long he lay there he didn't know.

I'm still alive, but for how much longer? The monastery can't have escaped damage.

There wasn't a sound to be heard. He could sense a light coming from somewhere.

It must be a torch ... but they can't have reached me already.

He opened his eyes and scraped off the dust from his face. He wasn't wrong, there was light, and it wasn't from his torch. He followed the source of light. It was coming from beyond the front wall, the direction that had been a dead end. It wasn't any longer. The wall had broken and collapsed to reveal a gap where light came shining through. Ladro stared, unsure what he was looking at. The gap was big enough to let him pass, but he was sure that the light meant it must be coming from the outside. He picked up the flashlight and hauled himself into a sitting position, before deciding it was safe to stand. Keeping his arms around his head, he rose almost upright and looked around him. Where he had been previously, was buried and no longer existed. Unless escape was possible, he knew he could die. He began picking his way towards the gap. He stood in front of it but was unable to see where the light was coming from. It was big enough to let him through if he turned sideways. He pushed hard, and with a sudden lurch, propelled himself into the space.

The source of the light remained hidden, but its glow illuminated and filled the entire space. He forgot his predicament and looked around.

What he saw shook him.

━ ━ ━

Abbot Louis didn't need a watch. He was used to time moving slowly and he could judge it within five minutes by what Office his monks were performing. 'Afternoon Prayers' were echoing across the courtyard.

He gave a satisfied nod. Ever since he was an aspiring novice, he had always harboured a benign appreciation for the Office of *None.* He associated it with a sweet, brief gentleness the major Offices lacked.

Señor Ladro has been a while. I did tell him there was nothing to see down there. He put it down to archaeological curiosity. *I hope he's not going to be too long.*

He walked out of his room and onto the parapet that gave him an uninterrupted view of the *semidesértico,* the half desert that had been his home and that of monks long departed centuries ago. He let his gaze travel across the plateau and the surrounding hills. The weather was warm and there wasn't a sound to be heard. How he loved this area. Its stark beauty had always attracted him. It possessed a mystical quality that in his more fanciful moments, he imagined as akin to the wilderness that Christ ventured into for forty days and nights. Whatever it was, it had been good for his soul.

He had long ceased to worry about the ground rumblings. Their frequencies were hardly noticeable and never amounted to much. Those of the last hour were no different. Like the others, they had stopped as soon as they had started. Señor Ladro was perfectly safe, and there hadn't been enough movement to make even one's feet tingle. He continued to stare out at the land outside the walls. He doubted that Ladro could have found a way through. Many had tried, but their efforts had proven fruitless. There was nothing to find there. What was needed was dynamite. That was the only way the place could be opened up, but using that could cause the whole complex to collapse. He wondered about the rumours of what the missing or lost painting might be. He'd heard many. As a monk for over twenty years, it would have been surprising if he hadn't.

He judged that almost an hour had passed since Brodie Ladro had made his descent underground. It seemed longer than necessary. He decided to check to see if all was well. The large trapdoor remained closed as he had left it. A swift yank on the large brass ring swung it open. What Abbot Louis saw filled him with horror. At first, he thought his eyes were playing tricks, but then it was obvious they weren't. A yellow cloud of dust and sand rose out of the opening, and in an instant, had covered himself and his office in a film of ochre particles and debris.

He gasped as he wiped his eyes.

This can't be possible! There wasn't a sound!

"Ladro! Ladro!" His voice went nowhere as he shouted into the choking filth that obscured half the descent in a pile of bricks and rocks. He shouted louder, but knew it was a waste of time. Even if he was alive, Ladro would never hear him through the debris.

I never heard a thing!

By then, he was already running to the nearest wall-mounted alarm bell down the corridor. He collided with the lame monk who was returning from his prayers.

"Brother!" he yelled, feeling uncomfortable at raising his voice. At the same time, he smashed open the glass on the general emergency system. "Shovels, spades, axes, NOW! All monks to the courtyard at once! Hurry, Brother. Hurry!"

The alarms shrieked throughout the monastery. Lame monk didn't hesitate and shuffled at speed to the central assembly point in the courtyard. Already, other Brothers were running to the spot, only to be told to sprint off again and return with digging tools, buckets and wheelbarrows.

Within minutes, they were assembled.

A grim-faced Abbot told them the situation. In his office, there was only room for one person at a time to dig, fill a bucket, and pass it to another monk, until it found its way to the surface. He watched as the monks worked at fever pitch and they still hadn't reached ground level.

This is going to take a long time. I pray for him and that he is still alive.

CHAPTER 56

idden in her hands, Ulla held the scissors with the blades concealed under her sleeve. They were no match against Throgmorton's weapon and she wished she had the Glock. Now she had to work out a way of using what she had to maximum effect. There was little chance of taking on two armed and dangerous men with just a pair of scissors. The Condesa was too frail to be of any use and just what Sister Agnes could do or how far she was prepared to go, she had no idea. What was needed was a gun.

How am I going to do this?

She looked at both men. Ox was the immediate threat. He had, she guessed, an animal violence and would lash out and kill anything or anybody that got in his way. His guarded posture, his arms folded over his chest, shoulders stooping, fat hands clasped together gave no hint of vulnerability. He sat down and had begun picking at his fingernails. The most frightening thing, she thought, was his total lack of expression. Throgmorton looked alert. His vulnerability was his preposterous vanity. The gun was resting on his lap and she knew he was listening and watching for Brodie to make an appearance. Different to Ox, but no less deadly.

She dismissed the idea of a sudden rush at one of them as she could be shot before she'd got halfway. No, she had to get one of them to her and they'd have to bring their gun with them or the plan wouldn't work.

I must pretend I can't move. Somehow, I've got to get one of them to come to me with his gun ... but how?

Ulla let out a long, low, soft groan and bent herself double, with her hands behind her holding the scissors. She shook her head from side to side.

Both the Condesa and Sister Agnes turned to her, and then at Throgmorton. He registered nothing, as if he hadn't heard.

"Shouldn't we be finding out what's wrong with her?"

"Please yourself, but no tricks. Ox, watch her, will you?"

Ox grunted, stood and walked towards Ulla.

Damn, he left his gun behind.

Sister reached her first. "Ulla, can I help?"

"Get his gun," she whispered. One look at the Sister's face, and Ulla thought she might have asked her to marry the devil.

Ox pushed the nun out of the way and hauled Ulla backwards into the chair. "Shut up, bitch. Stop snivelling." He backhanded her with force across the face.

Ulla felt her cheek explode with pain as her head jerked sideway. She clenched her fists and fought hard to resist the urge to sink the scissors into his leg. Unless she had a gun, it would be pointless. She would, without a doubt, end up dead.

She didn't expect the second blow that sent her face reeling in the opposite direction. "Sister, help me please!" Her tormented screech filled the air and galvanised the nun into action. It wasn't the reaction she expected.

Sister Agnes swung back her leg and with her stout sensible shoes, kicked Ox hard on his shin with all the force her tiny body could muster.

"God forgive me," she yelled.

If it hurt him, he didn't show it. His face hardened, as if

stopping himself from hitting the nun. He seemed to have drawn a line at that point.

Ulla shouted again, "The gun, Sister. Get it!"

She twirled around and headed for it.

"That's far enough, Sister. Another step more and your brains will be all over the floor." Throgmorton stood ready to fire at her. "Don't think your cloth is going to stop me either." He turned his head to Ox. "Get your gun. You're a bigger fool than I thought. Nuns, monks and priests are fair game and no different from anybody else. She got the better of you because you hesitated. Let me show you." He took three strides towards Sister Agnes and cracked the gun butt across her ribs.

She doubled up with an agonised squeal, her robes and crucifix swinging wildly in the air. Her pain was cut short as he finished the punishment by swinging the butt into the base of her neck, sending her crashing to the floor.

Ulla clenched every sinew in her body. To attack now was suicide. Either one of them would finish her off. She agonised for Sister Agnes but didn't dare move and reveal that she was free.

"You're a bigger, cowardly sewer-rat than I ever imagined," she spat with venom.

There was another sound. Throgmorton stepped back. Ox got his gun and they turned around to see the Condesa struggling to get to her daughter.

Ulla experienced a deep pang of pity for the two women. Maria, the Condesa of Toledo, was crawling in a slow and humiliating advance to her daughter. Kneeling next to her and using her scarf, she began dabbing at the blood covering her face and neck. Ulla could hear her whispering either endearments or prayers to her.

Throgmorton ignored the two women and spoke to Ulla direct. "Look and learn, my sweet. If you try anything, your punishment will not be so lenient. You're advised to behave as we may have a long wait. I may need you to make a phone call to Mr. Ladro.

Understood?" He poked the barrel of the gun under her chin and lifted her head with a savage jerk.

Ulla nodded. While Brodie was out there, a chance to finish off Throgmorton was very possible. *If he leans in any closer I can stab him.* She let her hand tighten on the handle.

His breath was hot on her face.

She flexed her wrist, held her breath ... *just another foot, please.*

CHAPTER 57

W here the light was coming from was unclear. The broken entrance gave no hint to what Ladro was looking at. The walls of the existing passageway had vanished to form a much wider passageway that rose overhead. The light illuminated the ceiling apex that curved upwards to form a continuous arched canopy that descended into smaller arched panels, each richly decorated with ornate, golden supporting structures. The entire area was a dome that covered an area the size of a small cathedral. The ground had been levelled flat and was made of flagstones. His astonishment increased as he gazed upwards. Each arched panel contained a painting.

He counted thirteen.

He then realised what he was looking at.

Oh, my dear God. I don't believe this! Brodie didn't know whether he should laugh or cry. *This is not possible. I'm in a dream. It can't be real.*

Common sense told him that while outside was a shaken mess of rocks and earthquake rubble; here, he was in an exquisite oratory of some sort, untouched, undisturbed and unknown to anybody. Somebody must know, for who put those thirteen paintings up there on those panels? He was speechless. The truth of the legend had become reality. What he had been seeking was real.

It was proclaimed in those thirteen panels, each one of the vanished works depicting the raising of Lazarus by a different artist, beginning with the original work by Annas Zevi who witnessed the event.

These must be all the missing Lazarus paintings!

The preposterousness of that thought, let alone it being *real,* swamped his reasoning. Any thoughts of the Abbot, Ulla, the Condesa faded away, overwhelmed by the immensity of his discovery. He grabbed at the wall for support.

This is not happening. It's not real.

He repeated it to himself until another thought struck him. *I've been brought here.*

That's rubbish, Ladro ... get a grip.

He had no idea what to do next. He moved forward, his eyes still scanning the paintings. He shouted out. "Is anyone here?"

It sounded ridiculous. His voice echoed and bounced around the smoothness of the walls, all displaying the curvature that led the eye upwards to the paintings. He found himself checking each one, the styles and techniques, and by that, he was able to chronologically estimate the time they had been painted. They were arranged in ascending order.

The last one of Lazarus being brought back caused him to gasp. It was unmistakeable. Cortez's missing painting. What the Condesa sought was hidden here all this time. He had no doubt of it. The style matched many of the sketches he'd seen at the Bodega. So many questions hurtled into his mind, he buried his head in his hands. *Who's going to believe me?*

He had no explanations. There were none that logically made any sense or would be believed. His recent visions offered a weird connection. *Madness.*

He reached out to the Cortez and could just reach the lower portion of the frame. He ran a hand across it ... Not a speck of dust.

Who placed them here? Who built this place? There's no record of this place anywhere, even in this monastery.

Where's all this light coming from?

He continued craning his neck upwards, unable to take his eyes off the paintings. He took pictures of them on his mobile phone. It was then he saw that next to the Cortez were mounted other panels. They were all blank, suggesting unfinished business.

How the hell am I going to get out of here? What about these painting?

Unless the monks dug him out or there was an exit from the mystery room he stood in, he could die here. He circled around looking for a possible way out. His attention became drawn to something standing under the Cortez painting. It appeared to be a tall chest cupboard made of dark oak.

His flesh tingled and he was certain that hadn't been there before. Or had he just not noticed it in his fear and excitement? It had nothing remarkable about it. It was plain, but it looked very old. Two large metal handles, possibly brass, offered themselves to be pulled open.

Ladro hesitated. Inhaling deeply, he grasped the two handles and pulled. At first the doors felt stiff, so he tugged a little harder, and this time they swung open with ease. He didn't know what to expect. At worst, all he wanted was a clue as to how to get out.

He gasped as the odour of centuries past blasted into his nostrils; the smell of ointments and herbs, of melissa, traces of mugwort, rue, cloves, and hints of myrrh. How he recognized them he had no idea ... he just *knew*.

He felt an eerie sense of peace. Had those strange smells caused him a deep quietness? A sense that all was well and he was in no danger? He couldn't answer that.

He wasn't surprised by what he saw next. He stared at the golden mantle hanging directly in front of him, untouched by the march of time. It glistened as new.

Ladro stood still, as his gaze took in what was in front of him. Its glow grew in intensity, holding him transfixed. Bit by bit, his defences fell away. The hardnosed realism, the functionality, practicality, Brodie Ladro, ace researcher, disbeliever in all ideas unless proven, all concepts and opinions were being stripped from him ... torn away in a soft pulsating field of gold. When he thought he could bear it no longer, the mantle fell to the floor.

It lay on the ground in the shape of a fan and revealed what it concealed. Ladro stared down at it, as if expecting it to jump back up again. But nothing moved. He then looked up at a blank stretcher-mounted canvas that had been placed on a large easel. There was no feeling of surprise. His entire attention focused on the canvas, as the chest faded away in a lateral split of light, leaving the easel and canvas highlighted in a space that stretched out into an infinite blackness.

His legs refused to move. He bent his head, unable to shout or scream, paralysed, powerless to prevent his inch by inch abduction, as the matrix of his being was drained from him.

With it went the last vestige of fear. He surrendered.

— — —

He wakes from a dream of death in the middle of a secluded field, wearing armour and the black cross pattée tabard of the Knights Templar. It is cloudy, chilly and windy, but he feels no cold. He hears the bells of God calling to him, and goes in a seemingly random direction. The bells stop. The field ... the clouds ... gone, as a shimmering path of glowing white marble and monks singing the Tibi Laus appear. In the sky, beautiful colours of blue and purple flash gently. He comes to a church, its portal aglow. He was home at last.

He pushes open the door and sees what he must do. It is ready for him. His brushes glide swiftly and confidently across the virgin canvas, giving vivid life and meaning where before only death had its abode. His entire being gives in to an ecstatic flurry. He works quickly, and he becomes the work ... is the work ... bringing him back from Hades as the eyes of Christ shine down on him and once more ... Lazarus is alive.

It is finished. His mission is accomplished and the world is reborn.

— — —

It was the influx of light penetrating his closed eyelids that prodded his consciousness to awaken. He realised he was lying flat on the ground.

"What the...?"

"There he is," a loud voice exclaimed.

He didn't recognise the voice or the outstretched hands shaking his shoulders and raking the debris from him. More lights appeared.

"Who are you? Where am I?" He shielded his eyes from the glare.

"Thank God you're alive. We were giving up hope. Are you okay?"

A concerned face bent close to him, and Ladro recognised a monk wearing work clothes. It was then he remembered. He made a mental check of himself; feet, legs, chest, ribs, arms and finally his head.

"Yeah, I'm fine, I think. What happened? An earthquake? Where are the paintings?"

Another voice spoke. "We had no earthquake, Señor, and there are no paintings. Part of the passageway collapsed while you were in it. This is a dead end. There's nothing here. It's a miracle you survived. One section has been completely blocked, but it missed you. It's taken us four hours to find you."

Ladro let the monks pull him to his feet and dusted himself down. "Four hours, what are you talking about? I've only been down here fifteen minutes."

"Check your watch."

One glance at his watch and he knew they were correct. "That's impossible. It's only just happened! Where's the room gone?"

"Señor, there is no room." He gave a knowing look at his brother monk. "How is your head?"

Ladro couldn't answer. Inside his mind, a black pattée loomed immense, followed by nonstop flashes of colour. The smell of oils, brushes, canvas, the dead, the living universe, and a matrix of DNA, gyrated through his head with breathless urgency.

"Whoa, Whoa, Whoa!" he shouted out to the roof, at the same time attempting to resist the tugs on his arms by his rescuers. A sense of powerlessness struck him and he knew he was meant to go.

"Quick, we must get you out of here. There could be another collapse." The monk shouted to his colleague and with force, began propelling Ladro through their excavated route.

He couldn't stop them. What was going on inside of him took all his attention. He had no idea what the visions in his head meant. One thing was clear: this was not the place for questions or answers.

Where is the dome? Where are the paintings? Where was I taken? I must have been dreaming.

His brain scrambled. Time had shifted into another dimension and what had seemed like minutes was in reality four hours. Stumbling over loose rocks and debris, he let himself be guided along as he began to recognise the route he had originally taken.

Ahead, he saw a glimmer of light. It was the original entrance and the spiral staircase that led back to the Abbot's study. Ladro could make out the concerned face of Abbot Louis, attempting to peer through the gloom.

"We've got him, and he's fine," the first monk shouted out.

Ladro was pushed and pulled to the top of the ladder and into the study of a relieved looking Abbot.

He couldn't hear what he was saying.

His eyes were shut tight, his mind ablaze and suffused with light and colours. Creeping into every nerve cell and sinew wove an awesome tiredness. He let the Abbot and his monks catch him as he began falling to the floor.

— — —

An unknown smell ... gurgling liquid pouring into something ... a hazy but smiling face ... he recognised Abbot Louis.

"Where am I?"

"You're in my quarters. You fainted."

"How long?"

"Ten minutes. You're safe and you can speak. Take this." He handed Ladro a steaming beaker of liquid."

"What is it?" Ladro grasped it as he struggled to sit up straight.

"It's a reviver made from rose, lavender, and henbane. Drink it, it won't harm you."

Ladro took several sips and put down the mug. It tasted sweet. "Father, I've got to get out of here. There's a painting down there I've been paid to find."

"I know that. You were talking out loud. It didn't make a lot of sense. It bore out local legend around here."

"What did I say?"

"A lot about Lazarus and why me? You said much concerning colours and paintings."

Ladro interrupted him. "I'm not making this up, Father. Look, I took several pictures of what I saw." He reached for his cell phone and pulled up the photo gallery. "Look." He jabbed at the buttons. "C'mon, c'mon," he shouted at the screen.

No photographs.

"What! They have to be here. It was working perfectly down there, including the flash. I *did* take them, Father. I took pictures of the paintings, I swear it."

Father Louis looked grave. "Your evidence is not good, Señor Ladro. That is a pity. I would have liked to have seen whatever you believe you saw. You also said other things; your fears for your friend Ulla, the Condesa Maria, and the blessed Sister Agnes. Are

314

they in danger?"

"I don't know." He speed dialled Ulla's number, and stared at the screen for a minute. "That's odd, she's not answering. Sorry, Father, I really have to go. My truck's some way from here, but I shall be back."

"As you wish, Señor Ladro. I look forward to your return."

"Of course, Father, and thanks for your help." Brodie headed for the door.

"And Señor..."

"Father?"

The Abbot had a strange expression. "It might be a good idea to clean up before you go." He pointed at Ladro's clothes.

Ladro looked down. He was covered in paint.

CHAPTER 58

F olded beneath her, Ulla's legs were becoming numb. Throgmorton had stepped back out of striking distance. She would have to wait. One false move and they'd cut her down without a second thought. She looked across at the Sister. She sat still with her head bowed and Ulla couldn't tell if she were praying or suffering from the ordeal. She willed her to look up and communicate. The Condesa lay prone on a sofa, with her eyes open wide but with a vacant expression, as if she were communicating with another dimension.

She's not going to be of any use if the going gets rough.

Ulla's mobile began ringing. Everybody heard it and froze. Throgmorton was nearest and looked at the caller display.

"It's him. We'll let him wait and get anxious. When he tries again you can speak to him and I'll tell you what you should say."

The phone stopped. Ulla knew what Brodie would be thinking. He'd suspect something was wrong. If that was the case, his behaviour would be unpredictable.

"He's not stupid, Throgmorton. He'll know something's wrong. What are you expecting him to bring back anyway?"

His face remained emotionless as he glanced at Maria. "The

same thing as that stupid bitch wants." He waved the gun barrel at Ulla. "It's a pity, Miss Stuart, that you'll not live to see a miracle."

For a moment, Ulla saw indecision register in him, whether to kill her or not. Her hand curled tight around the scissors. "Don't!" she yelled, ready to launch herself at him.

Sister Agnes's next move shocked her.

Her quiet voice became a roar. Her passive expression now resembled red hot coals. She sprung from her seat in a snarling rage and placed herself between the gun and Ulla, gripped the barrel with both hands, and at the same time, she pulled the gun barrel up against her head.

"Holy Jesus, you murdering bastard! I hope God never forgives you if you do this. Kill me now if you dare and may your corrupt soul rot and burn for eternity!"

She spread her arms wide open and lifted her head to stare into Throgmorton's face.

Ulla could only gawp. What humanity there was left in him showed itself. He wavered. Ox leapt over, ready to use his muscle, but Sister Agnes remained defiant and did not budge. Ulla knew this was the time to strike, but before she could, the ringtone of her mobile broke the tension.

Damn you, Ladro!

Everybody took a step backwards.

"Are you going to answer it?" Ulla snapped.

Throgmorton looked relieved and gave an exaggerated stare at the display screen. He picked it up, switched it to loudspeaker and placed it to Ulla's ear.

"Answer and be very careful what you say."

— — —

Angry flurries of dirt and grit flung upwards as Ladro brought the pick-up to a stop. He'd halted in the middle of the countryside away from the monastery. He needed time to think and make sense out of what had happened.

He couldn't explain the paint, but hell, there wasn't anything he *could* explain. All he remembered was the circular room, the paintings, and the shock of recognising the Cortez. After that, all was blank. He had collapsed, but had no visible injury to show that he had been struck. The room he'd been in had vanished. *No trace at all. It couldn't have been real. No photographs either.* The Abbot had said nothing more about the paint, but had gone very quiet. He had no explanation for how it got there.

I've got to talk to Ulla. Damn it. Unless there's an explanation or something happens, I think our mission is at an end.

He got out of the truck to get a decent signal and walked around to the back. A wide, thick roll of canvas, tied in three sections, located in the vacant space of the pick-up, caught his attention.

What is that? It wasn't there before.

He moved closer to examine it. As he ran his hand over it, he experienced a series of minor static shocks, causing him to jump back.

He pulled out his Swiss army knife and with caution, began to cut at the binding.

Thirty minutes later, he pressed the speed dial for Ulla's number again.

"Brodie?" She hoped he would pick up on the tension in her voice.

"Ulla, what's going on?"

Ulla looked at Throgmorton who nodded.

"Ask him what he found?" The gun barrel was now pressed into the side of her head.

"Not much. We're waiting to see what you've found." As the phone was on loud speaker, there was no way she could tell him what she wanted to.

"Nothing and everything."

His reply was odd, disembodied, and not at all what she

expected. It didn't sound like him.

Throgmorton gave her head a jab with the barrel while Ox kept the other two women covered. "Has he got a painting or not?"

"Do you have a painting or not, Brodie?"

Please, darling Brodie, understand what I can't tell you, please!

"I don't know what I've got. I really don't, so don't ask. I'll be about a couple of hours. How's the Condesa?

Is he being deliberately weird and suspects something?

"She's not well, Brodie. We're worried about her."

Sister Agnes again cut through the pretence and shouted out loud.

"Throgmorton has us as prisoners ..." It was all she could manage before Ox's pistol butt struck her hard across her mouth. She collapsed headfirst to the floor.

Ulla saw it coming. Her hand swung up, dislodging the phone from Throgmorton's hand and spinning it into his face. He staggered backward as he was caught off guard, and the pistol blasted off at the ceiling, bringing shards of plaster down. She flung herself forward into a shoulder roll, holding the scissors and knowing her objective was the gun or him or both if she could. Before he could turn, she had come up on her feet behind him and swinging back her arm, yelled out, "You bastard!" Her aim was anywhere soft on his body. She saw the look of alarm on his face and before he could bring the gun back down, she swung forward, arcing her arm upwards and plunging a single blade of the scissors into his spongy underarm flesh. Throgmorton gave a shriek of pain and fell backwards.

That was as far as she got, and it wasn't far enough. An iron like clamp descended and held fast to her arm, preventing any further movement. The cold pressure of a gun barrel hit her temple.

"I'll waste your fucking brains, bitch."

Ulla froze. She knew the trigger would be pulled if she as much as blinked.

"Let me finish her, boss."

Ulla felt the barrel push harder into the side of her head and heard the round drop into a chamber.

My God, he's going to let him do it!

Ulla closed her eyes tight, clenched her fists, dropped the scissors, and took what could be her last breath.

Throgmorton spoke. His voice had lost its cool demeanour and now croaked in pain. "An eye for an eye has always been my maxim. In law, those responsible are punished. Hold her arm out. Make it straight and let me see it tight."

She opened her eyes and could see the blood dripping from beneath his sleeve and onto the floor. For the first time she could remember since she was a child, real fear struck her. Ox jerked out her arm and held it as he asked. She attempted pulling back her arm, but he held it fast. Blue veins shone as he stretched it taut. She couldn't move.

"You'll pay for that, you stupid cow," Throgmorton snarled. "That hurt and I'm bleeding too much." He bent down and picked up the scissors. "You've also ruined an expensive jacket."

Ulla turned her head away with the gun still pressed into her head. She knew what was coming. She only heard him remove his coat, and a rush of air as his arm went upwards and then descended at speed. The force of the blow jolted her arm, but Ox held it firm as the point of the scissors split into her flesh, the tightness extending the slash and penetrating deep, before colliding with her radius bone.

At first, she felt nothing. There followed a sound similar to that of plaster being ripped from a wound. Unbelievable pain hit her as he jerked the blade out and wiped it on the end of her jacket.

"We're level pegging, Stuart."

Ulla turned her head to see the blood gushing out in a rapid flow, before she dropped to the floor.

CHAPTER 59

ULLA!" shouted Ladro, but got no reply.

Another yell, followed by a crashing noise. "My God. Throgmorton!"

It wasn't Ulla. It must have been Sister Agnes.

The phone went dead and he feared the worst. They were in danger. But since Throgmorton needed him to locate the painting, and as long as he thought he had what he wanted, then the women might not be harmed. Playing a waiting game gave them a better chance of survival. He drove slowly down to the highway leading back to the Condesa's. A plan formulated in his mind, but it was risky. *Anything is going to be dangerous.*

In spite of the perilous situation, he couldn't stop thinking back to the events beneath the monastery.

Something new and inexplicable had occurred. *That* lay wrapped in the back of his truck; mysterious, wonderful, and causing him to question his sanity. He had recognised it, the work of his human hands. Events were fitting together; the assignment, Throgmorton, the Bodega, Cortez, the Condesa, Valencia, Toledo, now Sister Agnes and Brother Louis, even stranger ... his visions, and now the unfolding saga. There was no way it could be explained. He had time and time again checked his phone for the photographs he knew he had seen. Abbot Louis had been correct, they were blank. But what he noticed was that each frame, whilst blank, showed a date and the time the blank image was taken.

There were thirty in total.

He continued on to the Condesa's home, aware of the gathering darkness. The blacker it became, the closer he could get to Throgmorton undetected. Navigating through the traffic, he reached the side road to Maria's house. Reaching the top of the ridge, he stopped the truck and killed the lights. Down below, he could make out the shape and outlines of her house. Apart from one light shining, it was in darkness. Cars were parked in the courtyard. He leant forward, gripped the wheel and placed his head on the steering wheel.

Focus, Ladro, focus. You know what you have to do.

A minute later, he got out and walked to the back of the truck. He tied the contents together with a long cord, which he lifted out with great care, slinging them around his shoulders. He reached for the backup pistol, but something stopped him. His hand hovered over it, but he withdrew.

His voice was telling him to leave it. There were no inner words.

He reached for the large knife and tucked it inside his jacket. He began the walk towards the house.

Keeping away from the skyline, he crouched low in a half run, going from bush to bush, getting closer but not knowing what he would find when he got there. The closer he got, the louder the chant ringing in his head.

Deus Vult! ... Deus Vult!! ... Deus Vult!!!

He knew what it meant. They were Latin for 'God Wills It!'--- a Crusader's war cry. This time he didn't fight it. He let it be, allowing it to flow through every sinew of his mind and body. The chant was accompanied by a vision of a black pattée flag. Ladro forgot who he was.

The mission was sacred and those who abused what had been freely given must die.

He guessed Throgmorton was not alone and the three women were there, but he was afraid they'd been harmed. The last phone call sounded bad. He knew what Throgmorton wanted, but now he knew the man would have to kill him to get it, and then he too would be destroyed.

Ladro realised it wasn't him thinking. Somebody or something else was doing it for him, directing and manoeuvring him, and whoever it was, he had to trust it.

Rounding a low parapet wall, he came to a stop and recognised the place. Not the Condesa's residence but the former monastery. He knew the layout as if it had been built only yesterday. He slipped by the remnants of the west wing that led down a small slope, into the rectangular area of the former cloisters that now held many guest rooms. Across the northerly section, he could see where the light came from.

What happened next wasn't expected.

— — —

Ulla watched Maria kneel beside her to bind her wound with her expensive Hermes scarf. The bleeding hadn't stopped yet but was congealing. An intense throbbing pain ran the length and breadth of her arm. The blade had missed vital arteries and veins and she knew she wouldn't bleed to death. She looked at Sister Agnes. She had managed to sit up and held her head in her hands. Blood stains covered the front of her habit. Ulla could only feel pity for her and rage at the moron who had struck her.

"Sister Agnes, how bad are you?"

"I'll survive, Ulla."

Ulla gasped at what she could see. A large bruise with a flow of blood had spread down from under her headpiece and her nose was swollen, her petite face bloated and now a bloody mess.

"My God, I'll kill the bastard!"

"A tempting mortal sin, Ulla, but don't do it, I beg you."

"Be still, please." The Condesa may have been frail but her voice maintained its imperiousness as she made the final tight knots as secure as her lean fingers would allow.

Maria continued. "Forgive me, please. I fear we have lost in this game and it is my fault. My pride and arrogance has landed you all in this mess. I am so sorry."

"Don't you believe it, Maria. Brodie can be very resourceful and I've seen what he can do. He won't abandon us, I promise."

Throgmorton sat close by, holding the pistol. He'd stopped bleeding and a close inspection showed his wound wasn't serious. He was alone. He'd sent Ox out as a lookout, telling him he didn't want any nasty surprises.

"Well, I hope our friend isn't going to keep us waiting too long. He must know you are being held and I don't think there's much he can do about it. One false move and one of you dies … it doesn't really matter who. The nearest is the most obvious. What do you think, Condesa? Not so high and mighty now, are we? But I don't think it will be you, well not initially. I still need you to test my theory."

He walked over to the window but could see nothing through the darkness.

CHAPTER 60

L adro's heart pumped hard. A figure had appeared through an opening in the ruined brickwork. Whoever it was wouldn't be friendly.

He pressed himself behind a pillar. The man hadn't seen him as he turned away to scour the far entrance of the building. There would be no second chances. Ladro centred himself, released his bundle to the ground, and let the strange force of whatever was possessing him assimilate him.

He was tired of being hunted and shot at.

He reached behind him and felt the handle of the knife. His heart skipped a beat as its grip filled his hand.

Transformation.

Either I will die today or God willing, the enemy shall perish. By this Sacred Patteè I live or die.

Deus Vult! ... Deus Vult!!... Deus Vult!!!

There was no cognition ... only hatred of the Godless usurpers and thieves.

Ladro shouted the ageless battle-cry. In a blur, he saw the man's startled expression at the suddenness of the attack, bringing to Ladro a taste of unknown pleasure. Leaping through the dark, he spun behind the confused thug and with a strength that was never his, gripped his arm around the man's thick neck and buried the blade, deep down behind his right ear.

There was no sound as he twisted the steel.

Ox's eyes rolled upwards in a final gesture as his hands waved in the air like a drowning man. Ladro let him drop as blood surged in a pulsating plume onto the cobbles. He yanked out the blade and stood on his victim's twitching body.

Who am I? I didn't do that ... I didn't do that.

Without thinking, he wiped off the blood and fleshy scraps across his trouser leg.

This is not happening ... it's unreal. Who is doing this?

A voice spoke to him and confirmed what he dared not admit.

"You know me. I am you, and you are me. Custodio Baez, monk, warrior, artist, and the Guardian of Christ's Sacred Relic."

"This can't be true. It's the twenty-first century, for God's sake." His voice bounced around the silent stone walls.

He wasn't going to argue with whatever it was, it just was, and he had to trust it. A major source of danger had been eliminated, although somehow, he felt detached from it all. Something or somebody was living in him and taking over when it had to.

He could see the faint glow of a light coming from an upstairs window and it was the only one in the place. It had to be where they were being held. He stepped out of the cover of the cloistered brickwork, recovered his bundle and began pushing his feet through uncut grass and weeds. Ducking low, he let himself be guided towards the source. The outside walls were covered in thick vines that led up to the window. As he approached, he spotted an opening between the boughs and made for it. He had to decide; climb the short route up the vine or head around the stairs towards the door? An entrance through the window would be less expected.

Peering through the intertwined branches, he began to climb.

It was a short distance. He caught his breath and waited to see if he had been heard. There was no activity from behind the window but he kept on high alert. He looked across at the row of grapevines and knew he could balance on one and gain full access to the window without being seen.

Holding on to the top branch, he looked over the top of it and what he saw caused him rage.

Blood.

The first person he saw was the unmistakeable figure of Sister Agnes. She was sitting on the floor facing the window, and her face was a mess. With an arm around her, was the Condesa.

Ulla!

He prevented himself from calling out. Ulla sat in a chair, her head lolling backwards, giving added significance to the uselessness of her left arm, which was smeared with large patches of blood and bound with a bright coloured scarf.

I'll murder the bastard!

He saw Throgmorton standing upright against a back wall, holding a pistol pointed at Ulla. Ladro couldn't make out what he was saying, but he didn't need to interpret the backhanded swipe that struck her across the face.

An inner voice prevented him from launching himself through the window.

Ladro saw him look at his watch and then stare directly at the window and begin to move towards it. He pressed himself close against the wall as flat as he could go, and hoped he wouldn't be seen. Throgmorton was looking for his man. If he opened the window, it could be the opportunity he was hoping for.

He watched the Judge release the catch to open the glass. Every muscle in Ladro's body tightened as he held his breath and prepared to attack.

He heard the metallic rasp as the bolt slid back and the window opened. It swung towards him and he realised he had misjudged the distance and angle, for the bottom frame slammed into his knee and ankle, sending him crashing down through the vine.

Holy Shit!

He lashed out frantically attempting to grasp at branches to break his fall, and hoping to God the inevitable bullet would miss him. He hit the ground holding handfuls of leaves, but unharmed. The shot was close, but missed him. Ducking low, he prepared to dive for cover. Throgmorton's yell bought him to a halt.

"One step more, Ladro, and I'll blow her head off!"

Ladro skidded to a stop behind a thick vine. He shouted back in a voice he knew wasn't his ... it was *his*.

"Judge, don't even think that's an option. One bad move and you will never see what I've got. I'll burn it and this place down, and you'll go up in flames with it. I swear by God that will and must happen."

The night froze and the soft moan of wind whistled its way through cloisters and the leaves of fruiting vines.

Silence.

— — —

Throgmorton stood still. He knew Ox must have been dealt with ... *but by Ladro?* That wasn't possible. If he was out of the game, Ladro must've had help.

If the worst happened, he reasoned, he still had De Witt's work. If played correctly, that could still be worth millions. But at the end of the day, *he* knew it was a fake. While if he killed Ladro, whatever he had would be his.

He moved to the side and grabbed Ulla by her injured arm causing her to call out in pain. He held it up at the shattered window and at the same time ripped off the dressing. The barrel of the gun was pressed firm into the side of her head that was bent sideways and bore an expression of severe pain.

"Is it worth it, Ladro? Her life for the secret you have." He pushed Ulla forward so that she was bent over the window frame and half hanging out, her bloody arm held upright behind her head and the gun to her head. He knew a shot from Ladro had a fifty-

fifty chance of hitting both him and Ulla. Ladro wouldn't risk it. "What's it to be?"

Ladro didn't reply and the Judge bent low and whispered into Ulla's ear. "I don't think he cares what happens to you. I might as well finish you off here and now." He shifted his body position and looked as if he was about to blast her.

"Don't do it, Judge," Ladro's urgent voice rang out into the night air. "I'm on my way up."

Ulla's wound had begun bleeding again and blood stained the front of her blouse and trousers. She looked white, her head hung low and she looked defeated. Both Sister Agnes and Maria got up to assist her.

"Over there, you three, sit on the floor and I don't want to see any of you move. When he gets here, you do and say nothing."

He thought he heard sounds from outside the room.

The door flung open with a crash. There was nobody outside where Ladro should be standing. Throgmorton blasted off three ear-splitting rounds in rapid succession into the vacant space.

"Damn you, Ladro. Show yourself or these women die… I'm not joking!" His voice rose to a screech. To emphasise his point, he fired another round into the wall next to the door, filling the air with plaster and the smell of cordite.

Maria and Sister Agnes curled up on the floor in tight foetal positions with their arms around each other. He swung around making a grab for Ulla, at the same time attempting to keep the doorway covered. Ulla ducked, but he caught hold of her hair and yanked at it with a vicious twist.

Ulla screamed out. "Take him, Brodie! Take him now!"

The Judge twisted her around using her as a human shield. "Try it if you dare, Ladro. If you do, she gets it."

There was no response. Ladro had disappeared. All that remained was an ominous tension. The three women looked at each other as the Judge shifted backwards gripping Ulla harder and knowing he *should* be in control but also knowing he wasn't.

"Get in here, Ladro, damn you, or I'm about to do something you'll regret."

"I shouldn't do that if I were you," said the quiet voice behind him.

CHAPTER 61

Disbelief registered on Throgmorton's face as he spun around still holding onto Ulla. The gun remained at her head. Unseen, Sister Agnes and the Condesa hauled themselves to a standing position.

"How the fuck?"

Ladro said nothing, his face remained expressionless. A night breeze from the open window caused the curtain to flutter. He saw Ulla's wide eyed look of desperation. He could read her thoughts.

Do something, Brodie ... kill him!

He ignored the request. In his outstretched hands was the bundle that had hung from his back. His eyes fixed firmly on Throgmorton who gave a quick glance at the open window.

"You came through the window."

"Whatever," said Ladro. "I think this is what you have been after." He nodded at the roll he offered to him.

The grip on Ulla relaxed. "How do I know it's genuine, a miracle worker?"

"You don't. Why don't you try it with the Condesa?"

"Of course. Now put it on the table over there, very, very gently. When you've done that, face me, take off your jacket, lift your arms, turn around and then kneel with your back towards me. No tricks or sudden movements or I'll pull this trigger."

Ladro knew Throgmorton had nothing to lose. He was already wanted for questioning over the De Witt murder. He began doing as he was asked. The women's lives had to be the priority.

In desert march or battle's flame
In fortress and in field,
Our war-cry is thy holy name.

Brodie glanced at the Condesa ... *she knows.* Her body had straightened, the sickness remained but her eyes shone with inner strength. As he knelt, he felt Throgmorton checking him for weapons. He would find none.

"Where's your gun?"

"I don't have one."

"Where's my man, Ox?"

"He tripped and had a nasty fall."

Ladro put up with another body search and was relieved the judge wasn't too good at it.

"You won't find anything."

"You're a bigger fool than I thought, Ladro. You could have left alive, but that's not going to happen now. None of you are going to escape to tell the tale. Why you walked in here unarmed, I don't understand, but you did and that was a big mistake. Giving me what I've been after isn't going to save you, either. You know too much." He gestured at Sister Agnes. "You, get over here next to him." He waved the gun at her.

She moved across with a look of immense disdain.

"That's right. On your knees facing the wall."

Ladro whispered to her. "Don't worry; we're going to be fine." She gave an appreciative nod. "How's Maria?" he added. She clenched her fist tight. At that moment, he recognized her strength.

A crash caused him to turn his head. Ulla lay flat on the floor and this time her hands were bound behind her. Throgmorton had his foot on her back and the gun pointing at the Condesa.

"You, your majesty, get over here and bring that bundle with you. Don't get any wrong ideas."

"Shit," whispered Ladro, "that complicates things."

Angustia superveniente requirent pacem et non eri...

The words tumbled through his mind. A black cross fluttered…

Destruction cometh; and they shall seek peace and there shall be none.

The knife pressed flat against his back reminded him of that. If he was to do anything, he would have to be quick. He accepted the force attempting to take him over.

Ladro bent his head ... he recognised who it was. Reverberating in his head like a thousand church bells, he heard him, and he knew.

I am Custodio Baez, Guardian of Lazarus and Christ's Holy Eyes. By Christ and Jacques de Molay's blessed name, the robber and heretic will not live or I shall perish.

He turned his head and saw Maria carrying the rolled-up bundle to Throgmorton.

She placed it in front of him and he gestured for her to begin unwrapping it as he covered the room with the gun.

The only sound Ladro could hear were the ribbons being untied by her trembling hands. An air of hushed expectancy filled the room. His fingers moved towards the hilt of the knife. Ulla had twisted her head around and was looking straight at him.

She mouthed silently. *Kill the bastard.*

All he could do was nod.

Finally, the ribbons lay undone alongside the roll of canvas. The Condesa stood back, and Ladro could see her face was a mixture of hope, fear and bewilderment, as she stared first at Throgmorton and then the canvas, uncertain of what she should be looking at.

"Lay it flat on this table," Throgmorton demanded.

Using both hands, she averted her gaze and began to unroll it, taking small backward steps alongside the table. She kept going until the canvas was open to its fullest extent.

The lights began to flicker.

CHAPTER 62

For a fraction, the brightness of the full moon shone like a distant lighthouse giving a momentary silhouette to the figures in the room.

Ladro released the knife, transferring it to the front of his belt.

The clash of armour ... horses shrieking ... the cries of wounded and dying men ... red and black crosses.

It was time.

The Condesa stood back, not daring to look at what she had unravelled. She placed her arms and hands across her chest and tilted her head back. Sister Agnes stood and moved beside her, clasping her arm.

Throgmorton said nothing and he kept his foot pressed into Ulla's back. Maria could see he had no idea what he was looking at. He made no move to prevent her daughter from being next to her. She detected a tremor in his hand and puzzlement on his face.

The clash of armour ... horses shrieking ... the cries of wounded and dying men ... red and black crosses.

She heard and saw them, and knew Ladro did, too.

Keeping her arms crossed, she lowered her gaze to look at the canvas. Her heart raced and her mouth went dry as she stared at a swirl of subdued colour. The work of the descendants of Zevi who had witnessed Christ's miracle, and whose secret was transmitted through divinely chosen guardians and artists up to the time of Cortez, and now, she believed, through Broderick Ladro.

She forgot about the dilemma they faced. Throgmorton wasn't there. All her prayers and lamentations over the last two years confronted her. The impossible had become possible. The room became gripped in an awesome stillness as she attempted to understand what was in front of her.

Christ stood to the left in a swirl of sand particles, reminiscent of El Greco meets Edward Hopper. He was dressed in black and his face shone white but dripped with sweat. His arms appeared to be raised but were lost in a blaze of yellow and greens. His gaze looked distorted. The tomb resembled the interior of a desert cave, dark and frightening as twelve faces stared out from the walls in expressions of wonderment and disbelief. Emerging from the tomb, a figure, expressionless and swathed in red and blue colours ... *faceless*. The initials *KORL* and a black pattée were in the lower right corner.

The risen Lazarus.

Its blankness, if it had a face, was positioned as if it would be staring out at the world from inside its potential frame. Outside appeared to be suggestions of indeterminate figures, staring into a promised hope.

It did not meet her hopes ... it exceeded them.

The painting was unfinished and Ladro had understood as she hoped he would. One ingredient was missing and she knew what that was.

The judge wanted a miracle and that he wasn't going to get ... yet. Never in her life had she been so certain of anything. She kept her eyes closed, aware of Throgmorton staring at her with the eager look of a man watching an execution. No one spoke and all she felt was her daughter's grip on her arm, and Brodie Ladro's thoughts. She let a minute pass by before she appeared to say a prayer, opened her eyes to gaze down on Lazarus and then, with the hint of a smile, lifted her head to confront the Judge.

The lights flickered once more, first bright and then dim, before a glowing dance restored normality.

CHAPTER 63

Whatever he anticipated happening, had not. Throgmorton's snarl filled the room as he attempted to keep Ladro and Ulla under control while he checked out the ageing Condesa in front of him. There were no cries of joy from her, and the painting looked incomprehensible.

"It hasn't worked, has it?" With blazing eyes his yell filled the room. He spun around and aimed his gun at Ladro. "What sort of crap stunt are you pulling, Ladro? If you think I can be fooled by this junk, then you're more pathetic than I thought. Answer swiftly or I start pulling this trigger." He clenched his teeth and fired a round into the wall close to Ladro, at the same time stomping hard into Ulla's back. With swift ease, he reloaded.

Ladro had ducked and barely had he begun to rise when the Condesa's voice, powerful and loud, rose over and above the drama.

"Stop! Stop now or you shall never know ... you shall never know." Her last words produced an enigmatic hush.

Throgmorton obeyed. He didn't know why he did but her entire presence was directed at him. He stepped off Ulla. "Get up and stand with those two." He gestured to Maria and her daughter.

She got up and shuffled over, her arm at an awkward angle.

"You, Ladro, get with them. I want you all where I can see you."

Ladro kept his head bent low,

Our war-cry is thy holy name!

He didn't look up but moved over to the other three. He placed his arm around Ulla.

"I've a feeling I'm missing something here." Throgmorton looked at them all. He had the means to finish them all off there and then and no one would be any the wiser.

Tempting.

"What won't I ever know, Condesa?"

"The truth of the Lazarus lineage. You see, there are things you don't know that have been known to my family and passed down to me across the centuries."

Her voice its clarity and confidence left Throgmorton in little doubt that she was speaking the truth as she saw it.

She continued. "The legacy of Lazarus has been known to our family since it all began through the early Mozarabs of this country, the Crusaders who were given the task to protect and guard our secret up to the time of Cortez. The artists were never random painters. They didn't choose to paint the event by themselves but were, believe it or not, chosen by Divine Ordinance. Although they never knew it."

"Legacy, my arse." His contempt was obvious. "So, how do you know this and nobody else does?"

"My ancestry extends back to the eleventh century Kingdom of Aragon. At the time of Queen Petronila, when the Moors were defeated in the thirteenth century, the painting was rescued and hidden at Valencia Cathedral ... before it too disappeared forever. Those who were in most need of its powers received healing, if they believed it was blessed by Christ himself. It was said that every painting is doomed to vanish or disintegrate, heralding a potential successor. That period can come to pass immediately or it may take centuries. I believed the work of Cortez still existed, I was mistaken. I know now that it has been replaced." She slowly and with reverence began to kneel in front of the large canvas, making the sign of the cross.

Total silence.

Throgmorton shifted, feeling ill at ease. He looked at them all and saw they all were transfixed on the Condesa, all apart from Ladro. He wasn't looking at her but his head tilted back and his gaze was fixed on the ceiling. His lips moved as if he was praying.

De Witt's painting had now become of more importance. This performance was going nowhere and he knew he had to make a major decision about them all. The entire episode was a step too far and a load of religious hysteria. He now wished he'd never got involved.

God, I'm going to have to do it.

His finger tightened on the trigger.

"Our war-cry is thy holy name! Beau-seant! Be glorious!" Ladro's immense roar filled the room.

CHAPTER 64

The veins in his temple stood out.

Beau-seant! Ad maiorem! Dei gloriam!

His grip tightened around the gnarled bone handle and the six-inch blade of his knife glittered and as if in slow motion, rose upwards. He raised his arm to its fullest extent, propelled his body upwards and towards the startled Judge.

Not yet! Not yet!

The voice of the Condesa rose in his mind. His attack faltered.

Throgmorton spun around, quick enough to sense his uncertainty. Ladro's arm struck down the barrel of the gun as the judge pulled on the trigger, twice. The shots peppered the wall behind Ladro, but his momentum sent him crashing onto the floor, still clutching the knife. He attempted to get up but Throgmorton had completed a full circular swing and Ladro took the full force of the gun butt on the side of his head. It sent him sprawling to the floor again in a bloody ball.

Throgmorton pointed the gun and aimed at his head, his fingers closing around the trigger.

"Stop! If you kill him, you will never know the final secret." The Condesa's voice, icy, high-pitched, sliced through the air and brought Throgmorton to a halt.

He didn't look up but kept his eyes locked onto the back of Ladro's head.

"You think I'm some sort of fool? You attempt to tell me this rubbish is a painting possessed with miraculous powers, painted by this idiot? I'm going to kill him and then all of you."

Ladro began to regain consciousness, enough to hear the exchange. He couldn't prevent the groan escaping from his open mouth. He managed to stutter. "Don't. She's right, there's more." He realised the longer he kept him talking, the greater his chances were for living. From the corner of his eye he could see Ulla and Agnes, and they looked like they were in a state of shock.

Brodie, I am here. Listen to me. I know who you are...

He was powerless to prevent the Condesa's voice and the images from breaching his everyday reality.

Flags fluttered in a strong breeze beneath a blistering sun. The call of Pope Gregory VIII, The declaration of Revenge for the Horns of Hattin. The desecration of Holy Relics must be prevented and despoilers put to the sword. Remember who you are.

Ladro squeezed his eyes shut and placed his hands over his ears but her vision and voice continued to fill his mind.

Saladin's crimes ... he is the devil, the despoiler, and he stands above you now. Do nothing apart from what I tell you ... and you will live.

He couldn't stop the process nor did he want to. He succumbed.

Custodio Baez lives. Zevi lives, and Lazarus will be raised again!

He lay still and prayed that Throgmorton wouldn't pull the trigger. From the conversation, he knew the man hadn't entirely given up the hope that his dreams of amassing a vast fortune from a miracle painting could still come true.

"I'll tell you what's going to happen next." He spat out the words like a machine gun. "You're going to tell me what this secret is and how it helps with what I'm looking for. You'd better make it good, because if you don't, he dies and then you. I've nothing to lose. I'm already wanted for one murder, and then there's your stupid maid to take into account. I know the European justice system, and I'll have nothing to lose no matter how many of you I kill. If your secret is valid, you might live. It matters little to me. So, start praying, Condesa, that your story is good enough for you to live."

Ladro waited.

She replied. "The painting is incomplete as they have been since Lazarus was first raised. A final ingredient is required to make it complete."

"I'm listening. What are you babbling on about?"

"The Lazarus legend has been traced back to the time of Christ, and has been known since the thirteenth century. Since that time, it has been protected from the Moors and nomadic Arabs by monks living around Toledo and Valencia. They guarded its secret." The Condesa began gasping for breath and her hand clutched at her throat.

"Now you've got this far, don't die on me just yet, you disgusting old hag."

"Let her sit down," Ulla snarled at him, and picked up a nearby chair for Maria to sit.

Without taking her eyes off Throgmorton, she sat on the chair. She paused before closing her eyes and Ladro understood her.

Custodio, I know you. Listen to me for this concerns you.

Ladro nodded and saw she had seen. A strange degree of pleasure coursed through him on hearing the ancient name being spoken, bridging the centuries. He had not been forgotten.

We shall all be leaving this room in a few minutes. He will then see what it is he wants and try to kill us. You must follow my lead. Our lives will hang in the balance. Whether we live or die will be in your hands. Beau-seant!

Ladro opened his mind and heart.

Our war-cry is thy holy name!

He heard her speaking to Throgmorton as he closed his eyes.

Her voice sounded a million miles away.

"Yes, you are right for once. The painting is incomplete and it will remain that way until the tabard is present and worn."

"Tabard? What tabard? What are you on about?"

Again, the Condesa appeared short of breath, her voice descending to a hoarse stage whisper.

"Let me explain. The Lazarus paintings have been produced by various blessed artists, and have been protected since the Crusades by warrior monks, some were the artist themselves. You will find a list of them in our family archives. But, I don't expect that will concern you, will it? Why do you think I undertook this venture even in my infirmity? Because I believed in fairy tales? I think not. I took it because I *know* it to be true. It's never been just a belief for me, it's fact. My cardinal error was using you, Maxwell Throgmorton, to assist in the search. But I now think that was meant to be."

"So, what's your point, your Highness?" Throgmorton sneered but never let his attention be diverted from any of them, especially Ladro.

She continued. "Borgoña's fresco collapsed in a pile of dust within the Cathedral walls of Toledo, but not before the new artist was selected."

"Selected? Selected by whom?"

"As all the painters had been chosen … by the mystical selection of Christ!"

"What a load of crap."

Ladro allowed the blackness to descend on him as his anger began to rise. His knuckles tightened ... his breathing grew rapid ... he tensed, ready to attack.

Wait, Custodio, wait!

Her plea cut through his rage and he halted.

I will tell you when.

He nodded.

She continued speaking to the Judge. "It was Francisco

Cortez's painting we so stupidly tried to find. It had already disappeared like all the other paintings before it. The successor has been chosen."

It hasn't, I've seen it.

The brief moment his message reached her caused her to falter. It wasn't noticed. "You wish to put this to the test? Then bring this painting with you and follow me. We shall soon see if it has the powers you are looking for."

CHAPTER 65

A s they descended a narrow corridor and marched through a cobbled arch, their footsteps echoed off the walls lit by emergency lighting. Ulla, still clutching her arm, followed the slow-moving Condesa, with Ladro in between them and Throgmorton following behind, his arm around the Sister's neck and the gun at her head. Ladro had said nothing but his mind was wide open, receptive and alert to every sound, and waiting for the Condesa's signal. They both had no doubts that Throgmorton was going to execute them all, whatever the outcome.

They reached a series of heavy wooden doors. Maria went to the central one and turned around. Throgmorton stood well back, his arm remained tight around Agnes's throat.

"Is this it?" he asked.

"Yes, part of the legend is here, where it has been for centuries." She indicated the large door, looked up at them all and knew Ladro could sense her desperation.

"Open it now and no tricks, or you know what will happen."

Her gnarled fingers had no strength to turn the large wrought iron latch.

Ulla spoke. "Let me do it." She moved to the door and gave the latch a vigorous shove with her good arm. The door moved begrudgingly before she kicked it hard and it reached its fullest extent. The room had full lighting, was circular and was as she had left it. Various devotional paintings and weeping Madonnas adorned the walls.

"Get in there all of you and line up around the wall where I can see you." He kept his grip on Sister Agnes.

Ladro stood between Ulla and the Condesa, who held the rolled canvas and had her eyes fixed on a large chest at the furthest end of the room. On it lay something folded.

It's the Tabard. The test begins.

Throgmorton moved to the centre. "This had better be good. What's going to happen next?"

Custodio, it's time to tell him.

"I will show you." Ladro stepped forward. He ignored the puzzled looks from Ulla and the others.

"What are you going to do?"

"The miracle of the painting, *The Eyes of Christ,* as we have always known it, is only brought to life when dire need asks it to, or when it chooses to do so. That need is amongst us. You shall see."

"More rubbish, but do what you have to, Ladro, but one mistake and her brains will be all over the floor."

The tabard. Put it on.

Ladro nodded and stepped across to the chest. He paused in front of it, looked down at the folded garment, and bent his head as he touched it.

The battlefield's clamour ... the sound of steel ... screams of men and horses ... warriors of Islam ... black and red pattée ... In God's name! Beau-Seant!

Custodio, put it on. It was yours and still is.

Centuries of spilt blood passed before him. A sensation of angry compassion took hold of him. With reverence, he picked up the tabard, held it in front of him and allowed the folds to drop down. He held it so all could see.

Without looking behind, he could sense their expectancy.

It was old ... very old. No longer white, time had changed it to a pale grey and wilted cream. Stains, their colour muted across the centuries, clung to it, proud emblems of forgotten battles. The edges were tattered, threadbare. Still on both sides, the black pattée, faded but visible. A series of minor shudders passed through him as he slipped it over his head. It felt as if he had never taken it off.

Throgmorton looked agitated. "Cut the drama and get on with it, my patience is going." He thrust the Sister in front of him. "Make it snappy or I will."

Maria, her face expectant but furrowed with pain, turned to face him. Behind her stood the easel and brushes as she had left them. Ladro stood as if in a trance; his eyes glazed. He was oblivious to all apart from her. She unrolled the painting, turned, and pegged the canvas to the easel.

Silence.

Thoughts of blood and violence abated and the focus of all pivoted on the contemporary work that glowered back at them.

It is time, Custodio.

I am ready.

Do it. Amat Victoria Curam!

My pain ensures my victory for the Greater Glory of God.

Ladro allowed his eyes to open and look at the painting. The shroud had moved. He ignored it. He was being asked permission. He agreed, lowered his head as if in prayer, and then stretched out a hand to grasp the largest brush.

"Brodie!" Ulla screamed out. "What are you doing?"

"This had better be good, Ladro, or you will die looking like a stupid fool."

Sister Agnes wriggled frantically, but couldn't break his hold on her.

Ladro turned and moved rapidly across the space that divided him from the others, ignoring their astonishment at his changed appearance. His hair had darkened, blood and filthy sweat dripped in large globules from his head, and his face grimaced in an unknown pain that had crossed the centuries.

Her voice was in his head.

Custodio Baez, Beau-seant! Beau-seant!

The tabard glowed with an unearthly whiteness. He held the large brush as an inverted spear.

The Judge froze at what he saw advancing towards him. It was Ladro, but it wasn't. It had become a distorted version of him. He couldn't pull the trigger against her head, but using his free arm, he flung the Sister forward at the advancing Ladro. Her impact sent him backwards and over as Throgmorton's shot whistled passed him to thud into an oak beam behind.

Ulla sprang like a wounded animal, eyes blazing, teeth bared and claws raised, she hurled herself on Throgmorton before he had a chance to let off another round. But he was too agile and strong, and his clenched fist smashed into her jaw, sending her crashing to the floor.

"Beau-seant!"

A bloodcurdling roar filled the room and a blur of motion fell on him. Another shot blasted through the air and hit nothing. Throgmorton fell backwards under the weight of Ladro transformed.

I am Custodio Baez, Protector and Guardian of Lazarus!

It wasn't Ladro speaking. It wasn't him fighting.

Ladro gripped him by the throat, and armed with only the sharpened end of the sable brush, he raised his arm high, poised to penetrate it deep into Throgmorton's frightened face. The Judge fought back, swinging his free hand in front of him as he kept his grip on the gun. He blocked Ladro's downward thrust by striking the descending weapon with equal force. Ladro ignored the pain, but was unable to stop the deflection, and found himself keeling in the direction of the blow. Throgmorton's next move was a follow through which flattened Ladro, as both men attempted to stand. He still held the improvised spear, but it would be no match against a gun. The distance between them meant he was out of striking range.

Throgmorton pointed his gun at Ladro's head and his finger tensed on the trigger.

"I've no idea what's going on here, but I do know one thing ... I'm going to enjoy this."

God forgive me, I have failed!

Ladro experienced eternity unfold before him as he closed his eyes, and tensed his entire body, hoping he wouldn't feel pain.

He heard shots, flinched, but felt nothing. The next thing he heard was a clatter, followed by a profound silence. He dared to open his eyes.

The Judge was farther away, bent on one knee, his gun out of reach. A dull red stain had begun its journey across his shirt front, and a low moan escaped from his sagging jaw. An expression of startled disbelief lodged in his eyes.

"What the fuck?" Ladro looked around. Both Ulla and the Sister had risen to their feet, equally astonished.

Stepping from a lazy wreath of gun smoke walked the Condesa. In her hand, she held a small silver Elite Beretta pistol. She approached Throgmorton, whose blood continued oozing between the fingers he was pressing to his body.

"Look at me," she demanded.

What was going through his mind, Ladro could only guess. Throgmorton made no sound but turned his head upward to look at her.

She looked taller and towered over his crumpled body. "Now, do you believe?"

"How? How?" His voice descended into a gasping whisper.

"There're things in this world you will never know, and this mystery is one of them."

Ladro's concern was for Ulla. He crossed over to her and Agnes and helped pull them to their feet. He started to ask if she was okay, but stopped halfway. Wide eyed he looked at her and ran his hand over her face, her nose, lips, and then down to her arm. There wasn't a mark on her. Any bruise, blood or cut had vanished.

"There's not a wound on you, Ulla." His voice rang with excitement.

She immediately checked herself. "I can't believe it," she gasped, turning to the Sister.

"The same with me. God be praised." She fell to her knees.

Ladro crossed over to the painting. "It has changed. It is finished. It has moved!" As soon as he spoke, he saw the shroud ruffle.

He reached out to touch it, but it was dry and static. The faces, formerly unfinished, were now identifiable; Christ, Lazarus, and the onlookers. Christ and Lazarus appeared to be looking directly at the viewer, and almost with a hint of a smile on their faces.

Did I do this?

You did.

The Condesa moved towards him. "You did. Throgmorton never understood and he never will. He's dead."

A glance put any doubt of that aside. His crumpled body was motionless, a small pool of blood seeping from under him.

"What are we going to do with him?"

"I'll show you all. Step over here, will you?" She stood against the far wall and pulled hard on a wall mounted crucifix. From beneath them came a rumbling and whirring sound of gears and machinery coming alive. "Watch."

Without warning, the central part of the floor opened, revealing a dark black abyss. Throgmorton's body fell swiftly and silently into it.

Sister Agnes bent her head and made the sign of the cross.

"That pit has been part of the monastery's secret history since it was built. It is over 150 feet deep. Undesirables found themselves plunged into it and it was also used as an escape route in times of war. Only myself and now you three know of its existence. He will find he's not alone and his remains will never be found."

Ladro spoke. "Reassuring, but more so to know that you are healed."

"Like Ulla and my daughter, I am. Thanks to you, Custodio Baez, I am. Look at me. I feel wonderful, unbelievably so. You are released, dear Brodie Ladro, to be yourself once more."

"Well, who was he then?" Ulla demanded.

"Let's say it's somebody I knew once."

"You also have a miraculous painting, Brodie." The Condesa touched it with reverence.

"No, I don't. It belongs to you. It's part of your legacy, part of this place, and for you to do with it as you see fit. You keep it, it's destined to self-destruct at some time in the future. I alone know where it will go when it does. That is my secret. I have seen all the Lazarus paintings since the revered original. They are all alive and will remain so until the end of time."

"I am jealous." She said nothing more but held Ladro's gaze as an understanding passed between them.

"We need to speak to Evita Cortez and her father to tell them as much as they need to know."

"I agree and I promise they shall want for nothing. I owe them much more than they can ever imagine."

"But what about Throgmorton? How do we explain him away?"

"We don't. If anyone asks, all we know is that he was called away. We do not know more than that."

EPILOGUE

London,
13 months later…

Money continued to pour into their bank account. Their discoveries were syndicated worldwide across satellite TV networks, and Ulla had the pick of the best possible assignments she could have ever wished for.

Sitting at her desk, she gave a long sigh. The letter was finished and she began to think of the events that had brought this about. She was pleased for the happiness that had befallen those who deserved it.

The Condesa, miraculously restored to full health, had given limited access to the media and had provided a new convent for her daughter, on the edge of the Tabernas desert. She had also rescued the struggling Bodega Cortez by giving them substantial funds and lending her name to their wines. Now, they were producing some of the finest wines that Spain could boast of. The Bodega's future was assured.

Her own personal sadness, Ulla had not spoken of.

Without him, her life lacked meaning. Brodie had left her two months ago, and she guessed it had been something he had been thinking of since their return from Spain.

He had left everything to her, including Gordian Knots, and had made certain she would lack for nothing. Every financial and business matter he had legally endorsed over to her, and that included his house. His actions, at first, caused her disbelief ... that was followed by deep pain. She should have seen it coming. He had descended into himself, a troubled being, locked away from her and caring only for his paintings. For days, he would barely speak. She had found him one morning staring at a blank canvas as tears rolled down his face. He had stood in that position for over two hours and refused to say a word. Whatever happened to him in Spain, he was now paying the price. She had asked him to see a doctor, but he had refused, saying that it was nothing to worry about, and he would soon sort it out. He did, but not in the way she expected.

It had never been in her nature to plead, and she wondered whether she should have. She had stood back and watched him go. He had loaded a suitcase, together with his art materials, into the back of his pickup truck, and driven away and out of her life with not even a farewell wave.

She read the letter through, folded it, and put it into the envelope, addressed and sealed it, ready for posting.

— — —

Monasterio de San José de Nazaret,
Nr. Segovia, Spain
A week later...

Abbot Louis, nodded his approval as he slammed the heavy iron grid gates shut, pausing a moment to savour the echo rebounding around the tunnel walls that led to his study. The air still carried the aroma of incense and spluttered candles carrying his prayers up to God.

Affixed to the wall, and covered in a golden mantle hung the monastery's most precious treasure, *The Eyes of Christ*, but to be referred to only as *The Raising of Lazarus*. Only his benefactor, the Condesa Maria Francisca de Toledo herself, and the newly appointed *Artista del Monasterio*, the official monastery artist, knew of its provenance, its power, and whereabouts. It was to remain that way until circumstances demanded otherwise.

Abbot Louis returned to his study, and as he had asked, the newly appointed monastery artist was there, kneeling in prayer before his personal shrine.

"Ah, Brother, you may finish your prayers and come over to my desk please."

The monk made the sign of the cross, stood, and let his cowl drop, bending his head before sitting where his Abbot was pointing.

"This draft you have produced, Brother, I am impressed with, especially the hands. Tell me, honestly, do you think I'm vain having such a work commissioned?'

"Not at all, Father," the monk replied, "it is expected of you and has been a long monastic tradition."

"That's reassuring, thank you. Tell me, who is the lady you have depicted as our Blessed Mary? She looks so serene."

"It was somebody I used to know."

"Remarkable." Abbot Louis looked thoughtful. "How long before the work will be completed, do you think?"

"Between the Daily Offices and ceremonies, it could be finished in three weeks, Father."

"I look forward to that, Brother. Before you go, I have a letter for you. It was addressed to the Condesa Maria, who forwarded it here. Rest assured your location is safe with us. Unlike some monasteries, we do not open personal correspondence."

The Brother took the letter and knew at once who it was from. There was no disguising her calligraphy style of writing.

Once in his cell, he put the letter to one side. The Office of Vespers and his obligation demanded immediate attention. During the recitations alongside his fellow monks, he allowed his thoughts to wander and saw her face in his mind.

Beloved Ulla.

If his heart lurched, he turned his mind back to Lazarus and the eyes of Christ into whom he had stared.

There was no turning back.

Later that evening, he unsealed the envelope and began to read. He noticed that his hand was shaking. It was much as he expected. It stabbed him in the heart as she described her feelings in a way he never thought she was capable of. She spoke of pain, anguish, shock and disbelief. She didn't ask him to return, but simply said:

"I never knew how much I loved you, and if you choose to return, I would take you back at once and unconditionally."

The next line caused him to cry out. He fell back and covered his eyes.

"I fear, dear Brodie, you may never do that … and that is what is so agonising for me. For you may never ever see our child due later this year…"

———

It was early evening and Brother Baez took a walk across the nearby hills. He wished to be far away from all people, but knew he could not. Inside, he felt only misery. He had taken the countryside and its people to his heart since his first arrival in Spain. Yet, his heart was imprisoned by what he had feared and now loved most, and it was not letting him go.

Ulla, beloved Ulla.

He could not support her as he had nothing to give. Yet, she would want for nothing. She had given her everything he had ever owned. He had stepped into another dimension, seen it, experienced it, and swallowed it whole, and knew he had been chosen. That, he knew. Ulla, too, understood. His heart screamed, but his path has been chosen for him. He would not reply to her.

He stood in a sacred line of artists who transcended space and time, chosen by Christ himself. From Cortez, all the way back to Zevi who witnessed the miracle of Christ raising Lazarus.

Now, he only had to wait for his own successor.

ACKNOWLEDGEMENTS

I would like to thank the following for their help and, encouragement in getting me to finish this book. *Linda Tolmie,* who pushed me along all the way and tirelessly read and reread anything relevant and gave me several ideas along the way. Her help was invaluable.

Sr. Assumpta, from Ladywell Convent. Her academic and professional skills improved my Latin, and my understanding of her vocation. Her sharp and keen observations helped me avoid some awkward mistakes in research.

Finally, *Jenni,* wherever she may be living in Cuba. She will never know how her actions impacted on me.

Amazon bestselling author, **Ken Fry,** holds a university Master's degree in literature and has extensively travelled around the world.

The places and events are reflected in his stories and most of his tales are based on his own experiences.

He was a former publisher before deciding to retire and devote his full time to writing. He now lives in the UK and shares his home with 'Dickens', his Shetland Sheepdog.

Fry has published 6 suspense thrillers to date, with more to be released in 2017:

The Lazarus Succession. Suicide Seeds. The Brodsky Affair, Dying Days, and 2 short stories, Check Mate and Is That You, Jim?

Join Ken Fry's Circle of Readers and get free eBooks and short stories.

www.booksbykenfry.com

Follow Ken Fry on Amazon:

Author.to/BooksbyKenFry

On Twitter:

@kenfry10

68905638R00204

Made in the USA
San Bernardino, CA
10 February 2018